A PERFECT
CORNISH SUNSET

Kelly Tink

Middlemist Publishing

To Mum, Dad, James and my boys.
You're why I believe in myself enough to do this.

Chapter One

Wandering the streets of the picturesque seaside town that is St Ives, Cornwall, pretending to be a tourist, when you have the privilege of living here, is one of my favourite things to do. Granted, these days, it's all swanky bars, restaurants and ice cream parlours, but the quaint book store, Jo Downs' handmade glass gift shop, and deli, up the grey and beige cobbled, narrow side streets, are where I go. So far, I've bought a paperback rom com and a samphire seahorse glass earring dish—to go alongside the dolphin and starfish ones in my collection. I love the fused glass designs and that her inspiration is drawn from the surrounding coastal landscape. It's a problem how many pieces of her collections I own, most of which are being stored in boxes until I have my own place again.

I'd spotted a couple of one-bed apartments to rent when glancing in the windows of the local estate agents, but I'm not really ready to leave the home comforts of my parents' place quite yet—ironic, given how reluctant I was to move in at first. The perks, however, were immediately evident, and for the most part, directly linked to my mum's cooking. Hydrangea

1

House guest house—my parents' dream, and my current residence, had won an award for breakfasts 'to die for' last year. Add to this my mum's homemade cakes and puds and there's really no sense in moving out anytime soon. The truth is, there's comfort being under the same roof as your parents. A sort of serene sense of security and the ability to switch off, or unplug from the stresses and strains of 'adulting'. It's as though I've escaped back to a time of feeling innately protected and nurtured—something I didn't fully recognise the worth of at the time, but which now I'm clinging to with both hands.

Next on my 'to do list' is coffee, plus or minus a second breakfast, though I suspect as soon as I smell food it will definitely be a plus. I'm working this afternoon, covering staff shortages, so I don't feel guilty for the indulgence when it's likely to be hours until I'll eat again properly. Taking breaks as a nurse, especially as I work in the Emergency Department, can be a little hit and miss. Particularly when I'll be joining a team who are on twelve-hour shifts and who'll need it more than me. Stuffing a biscuit or chocolate in my mouth and taking a slug of cold coffee is all I'll look forward to until I finish at ten tonight. The thought of leftover homemade lasagne waiting for me when I get home will have to see me through until then.

The compact café, with its whitewashed stone walls and matching wooden frame with blue writing, is as fresh as the sea air surrounding it. As I push open the door, the bell rings to announce my entrance. Frank, the owner, smiles at me from behind the counter.

"Morning, Frank," I say with a return smile, but his eyes flick towards a corner table and as my gaze follows my body stiffens and my heart rate picks up pace.

"The usual, Jo?" Frank asks, drawing my attention away from the couple in the corner and back to him. There are three tiny creases of skin between his bushy black, tinged with grey brows, which match his full beard, and the light from the window is shining on his bald head.

"Please. Er, take away, though," I add, sneaking another look back to their table, where I notice her mouth something to him and he turns towards me, giving me an unsure smile. It's a reflex of sorts.

"Any food?" Frank asks, his frown unwavering.

"No, thank you." I'm suddenly uninterested in the food I'd seconds ago been so craving.

"Are you okay?" he whispers, so gently even I barely hear the words as I reach my card over to pay, ignoring the fact that every fibre in my body's unanimously voting we leave, now.

I nod, and take a breath.

"Head up high," he commands as I move in the direction of their table. To do otherwise would seem petty and rude and I won't be those things, even if I feel them.

"Hi, how are you?" I ask Tom, noticing the uncomfortable expression on his face, and he only makes eye contact for a split second, before his gaze lands back on his half-eaten blueberry muffin. *His favourite.*

"I'm good. You?" He's rubbing his index finger over the ridge on his right thumbnail, the thing he always did when confronted. His mousy hair, which in sunlight has a hint of red in it, is short and casually brushed-up on top. I think about how I used to enjoy moving my fingers through his hair while we lay in bed together.

"Really good, thanks," I say, but wish my voice hadn't squeaked like an adolescent boy in puberty. *I'd quite like to leave here with some of my dignity intact.*

"This is, Sarah. Sarah, this is, Jo," he introduces us with a smile which wavers. My own doing the same as I force my eyes away from her perfectly round stomach.

"Congratulations." I nod as she instinctively rubs her tummy the way all expectant mothers seem to. My breath catches in my throat as I notice Tom scanning my face, no doubt seeing straight through my 'I'm going to smile like a children's TV presenter' façade.

"Thanks. We're having twins. It runs in my side of the family. A boy and girl …" she trails off, looking down, and her dark brown curls fall over her cheeks, as though they're trying to hide her flushing skin. Her perfectly manicured fingers circle her glass, which she lifts to take a sip of water.

"Jo, your Americano, extra shot," I hear behind me and turn to grab it with thanks.

"Congratulations again. I best be off. Take care," I say, not waiting for a return parting gesture from either of them, or Frank.

As I stumble back through the door onto the cobbles, unwanted memories rush at me as though I'm several gins in, and instead of everything appearing as it should, in the distance, it's as if my surroundings are up close, hazy and circling me. The steps in an alleyway where Tom and I perched to eat fish and chips on our second date, trying to hide from the seagulls. The spot outside Kelly's Ice Cream where mine was taken by one of the pesky beasts, its wing slapping against my cheek, leaving me shocked as it made its escape. Tom checking if I was hurt and buying me a fresh mint choc chip cone. The harbour view restaurant, on the first floor, where we went to on our one-year anniversary, and where he told me how much he loved me and we'd planned our future: three or four kids and growing old together. It had been the sort of declaration which made you believe it was forever. My eyes squint, trying to suppress the images. My legs feel unable to carry me away as fast as I want them to—it's as though they're a pair of windscreen wipers on full speed, struggling to keep pace with some torrential rainfall.

I don't stop until I reach the end of the pier, red-faced and hot, where I lean on the cold metal railing, looking out into the ocean, and gasp for air.

Tom is going to be a father.

The last time I stood in this exact spot the sun shone cruelly, as though it were taunting me. Not a single cloud or patch of grey sky for miles, as though it had no regard for what was happening to me. *To us*. Tom stood beside me, his arms encasing me, as though if he were to let go I might slip over the edge and into the water beneath us. On that day, I, we, found out I would never have children of my own. No tears came. It was as though they were trapped inside. Trapped behind the confusion. The 'what now' questions and soul-destroying realisation I'd never be a mother. I'd never bear his children.

Now, as my eyes sting with warm, unwelcome tears, I try to pretend it's from the breeze blowing into shore and push upwards with the back of my index finger to wipe them away. I sniff, sip my coffee and take a moment to compose myself, but soon the silent, forbidden sobs won't be stopped. As I bury my head against my coffee cup, my heart sinks to a depth not even this ocean could rival and I ask myself, *how can I stay here now?*

Chapter Two

My fob watch signals there's just one hour until my shift ends. My dark blue scrub top is sticking to my back, my feet ache, and I long to breathe some fresh air. The Emergency Department, or ED as we refer to it, has no windows. It could be hailing, snowing or a tropical rainstorm outside and I wouldn't know. Well, at least not until my patients come in soaked, telling me it's 'raining cats and dogs', or the ambulance crews stack up, bringing in elderly patients with fractured hips from slipping on the ice. It's muggier than usual inside, so I know the sun has continued to shine all day. When I left home at lunchtime, grateful for the distraction after seeing Tom, the air was already humid. Not like in the early mornings this week, when the air had been fresh with the promise of a glorious spring day. The birds had hummed and tweeted as they darted about, my only companions at such early hours. The benefit of starting work at seven a.m. is how quiet the roads are. It's less of a comfort in the dead of winter, but I love the spring. The clocks have gone forward and everything feels new. As I think of the word 'new', my stomach flips over, giving me a reminder of my midnight plan. Today had only served to reinforce my decision not to cancel.

"Must be near your home time, my dear." I look up from the arm where I'm drawing my patient's blood and smile warmly at her. Glynis doesn't look a day over seventy, not the eighty-four years of age her chart tells me. Her neat silver side-parted bob reminds me of Helen Mirren, as does her complexion.

"I'd love to know your secret, for how you've stayed so young-looking," I say. The glint in her pale powder-blue eyes tells me I'm not the first, but also that she doesn't tire of hearing it.

"Everything in moderation."

"Moderation, hey?" I've finished taking the samples, now I'm writing her details on the tubes ready to send to the lab.

"Yes. I've not denied myself the things I've wanted in life. I just made sure I—"

"Did everything in moderation, I see," I finish for her.

She nods. "Plus, I had a wonderful husband. Rest his soul."

"I'm sorry. When did you lose him?"

"Three years ago and it's been the longest three years of my life." I look at her, part of her fringe covering her left eyebrow, soft folds of skin framing those mesmerising eyes. There's a hint of berry lipstick on her lips, faded, but still showing. I find myself wondering what she looked like in her youth.

"It must be hard."

"It is. I wonder every day if today will be the day I can be with him again."

"Oh, there seems plenty of life in you yet."

"What about you? Do you have a nice young man waiting to run you a bath at home?"

I shake my head, pushing down the image of Tom and Sarah from before as I drop the tubes into a clear plastic bag, along with the paperwork, before sealing it.

"Choice or circumstance?" she asks, and its forthrightness takes me by surprise.

"A bit of both." I swallow and smile, attaching the blood pressure cuff to her arm.

"Well, these men can be troublesome, but I wouldn't change a single moment of the time I had with my Peter."

"It sounds as though you were very happy."

"We were." She nods. "Life wasn't always easy. We had our ups and downs. Lefts and rights, too, for that matter." Her eyes briefly close. "But marrying Peter, giving birth to my daughter … I have no regrets. So, maybe that's my secret."

"No regrets it is." I inhale and release. "Right, I need you to relax a minute while I do your blood pressure." The machine drones into action and Glynis is quiet. I enjoy meeting people, it's one of the reasons I love nursing. Especially older people, with their life stories and experience, though in ED it's rare to have the time to delve too deeply.

"It's a bit high, but I'll get one of the doctors to see you soon. Can I get you anything? Do you want me to call anyone?"

"If you could pass me my handbag, dear."

As I reach for her small black bag the scent of something musky, mixed with talcum powder, drifts towards me. She pulls out a mobile phone. "You'll struggle to get a signal in here," I say.

"Oh." She sighs. "I was going to call my daughter, so she doesn't worry when I'm not at home."

"I'll call her for you. Let her know where you are."

"Thank you." She gently squeezes my hand and I notice she looks tired.

"Why don't you have a rest, until your bloods are back and the doctor comes to see you?" There's a loud yell from a nearby cubicle of what sounds like an intoxicated patient. Also, a low murmur of someone in pain. "As best you can in here, that is," I whisper.

She nods, pulling her bag up higher, folding her arms over it before closing her eyes.

I'm barely at the nurse's station when I hear my name.

"Jo, we need you in resus," a colleague calls out and I run to the resus bay. It's a hive of activity. A young male patient is on the trolley, his shirt cut open, defibrillator pads stuck to either side of his chest. The air carries a heavy smell of alcohol and vomit and I have to try not to breathe in too deeply. Kate, my boss, is doing chest compressions as the airway specialist and their assistant give ventilations. Also present are the consultant, who's the team leader, a scribe making notes, another nurse, and a radiographer on standby for any imaging. The room is prepped with everything to hand. Oxygen, suction, monitors, ECG, BP, procedure kits for chest tubes, thoracotomies, etc. Sharps bins, IV and blood testing trays, X-ray, computer terminal and phone.

"Take over, Jo," Kate puffs out. The effort chest compressions takes means you have to rotate staff. I slide beside her, stepping onto a stool. Kate is taller than me and didn't need it—I do, to get the right angle with my arms straight and locked over the patient's chest. I place one hand over the other, entwining my fingers, and she counts me in.

"Three, two, one."

I start compressing his chest seamlessly as though Kate never stopped. Listening for the lead's commands in case they want to shock him with the defibrillator, or check for signs of life. It's only a couple of minutes, but it feels longer when I hear the command to stand clear while they analyse. A shock is required and everyone steps back, his torso lifting, before I continue. I feel a rib under my hands crack and I know I've fractured it. It's common in resuscitation, though still unpleasant no matter how many times it's happened before. I wince slightly, but don't lose my pace. I'm commanded to stop once more after a further cycle of compressions.

"We've got a rhythm," I hear and know we've managed to save his life. It was quick, too, so he shouldn't have any deficits. I breathe hard, stretching out my arms and rotating my wrists.

"He's a lucky lad," the consultant says. "Might make him think twice about what pills he swallows at his mate's next time."

"What did he take?" I feel a surge of annoyance rising inside me.

"What didn't he take!" Kate raises her eyebrows as she dumps her apron and gloves in the bin, which closes with a loud metal clunk.

I shake my head, wondering if it was worth ending up in ED, with me breaking his rib, trying to save his life. Looking down at my silver fob watch, a gift from my parents I've had since I graduated as a nurse, inscribed with the date on the back, I see it's ten-thirty. I'm half an hour late off shift, which is no great surprise. I suddenly realise I've not phoned Glynis's daughter and I wander back over to her cubicle.

"Time of death ten-thirty-one."

"What happened?" I whisper, a rush of coldness hitting my core.

"Massive heart attack. There's nothing we could have done."

I close my eyes before moving over to the trolley. She looks as though she's sleeping, like when I left her, but more still. I touch the back of her hand, a tear rolling down my cheek, and then cover her with a white sheet.

Wrapped in a grey towel, I perch on the edge of my wooden double bed, in my en suite room in my family's private residence of their guest house. The walls are painted cream, with a matching thick pile carpet, and roman blind at the small window. There's a black ceiling fan above me with lights below it, but my bedside lamp is on, its orange glow easier on my tired eyes. The room is basic, but comfy. Despite the months I've lived here, I haven't stamped my own style on it. Aside from my clutter. Every time I think I might change something, I try and tell myself I need to move out and start to stand on my own two feet again, but then I don't. Until now. I breathe in as I open my laptop. It's almost eleven-thirty and I don't have much time. I perched briefly on a stool in the kitchen to eat some of mum's homemade lasagne—so quickly it feels lodged halfway up my chest. I'm sipping a small gin and tonic, which my dad left out with a note saying, 'to settle your nerves'. I drag my cursor onto Google and search, opening the hospital's website and note its size and list of services. Inhaling, I continue my search, clicking through link after link, unsure of what I'm doing, but then I can't remember the last time I felt sure about anything. Shaking off my doubt, I finish the remainder of my drink, the alcohol taking the edge off as the liquid flows down my throat. My phone flashes, catching my eye, and I grasp at it, noticing the banner notification that it's my cousin, April, wishing me luck.

Once dressed, and by dressed I mean my bottom half in pale blue cotton pyjama bottoms and my top half a presentable lace yoke tie neck navy blouse, I turn on the main bedroom light. Seated at my desk, my

Post-it notes lining the wall behind the laptop screen so I can prompt myself with what to say, I open my video chat. I see Tom's name in my contacts and freeze before promptly deleting him—unsure why I hadn't already. The satisfaction in the small victory of deleting his number is quickly followed by the gut-wrenching ache in my stomach for a split second before I steel myself. *Now isn't the time to fall apart.* Perhaps the G&T needed to be a double, though there's no time now as the clock on the bottom right of my screen rolls onto half-past midnight. I enter the virtual meeting room and wait for what feels like longer than three minutes, when activity starts and I'm faced with a smiling woman with jet-black hair and thick-rimmed glasses, wearing a bright blue lanyard around her neck. Her name badge is just visible and reads: Kathy Thompson. Human Resources Manager.

"Jo, hi."

"Hello," I say, trying to sound both professional and friendly.

"It's good of you to stay up for this meeting."

"I appreciate you taking the time to talk to me."

"Not at all. I thought this would be the most efficient way of answering your questions, rather than back and forth with emails." Kathy smiles and I nod, returning with a smile of my own. "It helps give you a sense of who we are, too."

"It certainly makes the whole thing seem more real." I look at my empty G&T glass and think how much I'd love to take an unprofessional swig of alcohol right now.

"I've got your previous email in front of me, so I'll jump straight in with what you're going to need in terms of registration and documentation, and then you can ask questions as we go, if that's okay?"

"Sure."

"Firstly, do you mind me asking why you want to be a nurse over here in Australia?"

Leaning back in my seat, I sit in the silence of the house where everyone is tucked up asleep. I look up at the wall above me to see my canvas collage of my favourite pictures. There's one of me sitting beside my dad on a wall in the South of France; he has a scar above his right eyebrow from where he'd had a lump of some sort removed before we went away. One of my mum and I wearing aprons and Christmas cracker hats as we made Christmas lunch together. Several of April and I on my trips out to Oz to visit her. *Visit*, I think. This is just an elongated visit, I tell myself, casting another look over the photos of my parents. Wondering how much I'll miss them when I go. If. If I go, I tell myself.

Kathy from HR was lovely, and my pulse rate is only just returning to normal after hearing about the opportunities out in Australia. Everything about it was surreal. Daylight there, yet night here. Hearing her accent as she talked me through the steps I need to take to apply to work out there. Realisation dawning, this is no longer just a thought in my mind—a fun idea. Tonight, I put the cogs in motion and the step feels strangely liberating. My laptop screen lights up, catching my attention, and I see April trying to video chat me. I press accept and it loads the image of her pulled-back golden hair and smiling face, wearing a pink Barbie pyjama top and I can't help but chuckle.

"You still have those PJs?" I say, beaming at her.

"Yes. They're my favourite."

"I bought you them years ago."

"And your point?"

"Nothing." I remember buying them for her as a present, because as a small girl she wouldn't let anyone play with her Barbie dolls. Not even me. My aunt still likes to tell the story of when her friends came to play once, and she'd said, 'They're nice girls, Mummy, but can they go now because they're touching my Barbies.' She really didn't like to share them. Then when she was pre-teen, she went from keeping them immaculate to chopping all their hair into bobs and saying she wanted to be a hairdresser. I think at one point I wanted to be a hairdresser, too, just because she did.

"How'd it go?"

"Good, I think."

"Good, you think?" she asks.

"Come on, it's early hours of the morning and I'm exhausted, so I can't do better than that right now."

"Fair enough … did it make your mind up?"

"It made things clearer."

"Well, you know I'd be stoked to have you live with me."

"I know that, and me too. It's just—"

"A big decision."

"Yeah," I agree.

April is hugging her knees in front of her. She flips her hair to one side. "I get that. How are you?" Her eyes narrow.

"I had quite *a day*. We lost a lovely old lady, and had to save some idiot overdose …"

"Are you crying?" she asks.

"Sorry." I wipe my cheek with the back of my hand and clear my croaky throat.

"Hey, no. What's really going on? You lose patients, and treat junkies all the time. Sort of 'goes with the job description as an ED nurse', you always say."

"I saw them together, April!"

"Who? Tom and his new woman?"

I nod … "They're expecting twins!"

"What! Blinking heck, Jo!"

"Yeah."

"I'd ask if you're okay, but it'd be a stupid question about now. I really hate seeing you like this, Cuz."

"I'm sorry."

"Don't apologise."

I nod, staring at the screen.

"Do you want to talk about it?"

I shake my head. "Still processing … and slightly concerned that if I talk about it, I'll get so angry I'll break something."

"Do it. Maybe that's what you need. To smash a glass or something!"

"My parents are asleep. This is their stuff. I dunno.

Let's talk about something else." I notice April sigh, but she rolls with it all the same.

"Well, did you work on your bucket list?"

The change of subject I'm grateful for. I'm spent tonight, both physically and emotionally. "April, when you ask me like that, it sounds like I'm gonna die."

"Oh don't be so dramatic. Now read me what you have."

I roll my eyes and reach for my notepad.

Learn a new language
Be a nurse in Australia
Travel
Run a marathon

I read them out to her.

"Why did you cross out skydiving?"

"Because it was you who suggested it and I hate heights."

"It's all very generic, with *learn a new language*." Her voice took on a pompous tone.

"What do you suggest?"

"I dunno. Find a hobby. Learn to surf, or something. You live by the most gorgeous beaches in the UK and you only dip your toes in the ocean. Get in there, girl, and live a little. Besides, it'll help with the authentic beach babe vibe while you stay here."

"If … I still have to apply for a visa, register with the nursing council out there and convince work to give me the sabbatical I've been asking for."

"Well, you best get on with it then, instead of talking to me." She smirks and I know she's making light of it all. April really wants this, and slowly, day by day, I'm beginning to want it just as much.

"I'm going to crash in bed, and tomorrow I'll make a start. I promise."

"Love you."

"Love you. Night," I say and stare down at my list, my mind thinking back to Glynis and our conversation before she died. No regrets, I think as I scrawl *Surf lessons* on the bottom of it. Then I climb into bed and tell myself that tomorrow I'm going to tick something off the list.

Chapter Three

Stepping out of the car, I breathe in the fresh, briny sea air with my eyes closed. When they open, I watch the waves rolling in perfect lines as far as the eye can see, in the vast entity of bluey-grey ocean before me. The quartered black and white flags are visible from my lofty place by the bushes, looking down onto the sand. The people, scaled down to look as though they are toys from this distance, making the most of the waves on a good surf day.

I retrieve my straw tote bag from the passenger footwell, slinging it over my shoulder as I lock the car door to my little yellow Fiat 500. I woke this morning with the determination to 'be more April'—young, free and single, and also, to tick something off my bucket list. Since most of the items on my list require more time or planning, I'd decided it was going to be surfing.

My walk along the footpath takes me past the house I've always admired. Despite its derelict state, I've often wondered why no one has ever bought it as a project. Granted, it's an odd shape, more a rectangle than a square, but it looks spacious from the outside. There would be room for a couple of cars on the drive, too, which, in a bustling seaside town such as this, would drive the holiday-home rental price high. Assuming this would be the purpose for buying such a property. The views from the back of the house must be priceless, looking out over the crescent of white sandy beach, surrounded by high rocky headlands either side, with the sea a turquoise colour on a warm, sunny day. Oh, how I could lose myself in a good book by that view.

To my right is the cream imposing exterior of the Tate Modern gallery, though I don't pass it, turning a sharp left to walk down an uneven concrete slipway onto the peppery grains of white, black, yellow and grey sandy beach. I flick the heels of my leather toe-post gold sandals and remove them. The coolness of the sand in the shade is refreshing, compared to the warmer grains resting in full sun. It's balmy outside already this morning, and especially given it's only April—a freak early heatwave set to last the rest of the week, and not a bad time to have a few days off work. It's busy because it's the tail end of the Easter holidays, but not as heaving as during the peak of the summer. I prefer it when it's less busy, not having to share the beach or roads with quite so many tourists.

Pausing in front of a red wooden A-frame sign that reads 'Ben's Surf School' in white writing, with other services they offer and credentials, I notice a man just inside the hut. He's barefoot, with golden skin and a light dusting of sand over his feet and ankles, wearing a royal blue T-shirt and black board shorts. A strand of long dark brown hair, loosely tied back into a ponytail, falls over his face as he bends down, dipping a wetsuit into a bucket of water. Pushing a strand of stray hair behind his ear, he looks up at me. Our eyes meet, making me feel a blush sink over my cheeks, like the small glass vessels of a Galileo thermometer as they float to the bottom and I inwardly scold myself.

"Morning," he says.

"Morning."

"Can I help you with anything?"

"Oh, yeah. Sorry." I take a sharper than intended intake of breath and inch closer to the man. "I'm hoping to sign up for some surf lessons."

"Sure thing." He steps behind a small wooden desk and clicks around on a computer screen. "Beginners?"

"Pardon?"

"Are you looking for beginners lessons?"

"Why would you assume that?" My tone's clipped as I cross my right foot over my left before returning it to the floor where it had been.

"I've done this a while, so I can spot a newbie. No offence."

I wave the air nonchalantly, not bothering to get into a conversation with him about how arrogant he sounds.

"I can fit you in in about," he looks at his watch, "twenty minutes?"

"There's no time like the present, I suppose." I laugh, far longer than intended and feel a tingling sensation sweep up the back of my neck and across my face. *What's wrong with me! First I think he's arrogant, now I'm giggling like a schoolgirl.*

"Name?" he asks, his attention away from the screen in front of him and his gaze, once again, landing upon me. His eyes are a pale brown in this light, almost reflective, and from what I can see of them, beautiful. I blush further, realising I haven't answered him.

"Oh, um, Jo, Jo Mitchell."

"Well, oh-um-Jo Mitchell. You're all booked in. I just need to measure you for a suit." He scoots towards me from behind the desk in such an easy movement, shifting coat hangers about on a rail, pushing aside wetsuits until his fingers land upon his choice. "If you could spin around, so I can check this against your back?" He signals with his revolving index finger.

I do as he says, feeling an odd sensation as this strange man holds up a cold, smooth fabric close enough to feel it lightly graze my shoulders and the backs of my calves. There's further metal on metal scraping sounds as he pulls another suit from the rail behind us. The coolness against my skin once more. My mind wanders to when I was fourteen, on the beach at Sennen Cove with my mates and I used to walk across the car park to the toilets more times in a day than I needed to, just so I could see the guy who worked behind the surf hire counter. He was called James, with his perfectly sculptured body and tousled mousy hair.

"This one should be good." The man's voice pulls

me from my daydream. "Let me know if there's any problems. And you'll need this, too." He passes me a bright yellow shirt. "Lets the instructor know who he needs to rescue."

My heart sinks a little at the idea of requiring a rescue, but I notice the cheeky smile on his face and I nod slowly, softening. Regrettably, there's a smile burning into my cheeks.

"I'm Ben, by the way."

"I'm just oh-um-Jo," I say, lifting my shoulders.

He laughs, knocking back his head.

"So, this is your shop?"

"Yeah, the board hire, surf school and shop next door."

"It's great," I say and there's a pause, which runs on too long.

"Have a good time out there, okay!"

"I'll try not to drown."

"If you can. It's far too much paperwork." He offers me a bemused smile as my gaze lifts to him once more. Then I wander back onto the beach, pushing aside the encounter and my inner fourteen-year-old self.

Despite my petite frame, the all-black wetsuit is a perfect fit, covered with the T-shirt to make me stand out with the other learners—*at least it's my favourite colour*. While applying some suncream to my face, I hear one of the instructors shout the group over to where he and another guy are standing. The first instructor is younger than Ben, nineteen or twenty I'd say, whereas Ben's more mature, mid-thirties, at a guess. As an ED nurse, you get good at guessing people's ages. Triaging sick people all day makes you observant after a while. How tragic, though, when you're thirty-four and realise the man leading your surf lesson is far too young for you anymore. Not that I'm looking. A relationship is definitely not part of the 'be more April' plan. I'm just not blind. It's been six months since Tom and I broke up and instead of moving head first into another relationship with kids on the way, like he has, I'm going to focus on me and tick things off my bucket list.

As I reach the surf school with the others, I push my short, ash-blonde wet hair from my face. We'd carried the long boards back in pairs, which I'd seen people do during lessons before—it's not as hard as I thought it'd be. I can't say the same about trying to stand on one, although I managed it towards the end, feeling exhilarated when I caught the smallest wave to shore, raising a 'right on' from Ronnie, the blond-haired second surf instructor, who's more my age and just as handsome as his buddy—if not more so with the passing of youth.

Stopping by the double shower beyond the surf

school, beside the slipway, I wait my turn. When I press the silver button, the water cascades out of the slim metal showerhead and I peel the rest of the suit from my legs, wishing I'd taken it off at the water's edge. This is what I normally do when bodyboarding, the only type of surfing I'm accustomed to, until today. After fighting to get the wetsuit the right way round, I rinse off quickly in the freezing cold water—no wonder the others from my group didn't linger in the shower during their turn. Wrapping my grey geometric beach towel around my body, an odd swell of disappointment lands in my stomach as my eyes note the sign telling me to place my wetsuit in the bucket of water, and I realise Ben isn't there. He's a busy man. Probably married, with several perfect surfing children with even cooler names, like Tristan, or India, and I scold myself for a second time for having such thoughts.

For lunch, I indulged in a hot Cornish pasty, fries, and lemon San Pellegrino—surfing builds up an appetite, it seems, and I feel fantastic from being active and in the water all morning. Afterwards, I sunbathed, listening to the radio through my earbuds, where I drifted off to sleep. All packed up now, I pull my white, frayed-hem denim shorts and tribal print V-neck blouse over my now dry bikini and head back in the direction of the car.

"How was it?" a deep male voice bellows behind me and I turn to see Ben at the bottom of the slipway, awaiting my response.

"Really great!" I say, my fingers pulling at the top button of my blouse. "I suck at it, to be fair, but I enjoyed it."

"I don't think you sucked that badly. That wave at the end was pretty good for a newbie."

I bite the corner of my lip.

"Maybe you'll come back for another go?"

I nod.

"Well, I'll be seeing you, oh-um-Jo Mitchell."

As I reach my car, I think about how unexpected today has been, but tell myself that April wouldn't be averse to flirting with a man like Ben, in fact she would be all for it—*she* just wouldn't fall for him.

Chapter Four

My bones in my lower back crunch and click as I rise from my bed the morning after my first surf lesson. Sore is the least I can say about how my body feels. Then I think back to Ben and the sexy surfer thing he had going on and I run my teeth along my bottom lip. I'm unable to shake the feeling he was flirting with me and how good it felt. I've moved past the annoyance at myself for being attracted to him and now I'm left wondering what to do about it. There's a considerable part of me which wants to go back to the beach today, but I'd look like a stalker, needy, or both. I'd be going back because of the surf lessons, too, and not just because I have a bit of a thing developing for the owner. I felt so free in the water—so exhilarated and alive. I can't remember the last time I felt that alive. Probably when Tom and I were first together. That first year, when it was all about making plans for our future and being so in love.

My friend Emma, who was living with me at the time, had worried how serious he and I seemed, for fear she'd lose her housemate. She knew early on I wanted to have it all with him. House, marriage, kids.

Perhaps we would have, if things had been different. Still, I have my job, which I love, two amazing parents and awesome friends. My phone vibrates loudly on the coffee table, interrupting my thoughts.

"You must be psychic," I say.

"How so?" I hear the playful tone in Emma's voice.

"Because I was just thinking about you, and when we lived together before Stephen was born."

"You were thinking about how good you were to me, you mean!"

"Well, I don't know about that," I say and I can hear Stephen mumbling in the background. "Someone's very chatty."

"Stephen, come talk to Aunty JoJo."

There's a pause and I hear a shy, "'ello, Anty Jo-Jo."

"Hello, darling boy. I miss you. I hope Mummy's going to bring you to the beach sometime soon?"

"Go beach today," I hear him say and I feel bad, because I've probably dropped Emma right in it now, suggesting something that can't happen.

"Not today, sweetheart, but soon. I promise."

I hear further small protests, but it quickly settles.

"Sorry, I should have realised mentioning a trip to the beach to a three-year-old wasn't the best idea."

"He's gone back to bashing a car with his giant T-Rex, so it's all right," she says, with a rumble of laughter in her tone. "How are you?"

Emma's made a point of 'checking in' with me, or, 'checking up' on me, as I see it, since 'the split', though she doesn't have to. I keep telling her I'm all right.

"I'm fine, more than fine, actually."

"I'm listening," she says, a change of tone in her voice.

"I went for a surf lesson yesterday."

"And you didn't drown?" she says, exaggeratedly slowly, and then laughs.

"Ha-ha, no, I didn't drown. Very nearly on a couple of occasions, but Ronnie, my instructor, rescued me."

"Ronnie, hey." There's extra emphasis on the word 'hey'.

"Settle down, he wasn't my type." I hear a heavy sigh. "There was someone, though," I continue. Her sigh is quickly replaced with a sharp intake of breath and I can visualise Emma straightening up in anticipation of the news. "The surf shop owner, Ben."

"And?"

"And, what? For starters, I acted like a ridiculously infatuated schoolkid with a teacher crush, and more importantly, I'm sworn off relationships. It's part of my 'be more April' plan." I lift my chin, as though I've declared conquering some elaborate fear, such as confined spaces or touching a furry spider—to which I shudder at the thought.

"Oh goodness! Does April know of this plan of yours?"

"No, not yet."

"And you're sure about this? I mean, April will be thrilled, no doubt."

"I'm bored of being serious Jo. I just want to have some fun for a bit, Em."

"Well, okay then. So where does Ben fit into this grand plan of yours? Did you find out if he's single? Did he flirt? What would April do?" Her questions fly at me like tennis balls from an automatic launcher and I'm not sure which one to return first.

"April would make Ben her immediate plan without any hesitation what-so-ever," I say. "The rest, I'm not sure about. I mean, there was no ring and I thought he was flirting with me before I left the beach. He said he hoped he'd see me again, and that the only wave I managed to stay upright on was pretty good for a newbie. Surely that was just him being polite, though, to keep his customers happy?" I see his face and sexy smile as it replays in my mind.

"Oh, Jo. Have you seen you? I'm pretty sure men don't flirt with you just for return trade." She laughs with a familiar lightness in her tone and I smile.

"I miss you, Em."

"I miss you, too. Now, back to this Ben guy. I think you should go back to the beach and find out some more about him. Ask him out, for goodness sake."

"Right, because you would have marched up to some random man and asked him out?"

"What can I say? I'm a happily married woman now, so I can give wise advice."

"So, that's a no." I laugh and she joins me.

"I know how hard this past year has been for you. If having a fling with a hot surfer dude is what you want, then go for it. I just want you to be happy. You, more than anyone, deserve that."

"I know you do and I love you for it …" I inhale deeply and release. "I saw him," I say quietly, as though I don't want the words to be heard, but I do. I want to talk about it. I need to.

"Who? Tom?"

"Yeah. He was with his partner. Em … she's pregnant. Expecting twins."

"Oh, Jo. I'm so sorry."

"I heard a rumour that she was, but it was so real, seeing them together. Seeing her pregnant stomach. Seeing her living the life which should have been mine."

"Hence the surf lesson?"

"It was either that, or start breaking things."

"Ah, I see! Wise choice."

"I just need a different life, Em. I need to stop living in the past and do something. Anything … I … I applied for my visa." The line goes quiet.

"And," she says eventually.

"I haven't heard yet, but I'm going to go. It would just be for six months or so. You, Chris and Stephen could fly out and visit me while I'm over there."

"Until you love it and then never come home, like April did to you."

"Em, I'll always be there for you. No matter what."

"Me too," she says. "It's settled then!"

"What's settled?" I ask, my tone cautiously curious.

"Go back to the beach, walk over to this Ben guy,

and say 'Hi, I'm Jo, remember me? Would you like to go for dinner sometime?' What have you got to lose if you're planning on going travelling anyway?"

"Oh-um-Jo."

"Excuse me?" she asks, her voice rising.

"It's what he calls me."

"Now this, I have to hear."

I'm sitting in my car, in near enough the same parking spot I was yesterday, but I haven't moved from my seat. My conversation with Emma made me pluck up the courage to come back to the beach today, but now I'm here, I've sort of changed my mind. What am I supposed to say to him? Do people really have surf lessons two days in a row—aside from the tourists on holiday? Does he even work every day? I shake my head: *it's supposed to be a bit of fun.* Bored of my own analysis of the situation, and before I have time to *think* myself out of it, I'm throwing my tote bag over my shoulder and pointing the key fob at the car to lock it.

Standing opposite The Tate, I peer down onto the beach, where the surf school flags are flying proudly. It's cooler today, despite the good forecast; the sky is an overcast greyish colour with clouds aplenty. Hopefully the wind, which is blowing strands of hair in front of my eyes, will help push them away and bring in some of the blue skies I can see far out to sea. Weather is so changeable by the coast. As kids, we'd go to the beach in all elements, my dad making us a tent or shelter from tarpaulin. We'd play out in our swimsuits with jumpers and coats over the top, our parents making tea on a camp stove inside the 'tent', eating homemade cakes baked by my aunties or nanna. I was born and raised in Cornwall, but Dad's work took us to Derbyshire, where we stayed for many years. It had always been my plan to move back here, because I missed the beach, the lifestyle and my friends. Plus, Mum and Dad took early retirement and decided to open up the guest house, so I wanted to be on hand to help support them. Not that they've needed me, aside from the grand opening. They're naturals in the leisure industry. Still, I like to help out where I can. Especially for the free board I've had this year. My dad likes that I offer to pay, but never accepts the money, secretly enjoying having me back home, I think. I know he'll miss me when I leave, but he knows I need a change of scenery. My mum and I are close, really close and talk more, but, growing up, I suppose, I was more like my dad. He gets me, in an unspoken way. Our way.

I'm soon barefoot on the sand, one hand gripping my bag, the other swinging my flip-flops idly by my side. Bubbles are forming in the pit of my stomach, taking it in turns to pop, sometimes collectively. My breathing's so scarce I feel light-headed, too. I purse my lips and blow out a long breath, trying to steady myself as I round the corner into the shop. The desk is unmanned, so I wait in front of it, hoping someone, Ben, will appear. It's only a matter of minutes, though it feels far longer, until Ronnie pops his head out, recognising me.

"Hey, you felt the buzz and wanted more already?" he says, his shoulders back and chin high.

I tilt my head from side to side. "What can I say, you were a great teacher." *Oh, crap, now I sound like I'm flirting with him.* My face reddens and he gives me an easy nod. *Least if Ben does turn out to be taken, I could always search Ronnie out again … oh man, I'm channelling a little too much April.*

"I'll take this, Ron." I hear the smooth sound of a deeper voice behind me. Looking round, I see him standing there, his wetsuit round his waist, exposing his toned chest and ripped torso. I swallow again, trying to ignore the Belisha-beacon glow I'm wearing on my face. He places his board on the rack and steps past me, close enough for me to feel a light breeze between us, and moves behind the desk. "Hello again." He smiles, rubbing his hair dry on a towel; it is shorter at the front than at the nape of his neck and not com-pletely straight.

"Hi." My focus flits between the light dusting of sand on the floor and the exit.

"You flirting with my staff?" he asks when Ronnie disappears.

I inhale, looking up and shake my head. "No!"

"Relax, I'm just messing with you." He looks down, but his face is plastered with a wide smile—

dimples and all.

"You're mocking a customer? I'm not sure that's the best way to get return trade."

"You're right." His face becomes more serious. "I should probably make a better first impression."

"Second impression." I cross my arms over my chest. "I found you a bit arrogant the first time."

"Second impression … and wow, okay. I'm sorry about that." His eyes narrow. "So, how about I take you out on a private surf lesson, by way of apology?"

The remaining bubbles in my stomach pop at once and my legs do well to hold me upright. "I'd really like that, if you have the time?"

He nods, just once, unable to hide his pleasure in my acceptance, and I'm impressed with my cool, calm response. I appear to have left awkward oh-um-Jo from yesterday behind. Thankfully.

"No worries, just give me five and we'll get you suited up and down to the water."

The smell of salt and neoprene drifts up my nostrils from the wetsuit, which is cold against my skin. As we draw away from the shelter of the beach and nearer to the water, the wind picks up, making the waves fiercer than yesterday. I'm not sure my below-amateur ranking will match up to it. Ben's ahead of me, carrying the front of the board, and I can't help but stare at his broad shoulders underneath his suit. He's got the sort of physique where the angle of his upper body to waist form an upside-down triangle. There's no white instructor shirt today. I don't think this is an official surf lesson. I can almost hear Emma and April whooping in my head at the thought this might just be a little bit 'date like' for something which hasn't been branded anything.

We stop on a quiet spot of damp, firm sand and he sets the board down.

"Do you remember anything Ronnie taught you yesterday?" he asks.

I inhale, flicking my eyes upwards. "A little," I admit, hoping I'm not wrong.

"Let's go over a few things then, before we get you in the water."

I watch him draw round the board in the sand before moving it out of the way and finishing with a line down the centre of it. He stands up, flipping his hair from his eyes in one movement that's so natural and sexy I think this may be a terrible idea, having a surf lesson from a man who distracts me so much.

"Right, so, this is your board. Do you remember what the line down the middle's called?"

"A string something?" I grit my teeth, shrugging my shoulders.

"A stringer. You can use the line to make sure your feet are correctly placed when you stand up, but for now I just need you to lie on the board." He turns his hands outwards, in front of him, gesturing at the sand.

I self-consciously lie down on my fake board, keeping my legs together and my back arched—something I remember Ronnie telling me.

"Good, but shuffle up a tad."

I do this and pause, focusing on my breathing.

"Perfect. Now, remember, if you're too low down on the board, the nose will lift and it won't make catching waves easy, and if you're positioned too far up on the board—"

"I'll get dunked."

"You were paying attention. Okay, show me paddling."

I bring my arms up and rotate them, pushing away the sand beneath my fingers on the downward stroke.

"Cupped hands," he prompts.

I adapt my style, peering at him through the corner of my eye. He's nodding.

"Try and keep your back arched and don't over-stretch your arms. You want the power to come from your back and arms. What's next?" he asks, hands on hips.

"I practise paddling and belly-boarding to shore. When I'm ready to stand up, I paddle, put my hands down under my shoulders—"

"Good, a bit like chicken wings."

"Push my chest up, bringing up my back foot ..." I say and then lose what I'm doing. Ben crouches beside me, placing his hand on my knee.

"Twist your hips and bring your front foot through."

I'm standing, arms equal for balance, knees bent, resisting the urge to look at him, because I know he'll tell me 'eyes forward'.

"Point in the direction you're going with your front arm." He takes my hand, twisting it to the front and, despite how numb my fingertips feel, they are positively flaming when he releases his grip.

"Nice job. Good stance."

I breathe out and relax my posture before dusting some sand from the side of my cheek, which only worsens the situation. He edges towards me and lifts his hand tentatively.

"May I?"

I nod, and before he misses a beat, his fingertips are dusting the grains from my skin.

"Thank you."

"No problem," he says, with a slight dip of his head. "Let's get you in the surf."

I'm high on adrenaline already, with all the nervous tension and chemistry, feeling as if I can do anything right now. We head down to the water, past half-formed sandcastles and the rippling lines where tide pools of tepid water sit. I watch the sea rolling onto the shore, dissolving into foam, and as it retreats it's as though it leaves a mirror finish on top of the sand.

The freezing cold sea touches my toes, sending a rush through my entire body, but I'm surprisingly warm in Ben's presence. He sets the board on the wet sand and bends over to attach the strap to my ankle.

"Which is your preferred back leg?"

"My right," I say, and, as his hand finds my ankle it's as well the suit material is thick, because my nerve endings are in a frozen frenzy.

"You remember what Ronnie said about how deep to go out?"

"Waist height."

"Let's see what you got, 'oh-um-Jo.'"

I look at him, his mouth closed, one eyebrow raised. How can this man take one of my embarrassing moments and turn it into my favourite thing to hear him say?

"And, try—"

"Not to drown, it's too much paperwork!" I shout over my shoulder, waving my free arm above my head as I stride out further into the water.

I hear him laugh and I'm pleased I have my back to him, because my cheekbones are in danger of cracking from smiling so much.

As I settle into the sea, waist height, bobbing my shoulders under briefly to prepare my body for the cold, I let out an audible gasp. I don't look at him, standing ankle deep in the waves, watching me. I hold my board, nose end up, letting the waves go underneath it. Once I'm where the foamy, mushy-looking white waves are, I turn towards the beach, getting into position. Starting to paddle, I remember to cup my hands against the water and kick my legs as much as I can to pick up speed. Within no time, the wave picks me up and I wing my way towards Ben, who catches the nose of the board as I slide off, pushing my wet hair from my face.

"You nailed that! I think it's time to stand."

"Already?"

His eyes widen. "You don't get baby steps today. Popping up is what you need to practise. Now, I'm going to get you into position. Jump on."

I do as he asks and hold the rails of the board as he floats me over the waves, enjoying his close proximity. The sea has calmed since I arrived at the beach and the sun is breaking through the clouds, as I'd hoped it would.

"Next wave, you're going to paddle, then put your hands down, chicken wings, push your chest up, pull your leg through. *Don't* hesitate. Look and point in the direction you want to go." Ben pauses in the white water. "Paddle, paddle, paddle!" I hear him shout all of a sudden and I spring into action, my heart pounding.

My arms go, my feet kick, and without much thought, I push up, sliding my front foot forward, then I'm down, under the water briefly before I surface, my nostrils burning from inhaling salt water. I cough, trying to grab at my board, which is bobbing up and down. Ben grabs it and puts his hand on my elbow.

"You good?"

I run both hands backwards through my hair and pinch my nose, sniffing to clear it. "Yeah, I think so," I splutter.

"Come on, shake it off. Let's get you back out there."

I give him a wide-eyed expression.

"You've got this. Falling off is a given. Try and put your hands over your head, though, as you come up, in case your board is floating above you."

I nod, suddenly less interested in flirting and more interested in preserving my life.

We start the process again, and before long, I'm being propelled by a wave. This time I'm up, trying to stay crouched low, pointing towards the shoreline, eyes fixed on the quartered black and white flag stuck in the sand. The board slows in the shallow water and I step off, exhilarated, and turn to where Ben is now wading in my direction, smiling. I raise my fist and almost punch the air as though I've just surfed Pipeline.

As he approaches, I hear his thunderous claps. "You made that look easy."

"Oh, I'm not so sure about that. It was terrifying and …" I spread my hands out in front of me, "… such a rush," I say, letting out an elongated breath.

He shakes his head slowly from side to side, his eyes lit with a warm glow. I break eye contact, but the sensation it leaves me with doesn't retreat so quickly.

After a while longer, and several more 'wipe outs' and successes, we head back up the beach. Climbing carefully over the long line of grey stones, which rest where the tide come in, unsure what the time is, or how long we've been in the water. I drop down into the sand by the surf school, feeling exhausted. My arms and legs will do well to function tomorrow and my body is already starting to regret surfing for two days in a row. My heart, on the other hand, is not in the least bit sorry, especially as Ben takes a seat beside me, offering me a cold can of Coke.

"Thanks."

"Cheers," he says, touching his against mine before taking a sip.

"Today was great. Thank you for the private lesson. I'll drink this and then you can tell me how much I owe you?"

He waves his hand. "No charge. I enjoyed teaching you."

"You won't make a lot of money if you give away free lessons to everyone!"

"I don't give away free lessons to just anyone …"

A glow returns to my face instantly.

He puffs out a laugh. "Do you maybe," he rubs at his bottom lip, "want to grab some chips, and take a walk down the beach?"

I look down. "I'd like that, if you don't have to get back to work, that is?"

"I'm kinda the boss, so …" He gives a half-shrug.

"Let me get changed and then I'm all yours." The words topple from my lips before I consider what I'm saying. "In a manner of speaking," I add and jump to my feet.

Twenty minutes later, I'm dry and dressed, having made do with my hair and make-up-free face. We make our way, with our chips, down the beach, past broken crab claws and seagulls' footprints in the sand, past whitewashed beach huts and food kiosks, to the rocky area where people go looking for crabs. There's carpets of thick, dark green vine seaweed, which feels rubbery on the soles of my feet. Once we reach a flattish rock, we perch on it, and I stab my chips more earnestly to eat them, thinking I'm going to need more than these to replace the calories I just burnt off.

"So, I've seen you twice now and I know practically nothing about you, Jo."

"What would you like to know?" I hesitate slightly, hoping I've not given him too much free rein with his questions.

"What do you do for work?"

"I'm a nurse. I live with my parents in the guest house they own and run near Becks' fish and chip shop."

"I love Becks."

"Me too."

"Have you always lived here?"

"I grew up here, before we moved to Derbyshire as a family. I've been back a few years now."

"Are you planning on sticking around?" he asks, before slipping another forkful of food into his mouth.

"I hope so. It's home now, though I don't plan on living with my parents forever. It's just temporary, or should have been until I found another place to rent. I was living with my ex-boyfriend up until six months ago."

"What happened?" he asks, the can of Coke in his hand pausing halfway to his mouth.

"We wanted different things from life, I suppose. The house we lived in was his, so I decided to move in with my parents and I've sort of never left."

"I get needing some time to recalibrate."

Ben doesn't pump me for more details and I'm relieved. "What about you? You a born and bred local?" I ask.

"Near enough. I started the surf shop ten years ago, with my late wife."

I don't mean for my body to stiffen, or to inhale so sharply, but I do.

"Sorry, I'm not very good at dropping that into conversation."

"No, don't be sorry. I'm sorry for your loss … how, do you mind me asking, did your wife die?"

"It's another bombshell answer, I'm afraid."

I nod, looking into his light brown eyes and I feel as though I can almost see into his soul.

"Jen, that was her name, she died after giving birth to our daughter, Poppy."

My mouth moves, but I make no sound at first. "You have a daughter?"

"I do, she's seven."

I shake my head, my eyebrows lifting.

"Judging from the look on your face, I'd say I've shared a little too much!"

"No! My face isn't very good at hiding my emotions. I forget sometimes that it might come across badly. I just had you pegged as married with several beautiful children, all with very cool surfer names, and I don't know why I'm sharing that with you … It seems my mouth isn't so good at hiding things either." I grimace.

His laugh, soft and assured, is already a familiar and welcome sound to my ears.

"I like honesty. It's refreshing." He pauses, as if to examine me. "So, having a daughter doesn't put you off me?" he asks.

"Why would you want to know that?" I ask, feeling my blood pressure rising up a notch.

"You like to make a guy work for it, don't you, oh-um-Jo?" A beat. "I'd like to cook you dinner sometime. I'd take you out to dinner, but the aforementioned fatherhood doesn't allow me many evenings off—I'm not a serial killer or anything." He puts his head in his hands. "Now you totally think I'm a serial killer for mentioning it."

I laugh. "I'm pretty sure serial killers don't go advertising these things to their victims."

"Looks like you're not the only one whose mouth isn't keeping a lid on it today."

"I'd love to have dinner with you … sometime." I give him a slight smile.

Ben nods once, his composure returning, and we set back up the beach, towards the surf school.

"How's next Friday night suit, for dinner, that is?" he asks, opening my car door, after insisting he walk me back to the car park.

"Friday works for me," I say, with a wide grin. Unsure how I'm going to last until then to see him.

Chapter Five

The contents of my entire wardrobe lies strewn across my double bed. I've stubbed my toe twice in my haste to get ready, and now I'm standing in the middle of the room, wearing my best black lace bra and pants, hoping for inspiration to strike. He'd called me on Monday to arrange our date, joking about how he'd tried to leave it longer before calling, to play it cool, but he'd failed miserably. I love his honesty; how open and uncomplicated it all seems—well, aside from the single dad thing he's got going on, but then I remind myself I'm not marrying the guy and I breathe more easily. We'd arranged my arrival for eight-thirty p.m., to give me a chance to get ready, and for him to have time to settle his daughter, Poppy, into bed.

It's a little strange, the idea of going to a man's house for dinner, knowing there's a sleeping child. Not strange enough to stop me, or to dampen the excitement which is preventing me choosing an outfit. I'm certain my bra and pants aren't suitable, with a child, sleeping or otherwise, in another room. It's only spring, and though it's been warm on a couple of days, there's still a chill in the evenings. In the end, I opt for a casual black dress with pockets, tan ankle boots and a blue denim jacket. I've dried and straightened my hair and applied smoky eye make-up. I slip on my silver charm bracelet, and inhale fruity top notes of perfume as I dab a little on my neck.

Fifteen minutes later, by which time I'm ten minutes late, I pull up on the hilly, tree-lined road outside his house, checking my handbrake is securely on, and I'm in gear. The porch light has been left on for me and I can read the number fifteen, which is on the text he sent with his address. The house is a red brick, detached, two-storey property, with a hedge surrounding a tidy block-paved driveway. His black pickup truck is on the drive, and there's a pink scooter, with seventies-style streamers spilling from the handlebars in a matching shade, propped up against the house. Definitely no serial killer vibes yet. I inhale, smoothing hair behind my ears, before reaching for my bag and climbing out onto the pavement.

The pale green door opens just as I lift my hand to knock, and I bob my head to the side and see Ben appear from behind it.

"Hi. I saw you pull up, so I thought I'd open it, save waking Poppy with the knocking."

"Oh, yeah, of course. I didn't think about that."

"She's out for the count, so probably wouldn't have heard it if you had. I'm just so used to being a ninja."

"A ninja, hey. Do you have a costume too?"

"Skipping straight to the role play. I like your style," he says, nodding slowly with exaggeration.

I hold my face in my hands. My neckline's flaming hot.

"I'm teasing you again, sorry. In my defence, it's way too easy."

My left hand finds my hip and my face a fake scowl. "Well, if you're into all that, I could nip home for my nurse's outfit!" *My revenge, I can tell, is sweet.*

He coughs, his eyes widening as he tips his head to one side. "You win that round. Can I take your coat?" he says with a smile, arms out ready to ease me from my jacket.

"Thank you." I return his warmth.

"Can I get you a wine, or a hot drink?"

"Anything a bit stronger?"

"Gin?"

"Perfect."

"Not a wine drinker then?"

"Red on occasion, and prosecco, but usually when I'm with my friend. She's a prosecco kind of girl, which, don't get me wrong, I like, but not as much as gin."

"Is she local?" He's pouring a measure of gin into a glass, before opening the fridge to add the tonic and a slice of lemon.

"She and I lived together for a while, but she's back home in Derbyshire now, married with a child."

"Your drink, madame."

"Thank you." The coolness of the glass is welcome against my warm hands. I want to rest it on my bare chest, but I imagine how strange this might look, so I don't. "Whatever you have cooking smells amazing, by the way." I breathe in the warm aroma of what smells like roast chicken.

"I've made chicken breast, wrapped in bacon, with parmentier potatoes and a side salad. I hope you're hungry? And not a vegetarian. I forgot to ask you that?" A flash of alarm passes over his face.

"I'm not a vegetarian, but if my game face was better I would have totally gone for a round two win then." I take a sip of my drink.

"I've created a monster." He laughs, pulling on some oven gloves before releasing the oven door. The room fills with hot air and a more intense smell of chicken and salty bacon. "Another five minutes should do it." He places the oven gloves on the side and retrieves his beer bottle from the counter, taking a long pull. The kitchen is neat and well organised. It has grey cabinets on the floor and walls. A sink in front of the window and at the centre of the room is an island, behind which sits a breakfast bar, with three high-rise stools.

"I love this kitchen. Any I've ever had would look pokey and unsophisticated in comparison."

"I dunno about sophisticated."

"You have your own pasta maker, a granite pestle and mortar and this fancy coffee machine, which looks like some sort of alien spaceship from *Flight of The Navigator*."

"Great film."

"Classic."

"The pasta maker is mine; I love to cook Italian food. The fancy coffee machine, which shall now be named Max in honour of the film …" He smiles and I laugh, cocking my head back. "It was Jen's," he continues. "Her morning ritual was always an espresso, and when she arrived at work, she'd have a black Americano with an extra shot—you could say she was somewhat of a coffee lover," he says, busying himself getting white pasta plates from the cupboard.

"I'm with her … I mean … I love coffee too. Sorry." I shake my head. "I'm clumsy with my words."

"No, it's fine. I'm talking about my dead wife on our date, *again*."

"I don't expect you to hide the fact you lost your wife. She's the mother of your child and I don't judge you for mentioning her. I just don't want to say the wrong thing and upset you."

He moves in front of me, touching my wrist, which sends a warm tingle up my arm. "You won't upset me. Let's just be relaxed about it all and we'll both feel a ton better?"

I nod, rubbing my hand over his, where it's still resting on my wrist. Touching him feels surprisingly natural.

"What did she do for a job?" I ask when we've parted.

"She was a counsellor working for various charities over the years."

"Wow, such a worthwhile career."

"Tough going, but she enjoyed it. Yours is a pretty

worthwhile career, too. How long have you been a nurse?"

"Forever. I trained straight after my A-levels. I've always wanted to help people, I suppose."

He smiles at me, one that lingers and I want to look away, but don't allow myself, until the oven beeps continuously and he whips around to silence it.

After our delicious main meal and then some scrumptious salted caramel profiteroles and cream for pudding, I'm almost in a food coma. I'd offered to help clear up, but he insisted I relax in the living room, which is, again, surprisingly chic. Parquet butterscotch oak flooring and a white wooden hearth, with an electric-effect fire. There's a large wall-mounted TV and an inviting-looking silvery-grey corner sofa and chair. I ease into the chair and sip my coffee. Ben had offered me another gin, but I need to be able to drive home, so I declined. The last thing anyone needs is me passed out on the sofa and Poppy discovering me in the morning. Meeting her isn't part of my plan, or his, I imagine, given I'm a stranger. I'm intrigued about how she looks, though, and I remember seeing some photo frames on the mantelpiece, so I stand to examine them. Sure enough, there's a photo of Ben and a very smiley, long-wavy-auburn-haired little girl, with the biggest green eyes I've ever seen—Disney princess big. *And oh how pretty she is.* He looks besotted in this photo.

"That was taken about a year ago."

I jump, quickly setting the frame back down. "Sorry, I'm being nosey. She's beautiful."

"Thank you. I kinda think so myself, and don't apologise."

I smile. "Her colouring, it's so rare. Auburn hair and green eyes."

"Her mum," I watch as his Adam's apple rises and falls, "she had the same colour hair and eyes. I used to find it hard, how much she looks like Jen. Now, though, it's a sweet reminder."

"Can I see a photo of her? Your wife, I mean."

He hesitates for a moment, his brows pulling inwards.

My smile must reassure him, because he moves over to a sideboard, lifts a frame and walks it over to where I'm standing. He passes it to me and I examine the familiar eyes and hair from the previous picture, and I swallow down an odd feeling. "She's her double. Your wife was beautiful, Ben."

He takes the frame, breaking with a warm smile. "Do you want to watch a film or something?" he asks, swiftly moving on, and I'm pleased for the break in tension.

"I'm happy talking. I'd like to know more about you. Like why the surfing?" We move to the sofa, sitting beside each other.

"I just got into it from a young age. My friends all surfed. Their older brothers, sisters, dads. I just loved being out on the ocean. I always said I wanted to open my own surf shop; work on the beach all day."

"And here you are, living your dream."

He nods, a flash of nostalgia creeping over his face and I want to ask about his wife, but I don't.

"What else do you want to know?" He leans back.

"What did you want to be when you were at school?"

"I wanted to be in a rock band, like Bon Jovi."

I laugh, hard.

"Well, you do have the long hair for it."

"I'll let you into a little secret," he whispers and I lean towards him.

"I'm a little vain about my hair." He draws his finger to his lips.

I laugh once more. "Don't worry, I won't chop it all off while you sleep."

"I'd probably cry. Big, fat, ugly tears."

"Can you play an instrument?" I ask, my face aching with how much he makes me smile.

"Nope."

"Sing?"

"Not a note. It doesn't stop me belting out *Livin' on a Prayer* in the shower, or when Pops and I have a dance party here in the lounge."

"I can just visualise it."

"Can you?" he pauses, doing that smouldering, sexy stare into my soul thing he does when he's being playful. My insides twist into a deep, tight, pulsating knot.

"The dance party, not the shower part," I say, unable to break eye contact.

"You're incredibly sexy when you bite that bottom lip of yours."

"I didn't even know I was biting it."

"You do, when you're nervous."

"Oh, you think you make me nervous?" I lean away from him.

"I kinda hope so, because you terrify me." With that, he leans forward, smelling sweet and citrusy. Lingering inches from my face, his eyes flicking between my eyes and my mouth when, all of a sudden, he moves in, brushing his lips over mine. When we part, I try to remember to breathe. My heart is ricocheting off my rib cage—threatening internal damage. "I've wanted to do that all evening," he says, gently pushing a strand of hair from my face. His fingertips are warm, leaving a tingling sensation that remains long after his touch.

"So, we should go back to the part where—"

"You were imagining me naked in the shower?" He lets out a throaty laugh.

I shove him with the heel of my hand on his chest and he feigns injury, rubbing the spot with his hand. We lock eyes, laughing.

"No, the part where you have dance parties to Bon Jovi. I *need* to see this."

"All right."

To my amazement, he stands up, pressing buttons on his iPad, and before long the rising beat of *Livin' on a Prayer* fills the space around us. The drums have barely started their intro when he releases his hair from his ponytail, already pretending to hold a mic, while lip-synching and shoulder shrugging. I'm laughing from so deep inside and so hard, I almost forget the sleeping child upstairs and have to push my knuckles to my lips to silence myself. My amusement only adds to his performance, with hair flicks, air grabs, spins and leg kicking. By the second verse, I'm starting to see a career as a Bon Jovi impersonator, and what's supposed to be him making a complete fool of himself only adds to his sexiness. As I leave the sofa, moving towards him, he stills, the music no longer in control.

"I'm not looking for anything serious," I whisper, his lips inches from my own.

"Neither am I," he says, one hand finding my neck, the other my waist, and as he draws me into his body I start to question, just what it is I am looking for?

Chapter Six

It's my day off today, and Ben's got the surf shop covered for a few hours while Poppy's at school so that we can spend some time together. It's slightly against my better judgement to go on another date, but truthfully, the other night was the most fun I've had in a really long time. My mind hasn't left the moment he kissed me on Friday night and I've been trying not to count the seconds until today, when I can see him again. Plus, we're going to one of my favourite places: The Minack Theatre. Less than one hundred years old, it was the vision of a lady called Rowena Cade, and its name means 'rocky place'. Quite literally; it's carved into the steep cliffs to make a beautiful open-air theatre which hosts theatrical performances. I've actually never seen one, but it's on my list of things to do.

"Do you know she worked on this well into her eighties and died before her ninetieth birthday? The woman is a legend! Look at this place," I say to Ben as we stare down into the theatre spanning out in front of us. This once rocky gully was transformed into pathways which slope and wind beside an array of flowers and greenery towards grass-covered seating carved from the stone itself in a semi-circle to frame the stage. At the bottom of the theatre, there's a raised circular stage to one side, with stone steps to the left. The entire stage looks like multi-coloured honeycomb, with blocks of reddish, bluey/grey and pale green hexagon slabs. An archway in the centre, where the coastline drops away down a grass-covered rock face, has a path which leads below the stage. Every slab, post and pillar is carved and crafted to perfection.

"It's some legacy to have left behind, that's for sure," he says, hands on the metal railings. I can see his eyes scanning the ocean beyond the theatre, which on a sunny day could easily be mistaken for somewhere such as the Amalfi coast of Italy. "Shall we?" he asks, holding out his hand and leading the way down the many, many steep steps towards the stage.

There are no performances today, so we're just sightseeing, and I'm planning on dragging Ben into the café, for what is in my opinion the best cream tea for miles. Passing under the stone archway, behind the circular stage, we follow a path which runs parallel to the sea. Opposite a channel carved into the rocks sits a semi-sheltered bench in a stone alcove, which has a slightly cold, damp, mossy smell to it. As the waves roll into the channel, they're forced together, fighting for space as they lap the sides of the narrow brown rocks, tumbling loudly, creating a river rapid until they can flow no further and push back against the current. The white frothy water fizzes in the middle, resembling a bubbling Jacuzzi. We sit in contented silence and I appreciate how peaceful it is, despite the slight howl of the wind and the rumble of the sea, echoing in our shelter. I love the ocean. I find it grounding, its grace, strength, and power. Its ability to destroy anything and everything in its path.

My thick, ivory cable knit sweater with jeans and long brown boots were a good choice today as the weather's more like winter than spring. A shock to the system, after Mother Nature teased us with good weather this past week. I shiver, rubbing my hands together. Ben moves closer to me and I immediately feel his body heat. He takes both my hands in his, and as I turn towards him, he cups them, blowing warm air through his fingers towards my hands.

"Thank you." I smile, leaning into his body as he puts his arm around me, falling back into our silence with ease. "I love it here," I say. "It's perfect." My eyes are closed and I inhale the freshness in the air.

"You're a romantic, aren't you?" His head's tilted to one side.

"Huh?"

"A romantic!" He repeats himself.

"I heard you. I just don't understand how you've come to that conclusion based on my love of this place."

"Because it's magical and beautiful. There's the sea, and these little cosy places to sit and hold hands. You're a romantic."

"I'm not really. I'm a nurse, so I'd say I'm too

pragmatic for all that. Besides, romantics believe in 'happily ever after' and I've seen way too much real life to believe in that." I stop, noticing his expression change. "Sorry, I didn't mean to rant quite like that."

"No, I'm inclined to agree." His voice trails off and I feel like an idiot for mentioning the lack of a 'happy ever after', given he lost his wife so tragically. "Let's go with wistful then." He's staring at me, gauging my response, undeterred, despite my little outburst.

"Now *that* definitely doesn't sound like a compliment."

"It means reflective." He lets out a gentle laugh. "You like to sit and look out over the ocean, reflecting on your life and how you feel … That's why I enjoy surfing. I do the same. When I'm sat on my board watching the waves, waiting for the perfect set, I think. There's no interruptions out there. No one to answer to, be responsible for, or disappoint."

"Disappoint?" I ask.

"Oh." He shrugs off the question. "I just mean it's my sanctuary. Being a single dad isn't without its challenges."

"I can imagine … I mean, I can't imagine really, but you know what I mean." My words seem to tumble from my lips, then I inhale. As I breathe out, I look back at him; his eyes are fixed on my lips and I know what he's going to do. I'm willing him to—drawing an imaginary line between our mouths, using my mind to reel him in. He kisses me with the same familiarity of our second kiss on Friday night. Building up pace. Full of promise and wanting. When we part, I bring the back of my hand to my mouth and giggle as a passing older couple smile at our public display of affection.

"Good morning." Ben nods his head.

"It certainly looks good," the man says with a wry smile and I laugh harder. Ben, too, this time.

"Hungry?" Ben asks me, standing and holding out his hand once more.

"Always," I say, taking it.

On the way back along the path, we stop, noticing a small crowd gathered around a man who's on one knee in the archway by the stage. The woman facing him has her hands to her face as he reaches out to her. I know instantly he's proposing, so I nudge Ben and whisper for him to take pictures.

I can't hear the man's declaration of love, not that I need to. The way the woman's eyes glisten and her smile builds tells me more than his words ever could. A confident 'yes' drifts past us on a gust of wind and the couple fall into each other's arms and kiss, the air around them full of cheers and applause.

"Please tell me you got that?" I ask him, breathless and completely exhilarated from absorbing such a beautiful moment.

"I sure did. Come on, let's congratulate them." He pulls me quickly from our spot and we edge between the gathered people. The couple are hand in hand walking away from us, but we move alongside them.

"Congratulations," Ben says. "I hope you don't mind, but we took a few pictures of your proposal and wondered if you'd like us to send them to you?"

The woman, who looks about my age, smiles at her new fiancé before turning to Ben, her eyes soft, tearing up again. "Thank you so much. Would you mind sending me them on WhatsApp, if I give you my number?" Her phone's in her hand in an instant.

As we continue our ascent to the café, Ben turns to me. "No, you're right," he says, looking at me so directly it feels probing. "You're not a romantic in the slightest." I playfully tap him with the back of my hand on his shoulder as he swaggers off ahead of me, laughing, and my face aches from smiling.

I'm panting by the time we stop outside the café entrance. It's quite an ascent to the top. More people stopped the happy couple with their congratulations and I feel energised from being part of their story in some way. Ben opens the door for me and we drift inside, claiming a table by the large panoramic window which boasts the best views out to sea and over Porthcurno beach. The wedge of white sand meets a sea which turns turquoise as the sun, finally gracing us with its presence, shines down on it. The bay is sheltered by high cliffs on either side and it looks somewhat like a tropical island on a sunny day. It's a favourite of mine and I hope there's time to venture down there today, before our time together ends.

"Are you having a cream tea?" Ben asks, hovering beside our table.

"I'll get them, you paid the entry fee." I reach for my purse.

"It wouldn't feel right having you pay on a date. Call me old-fashioned if you like, but please let me."

I smile, placing a hand on my chest. The light resting on one half of his face makes his right eye look golden. My attraction to him is so strong, it's a struggle remembering to breathe, and I spend a good portion of our time together feeling giddy. As he walks away, I glimpse at his toned legs, uncovered in his light blue combat shorts. I'm not sure he feels the cold, and seems to prefer shorts above all other items of clothing, aside from his wetsuit. His waterproof coat has a thicker lining to it and is darker in colour than his shorts, but still blue. I'm sensing it's his favourite colour, especially given his paisley bandana, which suits him, is navy. I've never dated a man with the style Ben has and I like it. Tom was more of a chino and polo shirt kind of guy. My first boyfriend, who I dated from my late teens to early twenties, was a rugby shirt and combat shorts person. Perhaps I don't really have a 'type', certainly not one that relates to dress code.

The café isn't busy yet, and I'm secretly pleased we have the space to ourselves. Not having anyone listening in to our conversation, realising we're on a date, because I assume we scream 'only just met' in our body language—or at least I feel as though we do.

Through the window, I observe the darkness of the sea in the distance. The odd line of white water, rippling, but mostly the steady rise and fall of waves, which appear small from up here, on top of the cliff. A large ship sits on the horizon, just visible, and my mind ponders the creatures out there with it, in the depths of the ocean. My favourite sea creatures are dolphins. Wouldn't it be a treat to spot them off the coast? Not that I ever have. Perhaps today, with all the magic that's in the air, might be the day—I did just witness a romantic proposal, after all. With my eyes closed, I tip my head back, enjoying the warmth of the sun streaming through the large glass window.

I think of all the times I must have been to Porthmeor beach, or surfers as we call it, where Ben works and I can't recall ever seeing him. There's no recollection in my mind of noticing him, yet now I can't imagine how I would have missed him. I suppose I had no need to seek out the surf school, preferring to concentrate on relaxing in the sand, or wandering to the water on the swimmers' side. Perhaps I crossed paths with his wife before she died. There's something strange about living in proximity to a person you never knew was there, and wondering about the *what ifs*. What if I'd met him years ago, before he'd met his wife and before I met Tom? What if I'd met him when I wasn't sworn off relationships, could this be something more than a casual fling with a hot surfer? Sensing someone beside me, I see him drape his coat over the spare chair next to us and I shake off my thoughts.

"It won't be long," he says, sitting on the closest chair to me. His sunglasses are casually tucked into the neckline of his top. "After, I was thinking we could take a walk down on the beach, if you're up for it?"

"I was hoping you'd say that. It's one of my favour-ites."

"Mine too. Poppy loves to play in the stream that flows down one side of the beach. It's a great spot to take kids. Aside from the hike down the steps from the car park, that is."

"Yeah, this is true. Not so good if you need the loo once you reach the bottom."

"Ah, that's what the sea's for."

"Urgh. I'm not going surfing with you anymore." I draw my upper body away from him. He knocks back his head as he laughs and his hair falls across his face, which he pushes to one side with his hand. I watch him, unable to turn my gaze from his face.

"So, I have a question for you."

"Okay!" I draw my head an inch backwards, curious as to what he's going to ask.

"Don't look so worried, I'm just trying to get to know you better."

"Least it's not truth or dare. My friend, Emma, went on a date with a guy and they played that." I nod. *Oh heck, I really hope I didn't give him that idea now.*

He looks thoughtful for a moment. "Now that does sound interesting." He leans back in his chair, his arms folded behind his head.

I go to speak, but my lips only just part before I'm interrupted.

"Don't panic, I'm not going to suggest it, at least not today …" He relaxes then, tapping the table with both hands, a beat behind the other. "My question for you is best ever and worst ever date?"

"Hmm." I gently run my thumbnail under my

front teeth and release. "This one's turning out to be pretty good."

"Thank you, but you're not getting out of answering the question with flattery."

I run my thumb along my chin as I think over the dates in my life. Aside from my five-year relationship with my first boyfriend and then, lately, Tom, it had mostly been dates with guys who were okay, but not quite right, or the odd one who I liked more than they liked me.

"A guy I really fancied once took me to fly this enormous kite, which doesn't sound very romantic, but it was different and fun and quite tactile."

"Okay. Tactile. Fun. I can do those things." His tone reflects the mischief in his eyes. "And the worst?" he says, ankle resting on top of his knees, elbow propped up on the table.

"Oh, easy! I went out for drinks with a guy who was a dentist."

Ben nods, a little impressed by the dentist part, no doubt.

"It was going well, until he decided to examine my teeth."

"I'm sorry, what? He examined your teeth mid-date?"

"Oh, he got right on in there. Me, wide mouthed, unable to speak as his giant un-gloved fingers probed my molars."

I look at Ben, whose dazed expression makes me laugh.

"Firstly, I feel like this has changed my outlook on dental check-ups, and secondly, please tell me you never saw him again?"

I stare at him as if to say, 'Do you really need to ask?'. "I made my friend call me with a fake emergency, left and blocked his number."

Ben's laughing and he reaches for my hand.

"Here you are, my lovers. Two cream teas." The older lady with her strong Cornish accent sets down the tray, decanting the contents onto the table in front of us. "Say, you're not the ones who just got engaged, are you?"

I scratch behind my ear.

"No, not us, I'm afraid. We're just here for the delicious scones."

The lady stands up straighter, clearly as mesmerized by Ben as I am. "Isn't he a charmer," she says, shrugging her shoulders. I see a noticeable spring in her step as she retreats back to the counter.

"You have a gift with the ladies, Benjamin."

"Why, thank you." He bows his head. "Please don't call me, Benjamin, though. I hear that and look for my mother, which isn't a good thing."

"Why? Are you two not close?"

"Our DNA matches—does that count?"

"Ah, I see. Does Poppy get along with her grandparents?"

"She likes them about as much as I do these days, though she's only just working things out for herself. I tried not to taint her opinion of them. They're not the easiest people to get along with, and kids are very perceptive, especially as they get older."

"In what way aren't they the easiest people to get along with?"

"Let me eat this and I'll fill you in on our walk," he says, but I sense I've hit a boundary and I'm not sure if I have permission to cross it.

The scones were freshly baked and warm, with oodles of luxuriously thick clotted cream and sweet strawberry jam heaped on top. I'm never sure which way round you're supposed to make them. The age-old debate of cream then jam, or jam then cream? I prefer the former, but I could be doing it wrong. Ben joined *my way*, too, so we're probably both wrong, but, either way, they tasted delicious. Afterwards, we drove down the winding hilly road from the theatre to the beach car park and descended the steps to the beach. We're now ambling in fine white sand, my boots slipping with every step I take. Ben takes my hand and I love the feeling of his fingers interlocked with mine, radiating warmth through them, which seems to travel upwards and around my entire body, as though it were a separate circulatory system. I see a golden retriever bound towards its owner, a ball in its mouth, before it's thrown back towards the water, the dog disappearing over the sandbank and out of sight. No doubt into the water as his fur is already dripping wet. There are no children playing in the stream today. No piles of sand blocking the flow of the water while they try redirecting it into dug-out pools, attempting to stop it draining away. No smaller children, or mischievous older ones, destroying their efforts as they stamp on the heaped-up sand, creating springs which need plugging. I remember playing that very same game as a child, and momentarily my mind ponders what sort of child Poppy is, and what sort of father Ben is.

"You okay?" he asks me.

"Of course. I was just remembering playing here as a child."

"Happy memories?"

"The happiest." I smile up at him, his eyes fixed on mine in a moment of loud stillness as the next wave builds before rumbling onto shore. "So," I leave a pause for emphasis, raising both eyebrows, "I have a question, in keeping with our conversation in the café. *Your* best and worst ever dates, please?"

He pulls at his bandana. "Worst is easy. A mate of mine decided to set me up with his sister's best friend. We went out for a drink and she, not so subtly, dropped hints that she normally likes to be bought flowers on a first date."

My jaw drops. "How presumptuous and rude. Great first impression!"

"It gets better." He laughs, as though the punchline to a joke is already in his mind and he's braced for the impact. "She spent much of the night telling me I looked clean, like inspecting my fingernails levels of clean." He rotates one of his hands mid-air.

I place my hand over my mouth, my nostrils twitching.

"I think if I'd sat there long enough she'd have gone through my hair to check for nits or something." And at that, I almost snort out a laugh. "Later in the week, I got a message from her telling me the two main characters in her favourite film reminded her of us. It was a Nicholas Sparks film," he says and I'm gone. Flat out hysterics for all to hear on the beach.

"I'm sorry, that is all kinds of creepy and bizarre."

"I've never blocked someone so fast in my life."

"I'm impressed you know Nicholas Sparks films enough to get the reference, though."

"Jen loved a chick flick. Dragged me to the cinema to see every single one of them." He laughs. It's both warm and full of longing.

"Do you miss her?"

Ben looks down, his left hand flexing as he rubs his fingers with his thumb. "I'll always miss her. It's been so long now, sometimes it makes me sad, how fast memories fade."

"Have you been in another relationship since?" I ask.

"Nothing serious." The wall's up a little then, I sense.

"Just the clean police."

"Yep." He smiles at me, no more sadness clouding his features. It's blown over now, the moment.

"Best date ever?" I remind him of our conversation.

"Eating chips on the rocks after taking this amazing women surfing the other day. She's not bad for a newbie."

"Hey," I double take, "you can't use our date! It's against the rules."

"Well, it wouldn't be very romantic if I say otherwise, would it? It would also not be very truthful. I enjoy your company, Jo."

My heart flutters and my skin feels warm, as though all my capillaries just dilated, flooding my skin with blood flow. "I enjoy spending time with you, too …" I say, then immediately look away. "Did you know that *Poldark* was filmed here? This is Nampara cove." I gesture around the scenery.

"I didn't know that. You a big *Poldark* fan?"

"I was so sad when the last episode aired. I loved it … I mean, what's not to love about a floppy-dark-haired Aidan Turner, with his top off!"

"Oh, so it's dark-floppy-haired men in general, is it?"

I realise the irony in my statement and that I've inadvertently described him. "Well, yes, in general, but you in particular. Though if we happen upon Aidan Turner on our walk, you may have to make yourself scarce." I laugh and begin to run away, because there's something about his body language which tells me he's about to chase me and, most likely, dunk me in the sea for my last comment.

I scream, which carries on the waves, making it echo around the bay. The dog playing ball with its owner is now eyeing us curiously as Ben's strong arms grab my waist. He spins me around effortlessly, until I'm cradled in his arms and he's striding to the water's edge, no fear that his own boots are now soaking wet through.

"I'm sorry," I plead. "*Please* don't drop me. Argh!" I scream once more as he loosens his grip on me, making me drop an inch, before the tension is back in his arms.

"Ha-ha-ha." His face is soft, his eyes playful and bright. I'm in dangerous territory and I don't mean the immediate risk of being totally immersed in water.

Chapter Seven

Today, I'm sprawled out on my beach towel, toes dug under the sand, wearing a short summer floral print dress. Making the most of the beach and my close proximity to Ben, who has to work, but I've seen him briefly for coffee and he's going to join me for lunch any time now, I hope, as the smell from the bacon in the kiosk this morning, hot, crispy bacon on buttered bread, has been tempting me. There's a nice warmth to the day, as we're nearing the beginning of May. I have to work this weekend, as penance for requesting the following weekend off to go to Wincastle to see Emma for the Annual May Ball at her and her husband's lavish country estate. The ball is held at the beginning of May and I've been going for the past few years. Who doesn't enjoy the excuse to get dressed up and pretend to step into the world of Jane Austen for the evening?

Emma phoned me last week, checking I was still going to make it, and I don't know who was more excited, me, her, or Stephen, with his inordinately high-pitched squeals in the background.

I hear the dull sound of my phone vibrating and

search around in my taupe canvas beach bag for it.

"Hey, Cuz!"

"Hey," April says in a tired voice and I can picture her lolling against the throw cushions of her bed.

"You sound like you need an early one?"

"Yeah, busy week!" she replies. "I got your message about working the weekend and I know you'll be off to see Emma the following one for the ball, so I thought I'd best check in."

"I'm happy you did. I can tell you about my new dress."

"Describe!" Her tone elevates from tired to complete interest.

"It's a silk floor-length gown, with a sort of cross-over halter neckline."

"How chic. What colour?" she asks, but I'm distracted by the flock of seagulls who dive-bomb a woman walking past me with a tray of chips, and I flinch as they squawk loudly.

"Blooming seagulls," I mutter.

"Some unsuspecting soul decided to run the gull gauntlet then?"

"Yep. It amazes me when people try. I mean it's not like there aren't 'Beware of the gulls' signs everywhere, not to mention this place being infamous for the feisty beggars mugging people for food. Go fish in the ocean," I call out and a seagull waddling past eyes me as if to say 'Anything for an easy life, love.' "Anyway, where were we?"

"Colour?"

"Oh, yeh. I'd say it's a copper colour. I'll send you a picture."

"Please take several, especially from the ball itself. Speaking of, did you ask him yet?"

"No! Besides, he has Poppy to think of. I know he doesn't find getting a babysitter easy."

"Oh come on! You're making excuses and you know it. Can't he ask his parents?"

"They don't get along apparently."

"How come?"

"I'm not sure. We were supposed to talk about it last time we were out, but we got side-tracked."

"Side-tracked, hey? I like the sound of this."

"Don't get excited." My tone lowers. "We haven't been *alone, alone* yet."

"But the other night, after his Bon Jovi perfor-mance, you said—"

"We kissed … a lot … I didn't say more than that."

"The definition of 'casual' usually means sleeping with the guy. This sounds more like a budding romance."

"It is casual. I have no plans for a relationship, I just didn't feel comfortable taking it further with his daughter asleep upstairs."

"Man, you need to go to this ball! Have a night away together. Ask him … or give me his number and I'll do it myself!"

"Oh, no thank you! He's meeting me for lunch soon and I'll speak to him then."

"Skip lunch. I think the more immediate priority is

seeing the man naked!"

"April! You're such a hussy!" I laugh. More of a giggle really.

"Honey, I've seen the man's picture—he's fitter than some of the professional male models I get paid to photograph. If I were you, I'd be all over that!"

"I know, right!" My laughter doesn't subside, because I've always envied April's work as a freelance photographer and the men she brushes shoulders with. Now, for once, the tables have turned. I've never fathomed why she's always chosen casual relationships, though, and she doesn't care to talk about it, even with me, her favourite and only cousin. More than being family, we're best friends. Between April and Emma, I have every melodrama of life covered, and always have safe refuge, whether in person, or virtually speaking. I suppose the only sad part is the distance apart we all live. April and I grew up here in Cornwall and were inseparable. My mum would make us clothes from fabric bought at the local market. Floating pink skirts, paired with white tops and headbands, the padded sort, which were made from the same fabric as our skirts. Little lemon-coloured dresses, shorts and tops sets. We even had the same long-length hair, worn in the same style. Whatever the day or occasion, we always coordinated. There's a photographed period of our lives where you couldn't tell where I ended and she began. We were the sisters we never had, and still are, despite her living on the other side of the world.

"Well, try and get him out of your system by October."

"Don't worry, nothing's going to stop me jumping on that plane and travelling for a whole day to come and see my favourite cousin."

"I'm pleased to hear it. Right, I need my beauty sleep."

"Hardly, but sweet dreams anyway."

She laughs. "Love you and talk to Ben, or I will …"

"You won't." My words come out a little like a melody. "Love you. Goodnight."

"Hey." I feel a warm hand on my shoulder and a kiss on my cheek as he drops beside me in the sand. "Should I be worried, overhearing you tell someone you love them? You're not secretly married, living a double life, are you?"

"Ha-ha, no. That was my cousin, April. She lives in Australia."

"How long has she been out there for?"

"Years now. She lives in Sydney. Never was one to stay close to home. Far too adventurous and independent. It broke my heart when she made the decision to leave."

"Are you guys still close?" His elbow is resting over his bent knee.

"Like sisters. Do you have siblings?"

"No." He shakes his head. "I'd have liked a brother or sister."

"I'm lucky really. I never felt like an only child with April around." My gaze lands on the line of his gunmetal grey Billabong T-shirt resting over his smooth, taut bicep and I lean over, planting my lips on his, loitering for a few seconds before releasing.

"What did I do to deserve that?" he asks, his smile reaching those reflective eyes.

"Nothing."

"Well, remind me to do nothing more often." He leans down to repay the gesture and my breath stills.

"Hungry?" he asks.

My eyes widen. Thinking how April had mentioned seeing him naked.

"For food," he says, his jaw line flexing and I bite my lip. "Come on, before you start giving me other ideas." He pulls me to my feet and the hem of my skirt kicks up. I don't think I'm the only one who's feeling the lack of alone time and the amplified tension between us.

"So, what's the deal with your parents? You never did say." We've taken our lunch to the spot on the rocks where we first ate together. I'm perched on the flattest, smoothest surface I could find, surrounded by dark navy blue and beige rock faces in various textures. There are a few seagulls loitering close-by, so we're careful to guard our food from the pesky scavengers.

"My childhood was stifling. My parents are critical about everything. They disapprove of my life, my choices and my work. They never liked Jen, thought she wasn't good enough for me. Hoped I'd marry the daughter of someone from their wide circle of friends. I can't stand their lifestyle."

"They can't be that bad, surely?"

His eyebrows lift up as he cocks his head. "They can and they are. I'm a disappointment to them and it's taken me years not to care what they think and be happy living life on my own terms. When Jen died, they tried to make it into a positive, telling me I could start over and make a better life for myself and Poppy."

I shake my head.

"Yeah." He stares out deep into the ocean. "They think money solves everything and happiness can be bought for the highest price, but deep down, they're both miserable. My dad's so henpecked he wouldn't even know to have a thought of his own anymore. It's a shame, because growing up, there were moments when I felt he really loved me."

"So they're wealthy?"

"Stinking rich. My mum comes from a wealthy family and they exist in the higher circles of society and do little good."

"That's a shame. My friend Emma is married to a man who's from a wealthy family and they do so much with what they have."

"I wish my parents would, but they're too selfish … I know I don't exactly make a difference with my surf lessons, but I make an honest wage for myself. I know the value of a hard day's work."

"Hey, I'm sorry. I didn't mean to bring them up and upset you."

He places his hand over mine, its warmth never ceasing to surprise me against my perpetually cold extremities. "I'm not upset, they just make me angry. I've tried to keep the connection, seeing them every now and again because Poppy doesn't have any other grandparents, though even she protests these days. She's becoming old enough to realise for herself what sort of people they are."

"What about Jen's parents'?"

"Her mum died of a heart attack far too young. Her dad was never around, so she raised her alone. I think that's why she was so strong and spirited. Poppy has that quality." He huffs out a laugh. "When I'm a mess, she has this calm assurance about her."

"How sad about Jen's parents. Poppy sounds adorable, though, and I think you're doing an amazing job of raising her alone."

Ben's arm finds rest over my shoulder and I feel his soft lips press into my hairline, before silence surrounds us. The only noise is coming from the seagulls high in the sky and the waves crashing into the rocks. I've never been able to sit there with someone in complete silence and it not feel awkward. I'm the sort of person who will fill a break in conversation with obscure detail. With Ben, though, it's natural, unforced— cathartic even. We can be having the most in-depth conversation and pause for contemplation without either of us feeling the need to bridge the gap.

"I wanted to talk to you about something. I know you might not be able to. Or want to even and it's pretty short notice and a long way—"

"Spit it out, would you?"

"I go to see my friend, Emma, next weekend. It's becoming a yearly tradition to attend the May charity ball at the estate."

"The estate?"

"Emma's husband, Chris, the one whose family are wealthy, owns a country estate called Wincastle in Derbyshire. It's a beautiful place, and they have these grand balls, which are something else. I ... I'd love to take you with me if you can be away for the night?" My palms are sweating as I run my fingers across the honeycomb texture of a speckled rock face.

He twists his body to look at me. "I'd love to. Let me see if I can sort something for Poppy, though, before I confirm. Rita might watch her for one night."

"Who's Rita?"

"Rita works for me in the shop and manages the online store. She's the closest thing Poppy has to a grandma. One she actually enjoys seeing, but she has her own grandchildren sometimes at the weekend. If not, it's been ages since Poppy had a sleepover at hers and she's always pestering for it."

"I didn't want to put you on the spot or anything."

"I'm pleased you asked." He kisses me and I feel it. A flutter of nerves. The 'I've put myself out there' kind and now I'm hoping he doesn't say no. What if asking him to meet my friends and spend a night with me doesn't fall into the definition of 'casual'?

Chapter Eight

The mature lime-tree-lined canopy driveway leading towards Wincastle feels even longer today as I see the expanse of the house with its towers and turrets coming into view, framed by a gloriously blue sky and bright yellow sun. I don't think I've ever been here when the weather hasn't been perfect. It's midday on Saturday, the day of the ball, and a hive of activity, with vans and cleaners, gardeners and maintenance men all milling around the stable block and surrounding areas. I love this place. Everything seems to hark back to a gentler time, a place in history with fewer distractions. I don't presume it was an easier time, as it wouldn't have been without its difficulties and pressures; corsets for instance, something I could not get along with wearing. Or the pressure to find a suitable husband—Emma nailed that one, of course, but I, well, I'm not sure about all that 'happy ever after' anymore. Perhaps if life wasn't so unpredictable all the time, I might feel differently. Living in a place as beautiful and grand as Wincastle, now that's something I could get on board with. Though by living, I mean in the servants' quarters in charge of stoking the fire or washing the pots. I can make a bed with such military precision, you'd be able to bounce a coin on it. With proper hospital corners and pillow cases facing away from the entry door, which Florence Nightingale herself would be proud of. Yes, Emma would be my mistress and I, her ladies maid, which actually sounds pretty fun in a very *Downtonesque*, *Bridgerton* sort of way.

Climbing from my car, I pull out my small wheelie suitcase and dress bag from the back seat before making my way through the cobbled courtyard towards the entrance. I've barely lifted my hand to knock when the door flings open and I'm pulled into an excitable Emma's arms.

"You're here! Yay!" she says. Emma's wearing navy cut-off jeans, a plain round neck top and a tailored white blazer, which makes her wavy hair look chocolate brown in contrast.

"You look amazing, Em! Being rich suits you."

"Oh shush!"

"Okay, being happy suits you."

"I'll take that." She beams at me.

"Where's Chris?" I look around.

"He's taken Stephen for a walk. I've had so much to do this morning, he thought I could do without him under my feet."

"What can I do to help?"

"You can tell me everything about Ben over a cup of tea." She ushers me inside, taking my suitcase.

"Are you sure you have time to stop?"

"Are you kidding me, I'm making time for this.

Besides, we have to make the most of it before the boys return," she says and my smile, etched so deeply into every layer of my skin, can't be hidden.

"Aunty JoJo!" Stephen rushes towards me, throwing his arms around my neck. I squeeze him, planting a kiss on his soft cheek, observing how much he's changed. His round face hosts two perfect chubby cheeks that swell when his rosebud lips part, baring two rows of small white teeth. His eyes are bright, like his dad's, and his hair's whitish blond, styled short with a little waxed mohawk on his crown. I'm certain this means Chris dressed him this morning and not Emma, even more so when I see the curious expression she's giving her husband.

"I've missed you, baby boy," I say, sitting him on my knee, straightening his checked blue and white button-up shirt over his hips. "I have a little present for you." I reach down to the side of the chair and place a neatly wrapped gift on his knee.

"Thomas!" He points at the wrapping paper and is already delighted.

"Open it then, sweetheart," Emma says.

"Percys," he says, his pronunciation of Percy the train.

"Mummy told me he's your favourite."

"What do you say, Stephen?" Chris asks.

"Thank you." His tiny lips graze my cheek with a 'mwah' sound. Once Emma's removed the packaging, he hops eagerly to the floor to investigate his new toy.

"Hey there, thank you for his present." Chris leans down to hug me and say hello properly. There's one thing I've observed from my friends who have children, and that's the kids monopolise the attention so much, the grownups often forget to greet each other as would normally be the case.

I kiss his cheek. "No problem. Any excuse for spoiling my favourite little man," I say in a playful voice, listening to Stephen make full-blown train chuffing sound effects. "I had to stop myself buying a whole set of trains, because your wife here didn't want him to be quite so spoilt."

"There's only so many toys one little boy can play with," Emma says. "He's still young enough to be thrilled with the paper and boxes the things come in."

"Very true." I laugh. "I can't believe how big he is and how much he looks like you, Chris."

"Tell us about it and thank you." Chris smiles. "Did you girls have a good catch-up?" He's perched on the arm of the cream sofa, next to where Emma is sitting.

"We've been debriefing about the ever-so-lovely Ben."

"I'm being tag teamed now, aren't I?" I say, looking from one to the other.

"Chris just wants to know if he needs to be all big brother protective or full-blown bezzy mates tonight?"

"Ha-ha! Your cool, charming self will do just fine. It's casual, remember."

"So you keep saying."

"What?" I notice their exchanged looks.

"Nothing. It's just the beaming smile plastered over your face is enough for me to love him, even if you don't," Emma says.

"Steady on, Em." Chris feigns an uncomfortable shuffle and pulls at the collar of his powder-blue polo shirt.

"You're stuck with me, I'm afraid, Mr Golding."

"Glad to hear it, Mrs Golding." He leans in, kissing her.

I look away. "I might go dump my things in my room, if that's okay?"

"Oops, sorry." Emma blushes. "I'll help you." She smiles at Chris as she stands, and I follow her out of the room.

"You guys are still as cute as ever, I see."

"It's sickening, right?" She wrinkles her nose and we both laugh.

Emma handed me a crystal glass of ice-cold prosecco, before being whisked away to greet more guests by Chris. There's a statue of a Greek mythical man beside me, who is less than formally dressed in comparison with the other guests this evening. His Adam and Eve attire is the only thing distracting me from the bubbles forming in my stomach, courtesy of Ben's impending arrival and not the fizz in my glass. His message said he was parking, and since then I feel as though I've been standing here for an hour and not just the ten minutes or so since reading it. If he takes much longer, I might dissolve. After gulping back my drink, I slip my glass onto the tray of a passing waiter. *That needed to be something stronger.* I smooth a strand of hair from my face and catch sight of him, hands stuffed into his chic classic black tuxedo, a smile firmly positioned on his face as his eyes trace my form, feet to face.

He walks towards me slowly, his eyes drawing a line between him and me, reeling me in, even though my body doesn't move an inch. A few seconds later, he slips his arms around my waist, pulling my hips towards his, before placing his smooth, warm lips on mine. Despite being in a room full of strangers, he doesn't stop kissing me, until I'm out of breath and rosy-cheeked.

"You look beautiful," he says, taking my hand in his. A trickle of warmth travels up to my neck, making me shiver.

"Thank you." I bite my lip and he releases it with his thumb, parting them ever so slightly. "How early is too early to leave?" I say, laughing.

"We've got plenty of time," he utters, his eyes absorbing me and there's a pulsing sensation low down in my stomach. "Besides, I want to dance with you first," he says.

"Can you dance?" I ask, stepping backwards, eyeing him.

"You have to be pretty coordinated to surf. I might

even teach you a thing or two."

"I do hope so."

He shakes his head, eyes wide. "You're killing me … just so you know." He lets out a gruff cough and then spins me onto the dance floor, as though he's the professional and I the celebrity on *Strictly Come Dancing*.

After one hour of solid proficient dancing, we make our way to the edge of the floor panting for breath and I'm stunned, not least by Ben's stamina. Walking towards us, I see a beaming Emma, wearing a stunning white chiffon, one shoulder, A-line evening gown, with flowers covering the shoulder strap, clutching onto Chris's arm. Hiding underneath the fabric are her favourite, well-worn Jimmy Choos, and I know this because she's inches taller than usual. Within seconds, her arms are outstretched and Ben is being pulled into them. When she releases him, he turns to shake Chris's hand.

"I'm Chris, and this is my wife, Emma," he says.

"It's great to meet you both." One of Ben's hands finds mine, the other he slides back into his trouser pocket.

"We saw you two dancing and it seems you've got all the moves," Emma says to Ben.

"Thanks, I don't think oh-um-Jo here, thought I'd be able to dance."

Chris stifles a laugh with a heavy clearing of his throat, clearly having been let in on the nickname Ben has for me.

"I hadn't really given it much thought." I bounce my hip into him and he cracks a smile.

"Well, I may have to steal you for a spin around the dancefloor myself."

"I'd love to," Ben says, taking Emma by the hand, Chris laughing openly this time as he watches his wife being twirled to the music. He adjusts a cufflink on his white shirt and holds out his arms and I step into his hold.

"I like him, for the record." Chris stares down at me, swaying steadily, our bodies at a respectful distance apart.

"Really? You can tell already?"

"I'd like to think I'm a pretty good judge of character, with the bits Em's told me and his demeanour."

"Well, don't get too attached—"

"It's casual. I know. He's certainly a hit with my wife, so you might want to remind her again." He widens his eyes.

"She's so happy, Chris. You make her so *very* happy."

His smile says more than any words could as his gaze flicks up to where Emma is giggling to something Ben's telling her.

"I hope she's not doing a *Lucy* on me." I breathe in.

"Ha-ha. Don't worry, Emma knows not to meddle, unlike my sister. I like the 'doing a Lucy' reference. I may have to steal that phrase."

"Be my guest, just maybe don't tell her I said it."

"I won't. Besides, I'd prefer to take the credit, it

would annoy her more."

"Where is she, and Fynn?"

"Lucy's about to pop with their second child. Fynn hoped she'd want to come, but she didn't feel like squeezing into a dress. You remember what she's like?"

"I do."

"Will you and Emma have more children?"

"No, not after last time." There's a firm shake of his head. "We'd love to, of course, but it's too much of a risk and not one I'm willing to take."

"Emma said something similar before, I figured that wouldn't have changed. Stephen is such a cute little thing, though."

"Yes, and doesn't he know it. I love seeing him grow each day, discovering which traits he got from his mum and I. Praying none of Granny's slipped in there."

"Granny, yes, I've not seen her either."

"Oh, she's here. Poised and waiting to pop out at any moment no doubt, as opinionated as ever, though she's not in the best of health lately."

"I'm sorry to hear that. Your parents look well."

"They are. Stephen's mended something which was broken for a long time. It's amazing how much joy and healing a child can bring …" His words trail off, but he looks at me thoughtfully. I lift my eyes, catching Ben's gaze. "Would it be so bad if this thing with Ben wasn't casual? He makes you happier than you ever seemed with Tom. Just saying."

"Chris, I'm going to Australia," I say.

"You got a job?" He blinks, a half-smile on his lips.

"It's just casual work out there in a hospital, but I'll be able to take shifts to earn money and travel around. Spend some time with April."

"Does Em know?"

"She knows I've had my visa accepted. I'm just waiting on my nursing registration, but that can take longer. So there's really no sense in looking for anything long term. Ben is making me happy right now, but my mind's made up. I just want a change, Chris."

"I can relate to that. What about Ben, does he know what you're looking for?"

"We both agreed this isn't anything serious. His wife's dead and he's a single dad," I say, a little too resolutely.

Chris doesn't say anything more as we continue to move in time with the music. I get the feeling this isn't because he doesn't have more to add. There's truth in his words, I'm happier right now than I have been in months, years, maybe, but Ben is just a nice distraction. Settling on my new life and taking steps towards it are why the dark clouds are lifting. I will, however, continue to enjoy feeling as though thousands of dormant neurons in my body have finally switched on around him. I close my eyes, trying not to let the feeling overwhelm me. There's plenty of evening left before I can be alone with him, even though I know the fire searing away inside me can't be contained for much longer. Reopening them, an out-of-breath, laughing Emma is by our side, with Ben in tow, who has a glisten on his brow.

She hugs me close, whispering in my ear. "He's a keeper," before releasing her hold, and I can't resist an eye roll, or stop myself from smiling at her.

Ben and Chris are engaged in conversation as I feel the presence of someone else beside us.

"Good evening, Granny." Emma kisses her cheek, followed by Chris.

"Good would have been a quiet glass of sherry and an early night, my dear."

I notice Emma purse her lips to the side, her eyes lifting to meet Chris's.

"You remember, Jo, Gran?" Chris says.

"Ah, yes. The co-conspirator. How could I forget?" She scans my form, making me feel naked all of a sudden.

"Good evening," I say politely, a slight wobble in my voice.

"And this is Ben, a friend of Jo's."

Ben moves forward to shake her hand, but he's left hanging.

"More male-female friendships, goodie," is what she says, then she readjusts the lapel of her maroon jacket.

Ben furrows his brow as he glances toward me, his eyes pleading an explanation as he drops his arm by his side. Granny's footing falters and Chris steps beside her, propping up her elbow. "I'm perfectly fine, Christopher, no need to fuss."

"Come on," he says, "I'll walk with you to find a seat."

"Oh, very well." Granny doesn't protest further, which even I realise is most out of character, and Emma follows behind them, leaving us alone.

"I do hope she's all right, but what was that?" Ben asks.

"That's just Granny being Granny. I've seen her a few times, but heard far more stories from Emma. I think the words she uses for her are archaic and stubborn, with a few other choice things, depending on which story she's sharing."

"And you're a co-conspirator, how?"

"It's a long story. Let's go for a walk and I'll tell you the highlights."

I walked the path from the house to the bridge barefoot, swinging my heels beside me, on the grass which runs parallel to the yellow stone uneven path. We're staring down to the river beneath us, lit only by the moon and the lamps at either end of Lion Bridge. The large willow tree is bathed in shadowy moonlight to our left. The south side of the house is illuminated in soft spotlights and looks beautifully grand in front of us. It's peaceful here. Even with the sound of water trickling steadily downstream, and night creatures making their presence known as though they were a nocturnal orchestra, playing to the trees. The heat from my body has long since gone, leaving a chill creeping over my skin, but it's refreshing after all the dancing. As the breeze rolling off the river lifts the skirt of my dress, the fabric floats back and forth over my skin.

"Wow!" Ben says. "That's some story, but sounds as though they're meant for each other."

"I imagine you and Jen were meant for each other too?" My shoulders stiffen.

"We were." He sighs, gripping the stone wall, looking out into the darkness over the parkland. He often has a faraway look in his eye, when the conversation turns to his late wife.

"Sor—"

"Don't you dare apologise, we made a deal, remember?"

"We did. I'm …" I almost said it again.

"I don't find it easy," he glances at me, "talking about her. I do with Poppy, but no one else. Especially not you."

"Oh," I say and my body hugs the stone in front of me. The rough discolouration beneath my fingers is all patchy white, yellow and black.

"I didn't mean that the way it sounded." He takes a breath. "I mean, I feel guilty sometimes, getting on with my life and angry that hers was cut so short. Does that make sense?"

"Of course it does." I touch his arm. His skin is cool where he's rolled up his shirt sleeves.

"There was so much we were going to do together."

"Like what?" I ask, not moving from beside him. I

stroke his skin gently.

"Travel. Buy a Vdub camper and roam around. Then Poppy came along, but Jen would have taken her, too. Home schooled her by the sea in any and every location."

"She sounds amazing and very free-spirited."

"She was. I like a bit more routine, I guess. It's sort of how I survived being a parent on my own. We found our rhythm and stuck with it. I wonder, though, if Pops needs more spontaneity, like her mum would have been."

"I'm sure she just loves her dad the way you are." The trees in the distance feel as though they're shielding us. Encasing us and offering protection, with their height and fullness blackened by the night.

"Is it wrong that I want to kiss you now?" He's facing me, his eyes flicking from left to right.

I shake my head, slowly. It's all I want him to do and more. Especially now, somehow.

The bugs seem to quiet as though the orchestra have finished their piece. My breath hitches as his hand finds my waist, the way he had when he arrived at the ball, and I'm quickly enveloped in his arms, swaying as the instruments resume. The melody fills the air around us. His eyes are on mine—drawing me in as though I'm being willingly hypnotised. There are no words required for me to know what he's thinking; the thoughts which mirror my own so completely.

My back lands against the cool wall as the door shuts

behind us with a thud. We walked in silence back to the house, our fingers weaving in and out of each other's as the impatient coiled-up spring deep inside me wound tighter. His body presses against me firmly, my hands in his long dark hair, my fingers gently tugging at the strands. His hands are everywhere, as is my mind. Our lips meet eagerly, sliding along each other's. Our tongues dance and retreat, dance and retreat, as though making their acquaintance. A hint of plummy spice from the red wine on his breath. One hand finds my neck, the other the zip of my dress, which he pulls down, swiftly. As the next wave of tension builds, he pushes my hands above my head and I feel the silky fabric leave my body. He grips my waist, his fingers imprinting my skin, kissing down my neck, igniting tiny flames along the way. I fumble at his jacket, then his shirt as he helps me. When all that's left is our underwear, he lifts me, my legs circling his waist as he carries me to the bed, where he lowers me down, more controlled than at the wall. His hand softly strokes the side of my face, his breathing as fast as my own, my heartbeat ringing in my ears. I notice his Adam's apple rise and then he swallows. In the stillness he whispers, "You're beautiful." Shaking his head, in small movements, then he leans down and we give ourselves over to every bit of latent emotion we have within us.

Chapter Nine

The next morning, the air is crisp and the birds are chirping happily in the trees around us, darting and soaring in the treeline. There's a row of thick clouds in the sky above, which look like stepping stones towards a sun hiding behind them. Not quite ready to face the day and I know the feeling. I pull my navy longline knitted cardigan around my body, watching Ben as he throws his black suit bag into the back of his truck, along with his holdall. It's early, I'm not sure anyone's even awake yet, except for us and the birds. We've had just a couple of hours' sleep, but I feel energised rather than tired, at least for now.

"I wish you didn't have to make such an early start. How are you going to survive the journey on no sleep?"

He presses his body to mine, wrapping his arms tightly around my waist. "Graphic flashbacks!" he says with a smile.

"Oh really?" I shove him, laughing, though I fully expect to have one or two of those myself. Especially after having sex three times—twice last night and once this morning. In truth, I wanted to stay naked in his arms forever, and I could have.

"It's hard to leave you when you have that look in your eyes." He pushes his hair back from his forehead. His black V-neck T-shirt clings to his chest and abdomen, and my mind remembers every inch of what his body felt like under my fingertips.

"Then don't." I lean my torso into his, pushing him against the truck door. His lips meet mine with urgency, as they had against the wall last night.

"I have to get back to Poppy," he says, breaking away. "I'm gonna be driving most of the day, especially if I hit traffic."

"I know you do," I say. "I'm sorry it was such a long way for just one night."

"I'm not sorry." He pulls me back in for another kiss, but I'm once more reminded of his responsibilities in life. The thoughts of which I'd pushed to one side last night, after talking about Poppy and his wife. Hoping I'm not just a thing of comfort in his grief, but then maybe that's what this is for us both. His hands rest on the tops of my arms. "Last night was—"

"You don't have to say anything."

"I was just trying to tell you that I really enjoyed last night." His brow furrows.

"I did, too." I soften, but his look's unchanged.

Stepping back, I feel the cool in the void where our bodies have just been as Ben swings into the seat, pulling the door closed. The window opens. "Can I see you when you get back?" he says, holding still in expectation.

My soul is screaming 'yes', but all I say is, "We'll see."

He nods, lifting his hand and I wave back, then press my fallen hand into my stomach and breathe out.

"I thought I'd find you here." Emma strides over to me, dressed in a simple button-up khaki green shirt and leggings. Stephen trails her with a patient-looking Chris a few feet behind. The sun, though not warm, comes out of hiding and the clouds blow into wispy lines over the estate. The odd fuller cloud perches on a turret of the house, as if it were candyfloss on a stick. The view from my spot on the grass, beside a large lime tree, is spectacular. I can't believe Emma gets to live here. Everything is obscenely green, even the horizon of trees, in contrast to last night, but it still feels as protective and comforting. My bare legs are draped with my cardigan as I try to ignore the chillier than expected breeze. The fallow deer in the nearby paddock have been keeping me company since Ben's departure, looking up periodically from grazing on the tall strands of grass.

"You missed breakfast, so I smuggled you a crois-sant and a coffee to go."

"Why thank you," I say, gratefully receiving the cup and bag. "I'm sorry about breakfast, I didn't feel like the post-ball Granny experience. Especially as my new villainous co-conspirator self."

"Sorry about that."

"No worries. It's amusing, and makes all those tales you've told me come to life. She really is quite … unique."

"Let's go with 'unique'." We both laugh.

"Morning, Aunty Jo," Chris says as Stephen drops on me like a dead weight.

"Morning, handsome fella," I say to Stephen and make an 'oomph' sound, ever so slightly winded.

"Aunty JoJo play with me?" His puppy-dog eyes are adorable and hard to resist.

"I most certainly will. Is it okay if I just finish my coffee and then you can choose what we do?"

"Okay. Daddy play first?"

"Yes." Chris smiles at me and turns to Stephen. I'm sure he can sense a girl chat coming on and I need it. I need Emma's undivided attention.

"Tig." All I hear is excitable squeals as Chris lets Stephen evade his hands and they run off together. We watch them and I notice the fine lines around Emma's eyes, which signal how much she now smiles more than the passing of time. Her head tilts to one side as she admires the two boys in her life rolling around in the grass. There are no words for the look on her face. It's a contentment no amount of money could buy.

"You're happy, right?" I ask her.

She turns back to me, grabs my hand and squeezes it. "The happiest." She gives a small sigh.

"Are *you* happy, though? Because something is radiating out of you this morning, and I have a feeling it's to do with a rather gorgeous, tall, dark-haired surfer dude."

I shake my head, pressing my eyes shut. "Oh, Em!"

She makes a loud squeak and both boys look up like meerkats before continuing their battle. "You two had sex last night, didn't you?"

"Finally, yes! With us having to be at his place and Poppy asleep in the next room, I just—"

"You really don't need to explain yourself to me. Kids definitely put a crimp in your sex life."

"Last night, though …" I tip my head backwards and a cool sensation ripples over my skin. Emma is nodding when I look back at her. There's no need to finish my sentence, because the one person who will get *this*, without needing an explanation, is her.

"Jo …"

I look at her and, judging by her hesitation, I know what she's going to ask.

"Can you really do casual with him?"

"I thought I could. Then last night …" I sigh. "Em, he's a widower with a child. I'm not sure he's over his wife. I mean, do you ever get over that?" Em shrugs and the corner of her mouth turns up into a sympathetic smile. "Plus, I'm going travelling in a few months and I'm just not sure if I'm ready to trust my heart to someone again. Casual is all there is."

"I just don't want you to get hurt." She touches my shoulder.

"I'm already hurt after everything with Tom. How much more hurt could I get?"

"You know what I mean. Does he even know about Australia?"

"I haven't told him, because I wasn't looking that far ahead."

"Are you going to see him again?"

"He asked me if he could see me when I'm back, but I didn't commit to anything." I sip my coffee.

"But you're enjoying his company?"

"Of course. He's so easy to be around."

"Well, then, don't rule it out completely," she says and I stay silent. Emma's looking as though she's reading the air around me. "Has there been anyone else since his wife passed?"

"No, I don't think so, or at least no one serious. I feel awkward talking to him about it, though he's starting to open up more. He said something last night about feeling guilty for getting on with his life, when hers was cut short."

"That's understandable." Emma wraps her arms around her body. "It's so horrible what happened. It sends a cold shiver down my spine thinking about how I could have left Chris to raise Stephen alone."

I grab her hand, also feeling an odd, unpleasant sensation travel through me at the thought of a different reality, and it somehow makes what he went through seem more real to me. "You're here and that's all that matters."

"I'm surprised his daughter hasn't wandered downstairs when you've been over in the evenings."

"Ben says she's scared of the dark. She won't get out of bed once the lights are out, she just shouts him if she wants anything."

"Can I trade? Stephen started climbing his cots sides six months ago. I was looking for something in his wardrobe when I heard a loud thud, and I turned around to see him flat on his back on the floor. I didn't see the fall, but I imagine he flipped over the bars. Scared me half-to-death. All I saw when I closed my eyes that night was him doing it again, but landing on his neck or head. So we bought a toddler bed that's practically at floor level. It's fun getting him to sleep at night, because he'd rather run around his room until he's so tired he just passes out, half in, half out of the bed sometimes. We often find him in the morning sprawled out on his carpet."

"Thank goodness it was carpet he landed on, but I can imagine how scary that was. If you're trying to change my mind about being something more with Ben, you're really not selling this kid thing to me."

"She's older and past all that, but they really don't tell you about the perpetual worry you get when you have kids."

"Again, not selling it to me, which is good actually. Keep going," I say and she laughs. Something seems to spook the deer as they gather to run away further into the park. The clouds can't decide whether to stay or go either.

"Do you think she'd like me?" I pause, pulling at a thread on my cardigan. "I'm not her mum and surely it would be hard for her to accept a new woman in her dad's life? It's been just the two of them since her mum died when she was born."

"I won't say it wouldn't be hard. It would be uncharted territory for all of you." She leans over and brings me into her arms. "I'm here for you, no matter what. Moral support, any parenting advice I can give you. Though, if this does take a serious turn, you might be the one giving me advice, as you'd hit the teenage years before I do."

"Teenage years!" I rub down the side of my face. "I hadn't even considered that part."

"I'm really not making this any better, am I?" Emma sinks her head down into her shoulders.

"In an odd sort of way, you are." I watch the boys. Stephen is chasing Chris's shadow and whenever he almost catches it, Chris slides out of the way, making Stephen giggle. They go side to side this way and my heart aches. I wanted this. I wanted to watch the father of my children play this way with them. I swallow as an image of Tom passes fleetingly through my mind. "Em …"

"Yeah?"

"Is it bad that I've considered it? Meeting his daughter? Not that it's a thing, he probably wouldn't even want to introduce me to her, especially if I'm not sticking around, but I …"

"It's not bad."

"I'm not being very April, am I?"

"You're a terrible April," she says and I bury my face in my hands.

It's late, far later than I wanted it to be driving home to Cornwall, but I couldn't drag myself away from Stephen's cuteness, and being in the familiarity of Emma and Chris's company. Staying awake is hard, especially on next-to-no sleep, though thoughts of Ben and regretting my cool goodbye to him this morning are keeping me alert. As is my third coffee of the day, four if you count the one Emma brought me for breakfast. I lift my eyebrows and crunch my neck from side to side, seeing the oncoming lights of other vehicles, which are making my eyes strain. The bonus is the roads aren't busy at this time of night and I've made good progress. Ben's journey had taken him longer than he'd have liked, spending a good hour or so nose-to-tail with other cars on the busiest stretch of the A30. Another reason I didn't set off as early as I'd planned, Ben suggested as much when he text me from the services. Another bonus of night-time driving is seeing everything bathed in silvery moonlight, and my bespoke playlist to sing along to, knowing I can fully invest in the song without other passengers spotting my steering wheel performance.

The default iPhone ring melody fills the car, replacing my music, and I press the button on my steering wheel to answer it. "Hello."

"Hey." I hear the deep tone of his voice and my

insides awaken. No coffee on the planet would have the same stirring effect he has on me.

"Hey," I mirror.

"Hope you don't mind me calling? I just wanted to see if you made it home safe?" His tone reflects his uncertainty and I hate that I put it there.

"Of course it is. I'm sorry if I was a little cold when we said goodbye."

"I *was* wondering if I'd done something wrong?"

"No, you really didn't." I want to tell him last night was perfect, but it sounds too cheesy. "I had a great time. I think you know that."

"Well …" He lets out a low cough sound and I know he knows. "You're still on the road then?"

"Yes. You interrupted my jam. Whitney and I were having quite the duet."

"Dang, I wish I had a dash cam pointing at you right now. How's the journey?" he asks, in a light tone.

"Slow. Long, Boring. Would you care for any more adjectives, because I could probably go on?"

"No, they about cover it." He laughs. "I do hope Whitney is helping you stay awake?"

"Whitney, Mariah, Celine, Rod, Michael."

"Wow, you've got some power ballads going on there!"

"Despite that and my fourth coffee of the day, my eyelids are threatening to close on me every second."

"You think you should pull over at the next services for a rest?"

"I don't think I'd settle in the dark car by myself."

"That's a point. I don't think I'd like that either. *Me*

in the dark car with you is another matter entirely."

"Oh, I see your plan. You're going to start that kinda talk to try and keep me awake, huh!"

"Is it working?" I can hear the edge to his voice and see the cheeky smile that accompanies it in my mind.

"Absolutely, do continue." My insides are pulsating again.

"I haven't been able to stop replaying having you pinned up against the wall all day."

"Me neither." I run my teeth along my bottom lip as a hot prickling sensation floods my body.

The line goes quiet, but I know he's still there, his gentle breaths just audible against the sound of my heartbeat, amplified by the silence. I feel him; his fingertips pressed into my skin, the taste of his warm breath as our lips met. My eyes are set on the road ahead, but my imagination is right there with him, replaying every part of last night. Every time his hand slid over my skin, my back arching. Wanting him. Aching for him. The self-contained flames which seared within me blazed nightlong, and the spring slowly uncoiled, loop after loop, until only unravelled metal remained.

"Jo." My thoughts are broken by the sound of my name.

"I'm still here," I whisper.

"How long's left of your drive?"

"Not long, half-an-hour or so," I say.

"Come round the back, the door's quieter."

I nod, but remember he can't see me. "Okay."

Chapter Ten

The light's streaming into the room through slats in the white wooden blinds when I wake, alone. Jolting forward, I realise where I am and that I've inadvertently slept over. Pulling the duvet over my naked skin, I reach for my phone. *Nine-thirty a.m.* A notification tells me I have a message from Ben: *Don't worry, she doesn't know you're there. I distracted her until it was time to go to school. I'll be back soon, with breakfast. Sit tight. Ben x*

Lying back, my breathing returns to a normal rate. Following the initial panic, I think how sexy it is, sneaking around. Not that I'm the sneaking around kind of a girl, but even I can't deny enjoying the surge of adrenaline it gives me. Besides, we're not doing anything wrong. We're both single; it's just a little complicated.

With the coast clear, I decide to shower. Wandering into the en suite, I find a stack of dark grey Egyptian cotton towels on the shelf above the chrome radiator. The compact space has simple white tiles on the walls and black larger ones on the floor, leading to the lip of the walk-in shower tray. It's minimalist and as stylish as the rest of the house. I step behind the glass panel and turn the tap, feeling the water land on my shoulders from the large rainfall showerhead above me. My hand feels for the bottle of shower gel resting on the niche shelving cut into the tiles. When I release the cap with my thumb, the smell of him drifts up my nostrils and I breathe deeply, inhaling the humid scent, as the space around me fills with swirls of steam.

"I'm back." I hear his muffled words through the patter of water and my initial thought is, will he mind I'm taking a shower, but this is soon replaced with ideas of him joining me. When I see him through the shower screen, his soft, shining eyes and tilt of his head tell me I'm not alone in this. He lifts his white top over his head, his shorts and boxers hitting the ground with ease. My heartbeat is so loud in my ears, I feel as though it's on full blast through a headset. Suddenly, I'm against cold tiles, shivering, the water flowing over his head, spraying me between each movement of his lips on mine. My nerve endings are charged, stirred up by his touch, which feels silky over my wet skin. My mind empties.

"Sorry, the coffee and pastries are probably cold," he says, with a not-at-all sorry expression resting on his satisfied face.

I sip from the takeaway cup, wince slightly, confirming his suspicion, then press my lips into a smile. "It's the thought that counts." I shrug. "Besides, I should be the one apologising for distracting you and ruining breakfast." I give him a knowing look.

"Feel free to distract me anytime you like." He's shaking his head. "I could get used to coming home and finding you naked in my shower."

My fingers set to shredding pieces of pastry from my buttery cold croissant.

"You okay? Did I say something wrong?"

"No, not at all." I'm holding a thin flake of golden pastry between my fingertips, examining it. "I was worried in case Poppy realised you weren't alone when I woke up this morning."

"I knew you would be, but I didn't want to wake you. Not after all the driving and the deprived sleep of the previous nights." His smile is loaded with mischief. "Besides, she's usually so chatty in a morning that she wouldn't pay any attention to anything else. Kids are really good at being self-absorbed."

"I can imagine. Still …" I swallow, my heart thumping in my chest. "Finding me naked in your bed wouldn't be the best first impression."

"First impression?" His head jerks back.

My lips part, but I'm silent.

"You want to meet her?"

"Was that a question or a statement?" I ask, fiddling with the back of my earring.

"I'm not sure, which would you rather it be?"

"We agreed casual," I say, half wishing I hadn't started this conversation. My heart rate is unable to find its way back to a resting rhythm.

"We did, and meeting Poppy isn't casual." He

sounds calm, but his chin lifts, his narrow eyes remaining focused like the lens of the camera zooming in on the object of interest. He isn't frowning, but there's no smile on his lips.

"I know it's not. You don't have to if—"

"I want you to meet her." He takes my hand. "But, perhaps we tread lightly. You're Daddy's friend."

"As opposed to?" I'm not sure why this slightly smug-sounding comment leaves my lips, but it does.

"You're right! It's not exactly like we're going to share with her that we're friends with benefits."

"Friends with benefits, hey," I say flirtatiously, to lighten the mood. "It works for me." He kisses me then, reminding me of just one of the perks to this ever-evolving arrangement.

"So …"

I bury my face beneath a cushion.

"Why are you hiding?"

"Because," I say, my voice muffled, "you say 'so' and then ask me things. Like what I was like as a teenager, or something."

"Actually, what were you like as a teenager? It wasn't my question, but I'm intrigued."

There's silence, so I peek at him, as though he were a scene in a scary film I'm checking is over. "Okay, fine." I sit up. I'd protest, but I actually enjoy our 'so' game. It makes me feel safe, content and terrified, all at once. "I was a goody-two-shoes, or so the mean girls in class called me. I mostly didn't care. I did the work, stayed out of trouble and didn't drink—aside from trying Thai whisky at my friend Amber's house when we were like sixteen. We only had a sniff, to be fair, but afterwards we felt tipsy, or at least we acted as though we were."

He's laughing, his eyes bright and sexy. "Go on."

"I didn't smoke, or sleep around. Enjoyed spending time with my parents, I still do." As I say those words, I instantly feel a pang of homesickness at the idea I'll be leaving them behind for a while.

"No rebellious streak then?"

"Nope. There's still time, though, right?" I chuckle.

"I'm very down with a rebellious streak, assuming you have it with me!" He kisses me then. Long and full of passion. When we part, I'm deliciously giddy, though I manage to bring myself back to the conversation.

"My parents were probably a little relieved when my cousin, April, went to Australia, or there may have been trouble."

"She's the rebel then?"

"Oh, she is. We're very different."

"How about you?" I enquire. "Rebellious or goody-goody?"

"Both. Goody at school. Rebel at home, just to push back at my folks."

"Drugs? Alcohol? Sex?" I lean forward.

"No drugs. Not my style. A few spectacular benders as a teen. Vomited all over my mum's friends' shoes as they were leaving our house after a dinner party. My parents had been so busy entertaining, they hadn't noticed me pouring myself drinks all night."

I grimace. "Grounded?"

"Nope." He shakes his head. "Wish they'd cared enough to bother, if I'm honest. I had to listen to mum moan about 'the embarrassment of it all, Henry'," he mimics what sounds like an older and well-spoken lady—I assume how his mum sounds.

I loosely fold my arms across my chest. "I can't imagine not having parents who are also my friends."

"Can't miss what you don't know!" he says, a little too dismissively, but the flicker of something pained flashes over his face. "Teenage crush?"

I hide behind a pillow again and he pulls it away this time. "You'll laugh," I say.

"I promise, I won't."

I wiggle my shoulders, puffing out my chest. "Boyzone—"

He sniggers instantly.

"Hey!"

"Sorry." He holds his palms out, his lips a flat line.

"I was madly in love with Ronan Keating. Well, me and my friend, Sally, who I spent each and every maths lesson discussing all things Ronan with. I'm terrible at maths, too, so I should probably should have paid more attention." I laugh.

"Oh, the cliché." He looks up at the ceiling. "It's the Irish accent, right?"

"Hmmm, I mean I did fall for a boy in year seven, who read *Across the Barricades* lead male character entirely in a Dublin Irish accent." I shrug and he puts his head in his hand. "So, yeh, the accent, the cheeky grin, and gorgeous eyes." I swoon.

"We did leave this crush in the nineties, right? Also, he's not very tall, dark and broodingly handsome … you know, like Aidan Turner."

"My tastes are eclectic and ever-evolving." I confirm. "I also once wrote him a poem."

"Ronan?" he asks. "I have to hear this, please tell me you remember it?"

"I absolutely don't remember." I turn from him, my face aching with happiness.

"You do! Word for word! Come on. I did my Bon Jovi solo for you."

I blow out a fast breath.

Ronan, you're the very best and you will always be my one true love, this is for sure, this is a guarantee.

So special's how you'll make me feel, when I look in your eyes. And when we kiss, well that's still to come, but this is no surprise.

On this one thing, I cannot say, but one thing is for sure, my love for you will always be the best and so much more.

"You had it bad!"

I nod, hugging my legs. "Wall to wall posters, every concert I could go to. I wrote that very poem out, tied it to a teddy and handed it to a security guard inside the arena to give to him." I can't look at Ben now, but I feel every inch of his amusement. "I even sobbed on my dad's lap when I read he'd got married."

He howls at this, laughter raging from him and I fear he might actually stop breathing. "Oh, I'm sorry." He pats his chest. "I promised I wouldn't laugh, but I'm half picturing you as a cute girl getting all emosh and half crying on the inside that I have a girl and this is going to happen to me someday!"

"Jokes on you, my friend. Jokes on you! Now spill. Teen crush!"

"Easy. Liz Hurley!"

"Liz. Hurley?" I give a beat between her first and last name, cocking one eyebrow.

"It's the accent. Kate Beckinsale, too," he admits.

"Now that I can understand, but not Liz Hurley."

"Her dress sense helped. Liz, I mean." He gives a slight shrug.

"I do not want to know what Liz Hurley's dress sense helped you with as a teenage boy." He's looking at me, his lips curled up, his eyes doing that thing where they flick from left to right as if he's taking me in.

"This is good," he says.

"It is." I nod. *It's too good.* Dangerous levels of good.

Rather than the encore Ben suggested, I'm downstairs, in yesterday's clothes, washing up breakfast things while he showers. Actually showers this time. It's almost time for Poppy to be collected from school and I'm going to meet them at the beach afterwards for ice cream. As I wash up the purple princess cup of the little girl I'm soon to meet, I have an empty feeling in the pit of my stomach, mixed with a lightness in my chest.

"Penny for your thoughts?" I feel his hands slide round my stomach as he joins me, the smell of his freshly showered body dragging my mind back a few hours.

"I'm happy, is all." He spins me round and soap-suds drip to the ground.

"Good, but you sound as though that surprises you?"

"I guess it does a little."

"We've," he pauses. "We've never really talked about your last relationship and why it ended. I can tell you're still pretty cut up about something."

"We haven't," I say with far more abruptness than intended and turn away. He pauses again, unfazed, but silent. "There's just nothing to say. I'd rather not talk about it," I continue.

"Okay. Can I ask you one question?" he says, and I don't answer, but my lack of protest gives him a green light. "Are you still in love with him?"

My head jerks back. "No."

"No, you're not in love with him, or no, I can't ask the question?"

"I'm not in love with him anymore. I'm a little bit broken, but then, so are you."

He nods, hanging his head, and I'm aware I've touched a raw nerve.

"I'm sorry," I say. "Of course you're broken. You

lost your wife." I sigh.

"Well, aren't we just two together people." He laughs.

"Indeed we are … Are you sure you're okay for me to meet Poppy?" A cool sensation rolls up my arms, making the hairs stand on end.

"I'm running out of reasons in my mind for you not to."

I nod. "Meet you at the beach in an hour?"

"We'll be there."

Stepping onto the sand of the fairly empty beach, I see the odd couple walking, kids running in and out of the sea and a dog or two, but it's not busy. Ben's lifting up the A-frame sign when he spots me. I see Poppy, her auburn curls pulled back into a neat ponytail, perched on the step outside the shop, sifting sand through her fingertips. The air smells of chips, pasties and a hint of diesel as a bus chugs up the hill behind us.

As I edge closer towards them, Ben mouths something to her and her eyes meet mine with a sincere smile. Even from here, I see how green they are, and the nearer I get the more strikingly vivid they become. None of the photos do her beauty justice. Then, I imagine, neither do the photos of her mother, and I have to shake off the thought, which leaves a slight burning sensation in my chest.

"Poppy, say hi to my friend, Jo."

"Hello," she says, her ponytail swishing with her movements.

"It's really nice to meet you, Poppy." I rub the top of my arm.

"Do you like ice cream? My daddy says we can get some."

"I happen to love ice cream," I say, admiring the innocence and simplicity of her tone.

"My favourite is strawberry, but Daddy loves caramel." She looks up at Ben, her face glowing.

"I'm a mint choc chip kind of girl," I reply, flattening my lips into a smile.

"Urgh, mint-flavoured ice cream." Her cute button nose wrinkles.

"Have you ever tried it?" I ask.

"No," she replies through crumpled features and I'm not sure I'm winning her over.

"You might like it."

She gives a firm shake of her head and I laugh, catching Ben's gaze.

"Mint ice cream was always going to be a hard sell," he says to me as he pinches the end of Poppy's nose.

"Hey!" She reaches up to his closed fist. "Give it back." She's giggling as her dad moves his arm around, evading capture.

"I think I'll have bogey-flavoured ice cream," he says, pretending to gobble something from his fist. Poppy and I are both laughing. "Come on, let's go before I have to steal yours, too," he says, touching the end of my nose with his index finger. When I meet Poppy's eye, her smile is so sincere I almost melt, as if

I'm fresh snow hitting warm tarmac.

With the last morsels of our treat polished off, we explored the rocks for anything the tide left behind. Poppy dipped her orange fishing net into every pool of water we came across, checking it for anything resembling a living creature. Today had been overcast, but not cold, so it was still pleasant outside, even though it was now late afternoon.

"Got one," she calls out, waving her net in the air. I can see two sharp-looking claws in the orange netting. "A crab, see." She holds it out for me to look inside.

"Well done," I say, peering down at the small creature. Poppy grins before turning in her dad's direction, who, with such light footing, springs across the rocks towards us. I watch as he unravels the crab from the netting and holds it between his fingers, facing in Poppy's direction, pretending it's talking to her. The delicate ripple of joy in her laugh makes my heart lift. Ben releases their catch, and we set back the way we came, trying to negotiate safe footing around slippery, mossy, seaweed-covered rocks, which crunch and pop underfoot. Ben holds out his hand, feet astride, helping Poppy and I over more tricky terrain. As our feet find the flat sand, I feel a hand in mine and, to my surprise, it's small and soft. I turn to look at Poppy, swinging our arms between us.

"Shall we look for shells?" she asks, and I struggle to form words in return. Instead, I nod, smiling down at her. The only time she releases me is to drop towards the ground, picking up various shells before placing them into the bucket I'm holding. Otherwise, she's attached to me. I don't look back at Ben, who seems to be hanging back on purpose.

"What are your favourite shells?" I ask.

"The little pinky ones." She holds up one the size of my thumbnail. It's a pinky-white colour, rounded on one side, with big ridges running to the edge.

"That's a scallop shell," I tell her, stopping to kick a ball back to a boy playing football with what looks like his older brother, who waves in thanks.

"Do you know the names of all shells?" She's beaming up at me now.

"I know a few."

She takes the bucket and pulls out a brown shell.

"That's a common periwinkle. Its tip is fairly rounded, see?" I say, rubbing my thumb along it. Copying me, she nods, before placing it back into the orange bucket.

Next, she hands me an upside-down cone-shaped one.

"This is a limpet shell."

"I know this one." She holds out a blueish/purple oval. "It's a mussel."

"That's right. Have you ever tried them?"

"Yuk." She turns her chin over her shoulder, making retching sounds, and I laugh at her theatrics.

"Me neither." I wink at her. Next, she pulls out a pure white shell. "See, this one looks just like the periwinkle shell." I retrieve it from the bucket. "But its tip is pointier—do you see the difference? This is called a dog whelk."

"I love it," she says, grasping my hand once more.

"Me too. They're my favourite."

"And mine," she points out. When I glance up, meeting Ben's steady gaze, his eyes are shining.

After our successful first meeting, I was invited, by Poppy, to join them for dinner the next evening. Ben has just finished shaping the dough with his fingers to make pizza bases—something I've never made from scratch before, though the smell of the dough reminds me of my mum baking bread. Poppy's standing next to him on a step and I slide the dish of passata sauce towards her. She spoons out just the right amount, spreading it with the back of the spoon.

"You've done this before?" I ask, watching her masterful skills.

"Me and Daddy love making pizza, don't we?"

"We do." He touches her nose, leaving a dusting of flour on the end of it.

"Hey!" she protests, trying to reach him to return the favour, but he moves too quickly. Next, she tears off chunks of fresh creamy mozzarella, arranging them delicately. I can smell sweetness coming from the fresh pineapple chunks, tinned sweetcorn, red peppers, and onions. There's saltiness from the thin ham, an earthy smell of mushroom slices, and smoky pepperoni. I'm amazed how professional-looking all this is and just how much choice we have.

"So, if you didn't already own a surf shop you could totally open an Italian restaurant."

Ben laughs. "My second passion, Italian food and cooking."

"I want to be a chef when I'm older," Poppy chirps up as she finishes adding the mozzarella topping to all three bases before pushing a left-over sliver of cheese into her mouth. "What topping do you want on yours, Jo?" she asks me sweetly and with the upmost concentration.

"Ham and pineapple, please."

"You're as bad as Daddy. He loves pineapple pizza."

"And you don't?" I'm leaning my hip on the counter top.

She gives two firm shakes of her head, while arranging my toppings with precision.

"If you had to choose between eating a mint choc chip ice cream and putting pineapple on your pizza, which would it be?"

"Pineapple, I guess." She moves on to the second base, which mirrors mine, aside from the addition of sweetcorn and onions.

"Sweetcorn?" I look at Ben.

"Daddy loves sweetcorn; he eats it straight from the

tin, normally."

"I pinch a bit from the tin. I don't sit there with it for my dinner or anything."

I'm laughing at Poppy's honesty, and Ben not used to having his quirks outed.

"Your turn, miss. What's Poppy's favourite topping?" I twizzle her ponytail between my fingertips.

"You're gonna love it ..." She takes the pepperoni, placing it carefully around the edges. Then the ham, then the mushrooms, then the red peppers, all in circles until she sprinkles some sweetcorn in the centre. It's a work of art.

"Wow!" I've never seen a pizza that looks quite so tidy before.

"I'll let you try some. It's the best."

"I'd love to," I say and squeeze her arm.

"Oven's ready! We can get these cooking," Ben says, sliding each pizza in one by one.

"I think yours reminds me of the Skittles experiment," I say to Poppy, who gives me a blank look.

"Do you happen to have any Skittles, Ben?"

"We might have in the treats drawer." He points across the room.

"There's a treats drawer?" I say, widening my eyes, and Poppy nods enthusiastically.

"If we get sweets and chocolates, they go in the drawer for us to choose from when we've been good."

I love that her explanation of being good involves Ben in the equation. She takes me over to the top drawer and I sift through the piles of goodies, seeing a bag of Skittles hidden under some Haribo.

"Perfect. Can I have a small plate, please?" He passes me one and Poppy watches me open the bag of sweets. "Now, we need to arrange these around the plate." She picks up individual sweets, doing as I said. "Make sure you mix the colours up." She swaps out a red for a yellow one, then sticks to the same pattern: orange, yellow, red, purple and green, until the circle is complete.

"Done." She beams at me. "What now?"

"Now we get some warm water and pour it over them."

"Water?" Her little features crumple together.

"Trust me," I say, and she does. Ben fills a Pyrex jug and hands it to Poppy, who carefully fills the plate with water. Nothing happens straight away, but I nod, almost encouraging her to be patient as the lines of colour drift towards the centre, the white circle getting smaller and smaller, until there's an explosion of colour—like a rainbow. She inhales, her reaction every bit as awe-inspiring as if we were seeing the arc of colour splashed across the sky, and I'm already a little smitten with her.

After Poppy lets me try some of her pizza, I have to admit her way of making it may be the way forward, though all of our pizzas were delicious. I'd whipped up some brownies while our food was cooking and Ben has gone into the kitchen to clear our plates and serve up dessert.

Poppy's flicking through Disney+ when he enters the room, carrying two blue bowls.

"Please don't make me watch *Frozen* again. One, or two," he says firmly, and she presses the arrow button so that it moves away from her almost selection.

The smell of rich, dark chocolate reaches my nostrils as he hands me a bowl, and I can't resist lifting it up to my nose. "Thank you," I say. Other than a 'thank you', Poppy falls silent, making no protests about not being able to watch *Frozen*, one, or two, and I watch her spoon far larger quantities than should be possible into her mouth, lifting her bowl to catch any spillages.

"Pops, put less in at once, please."

She nods, wide-eyed, the goo of the brownie preventing any words leaving her hamster cheeks. Ben looks at me with a 'kids' eye roll and I smile.

"I think Jo will have to come for tea more often if these brownies are anything to go by."

"Mmmmm." Poppy nods again.

"I'm pleased you're both enjoying them."

"I enjoy you being here with us," Ben whispers, squeezing my knee, the heat from his touch radiating through my entire body. I feel the same, though say nothing, because my mind keeps coming back to the thought that *I'm leaving soon.*

Chapter Eleven

After a run of back-to-back days at work on twelve-hour shifts, my room looks a state. People have always envied my job and working long days, because you get more days off. In reality, though, you just spend those days in bed, exhausted, or catching up on chores. At least living with my parents means I don't have a whole house to keep clean. I like to help them when I can, as a thank you for my protracted stay. My laundry isn't too bad, aside from my uniforms, as I normally only wear pajamas either end of the day. This morning's the first time I've been up and dressed in actual clothes all week, and I'm enjoying my summer wardrobe. Today, I've chosen to wear a white vest top and my favourite red floral, mid-waist, ruffle hem shorts, which look like culottes. I'm supposed to be meeting Ben for lunch and then helping my parents this afternoon. My en suite is desperate for a clean—bathroom cleaning is my least favourite chore, Mum's too. Dad is normally designated loo cleaner in this family. He makes the shower sheen better than Mr Muscle himself. I miss having my own place, but moving here was only supposed to be temporary, as

Tom wanted to keep the house when we split. It was his before we lived together, having decided to move to his place, instead of the house Emma and I had shared, because his was the bigger of the two. It's odd because I felt as though it were a step back, moving in with my parents. I used to speak to Emma about it, because she knew how that felt. Now, though, I love how homely it is. It's different from Ben's place, though I really like his chic interior; it's a contrast to my parents' rustic, cosy quarters. The lounge has a stone hearth and electric fire. Cream shutters line the bay window and a large wooden bookcase sits beside the window seat where I love to curl up and read on my days off. There are ethnic print throws over both the leather sofa and matching chair, with a mahogany coffee table in the centre. The small kitchen sits behind the leather sofa, with a dark-stained worktop, neutral painted cupboards and a white ceramic sink. There are French doors leading onto a square patio, fenced on all sides—a piece of privacy, away from the guests. I think my parents' style has been a huge influence on my own, and I wonder what Ben would think of this place. It's not been practical to be here together. We spend most of our time at his house, and I've wondered on more than one occasion if it's difficult for him to have memories with his late wife there. I'm not sure I could have been with another man in the house Tom and I shared, if things had been different and I'd stayed there. Perhaps it's okay, because no matter the darker memories, I suppose there are happier ones to treasure, too. Despite how much we've started to open up to each other, there's still things I'd love to know. Things I wish I was brave enough to share with him, too.

"Hey," I say, answering my phone on the first ring after seeing the backlight flashing beside me.

"Morning. I'm going to have to cancel our plans." His speech sounds rushed. "Rita's called in sick, so I have no one to watch Pops. It's half-term and I'm slammed at the shop. Ronnie's out because he's sprained his ankle, so I'm short-staffed for surf lessons, and it'll be busy with it being school holidays. I'm sorry."

"Hey, relax. It's fine," I say, not used to hearing Ben in a flap about anything.

"Pops normally hangs out here with me, or with Rita next door, but she's already bored and wants to go for a walk down the beach. It's not helping."

"Can I do anything?" I hear my mum's voice in my head. I sounded like her then, how she asks me 'if there's anything she can do for me' when I'm stressed out.

"Not unless you can teach a surf lesson for me?"

"No, but I could take Poppy for a couple of hours. If you like?"

"Are you sure?" I hear a flicker of hesitation in his voice, which matches the feelings I have on the inside. Once again, I'm left hearing a voice asking me what I'm doing.

"I'm sure," I answer, in spite of my reservations and the not-so-quiet guilty conscience sitting on my shoulder, whispering in my ear. "Tell her I'll be there in half an hour and we'll get some lunch and have a picnic."

"You're a lifesaver and I owe you."

"I might have to hold you to that." My tone is light and more flirtatious now.

"Anytime," he replies and it's as though someone blows lightly over my neckline, because I shiver. These feelings Ben gives me, they're getting more intense by the day.

The second we hang up the phone, I feel a pang of guilt. The truth is, I want to see Poppy again and spend time with her. I also want to help Ben out, try and take some of the burden from him. Even though my mind's made up about Australia, which makes me feel awful that I allowed him to introduce her to me. It was knee-jerk and rash and now I don't know how to tell him the truth—I just know it needs to be soon.

Outside, it's nineteen degrees with a full sun, bright enough to lift anyone's mood. I've packed my swimming things and some other beach activities to keep Poppy entertained. Plus a cardigan for if the weather changes. I figured we could walk the rock pools and maybe collect more shells—she seemed to love that last time. Despite my reservations about offering to look after Poppy, I'm keen for the excuse to spend the day outdoors and to see Ben, even if he has to work. I did, however, promise Mum I'd help her this afternoon, but I'm hoping that turns into a baking session, where we drink coffee and natter.

"Hi," I say, and Poppy's soft expression reflects her excitement that I'm here, which makes my heartbeat quicken a little.

Ben grabs Poppy's backpack from behind the desk and places some cash in my hand before I have chance to register what he's doing. "For your lunch and to say thank you."

"You don't—"

"I insist." He withdraws both hands as I try and push the money back towards him.

I take a breath, realising it will be pointless trying to refuse. "Thank you," I say, wishing I could kiss him. He leans ever so slightly, his pupils dilated, and I know he feels the same. "I've got a couple of hours and then I need to help Mum at the guest house."

"Can I come too?" Poppy chirps up, watching me with her big green eyes.

"Pops, you can't just invite yourself places," Ben chides.

"It's fine. If you're okay with it, I mean?" I don't stop to consider the implications of introducing her to my parents, but the way she looked at me when she asked. I think how terrible a parent this would make me if I can't resist the 'puppy-dog eyes'.

"Can I, Dad?"

"Sure. If Jo really doesn't mind."

I give a casual 'fine by me' shake of the head.

"Be good and listen, okay?"

Poppy's fist pumps the air.

"Now, what do you fancy for lunch, miss?" I say, winking at Ben over my shoulder. It's girl time and we don't plan on eating sensibly. Poppy is going to be my guilt-free reason to eat chips and ice cream for lunch.

"Have a good time, girls," he calls after us.

"We will," I say, already knowing this is one-hundred-per-cent true.

After lunch, some crab-catching and shell-collecting—of which she remembered the correct names clearly—I suggested a paddle in the sea. Poppy, however, wanted to build sandcastles together and tasked me with making a unicorn. I wasn't sure my modelling skills were that great, but I gave it a good go. As we stand back, appraising my efforts, she tips her head from side to side.

"Daddy's better at it, but it's still a great try." She has a maturity beyond her years, and her honesty is as refreshing as the breeze rolling into shore.

"Thank you," I say. "I never was very good at art, so I'm pleased you think it looks okay."

"What's this I hear about mine being better?"

We look up to see the stature of Ben behind us.

"Daddy!" Poppy flings her arms around his bare shoulders and he swings her round. "Jo made me a unicorn."

"I *tried* to make a unicorn." I turn my palms upwards and shrug.

"I see. Hmmm." He rubs his chin, his eyebrows raised.

"Hey!" I say, reaching out to playfully push his shoulder.

"I'm joking." He chuckles lightly. "It looks every bit a unicorn."

"Take a picture of it, Daddy." Poppy kneels beside my masterpiece as he pulls out his phone. "You need to be in it, too, Jo," she says, tapping the sand beside her. I fluff my hair and kneel, leaning on her shoulder.

"Say cheese!"

"Cheeeese!" we say in harmony.

"Let me see."

"Manners," he says, with intonation and an ever so slight frown.

"Please can I see?" She looks at the image and beams.

"I came to see if everything's okay, but it seems you have it well and truly under control."

I can't help but feel his approval and it sends warmth through me, as if I'd just taken a sip of hot coffee on an ice-cold winter's day. "We're having fun."

"Thank you for this."

"No problem. I had some spare time. My FWB cancelled our lunch date," I whisper.

"Oh they did, did they?" he whispers. His eyes lock on mine. "Perhaps I can cook for you tonight, to thank you properly for today?"

"Please, Jo, please?" Poppy hears Ben's request, but thankfully not what I said. I'd die if she asked us what a FWB was. After more fluttering of her long eyelashes and the look in Ben's eyes, I can't resist. They're a formidable pair, to be honest.

"I'd love to."

At the guest house that afternoon we're greeted with Mum's warm arms, and Poppy seems to immediately relish the attention. The house is one mile from a small local cove, where the sea is normally calm. The front guest rooms all have a sea view and large bay windows. The whitewashed exterior walls feature a sky-blue sign above the porch which reads: Hydrangea House, its name inspired by the lush pink, purple and blue hydrangea plants surrounding the property. One of my favourite plants. The driveway is a large gravel space, with formal vibrant green grass borders. Alongside the bottom two bay windows is a wide bi-folding patio door, which leads out from the dining room onto a dark brown decking area, with some outdoor wicker tables and chairs. The second to greet us is my parents' 'Lassie' dog, Cassie. She's a beautiful collie, but loud by nature. Barking at everything and everyone when she's hungry, excited or just simply bored. My dad's trained her to bark less over the years, and the guests love her as much as we do. Straight away, Poppy is stroking her long, soft, tri-sable and white coat, which ranges from pale tan to dark mahogany in colour. Cassie rolls over onto her back for Poppy to stroke her belly and they become fast friends.

"She's always wanted a small person to play with. You've made her day," my mum says. She didn't mean anything by it, but the comment stung me all the same, though the touch of her hand on my arm tells me she realises how it sounded.

"Can we take her for a walk?" Poppy asks. With that, Cassie's on her feet and barking.

"Oops." She grimaces.

"Cassie, sit." I turn to Poppy. "We'll take her out before we go, okay?" I whisper so Cassie doesn't pipe up once more. We follow Mum into the kitchen, where the wide range oven is still on, and the island in the centre of the room is laden with pastries. There's an aroma of sweet cherry, subtle vanilla and creamy almonds.

"What's that smell?" Poppy asks.

"My cherry Bakewell tarts."

"Can I try some, please?" Poppy looks at me and I'm all of a sudden aware of my 'responsibility' in this decision. Shouldn't I be worried about it spoiling her dinner or something? It's two p.m. and I'm sure my own mum would have said something along those lines.

"I'll wrap some up for you all. Perhaps you can have it later when you've eaten your dinner."

I breathe a sigh and Mum smiles at me. Clearly my 'rabbit in the headlights' look gave me away. I don't know much about children.

Hydrangea House is my parents' lifelong dream, and they've succeeded. It reminds me of staying in places just like this as a child. The sound of crunching gravel from the car park, the ding of the bell at reception. The wafting smell of fried bacon and eggs of a morning as you make your way to breakfast. Waking up to the sound of seagulls in a bright room, in crisp white linen, which smells laundered—in a way only holiday sheets do. I hear Mum out front with some guests. Two small children, about five or six years old, are standing in front of her, heads cocked back and smiling.

"Have a lovely time at the beach. I'll turn up the thermostat to warm the sea up for you." The corners of my mouth curl into a smile as I remember being told the same thing by my nanna, who lived up the hill by the beach where Ben's surf school is. It was magical. I also remember how steep the climb back up from the beach to her house was. It felt as if we were climbing a mountain at the time. Mum would often guide me, placing her hand on my back for assistance. Sometimes my dad and I made train noises, our legs moving faster the quicker we spoke. The beach, that hill and my nanna's house were part of my childhood. Now, my wonderful childhood, my mum and this place will be these kids' memories one day, I think as they thank her, giggling excitedly. Their parents wink at her on their way past.

Mum turns to catch me watching her, and I know from the look in her eyes she's right back there, with us as children. Full of innocence and joy in the simple things.

"Can you really warm the sea up?" Poppy appears beside us, head cocked to one side; she looks just like her dad all of a sudden.

"I most certainly can. You just wait and see. Next time you're there it'll be warmer." Poppy's look is one of trying to believe her, and the rational part of her brain which is developing thinking it's far from possible. Her smile, however, reaches her eyes and they twinkle with the magic she's holding fast to. The magic we all held fast to for as long as possible at her age.

"Who wants to help me make a cake?"

"Who for?" Poppy asks.

Mum leans and whispers in her ear and she gasps, staring at me.

"Jo, it's your birthday tomorrow?" Poppy squeaks.

"It is, but it's not a big birthday. I don't want a fuss."

"Are you not having a party?" Her narrow shoulders slump.

I look at my mum, who's most definitely enjoying this more than she should, having been trying to get me to celebrate it this year herself. Truth is, I hadn't really thought about it. I've been so wrapped up in Ben lately, and planning Australia, I sort of forgot, or at least it crept up on me. After the year I've had, there didn't seem a huge point in making a fuss. Another year older was no longer something to celebrate. Birthdays seem a reminder of the things undone for some reason. Though I said as much to mum and she told me I was being 'dramatic', followed by, 'Wait until you get to my age.'.

"I'd not really thought about it," I answer, finally.

"You're coming to my house tonight, so we can make it a birthday party. I'm really good at throwing parties, you'll see," she says, smiling. With that, she takes my mum's hand and almost leads her back to the kitchen. *Another formidable pair in the making.*

"Now might be a good time for those chores, Josephine," Mum calls over her shoulder, the biggest smile I've seen on her face in years and my heart swells.

"Looks like it's just you and me, Cass. How do you feel about cleaning bathrooms?" Cassie flops down, her head between her paws. "It's not what I'd rather be doing either," I say, tickling her favourite spot, behind her right ear. "How's about you keep me company, until the bakers have finished? Then we can steal back Poppy from Grandma ..." I don't know why that particular word slipped out instead of 'Mum'. Perhaps it was the way she stepped into the role so comfortably, and Poppy for that matter, or maybe it was the throwaway comment my mum made earlier. Whatever the catalyst, it crept out of my subconscious and I wasn't sure if I should enjoy how it sounded. I need to face the facts, this casual thing with Ben is turning into something way more than either of us set out for. I have to tell him about Australia. *Tonight. I'll tell him tonight.*

When Poppy claimed to be an expert party planner, I hadn't known what to expect. She'd banned me from the kitchen all afternoon, which was long enough to complete my chores and shower, while Cassie napped on the landing, opening one curious eye as I moved from one place to another. She seemed to sense Poppy being done, because her tail was wagging before she even came into view, holding Cassie's lead and recreating the scene from earlier today. The sight of said lead being as exciting, if not more so, than the word 'walk'. Afterwards, Mum helped Poppy, in a clandestine fashion, deposit things into the boot of my car. I'd tried to look, but had been promptly shooed by two small hands.

When Ben arrived home, he hadn't seemed surprised by the sight of Poppy kneeling in front of me, a towel under my legs, her hands massaging cream into my feet so lightly it tickled. He simply disappeared into the kitchen, laden with heavy bags, and didn't return. I'd told Poppy I would go and see if her daddy needed help, but she made me put my feet up on the sofa, handed me the remote, and fetched me a cup of coffee, which Ben made. Then she ordered me to stay there and disappeared herself.

Eventually, I'm fetched by Poppy, who is dressed in her Elsa outfit, wearing a gold party hat. She attaches a silver one to me, and leads me by the hand into the dining room, which looks out over the garden through the patio doors. The table's set with silver crockery and wine glasses, a posy of daisies in a vase beside some quietly burning candles. There are six chairs, one of which is already occupied by Pinky the Flamingo, wearing a blue party hat. Ben enters the room moments later, carrying plates full of steak and thick-cut chips, with mushrooms and roasted tomatoes. Poppy is having chicken nuggets, chips and peas for her meal. Even Pinky has a plate with two chips on, and a solitary pea. She notices me looking at Pinky's plate.

"He doesn't like to eat chicken," she whispers. "It's his cousin." Her deadpan delivery makes my insides cry with laughter, but I don't let it out. I give Ben a knowing smile at how unbelievably cute, and inadvertently witty, she is.

"I see you had some help from," I pause, checking the words I'm about to say aloud, "my mum."

He shows me a bottle of red wine and I nod for him to pour me a glass. It's an Australian Shiraz, so I'm sold, though the thought of Australia sets me on edge, but I shake it off.

"I had the most interesting phone call. Apparently it's a certain someone's birthday and she's been hiding it." He theatrically widens his eyes at Poppy, who's nodding.

"Hiding is a little strong. I prefer *pretending* it's not my birthday."

"Birthdays are kind of a big deal in this house, aren't they, Pops?"

She moves her head up and down, exaggeratedly.

"Well, I can see why, with how amazing this all looks and smells. Steak is my favourite."

"We know. Linda told us."

"I figured as much. Thank you." I start to lean over, but retreat, remembering I can't kiss him. "And thank you, super party planner over there." She bounces her shoulders with excitement and we begin our meal.

Afterwards, Poppy jumps down, dragging her dad back into the kitchen, leaving me sipping my wine, contented. They return moments later, turning off the lights as a yellow glow appears and they sing, 'Happy Birthday'. When the cake, red velvet judging by the look and smell, with buttercream frosting, is placed in front of me, I blow out two candles.

"Make a wish," Poppy whispers, as though even the idea of it were a secret, let alone the wish itself. When the lights are back on I look at Ben, who's watching me with a look I can't fathom, and for a second, the hope from the moment is lost. Replaced by an odd wave of apprehension.

I wait in the lounge for Ben to return after putting Poppy to bed. She asked for me to join them in a bedtime story, but he was quick to squash the idea, making it sound as though I should be the one who sits and puts my feet up because it's my birthday tomorrow, though I read more into the situation—even if I don't understand what's going on. I see the lounge door push open and he closes it quietly behind him, retrieving his half full glass of red wine. He does sit next to me on the sofa, but there's more of a gap than usual.

"Are you okay?" I ask, turning my body angle towards his.

"I'm good." He sips his wine, a steely look in his eye.

"Have I done something wrong?" I touch his arm and he closes his eyes before mirroring my body position.

"I really don't want to ruin your birthday eve."

"Okay. Sounds ominous." I lean back. "Whatever it is, just say it." I take a breath, my mind waiting for him to deliver whatever blow is coming. As if the axe hanging over us is poised and ready to come down on this *too good to be true* situation.

"When were you going to tell me about Australia?"

I freeze as his gaze meets mine for the first time since he sat down, and I see hurt in his eyes. Pain almost.

"Mum?" I ask. I'd not even considered her telling Ben a possibility. *Why did I take Poppy to the house today! Why hadn't I told her about Ben not knowing? I know why. She'd tell me I was wrong to keep such a thing from him. Wrong to get involved with that little girl, I hear her say and she's right.*

"She thought I knew. In fact, she thinks I do, because I played along … six months to a year! You're going away and you just didn't think to mention it?"

"It's a year's working visa. I'm not sure how long I plan on being away. It depends on how it goes. And I was going to tell you, tonight." I lean towards him.

He huffs and stands, making his way to the hearth, where he sets his wine glass down on the mantel with a small thud.

"Ben, I said I wasn't looking for anything serious and so did you." My tone is level and quiet, though there's heat bubbling inside me.

"I wasn't. I'm not …" His head dips towards his chest. "Jo, I introduced you to Poppy. Who happens to love you, by the way." He raises his voice. "What am I going to tell her when you leave? Did you consider that?" His stare is cold.

"I'm sorry. I didn't—"

"You didn't what? Care?" Both his arms lift, tapping against his thighs as they drop back down.

"How can you say that!" I almost shout, but lower my tone so Poppy can't hear me. "I do care. More than you know and more than I thought I would." I look towards a photo of Poppy, the one I held in my hand that first night here.

"What's that supposed to mean?"

"I don't know, Ben! I was just looking for some fun before I go away. I was honest about that. Not long before we met, I'd bumped into my ex and his pregnant partner and I was rebounding. My friends were encouraging me to start living again, so I went surfing and met you. I figured there was no harm acting on an attraction, especially when we were both clear on what *this* was."

He rubs his fingers over his forehead. "Was?"

"Is. I don't know!" I sigh, brushing hair from my face.

"Why are you leaving?" His stillness and deep gaze makes me shift uncomfortably. I wrap my free arm around myself and rub my arm.

"Because it's a great opportunity to see some of the world."

"That's not the real reason. Why are you leaving?" he asks again, shaking his head.

"I told you, I want to see some of the world." I let out a noisy breath before swallowing down tears.

He's leaning on the mantel, his open palms resting over his lips and chin. "I think you're running away." He looks at me over his shoulder.

"I'm not running from anything. I just want a change." I gulp the remainder of my wine. It's sour and makes my cheeks tingle.

"Why won't you open up to me, Jo? You know everything there is to know about me. Everything."

I don't respond. The heat is now flushing through my body.

"You said it yourself, you bumped into your ex and then, bam, you hook up with me. You're still in love with him, aren't you?"

"You make me sound like a hussy when you say it like that and no, for the final time, I'm not still in love with him." I breathe out, standing. The wine has made my legs feel hollow, heavy.

"I'm sorry. That's not what I meant. I just wish you'd trust me with this. Explain to me how you're feeling. I might be able to help."

"Ben, I don't want to talk about it. I've done nothing but talk about how I feel for months. Now what I need is to go away for a while. I just wasn't banking on meeting you, or Poppy."

"You should have told me." He moves towards me. "It would have made a difference in my decision to let you meet her."

"I know. I realise that now. I'm sorry. I don't want her to get hurt. That's the last thing I want." I feel myself losing him. Both of them, in this moment and I'm terrified—room spinning, ringing in my ears, afraid. "What do you want from me?" I ask, our bodies parallel in the centre of the room.

"I don't know." He's looking down, as though the solid floor beneath us holds all the answers.

"This is exactly why we agreed to keeping things casual. Neither of us is in a place for this …" I'm retreating now. A wall going up between us.

"It was my call to let you meet her. Australia or not, we both agreed what this was, and I should have kept her out of it."

My heart deflates a little at the thought of not knowing her. "I'm not sorry I got the chance to meet her. She's amazing."

"She is."

"You're amazing," I find myself saying, the half-built wall inside me crumbling as though the bricks were laid by an amateur in the rain.

He pushes a strand of hair from my face. "Where does this leave us?"

"Maybe we walk away now, before things get more complicated."

He takes a step back and I see his nostrils flare ever so slightly. "What if I told you I don't want to walk away?"

I close my eyes, focusing on my breathing, and feel his hands clasp mine, pulling them towards him, resting them between our chests and I look up at him. "I've—"

"Ben!" I shake my head. I know whatever he's going to say will change everything and I'm not sure I'm ready. I'm not sure if I'm brave or strong enough.

"I need to get this out," he says and I still. "I've not entertained the idea of a serious relationship since Jen died. I couldn't imagine loving again or bringing someone into Poppy's life. I couldn't imagine allowing myself to be that hurt again. Allowing someone to hurt her that way. She doesn't remember her mum. She knows about her and loves her, but the loss she feels is different. It's a sense of missing something she's never experienced, as opposed to grieving someone who's no longer there. The truth is, I let you meet her because I wanted you to. I wanted to see what it would be like having a woman in our lives. Having you in our lives, Jo."

I swallow, the reality of Ben's history and meeting

Poppy finally hitting home.

"I told you I wasn't looking for anything serious, but maybe I am. Maybe I'm just afraid of losing someone I care about again. Giving Poppy a mother figure and it being taken away from her."

My eyes are stinging more now, with unfallen tears.

"I'm not sure how to navigate all this, or if we could even make a go of things … I just know that I'm in too deep already and it's going to hurt, losing you. However that happens."

"Ben, I'm not going to change my mind about going to Australia. I can't ask you to put your life on hold while I do this …"

He looks down.

"But I'm already in too deep, too."

Chapter Twelve

Somehow, Poppy and I talked Ben into taking the day off, but trying to get him to forget about work might not be so easy. This week marks the start of the school summer holidays, and Ben's busiest season until September. Business has been ramping up steadily over the course of the last few weeks, and now it's positively bonkers. We'd still planned some things we can do together over the six weeks school break: theme parks, overnight camping—to which I suggested glamping. I'd promised Poppy we'd have a sleepover at the guest house, see a film, and have some girl time. Maybe even take a shopping trip. I'm excited. There was even a possibility that Emma, Chris and Stephen would be coming down for a week's holiday and I was praying for it. I could just imagine them in Ben's back garden, having a BBQ, the warm, smoky aroma of succulent pork sausages and beef burgers cooking over the coals. Opening a bottle of Bud, because I've always associated a summery evening with a BBQ and a bottle of Bud for some reason. Poppy and Stephen playing together, running around. When they're both in bed, sitting out talking under the stars, with blankets, around the fire pit.

The night we talked, after Ben found out about Australia, we decided not to plan too far ahead and see where life took us as a potential couple. It hadn't been part of the plan for either of us, but I wasn't ready to walk away. Ben had spoken to Poppy about us being more than just friends and that I was going away in a few weeks, to be a nurse in Australia. Our relationship status didn't seem to surprise her, but I'm not sure she fully grasped the concept of me leaving, preferring to live in the moment, as kids do. Everything being out in the open feels more relaxed, despite the question marks surrounding our future.

"Try and get Daddy to chill out today, Jo," Poppy says, snapping me out of my daydream. She's shaking her head at Ben, who's on the phone to Ronnie.

"He will, once he's sorted stuff at work." I place my hand on her shoulder.

"It's his birthday. He shouldn't work on his birthday."

I rub Poppy's arm, wholeheartedly agreeing with her. Ben's stressed, what with it being peak season. I know he feels as though he should be at the shop, but it's his birthday and we're up early to go to the Eden Project for the day. I've never been, and Poppy was a lot smaller when she last went, apparently. There's no sign of his conversation ending, so I steal the phone from his hand, leaving Ben open-mouthed, his hand mid-air.

"Ronnie, hi, it's Jo. You've got this, right? … Perfect. Don't call him unless it's an emergency … you too." I hang up and put his phone in my handbag, hearing a low snigger beside me.

"I was—"

"You," I say, wrapping my arms around his waist and kissing his lips, "are spending the day, your birthday, with us. They're a big deal in the Campbell house, remember!"

"You win." He kisses me. No longer hiding our affection from Poppy feels good. "And you." He scruffs the top of her head, making her squeal. "I heard you sniggering."

The air fills with Poppy's laughter and I feel a warm glow spread over me, watching them together, and how truly unique their bond is.

"Let's go, family," he says, taking me by surprise and leaving me a fluttery sensation in my stomach, as though someone lifted the lid on a jar full of butterflies inside it.

I'm not sure who's more excited when we arrive, Poppy or me. The site is so vast and impressive, far more than any of the photos I've seen. From up here, by the entrance, I can see a trail of zigzag walkways, which gradient down to the valley at the bottom. The domes are a spectacular sight. Like enormous half-cut golf balls, or oversized bubble wrap. The gardens are most perfectly landscaped, with luscious, vibrant plants and flowers; hot pinks, purples, yellows and blues. The bushes and trees the colour of ripe limes appear to go on forever. Everything's a different height, colour and texture. All my senses are heightened and we aren't even inside one of the biomes yet.

"Hey, you good?" Ben asks, touching my hand.

"I'm great. This place." I pause, unable to find quite the right words.

"It ticks your wistful box."

"It does." I jut out my chin and shake my head.

Ben grabs my waist and pulls me in for a kiss. Poppy's beside us, studying a map.

"Where to, Captain Popsicle?" he asks.

"Dad!"

"Sorry!" he says, exchanging a knowing look with me. Poppy used to love that nickname, but now she cringes whenever he says it. There's still the trace of a twinkle in her eye, however much she protests, and I think that's why he still does it, while he can.

"We should go into the Mediterranean biome first," Poppy says. "It's cooler than the rainforest, and it means we can acclimatise."

"Excuse me? Acclimatise!" Ben does a double-take.

"It means get used to something."

"I know what it means, kiddo, I just didn't know you knew such big words."

"Dad!"

He holds out both hands, palms forward, retreating. "Am I not allowed to be impressed by my baby girl?"

"I'm not a baby anymore." Her arms fold over her chest.

"My mum calls me 'baby' all the time," I say, "and

when I say 'I'm not a baby', you know what she says back to me?"

"What?" Poppy asks.

"She tells me I'll always be her baby."

"Do you mind her calling you that?"

"Not anymore. I like it." I shrug.

The corners of her lips curl and a dimple appears on her left cheek. What I love most about Poppy's smile is that every time, without fail, her green eyes sparkle. It's the sort of twinkle you want to see again and again. I find myself saying or doing something to make it happen.

"See, baby girl." Ben wraps his long arm around her slender shoulders and squeezes, knocking me a sideways smile, and this time she accepts the gesture.

On our walk to the biome, we pass a giant bee sculpture and stop to admire it. Its metal wings are positioned upwards for flight. It's nestled in the flower beds, with huge alien like eyes, coiled springs for antennae and black legs which look like those of a spider.

"That's amazing," I say, taking out my phone to capture it.

"You know, bees are the most important thing," he tells Poppy.

"Why?" she asks.

"Because pollinating insects are key to the environment and both humans and animals. Lots of foods we eat wouldn't exist without pollinating insects like bees."

"Really? What food?"

"Like broccoli."

She wrinkles her nose.

"Or … strawberries and raspberries."

Poppy gasps.

"Chocolate and coffee!" Ben finishes his examples and this time I gasp, too.

"I love bees," Poppy says.

"Me too, Pops, me too," I say in return.

"Your mum always made sure the garden was a sanctuary for bees and insects. I've not managed to keep it up in the past few years."

"She wouldn't have liked it if coffee disappeared, would she, Daddy?"

"No, baby." He looks at me and I tip my head to one side.

"Maybe we can plant things in the garden to help the bees this year?" Poppy asks.

"I'd love that," Ben replies, trying to hide the emotion stacked up behind his eyes.

I know Poppy doesn't have any memories of her own when it comes to her mum, she was just a baby, so it's lovely hearing the things she's learnt from Ben, who has worked so hard to keep Jen's memory alive for his daughter. I watch him, sensing his conflict between the warmth in his emotions and a pain only someone in his situation can comprehend. It's during these moments I can't help but wonder if he can ever fully give his heart to someone else, and if not, am I okay being the woman he loves, but not quite as much as he loves his daughter, or loved his late wife? Then I shake my juvenile, selfish thoughts away, as I've done before, more times than I care to admit of late.

We've eaten sausage rolls for lunch and our next stop is the rainforest biome, reported to be a warm, mid-twenty heat at ground level today, with a temperature in the high thirties up on the canopy walkway. I, for one, am grateful it's not a hot July day outside, given that would only elevate the inside temperature. The balmy air hits me as I step deeper inside the biome and it strikes me how bright it is in here. I can hear birds chirping in the canopy above us, and the sound of water. There's a noisy river, which is flowing through large boulders covered in mossy green plants, running away from me, deep into the undergrowth, with waxy-looking leaves overhanging the rocks. When Ben stands beside me, I pull my phone out to take a selfie, our heads touching, and our smiles wide and matching. Poppy joins us for the second picture and Ben makes bunny ears behind her head—it's a keeper.

This place is incredible and I've forgotten we're in the UK, feeling as though I'm abroad, or I've stepped into a different world entirely. It actually makes me want to visit South America or Southeast Asia for myself. Though I imagine this jungle is a little less intimidating than the real thing, and I certainly don't see Ben as any kind of Bear Grylls or Ray Mears.

"Hey, Pops, look at these." He turns to me. "She loves lily pads."

"Wow, they're really big!"

"Santa Cruz lily pads." I read the display sign and then take some more photos.

We learn about the cacao trees, which grow beans used to make chocolate, and I lean forward. "I didn't know any of this!" I say, reading all the information around me.

"We're educating Jo," I hear him say, bumping his shoulder with Poppy, and she giggles. He then stands and whispers in my ear, "There's a few more things I can teach you, if you're interested."

I breathe in, feeling my pulse quicken and lightness in my chest, unsure if my current core temperature could possibly get any higher.

"Maybe. It's your birthday, after all." I wink and he lifts his chin, exposing his neck, and I see him gulp.

As we reach the waterfall crashing through the South American rainforest, I shake my head in disbelief at how incredible it is. Looking over to where Ben and Poppy are standing still, I know the feeling's mutual. The sound of the water takes me back to when we sat watching the sea at The Minack Theatre, and the calming, grounding sensation water has on my soul. Perhaps this is why I'm so drawn to Ben—he's a man of the sea and has the very same effect on me.

I've walked around behind Poppy, beside Ben, holding hands and watching her glance over at us, to check we're seeing what she's seeing. Or listening to her say, 'Look at that!' and 'I can't believe it!'. We've passed over a misty walkway, over wobbly rope bridges. Stopped for a group of nine Roul-Roul, or red-crowned wood partridge, some of which are blue, almost peacock-coloured with a red crown and some bright green. A boy tried to pick one up, despite the signs saying don't touch.

"Time for the canopy walkway," Ben says, rubbing his hands together.

"Do we have to, Daddy?" Poppy's shoulders curl forwards, caving in her chest.

"You'll be fine, kiddo. I'll walk with you." He turns to me. "She's terrified of heights," he whispers.

"You know what. You could hold my hand?" I say, in a gentle tone. "I'm not a fan of heights, but I'd really love to go up and see what it looks like from up there," I lie. I'd rather stay here. Go back the easy route. I look at the metal mesh platform above us; up there looks high and hot, but Poppy makes me feel brave. I want to be brave for her.

"You aren't?" Poppy's big green eyes are shining as they meet mine.

"Never have been." I shake my head and wrinkle my nose ever so slightly. "But I still do things because I don't like to miss out." My voice is low, just above a whisper, as though my words are just for her to hear.

"So we could hold each other's hand and feel bet- ter?" She places her little paw-like hand in mine and I grasp it tight.

"Exactly, with your dad beside us to make us feel safe."

"Daddy always makes me feel safe," she says in a soft tone, a radiant glow on her face that melts my insides. My pulse feels as though it's in my throat as Ben breaks from Poppy's gaze and finds mine.

"Thank you," he mouths. His brow dips fleetingly.

I smile in response, my heart so full of this strange, cosy warmth I need a sign, like a car park with no spaces left. Big, red capital letters. FULL.

Emma, Chris and Stephen are en route and will be staying with us for a few days, so I'm extra excited today. It's just over a week since our 'family' outing to the Eden project, which was the best day I've had in my life. The photos taken that day arrived from the printers this morning, and Poppy and I have been looking through them over our breakfast, which consists of homemade Nutella pancakes. Ben left the house for work early and we don't expect him home until late.

"Oh, I love this one," she says, not touching the picture this time, as she managed to smear chocolate spread over the last one. Thankfully, it was a less flattering shot of me eating—such a shame I needed to rip it up. Unsalvageable it was, even if I can hear Ben telling me to keep them all. *They're memories.* Poppy wanted actual prints to put in her scrapbook, so we'd printed them all and it's lovely having something so tangible.

"Me too. It was so realistic."

"I'm pleased bees aren't that size in real life," she adds.

"It would be a little intimidating, yes."

"I don't know what that means?" She looks blankly at me, which is adorably cute.

"Intimidating means sort of scary, or threatening."

"Oh. Maybe I'll use that word in front of Daddy and surprise him again."

I laugh. "What word was it you used last week?"

"Acclimatise."

"That's it. I was very impressed, too."

She beams, her shoulder lifting toward her ears.

"Finished?" I ask, my right hand hovering to take her plate away, and she nods.

"Perhaps wash your hands, miss," I say as she sucks chocolate off her thumb, before hopping down from the breakfast bar and disappearing into the downstairs toilet. When she returns I can almost see the cogs in her mind turning.

"Jo?"

"Yes?"

"Daddy seemed sad when he talked about Mummy on his birthday."

"He did, you're right," I say, feeling coolness wash over my skin.

"Do you think we could surprise him with a bee garden to remind him of her when he's sad?"

"Would you like a garden to remember your mummy by?" I ask softly, in a voice which sounds as though I'm offering to kiss her grazed knee better.

She gives three confident nods of her head and smiles at me. Her hair is unruly and her eyes stand out even more at this time in the morning.

"Well," I touch my chin with my finger, "I don't know much about gardening, but I know a couple who do."

An hour later, Emma arrives and Poppy and I are both dressed in our shorts and tops, smothered in factor fifty suncream, rocking our baseball caps—mine happens to be Ben's. Ronnie's off today and was happily enlisted to help with any heavy lifting, alongside Chris, who got stuck in, moving the planters and mowing the overgrown lawn, despite the long drive. My mum and dad arrived a few minutes ago and Poppy and I are helping unload the back of Dad's car, which is packed to the brim with tools, pots, flowers and compost. She's working so hard, carrying as much as her dainty hands allow. Dad has set about digging up a patch on the left-hand side of the garden, by the fence. To the right, is a garage, with a netted pink trampoline in front of it, and along the brick side, a mud kitchen. It's personalised with Poppy's name, made from old pallet wood, with a metal sink and various size pans. A paved path runs the length of the garden, with a few weeks' growth of vibrant green grass either side. The overgrown nature area at the very bottom is dotted with wildflowers;

blues, pinks, yellows and reds—poppies, of course—all waving in the breeze. This was by no means a small garden and already a wonderful space. It was just lacking someone's attention. As Poppy's sole parent and working full time, it isn't a surprise Ben hadn't been able to keep up with its maintenance.

My eyes find a faded light brown wooden bench, almost hidden in the overgrowth. The inscription on it reads:

In Loving Memory of Jennifer Chapman.
May you sit on clouds, touch the stars and dance in
fields of Poppies.

"That just needs a little sanding and a coat of varnish. Ben should have some in his garage," Ronnie says as I rub my hand along the rough edges. "As soon as I've finished the lawn, I'll start on it." There's a hint of sorrow in his tone and I realise he must have known Jen well. He wasn't just Ben's employee, but, for a number of years now, his best friend. Perhaps this is why there had been no hesitation when I called him to ask for his help this morning. I only wanted him to lift a couple of heavy things, save my dad having to, but he'd stayed and seemed committed to the project.

"Thank you," I say, meeting his sad eyes. He tries to raise a smile.

"You all good?" Emma strokes my arm and I turn to hug her.

"More than, with you here." Stephen is napping inside, having refused to sleep for much of the car journey here, which backfired on them setting off in the early hours.

"Such a beautiful inscription." Emma stands closer to admire it.

I nod. "I hope he doesn't mind, all this." I gesture to our mini DIY SOS team.

"I think he'll be blown away. It's thoughtful of you to help Poppy do this. It can't be easy sometimes, being reminded of his past."

"I'm learning how to make room for it, for both of them. It doesn't mean I'm not a little overwhelmed and intimidated sometimes."

"Of course. You're only human, Jo." She touches my arm lightly.

"I'm so happy you're here." I pull her towards me again. "I'm sorry for using your husband for hard labour, though. This wasn't my intention when I invited you all to stay."

"Oh, no worries." Emma crosses her arms over her chest, smiling.

"You just natter, ladies," Chris jokes, a bead of sweat on his brow as he helps Ronnie move the bench. "We'll, you know, do all the heavy lifting." Emma slaps Chris's bum and Ronnie laughs.

After bringing through the last of the plants, I'm feeling a little overwhelmed by the task. Not Poppy, though; she's wearing small pink gardening gloves, kneeling on a ladybird foam knee pad Mum bought her from the garden centre. They're side by side assembling some wood in a square frame.

"What's this, Pops?" I ask, crouching beside them.

"It's a bee hotel."

"A hotel, hey?"

"Yes, they lay eggs in here." She puts her tiny finger through the centre of a hollow stem.

"How clever. Where do we put it?"

She turns to my mum and shrugs.

"In full sun's best. When it's finished, you can choose where it goes. Then we need to get started on the bumblebee pot."

"A bumblebee pot?" I eye Mum with amusement.

"It's a clay pot filled with moss, then hay, and turned upside down in the soil. The queen bee goes inside this hole to keep dry and warm in winter." She places her pointed finger to the hole to show us.

"Mum, how on earth do you know all this?"

"Gardening programmes. I've seen enough of them over the years with your father and his green fingers."

Dad and Chris had the soil dug over and had shaped the flower bed in no time. The garden wasn't in as much disarray as I first thought, especially for our little army. Before getting back to their guests, Mum helped us to arrange the pots on top of the soil to show where to plant them. Poppy, Emma and I tip out various flowers: antirrhinums, or snapdragons as I know them, in bright shades of tango orange, yellow, pink and violet. Dahlias, Mum's favourite, we have those in peaches and purples. My favourite is the salvia plant, called 'Hot Lips'. Its bicolour flowers, in red and white, rise above a bush of green leaves. Campanula, delphiniums, geraniums—my parents hit the bee-friendly flower brief with ease. We have an ombre effect from the brightest orange to the palest tangerine, deep hot pink to faintest blush and bright blue to deep purple. There's height, depth, colour, tubular plants and single flowers, all of which appeal to pollinators, or so I've learnt. The already established lavender is in bloom and has plenty of visitors on it. Hopefully they'll enjoy the other additions. Plus our bumblebee pot and hotel, which Poppy found the perfect spot for in the foot of a hedge at the back of our flower bed.

Running her fingers over the stems of lavender, Poppy sniffs her hand. "Did you know, bees find purple the easiest colour to see?"

"I didn't, though it makes sense with how much they're attracted to lavender. I assumed they just loved the smell. Did you do some research about bees?"

"When we got back from the Eden Project, I borrowed a book from the school library all about bees, plus your mum taught me lots today."

"Did it suggest we do anything else?"

"Bees like fresh water to drink, but can drown easily. We need a shallow lid and some stones for them to stand on."

"Well, let's see what Daddy's got in his garage, shall we?"

Emma was already inside, giving Stephen a snack. Poppy vanished to find her coloured stone collection and I claimed a shallow tray from the garage. She emptied the velvet bag of stones onto the tray and we poured in some fresh water, ensuring not to go above the height of the stones. We set it in a patch of shade near the flower bed and stood back, watching our creation.

"I think Daddy's gonna love it," she says.

"I know he will," says Ronnie, who's just finished varnishing.

"Especially the memory bench. Thanks for doing that," I say as Poppy disappears onto her trampoline.

"It might need another coat, but it's no trouble. I loved Jen. She did a lot for me, so this is nothing in return."

"She sounds like a special lady."

"She was." He sighs and turns to see Poppy leaving the sprung mat, her hair going in every direction, as do her arms. "I'm pleased she's got you." He glances sideways at me.

There's a burning sensation in my chest and my eyes sting back hot tears. "Ben, too. He was in a dark place for a while after she died."

"What happened?" I ask, hoping to learn some more of what he went through.

"He stopped talking. Stopped asking about the business. Started smoking again."

"Again?"

"He used to smoke before he and Jen got together, but she put a stop to that. He'd never touched one while they were together, but he did for a year or so after she died."

"And now?"

"He doesn't anymore. Well, the odd one with a pint, but hardly ever."

"I don't know how he coped with a newborn and the grief of losing his wife." I cradle my left shoulder and rub my skin.

"I don't think he remembers much about that time in his life. It's as though he were on autopilot, taking care of Poppy, and he did, even though he was broken. She had every bit of his attention. His parents helped for a while, mostly because he didn't have any fight in him to try and stop them. Then, as time went on and he grew stronger, he thought she deserved some grandparents. Hoped, I think, that they'd mellow knowing her. I know he was lonely. Before you, the most he had were a few dates, no one that mattered to him. I knew the right girl would come along one day." He nudges me with his elbow and I knock him a sideways smile.

"I can't imagine seeing Ben be anything other than strong." I feel a sudden chill run through me.

"No, it was hard to watch. I tried to keep the business going as best I knew how. Give him time to recover."

"He's lucky to have you," I say.

"I'm the lucky one. Don't know where I'd be without him." We both take a breath and exhale in unison.

"Uncle Ronnie, come bounce with me!"

"I'm coming, kiddo," he says, sounding just like Ben and jogging over to her, unzipping the net. He climbs in and grabs her hands, making her fly even higher. She does scissor kicks and tucks as her breathy laughter rings out around the garden.

Ronnie has been his support system. In the absence of grandparents, or uncles and aunts, he's been there. I can't imagine going through what he has alone, and I'm so pleased he didn't have to. This is the first time I've seen Ronnie away from his work and had a chance to speak with him properly. I'd been guilty of stereotyping him as just another hunky surfer dude, but there's more to him than that, and I look forward to learning his story.

Later that evening, I find Ben in the garden, illuminated by silvery moonlight and the glow from the crystal-shaped solar garden lights we repositioned this afternoon. He's standing beside the memory bench, holding a bottle of cider as I reach him.

"Emma and Chris said to say 'night'. They're trying to get Stephen to settle after his monster long nap and are both tired from their early start. They also said to say thanks for the BBQ—another one of your culinary talents." I bump my hip on his. "Poppy's out for the count. I think manual labour exhausted her. You okay?" I ask, when he doesn't say anything. Poppy had been so excited to reveal our surprise. I'd seen how emotional Ben felt, trying to cover it in smiles and hugs. Poppy may have sensed it, too, but pleasure was the predominant reaction, as she led him through the design of our bee sanctuary.

"That kid …" He swallows. "She knocks me on my ass so often, I'm surprised I can still stand."

I laugh, rubbing his arm. "She's a great little girl."

"And this was all her idea?" He gestures around the shadowy space.

I nod, gently. "All her. The queen bee and us, her army of helpers. She's been reading up about bees since our trip last week. My mum helped her along with some ideas, but it was her idea to give you a place to remember Jen."

Ben blows out a long breath. "And you're parents helped?"

"Ronnie, Chris and Emma, too. They all chipped in. I have zero gardening experience, so …" I pause. "The bench is beautiful. Did you choose the words?"

His nod turns to an ever so slight shake of his head. "She loved poppies. When we found out we were having a girl, there was no other name on the cards." He huffs out a nostalgic laugh. "I think even if the hospital had got the sex of the baby wrong, he would have been called it, too."

I laugh, enjoying hearing his memories.

He's nodding again. Loud, stilted breaths rage from his nostrils as he tries to hold onto the wall of emotion threatening to cave inside. I turn to him, moving slowly closer, and reach my hand behind his neck. As I pull his head towards me, he crumbles.

"She would have loved her so much." His words come out like lone syllables and my grip on him tightens.

Chapter Thirteen

I'm in the kitchen, making Poppy's lunch for her first day back at school. She wanted ham and cheese sandwiches cut into triangles, which I happily indulge. I wrap them in cellophane and place them inside her unicorn lunch box, alongside her other snacks and juice bottle. She's sitting at the breakfast bar, eating her square-cut jam on toast. This week, it's all about the shapes with food. A couple of weeks ago, it was about making foods into faces. Like the pancakes we made, where we chopped up bananas and added them to make bunny ears. We squirted cream onto the back to make a fluffy white tail and drizzled on some honey for extra yumminess. We even put fruit in her dad's porridge to make a smiley face using blueberries.

It's my day off today, so I'm joining Ben in taking Poppy to school, at her request. I felt very honoured when she'd asked me last night, before bed. As I look at her, all dressed in her red jumper, white polo shirt and dark grey skirt, I can't help but feel proud. Proud to be allowed to experience these things. Proud to have met her and be able to watch her grow. I'm practically living here these days, and have been for most of the summer, though the school routine is new to me, and it's exciting. I know it will wear off over time, turn into a chore perhaps, but for now, it's what I want to be doing.

I can't remember the last time I slept at my parents' place, and the times I've suggested it to Ben, he always asks me to stay, or Poppy does. It's odd how 'at home' I feel in somewhere I'm only a guest, and even stranger to think I'll be leaving in a few weeks for my adventure. Not that Ben and I have spoken about it. I'm pretty sure ostriches bury their heads less than we are doing. It was odd, the mixture of emotion I felt when I popped home to check my post, seeing my application to AHPRA—the Australian Health Practitioner Regulation Agency—had been approved. I now have everything I need to go over there. Everything but the two people in this room and it scares me, how much I'm going to be leaving behind.

"Eat up, Pops, or we'll be late." He's in a blue top and board shorts, with tousled hair. A standard look, which I happen to love. "Thanks for making our lunches." He leans over to kiss me and I feel a familiar jolt of electricity surge through me.

"My pleasure. I have to earn my keep somehow." There's a passing mischievous expression on his face, which I assume is one-hundred-per-cent rude and he doesn't say the thought aloud. Not that he needs to.

"You still hanging with me at the shop after we've done the school run?"

"I am. It's supposed to be a glorious September

day and I plan on spending it on the beach, reading a book and watching you hard at work."

"Charming! You hear that, Pops? Jo's going to watch me working hard all day."

"Dad, you own a surf shop, which is basically your favourite thing to do on the entire planet." It's so matter of fact I fist bump her.

"She's got you there."

"I wouldn't say it's my favourite thing to do …" He flicks his eyes up to meet mine and smiles, which makes my cheeks flush with colour. We both know this innuendo will be lost on Poppy, or he wouldn't have said it. "I do love my job, though, not as much as I love you." He stalks over, grabbing Poppy for a quick kiss and cuddle. "You too," he says and I inhale as his lips meet mine. As they part, our eyes lock and I can see he realises I'm wondering if he means what I think he does. It may have been five months since we met, but we've never said 'I love you'. Not in as many words. He didn't even say it then, not really, it was more implied than anything.

"Dad," Poppy says, pulling at his elbow. "We need to go, remember."

"Bag, lunch box, shoes, go, go, go!"

We pile out of the door and Ben stops in front of his truck, but Poppy's waiting by my car.

"Come on," he says, pointing his thumb at the doors.

"I want to go in Bumblebee." Which she named not after the Transformer, but simply because it's the correct colour for a bee.

"All right." He puffs out a breath, realising it would be futile at this late hour to try and change her mind. I smile, unlocking the car, and we pile in. Ben looks far too big for the compactness of my car, but Poppy, as usual, looks right at home. We've cruised around in Bumblebee many times over the summer, when Ben's been busy working.

"Can we put the music on, Jo, please?"

I press the button and pull out of the driveway as the stereo kicks in with the sound of engine revs and heavy beats from an electric guitar. I catch Poppy rocking in the back as the first lines of Little Mix *Power* play out, the original, not the most recent one featuring Stormzy. Ben's stare, burning a hole in my temple no doubt, with the opening lyrics—it's a girl power song and a little sensual, but I know Poppy's young enough not to know the connotations of the words. My knees start to bounce, followed by my shoulders. I'm rocking with her, backwards and forwards as we always do to one of my old albums. Then with her laughing, I start to sing, casting Ben a sideways glance. He's just staring at me, with his sexy smile.

"I had no idea you could sing," he says over the music. I keep singing, with a smile on my face, blasting out a line in higher notes about being in control.

"Yeah, you are," Ben says, in a volume just for my ears.

Then it's Pops' part of the song and she mirrors the deep male voice on the track. Ben cracks up laughing, turning his full body to look at her. I'm not sure which of us is taking him more by surprise.

"There's so much sass in this car right now," he says, trying to outdo the decibels of the music.

As the song builds, Poppy gives a ponytail flick and we both give the odd head roll. Especially in the rap verse, where she is wagging her finger and waving her hands around. Ben's mouth is open, unsure what spectacle this is before his eyes.

"So this is what you've been teaching my daughter all summer, when I've left you two alone." His tone is light and playful.

"To be a strong, independent female. Too right! Besides, you started this with the Bon Jovi dance parties." As the tempo slows, I squeeze his knee as I sing a more seductive line. Poppy is oblivious to her dad's sudden distraction as she carries on her dance party in the back seat. I concentrate on the road, feeling every bit of heat from Ben in the passenger seat, but this is Poppy's favourite part. "Go, Pops," I blurt out as her cue and she gives it her all, with one more ponytail flick. As I belt out the chorus for the final time, I can see Poppy through my rear-view mirror.

"Join in, Daddy!" she shouts.

"Oh, I don't think I've got the right body parts to do this song justice!" he says and I catch her shrugging off the reply she clearly did not comprehend, unfazed and swaying to the song's conclusion not far from the school gates.

It's almost lunch and I'm at a crunch scene in a psychological thriller I've been reading by a debut author. It's gripping and I've forgotten where I am on several occasions this morning. The sun is bright and hot, or getting that way. I might even have to venture down to the water to cool off soon. The beach is fairly quiet, though not deserted, with plenty of tourists still lingering around for a few more weeks yet. Ironically, it'll soon be Ben's slower season, and the first time in our relationship where we would actually get to spend some quality time together, away from the beach and his work, but then I'll be gone. I've been to visit April in Australia every couple of years, saving up money and holiday days—usually going for three weeks, not six months or more. There were plenty of times I thought about joining her out there. My nursing career makes it more straightforward than most professions, but I always told her I was a home bird and that I'd miss my friends and family too much. In many ways, I wish it wasn't this year I'd changed my mind about that, though a big part of me knows I'm doing what I need to do. When I think back to Tom and everything which happened, my resolve strengthens.

Two freezing hands grab my waist and I let out a little scream, making a couple flinch beside me. "Don't do that! I'm reading a book where the main female character is being chased by her crazed ex-husband."

"Ha-ha-ha. I'm sorry. You look so hot, I thought I'd cool you off."

"I was about to go for a dip in the sea."

"Well, let me help you with that, madame." He picks me up, cradled in his arms.

"My stuff!" I screech.

"Hey, Ron."

"Yeah."

"Keep an eye on Jo's stuff, will ya?"

"Sure thing." He laughs at the sight of Ben man-handling me down to the water's edge, and I give him a 'thanks for nothing' smile.

"Put me down, Ben … Ben, don't you dare chuck me in the sea! I'm warm, but not that warm. Benjamin …"

"You're Benjamin-ing me! That definitely deserves a dunk."

I tap his shoulder and my lips tighten into a line.

"Ha-ha-ha, it's just too much fun, oh-um-Jo."

"Are you ever going to stop calling me that?" I plead.

He shakes his head slowly, from side to side, wearing a smug expression.

I squeal as the spray of a wave hits my outer thigh. "Ben!"

With that, he lowers my feet into the shin-deep water and a cold sensation rushes up my body. My hair's standing on end as he pulls me towards his warmth.

"You're incredibly—"

"Endearing."

I draw my head back, eyeing him, thinking what scathing word I wanted to use.

"You started it in the car, with your sexy singing performance. I thought we could both do with cooling off a little."

"Remind me not to sing to you in the future if this is what follows."

"Please don't. I loved it. You, Poppy. It was like watching a part of her I haven't seen. She gets into our dance parties, but it was the connection you both have. The ease in how she is with you, I've seen it grow over the summer. I've watched her blossom having you around, Jo."

"Well, she's fun to be around. You've raised a happy, intelligent, fun little girl," I say, though guilt rests deep in my core.

He smiles proudly, as though hearing it from someone else, however much he knows these things to be true, is worth so much more to him. Neither of us moves, aside from being rocked by gentle waves.

"About this morning," he says. I shake my head and he uses his hand to turn my face to his. "I meant it … that thing we haven't been saying."

My feet sink into the silky sand beneath them and my limbs are no longer aware of the cold water in which they're submerged.

"I love you. I'm in love with you."

"Ben …"

"You don't have to say it back." His hands fall beside him and I take them in mine.

"It's not that."

"What then?"

"We decided to see where this takes us and it's been amazing. This summer with you, being part of your lives."

"I sense a but …"

"The elephant in the room. I know Poppy knows I'm going away, but I'm worried, especially when you talk about her blossoming around me."

"I didn't say it to make you feel guilty, I said it because it's true. Jo, we went into this with our eyes open. I've not asked you to change your plans and if your registration is accepted then I'll be happy for you."

"It was accepted. I'm all set." My arms hang loosely by my side.

He nods. "The waters cold, let's go in," he says.

As we make our way back to my things, I grab a towel and Ben wraps it around me, rubbing his hands up and down the lengths of my arms to warm me up. Thankfully, the sun hasn't disappeared, so it shouldn't take long to dry off before we grab some lunch.

I turn to him beside me on the sand. "You said you'd be happy for me?"

"I am happy for you, but it's not the same thing as being happy about you leaving."

"I'm coming back." I move my head until our eyes meet.

He nods once more.

"Don't you believe me?" I ask, sensing his nods are in place of his real thoughts.

"It's not about believing you, it's about not really understanding why you're going in the first place."

"Before you and Poppy came along, this place was full of painful memories."

"The memories are painful if that's all you choose to see them as," he says. "What about all the good ones? They're usually worth sticking around for."

"That's why I need to get away. So that I can let go of the bad and remember the good. There are … things, I need to deal with, Ben."

He nods, though it's different this time. It's acceptance. As my ears tune into my surroundings: the flapping of the flag in the breeze, the squawk of a seagull overhead and the hum of a bus passing on the road above us, a question builds in my mind. "You could come with me."

"To Australia?" he says, drawing his head back.

"I don't mean for six months, but for a couple of weeks, on holiday. My cousin has the space, and I could fly home for Christmas. Ben, when you told me you love me before, I didn't say it back, not because it's not true, but because it's getting harder to leave you behind.

I love you," I say. Leaning towards him, our lips meet as I steal the warmth from his. "I wanted to tell you I love you for weeks and hear you say it. I just, I wasn't sure."

"About whether you did love me?" His brow furrows.

"No … You married the love of your life and I—"

"You're worried I won't love you as much as I loved Jen?"

I nod, softly, ashamedly. I want to bury my head in my hands.

Ben takes my hand and swallows. "Jo, I loved Jen and I will always love her, but I had no idea I could feel this happy and in love again. I thought it was a onetime deal. That I got lucky to experience it once and that was my shot. I was wrong. I'm madly in love with you. So much so that I'd jump on a plane and travel across the world to spend a couple of weeks with you in Australia."

"You mean it?" I almost shriek.

"I'd love to. I just need to sort work and school, but I'll make it happen. I promise." He draws me in for a long kiss.

"Get a room, boss!" Ronnie calls out from behind us, and we part, laughing.

Chapter Fourteen

I'm standing in arrivals, waiting for Ben and Poppy to walk through any minute. I've been here in Australia for just over three weeks without them, missing them like absolute crazy. Pops didn't break up for October half-term until two days ago. Ben is taking her out of school for an extra week, which he was happy with, and the fines are just about affordable, alongside the astronomic price of flights. At least they don't have to pay for accommodation at Chez April. I wish they could stay longer than two weeks, but I understand why they can't. Catching up with April the past few weeks has been fun. A welcome distraction from my pining, though the fact I'm pining so soon into this time apart doesn't bode well for the months ahead. April's regaled me with many exciting stories of photo shoots in lavish locations, or with famous people. She even did a photo shoot with Elsa Pataky, who's married to Thor—well, Chris Hemsworth. The first thing I'd wanted to know was had Chris been there, though sadly he had not. Just as well, my jealousy couldn't have handled her meeting them both. April earns a decent wage from a job she thoroughly enjoys.

The jet-setting, up at the crack of dawn, rubbing shoulders with celebrities and partying till the early hours lifestyle suits her entirely. As does her swanky three-bed apartment near Manly beach, with a shared pool in the complex. I'm not sure why she rents such a big place just for her, but I know she has a never-ending stream of UK visitors and the odd stray cousin who decides to move in, albeit temporarily.

My attention is caught by Poppy's auburn tousled hair in the crowd of people spilling through the arrivals gate. Hugging Pinky with one arm, her other hand pulling a wheelie suitcase behind her, she looks every bit as tired as I felt when I arrived. By her side is the man who makes my heart feel full, wearing shorts, a plain steel-blue shirt, with a hoodie tied around his waist, flip-flops on his feet and his sunglasses pushed into his hair. There's a wave of apprehension rippling over me as they near, wondering if our time apart has changed anything. Wondering if I'll still feel the same connection with Poppy that I never imagined possible for a child who isn't your own flesh and blood.

"Jo!" a small, high pitched voice calls out and she's in my arms in an instant. I squeeze her so tightly, I fear she might pop. *There's my answer.*

"Can I get one of those?" Ben's mellow tone warms me like a comforting mug of hot chocolate.

"Get in here, Daddy. You two can be the sandwich and me the ham," she says and climbs between us as we do back home. Ben leaves his lips on mine a while and I breathe him in. He's a crumpled warm mess, smelling of faded aftershave, but he's mine.

"Hello, you!"

"Hello, yourself!" I say and nip the corner of my lip beneath my bottom teeth. His thumb rubs it free, as always, and he shakes his head. His eyes scan me like the X-ray machines used to check your luggage; everything is visible, including my feelings, which tell him I can't wait to be alone with him later.

"April's getting coffee, and we're going to take you both sightseeing to keep you awake."

"I'm really tired …" Poppy groans, leaning her head against Ben's stomach, her eyelids only half open.

"I know, Popsicle, but Jo's right, if we don't stay awake today it will be harder for our bodies to get used to the change in time zone."

"Okay," she says, her voice barely audible. The lack of complaining about her nickname makes me realise just how tired she is. Poor kid. She'll rally when the excitement of being in such a big, beautiful city kicks in. I remember the first time I came here to visit April. The buildings are tall, the roads are wide and most places are accessible by water, either by ferry or boat. You strain your eyes to keep those heavy lids open for as long as possible, to be able to take it all in.

"Hey!" my cousin says, a hint of an Aussie twang in her voice, appearing beside us with a tray of hot drinks.

"April, meet Ben and Poppy."

She smiles warmly.

"Hello. Here let me get those," Ben says, taking the tray of drinks to hold.

"Cheers," April says, removing a cup and handing it to me. "Cuz, I got you an Americano, extra shot. Ben, mocha for you." She points to the medium size cup on the back of the tray. "And for you, Poppy, a hot chocolate, extra marshmallows and cream—just don't tell, okay?" Her voice trails off on the last part, almost whispering it in her ear.

"Thank you." Poppy breaks into a wide grin and I can immediately see they're going to get along. April's a natural with kids, having been both a babysitter and pre-school assistant in the past. In fact, she's done many different jobs and always been successful at them.

"Thank you. This is great," Ben says to her before turning to me. "I could do with changing my shirt and brushing my teeth. You too, Pops. Drink up and we'll find your toothbrush."

Today's a great day for a ferry ride from the bustling Circular Quay across Sydney harbour, in full view of both the enormous harbour bridge and the glistening Opera House. Our destination is Watsons Bay, an old fishing village, and one of my favourite spots to explore in the city. The views, gardens and golden sandy beaches are something else. There's also the best seafood restaurant called Doyles. Their fish and chips from the wharf are the best I've tasted, especially the barramundi, which is my favourite. Although dining in on fresh fish is a blissful experience, we won't do that today. I'm not sure it's high up on the list for entertaining a seven-year-old, and a tired one at that. As the ferry pulls in, I see an awestruck Poppy watching the astounding city skyline behind us, with the high-rise buildings and arch of the harbour bridge. I know exactly how she feels. No matter how many times I've seen it, it never gets old. I often wonder if people who live here take everything for granted. The sights, scenery, close proximity to the beaches and the array of wildlife.

We climb down the ramp of the emerald-green and creamy-yellow ferry, the sound of metal clanging under foot. Poppy practically skips in front of me—a change to the jet-lagged slump at the airport. No doubt the sugar hit from the extra marshmallows in her hot chocolate, though if I've learnt anything about children, it's not the sugar rush you have to fear, it's the sugar crash which follows.

"This was a great idea." Ben kisses my cheek.

"I'm full of them." I wink at him, feeling so natural flirting with him. We're nowhere near out of honeymoon territory yet and I hope when we are our flirty banter remains.

As we pass Doyle's, my nostrils start twitching and my stomach groans. It's not quite time for lunch, but my senses are trying to convince me otherwise. On the edge of Robertson Park, I see a cockatoo with a yellow crest wandering on the grass near the path we're on.

"Look, Daddy!" Poppy points and I tell her what it is. There's something so magical about a child's face, seeing them *see* something for the first time. I find myself looking for her reaction to everything and enjoying it even more than my own.

"I love the pink ones," I tell her.

She gasps. "They have pink ones?"

I nod and watch her eyes scanning around hopefully.

"You do realise she's going to want one now, and I'm going to have to break her heart when I tell her she can't," he whispers to me.

I shrug, smiling, and he rolls his eyes.

The walk is pleasant. We are soaking up rays of sunshine, with Ben holding my hand and Poppy still searching for pink birds. April is taking pictures behind us somewhere. I've become accustomed to her disappearing skills—there one minute, gone the next. I call her Walkabout April. If we ever go anywhere unfamiliar, I have to hold on to her so as not to lose her. I pause, looking back to see if there's any sign of my gorgeous cousin. I see her, all bouncy long golden hair, striding confidently towards us, black camera strap around her neck, her pale blue denim shorts and vest top showing off her pear-shaped figure. April's not super skinny, and despite much of her life being around size nothing models, she's not in the least self-conscious of her curves.

"Daddy, can we go to the beach?" We see Poppy

standing in front of a grey slatted wooden sign, which reads 'Lady Bay Beach'– a nudist spot, the arrow pointing to our left. I pause, as does Ben, and April, as she reaches us—Poppy innocently awaiting our reply.

"Well, oh, um," he says.

"Actually, Pops, I've always wanted to walk to the lighthouse. How about we do that and then we can go to the beach tomorrow?" I jump in.

"Okay." She shrugs, and I'm relieved she doesn't have a meltdown about it. I've not seen her have many; however, the odd one she's pulled out of the bag had been a real eye-opener. Like in Clarks shoes shop, when she wanted pink shoes and not the boring black ones stipulated by school uniform rules. She'd been coming down with a cold that day and I think it was fuelling much of her behaviour. Needless to say, I didn't want a repeat show, one fuelled by jet lag this time.

"Thanks," Ben says as we walk on.

"No worries, oh-um-Ben!" I say and even April laughs behind us.

"Touché!" He slowly shakes his head, but the dimple and two perfect creases on his cheeks are unable to hide his amusement.

It takes just five minutes to reach the lighthouse— an impressive red and white structure on the cliff edge, which looks like a helter-skelter ride at Skegness, but the view is stunning. A jagged cliff face. White, foamy water beneath us over submerged rocks. Ferries crossing the ocean and sailboats floating on shimmering blue water. Poppy's interested, but for less time than it took to walk here, and I think she's going to wish we'd gone to the beach instead.

"Can we go back to the beach now?" she asks on cue.

I look at Ben. "Tomorrow we'll do the beach, sweetheart."

She makes a huff sound.

"If we walk this way we get to The Gap and can see for miles," April tells Poppy, her tone light and mysterious. Even I'm enticed into going—though I actually know The Gap and it does have the most breathtaking views. A photographer's dream, being able to take panoramic shots of the ocean, harbour, south head and cliffs. It's both sad and hard to believe The Gap's infamy as a suicide spot, given how beautiful it is. Much of the mesh walkways around the bay are covered with large metal builders' fences protecting the high spots.

Twenty-five minutes later and we're approaching our destination. It would have been quicker, but Poppy got tired halfway and Ben needed to carry her on his broad shoulders. To my surprise and relief, she jumps down, aided by Ben, and runs off to the wooden barrier where the warm yellow-brown sandstone cliffs fall away to a wavecut ledge overlooking the Tasman Sea.

"Do you think there's dolphins out there?" she asks, scanning with her eyes.

"For sure!" April says, leaning on the barrier beside us.

"And sea turtles?" Poppy stands straighter.

"All kinds of sea-creatures live out there."

On the rocks, I breathe in the sight of royal-inky-blue water, flowing into light turquoise near the rocks, the feeling that we're miles away from anywhere. I turn to my left and see Ben staring at me, a familiar look on his face. He slides in front of me, his hands on my waist, and he pulls me towards him until our lips meet.

"Thank you."

"For what?"

"Inviting us. We haven't taken a proper holiday before, and it's nice to think I get a couple of weeks' quality time with Pops … and you. Plus, the scenery isn't half-bad." His eyes don't leave mine.

"What's nudity?" Poppy asks, interrupting the moment. My gaze finds April, whose mouth opens before transforming into an amused smile.

"What, darling?" he asks.

"That sign from the beach earlier said nudity. What does it mean?" She pronounces it with an 'ud' sound as she did before.

Ben shifts from one foot to the other, running his left hand through his hair. I'm semi-frozen to the spot, enjoying this playing out in front of me. Waiting to see what parenting gems Ben conjures up.

"It means no clothes," he says, going with straight-up honesty.

Poppy's eyes move left then right; her other features remain static. "People wear no clothes on that beach?" she announces, the disgust rising from her like dust being whipped up by the wind. "Gross! I'm never going there." She pauses. "Are all the beaches here like that?" The genuine look of concern on her little face is so endearing, I want to run over and bear hug her.

"No, sweetheart," I say.

"Phew!" she puffs out.

We all chuckle a little as Ben throws his arms around her.

We ate a late lunch, which was almost an early tea—ice cream may have been our lunch, though Ben and Poppy have no idea what time of day it is. Doyles didn't disappoint, either. Still the best fish and chips I've ever had. Now I'm sitting beside Ben on the return ferry, his arm around me, keeping me warm. I feel a gentle nudge and look beside him to where Poppy has her eyes closed, her head lowering to her chest, before she startles and sits upright, her eyes wide, only to start the process again. April is opposite me, and as I catch her smiling eyes, she raises her camera and snaps a photo, as she's done several times throughout the day. I want to remember to ask her for some of the shots, because we don't have many of the three of us all together. Is it wrong to wish there was a picture of the three of us in Ben's house, on his mantel, next to photos of his late wife?

Chapter Fifteen

Only in Australia do I enjoy waking up at six a.m., and not because I'm jet-lagged, but because I love the mornings here, and going for a run. Ben decided to join me, leaving April and Poppy sleeping. There's no way either of them is waking up for a good couple of hours yet. The sky is a clear powder blue and the air is clean and fresh. Birdsong is loud and lively, awakening my senses to these foreign, yet familiar surroundings. We run along the block-paved path, past closed shops and a volleyball net on a grassy area, lined with tall pine trees. Most of the runners are on the path which runs alongside the beach, but we take the steps onto the sand. My trainers slip and slide, making every stride feel cumbersome, until we reach the wet, firmer sand on the shoreline. I step over a washed-up jellyfish and shudder at the thought of landing on one barefoot.

Only two things dampen my love for Australia. The first is the infinite array of insects and creatures that can do an unnerving amount of damage to someone. The second is it's a blooming long way away. The relative distance from my life back home had been a happy prospect when I'd wanted to take off to

Australia after Tom and I split. I hadn't the funds, or time off for it, and so planning this trip had been my focus. How the escape would have been so welcome back then. At the time, I remember an old Kelly Clarkson song playing out on the car radio, taking me back to lying on Manly beach with April beside me. The sound of the ocean and nothing but blue sky and the sand between my toes. It's funny how music can do that. How it taps into your memories and retrieves some of the best and worst moments of your life, the melody bringing total recall of first loves, first heartbreaks, songs danced to on favourite nights out, songs which remind of old friendships, or those no longer with us. *That* song that makes you want to wind your window down at the first hint of summer sunshine and belt out lyrics, all hope and positivity. It's like the soundtrack of your life; some you run from, and others, you run towards. Australia is a happy place for me. Unspoilt and full of magical memories. It's *that* song I wind down my window to and the feeling inside when I do.

"You know, this would be easier up there." He points to the path behind the low-rise wall.

"I know, but less of a challenge." I'm panting. A thin film of sweat is gather at the band of my crop top. "Are you not feeling up for it?" I say.

"Oh, I'm up for it." His voice is breathy, too, and I'm certain we're not talking about the run any longer. Our pace quickens then, over footprints and shadows, which look like giant Christmas trees in the sand.

Back at the apartment, there was silence, and we managed to take advantage of some *alone* time together in the shower, before dragging Poppy out of bed for breakfast. April has work commitments late morning, so it was just the three of us who boarded a ferry to the city, and then from the city to Taronga Zoo—I love travelling by water. It's quite possibly my favourite way to get around. On our second boat, just a short ride, my palms start to sweat, thinking of the sky safari cable car we need to take up and over the zoo. The bird's eye view above the tree canopy and animals below, with the backdrop of the city skyline behind, is the *only* reason I do it.

"Shall we hold hands?" Poppy appears by my side as we await our next mode of transportation.

"I'd like that very much." I take her hand, climbing into our cable car. We begin our ascent and I hear Poppy say 'wow', faintly, as though she inhaled the words, rather than spoke them. She turns to look behind us; the expanse of piercing blue water and sky frame the city skyline and all its iconic features.

"Look!" Poppy's attention has moved on to the animals coming into view. My favourites here at the Zoo are the Asian elephants, red panda and sun bears—I love the patch of yellow on their fronts. If smuggling one through customs were allowed, I'd probably want to take one home with me. Poppy, I imagine, is going to want to adopt several animals here today.

"Daddy, I love Australia," she says, with such conviction her face glows.

"Me too, Popsicle, me too." He looks so relaxed as he gazes from her to me. I draw in a small breath as my stomach flips and not because we're goodness knows how many feet off the ground right now. I soon forget all about my fear of heights, even when the cable car rocks back and forth. I just want to absorb her infectious energy, savour the happiness in Ben's eyes and delight in these moments. It's worth facing all my fears for.

Later, while we stroll through the Australian walka-bout, kangaroos and koalas have Poppy's attention. Mine is taken with mums pushing prams, or holding small babies to their chests in carriers. There's a mum breastfeeding her baby on the bench, her youngest playing at her feet on the grass.

"Jo!" I give a slight shake of my head and turn to Ben, who's staring at me. "You all good?" he asks.

"Yeah!" I swallow, then smile.

"Pops and I are thinking we should eat, if you're hungry?" He raises the palm of his hand.

"Food is fine by me," I say, pleased to be pulled back into the present.

We're waiting on a picnic table, in the shade, for Ben to bring over our food. Poppy gives me a surprise side hug.

"What was that for?" I ask.

"Thank you for letting us come on your holiday."

"You're welcome." I stroke her rosy cheeks. She

has the most perfect dusting of brown freckles across them and her nose. "I love having you here!" My heart feels light in my chest.

"You make Daddy smile."

"Aw. You make him smile, too."

"I know, but he still got sad. I heard him crying for Mummy sometimes … he doesn't know I know."

The word 'Mummy' from her small lips pierces the depths of my soul. This poor, beautiful little girl never knew her mum and her mum never got to know her. The lightness in my chest is replaced by heaviness, weighing me down. As though a scale had been tipped. I look to where Ben is paying for our lunch and have this overwhelming urge to hug them both. I pull her towards me, kissing the top of her hair, which smells like strawberries—her favourite shampoo and one of my new favourite scents.

"He misses her, but he has you," I say.

"He misses you, too," she says softly, staring up at me through thick, full lashes.

"I miss you guys, but I'm coming home for Christmas."

She nods in acceptance, the conversation over, but I feel a pang of something. It doesn't feel like guilt, though maybe it is.

"Hot dogs and fries all round," he says, reaching us and Poppy and I smile, as though we'd been chatting about our favourite animals and not just how insightful his daughter is.

When the last of our lunch is gone, Ben and I sit together while Poppy plays happily on the grass in front of us.

"What are you thinking?" I ask.

He shakes his head. "Nothing."

"Oh come on," I say. "You have a look and I want to know what it's for." I use my best pleading eyes and it seems to do the trick as I watch his shoulders relax and his eyebrows flick together as though he's shaking something off.

"I've never thought this before, but I was just imagining having another."

"Another what?"

He tips his head in Poppy's direction and my chest feels as though someone's placed a bolder onto it.

"You want a baby?" I swallow.

"After what happened to Jen, I never thought I'd entertain the idea, but I look at her …" He's gazing at Poppy, his expression soft and his eyes bright. "She makes my heart so full." He lets out an appreciative sigh. "Do you want children?" he asks, so matter of fact it makes my body tense up. "We've never spoken about it."

"I … where's Poppy?" I stand up, searching the space around us where she'd just been. I don't even remember taking my eyes off her.

"Poppy!" Ben calls out, already moving away from me and my heart races as though it might explode.

"Poppy!" I call louder and walk in Ben's direction. As we round a corner, I see her walking back towards us. We rush to her, Ben pulling her into his arms.

"Dad!" She sounds winded.

"I've told you, never walk off!" He gently holds her cheeks in his hands.

"I'm sorry." She wiggles free. "I thought I saw one."

"Saw what?" I ask, the sound of my pulse slowly retreating from my ears.

"A pink bird."

I laugh, a borderline hysterical laugh at the idea she wandered off in search of a pink cockatoo, which I told her about.

"Just tell us next time, you scared me," he says deeply.

"And me," I say.

She hugs us both sorry and we hold a hand each, but my relief is short-lived, knowing the conversation which was interrupted is something I'll have to face. Sooner, or later.

As far as beaches go, we've already been to Manly and Palm Beach—my ritual visit to see if I can bump into any of the *Home and Away* soap stars while filming, though I'm yet to be successful. Still, it's a great place to take a picture among the recognisable landscape I so often admire on the telly; all the same. I did have to explain to Poppy what the show was, and why I'm so interested. I would have offered to show her an episode, because I used to watch it with my mum when I was her age, but the content has changed over the years, and I'm certain it's not appropriate for a seven-year-old these days.

The next beach on our list of attractions to visit is Bondi. Ben's been angling to go there for a surf since we got here, and we're planning to do it later. This morning, though, after our customary early run, *shower*, and breakfast, we're on a sightseeing, hop-on, hop-off bus tour. We start at bustling Circular Quay, the transport hub of ferries, cruises, trams, trains and buses, not to mention home to street performers, food vendors and coffee shops. It's vibrant and exciting. We stop at Sydney Tower to take in the observation deck boasting views of the Pacific Ocean to the east and Blue Mountains to the west, where we'd spent the day only a few days ago. Memories are still fresh in my mind of the blue haze meeting white clouds over the eucalyptus forest, which goes on as far as the eye can see. Majestic waterfalls, steep sandstone cliffs and forest-filled valleys. Ben and I had walked down and it was a trek. I'd freaked out several times when I thought something touched the back of my ankle, usually a leaf skimming my skin. I'd imagined snakes, or spiders; tiny redbacks, waiting to attack my nervous system with one venomous bite. We descended in equal parts of terror, awe and hilarity. Exhaustion and heat, too. It had been so warm. If only I'd been brave enough, like Poppy was, to use the scenic cable car with her and April, but if we had we'd not have made a few wrong turns, following others, onto epic lookouts, the views of which should not be missed and won't be erased from my memory. It was definitely a trip highlight and we took lots of amazing photos I can't wait to look at properly.

We pass the war memorial El Alamein fountain, the sprays of water looking like the fluffy seed head of a dandelion and I wish we'd had time to get off and investigate. We leave the bus to walk around the Opera House. This beautiful structure deserves its worldwide recognition. What strikes me every time I'm up close is how the ceramic tiles of the roof look more cream than the white shown on pictures, and also just how many steps there are. Not that either of those things faze me. I'd love to go inside and watch a performance, but it's never been ticked off my bucket list, despite how many times I've visited. Judging by Ben and Poppy's quiet appreciation of the structure, they're as captivated by it as I am. I've spent many a happy evening under the lit sails of the Opera House, in a bar with April, watching as the water in the harbour glows in the moonlight. An inky-black pool with patches of white and yellow from the surrounding lights. Night time is my favourite time to be here. It comes alive after dark. Now, it's touristy. All phone cameras aimed at the buildings and scenery. Crowds of people sitting, standing and marvelling at its magnificent stature.

We visit both the breathtaking Royal Botanical

Gardens and Hyde Park, noting the bats who reside in the trees of the latter. The grey-headed flying fox is massive—thankfully, a fruit bat, but I wouldn't want to meet one after dusk, and Poppy was somewhat nervous after seeing them. I've never seen so much colour as I did in the Royal Botanical Gardens. It was tropical; vibrant pinks, purples, reds and yellows. Precision lines and shapes. A bee sanctuary if ever I saw one. It reminded me of home. Home, with Ben and Poppy, and I'd felt sad and happy. I love Australia. The life, the skyline, the beaches. Everything seems to be in the backdrop of the harbour, but I miss them.

The idea of visiting the fish market met an up-turned nose of a disapproving seven-year-old, as did the maritime museum. Not her 'thing' apparently, which made April giggle into the back of her hand. Ben was quietly pleased, because although he was massively enjoying our tour, fewer stops meant getting to the beach quicker. We had a brief stop at the harbour bridge, taking in its coat hanger shape and the small dots of people we could just make out doing the bridge climb—where you literally climb the arches of the bridge. I had to dissuade Ben from booking us tickets by telling him the cost per person, and that we'd need a good three or four hours spare. I draw the line with that kind of height, no matter how fabulous the views would be. We'd visited the Sydney Aquarium already, so didn't stop there again, despite Poppy asking if we could go back inside. I don't blame her; the exhibits were as bright and enchanting as I remember. I love the large glass display, where you feel the tranquillity of being surrounded by sea creatures in every size, shape and colour, with their grace and hypnotic, slow, steady movements.

Passing Bondi on the tour only added to Ben's growing excitement and I could see him physically twitching to get out on those waves, craning his neck to get a better look, and lingering for as long as possible.

Bondi, with its crescent-shaped beach and gloriously smooth white sand has the bluest of seas—painted-on-a-canvas blue. Unspoilt, clear and bright. Like on the perfect postcard. The first time I visited this beach, I was impressed with the sand and surf, but the sur-rounding headland is somewhat plain and not as you'd expect. The beach is the attraction, but even in Cornwall you have an impressive cliff or two to make it more visually pleasing. My toes sink into the warm, silky grains and I feel contented, which is good, because I've been a little on edge since Ben mentioned wanting more children. I don't know why I hadn't considered this a possibility. Denial perhaps?

"Are you going to join me?" he asks.

"I'll admire you from up here!" I say, placing my towel on the ground and inching my dress over my head to reveal an orange floral bikini. "All that sightseeing was exhausting."

"I'm suddenly not interested in the waves …" he says, leaning towards me and brushing my lips with his.

I roll my eyes upwards, my cheeks twitching as I try

and hide my delight.

"You came here to surf, so go! April, Pops, and I will cheer you on. Just don't get eaten by any sharks." I whisper the last part and kiss him on the mouth, pushing my tongue slightly between his lips, as I had done in the shower that morning.

"Sharks aren't the only things around here that bite you know," he says, and I inhale, seeing him remove his shirt, before making his way to the surf hire. He looks gorgeous. Like front cover of a magazine gorgeous. All broody, holding a bottle of aftershave to his cheek.

April and I apply suncream, and I make sure Pops is slicked up to her eyeballs in factor fifty, plonking a hat on her head, which she half protests at, though not enough to remove it. She's happily playing with the bucket and spade set we bought at the shop. I can see Ben, albeit not well; he's a speck on the horizon, but I can see when he's on a wave and when he wipes-out.

"Ouch," I mutter quietly, my shoulders rounding, as I see his board lift and his body fall. I know he's not hurt. He's a confident surfer and swimmer, but I wouldn't be surprised if he wasn't a little winded.

"Pops, shall we go get some action shots of Daddy?" April asks her, turning to get a nod from me.

"Good idea," I say.

"Are you coming, Jo?" She's taken April's hand, but turns to me.

"You guys go. I'll watch the bags."

"See you soon." April smiles and sets off with a

chatty seven-year-old. It amazes me what conversations they can hold about absolutely nothing; all the while, you have to look and sound completely interested. I usually am, but mostly because I enjoy seeing her sound and act so animated, as opposed to hearing some of her actual words.

I'm exhausted. There isn't a moment to relax, which means by nine p.m. Ben and I are yawning and off to sleep. I think that's why we're up and out so early, plus the prospect of some alone-time in the shower is great motivation for the early starts. It's a different type of holiday with a child in tow, a good sort, despite it being all go from dusk till dawn. Especially because they haven't been here before and only have two weeks to see as much as possible.

My time alone sunbathing in the relative peace and quiet was just what I needed. I'm starting to feel hungry as I notice the three of them wandering back up the beach. We had brunch while on the tour, which feels as though it were hours ago. Ben sets his board down beside his towel, which he scoops up and dries the droplets of water on his chest. I stare at him, warmth trickling over my skin thinking how he's mine. How I get to touch and hold him.

"How was it?" I ask.

"Great! I caught a few barrels, but it was heavy out there. You should have joined me for another lesson. Then you can say you've surfed Bondi."

"Maybe later if it calms down and you promise to

be gentle with me."

"Always!" he says, but looks away.

"My shout for a late lunch. Shall we get takeaway pizza?" April asks.

"Yes!" Poppy jumps up on the spot.

"How's about you help me then, Pops?" She tips her head in the direction of the shops.

She runs off with April without a glance back towards Ben and I, though April looks at me, a sort of grimace. Apologetic.

"Friend for life, right there." I laugh, trying to ignore a growing hollow feeling in my stomach. Like an expanding fault line—slow, creeping. Ben is staring towards the ocean. "You okay?"

"Yeah."

"Ben, what's wrong?"

"Poppy asked April why you didn't have any children. She told me when Poppy was jumping waves, saying she wasn't sure what Poppy knew, so she didn't give her an answer."

I freeze. My heart's fluttering so quickly inside my chest, I feel it might take flight. I swallow, trying to moisten the dryness in my mouth, but it doesn't work. I just listen to him as he goes on.

"I nodded like an idiot. Just like I did when your mum told me about Australia. Pretending, again, to know what she was referring to, while asking myself what April thinks I should know about you, which you didn't think to tell me?"

"You seem upset," I croak, because the air feels as

though it's caught in my throat.

"I'm not upset." He takes a breath and the frustration in his demeanour seems to lessen. "I'm just confused that there's still things I don't know about you, when I've told you everything there is to know about me. I wish you'd let me in. Whatever this is. Whatever you're holding back from me." He rests the back of a balled fist on his forehead. "You can trust me."

"I know I can. I do trust you!" I go to reach up to him, but my hand drops away.

"Do you?"

"Of course, just not here, though. I don't want to talk about it here." I pull at a loose thread on my burnt orange beach towel.

"Okay." He pulls me to my feet and into his arms, the heat from my sun-drenched body cooling slightly as our skin meets. Inside, the fault lines have moved rapidly and my dormant emotional volcano is expelling ash and steam, leaving me to decide on my course of action. I do trust him. I meant those words, but there's a part of me which, instead of facing up to this, wants to evacuate.

We spend the remainder of the day at the beach and, as promised, I try surfing with Ben, as does Poppy, and even April has a go. It's not the first time she's surfed. A former boyfriend was a surfer and she learnt from him—she can take it or leave it, though it was fun us all mucking around together and taking some action shots as mementoes of our trip. There's tension though. Subtle. Unspoken, but there. We BBQ back at April's place and then she'd offered to babysit while Ben and I see the sights of Sydney by night. Despite dwelling on our conversation at the beach, unsure still what to do about it, I'm excited and more awake than usual at the thought of an evening alone with Ben in the city. I put on a deep V-neck black maxi dress with a thigh-high side split, my silver leaf drop earrings and matching necklace. My wavy hair frames my face. I grab my black purse and denim jacket and we head out to Darling Harbour.

Seated in the window seat of a chic bar, I'm presented with a cocktail Ben's ordered. It's huge and strong, with real fruit on sticks and an elaborate straw. As I take my first sip, I realise I might be gliding home later.

"Woah!" I raise both eyebrows and inhale. "Are you trying to get me drunk?" I ask.

"Well, if I am, it's your fault for sticking that tongue of yours in my mouth at the beach and wearing the sexiest orange bikini."

My cheeks hurt from smiling so widely back at him as his hair flops over his forehead and he pushes it aside in such a familiar movement. His eyes appear brightened by his even more tanned complexion and the change in pace. He doesn't get much time off back home. I think having both April and me on hand to help with Poppy and the fact that he's away from work has really helped him look more relaxed. Not that he usually looked stressed, it's just a visible change I can see out here.

"I love you," I say and breathe in.

"I love you, a ridiculous amount. I hope you know that?" he asks, his eyes almost the colour of honey in this light.

I nod and look down, aware of where this conversation is going. He doesn't ask, not in words. The air between us feels open, inviting, as if this is the safe space I've been waiting for to share it with him. There have been so many times when I've thought about telling him, but I just couldn't find the words, or I was too scared of what they might do to us.

"My ex-boyfriend, Tom and I, wanted to start a family," I begin. "We were happy and in love, or at least I thought we were. I wanted a couple of kids, he wanted four." I laugh, but not because I'm amused. "I'd always had problems with my periods. Pain so bad I used to pass out as a teenager, that sort of thing. Mum took me to the doctors, but we never got to the bottom of it … Tom and I tried for over a year to have a baby and nothing happened. We paid privately for tests and surgery and the doctors told him everything was fine with him, but I was diagnosed with endometriosis, and … well, the short story is that I can't have children of my own …"

"I'm sorry," Ben says, taking my hand as a tear escapes my eyes. "I know people who have endometriosis and have children," he says tentatively.

I move my head up and down slowly. "People can

and do … In the beginning, you have this hope. You cling onto the statistics of all the people who have this condition and go on to have a baby of their own and so many do. You have the surgery, medication and painkillers. You believe it's fixable … *You're fixable*," I whisper. "Over time, though, you start to realise yours isn't the type which gets fixed, and so do the doctors. Hope is quickly vacuumed up. Every test, every procedure, every appointment, it sheared another piece of us away—another piece of me, gone. Tom and I fought a lot because of it." I sigh. "The pressure it put on us was huge."

"Did you think of having a family another way?" he asks softly.

"We talked through our options, but both of us had our reservations and decided they weren't for us. In the end, he wanted children of his own, so we broke up. He's now with someone else, expecting twins!" The last word I utter through gritted teeth.

"Jo!" His arms are around me and I'm swallowed into his broad chest. He smells warm and fresh.

"The speed in which he moved on, and how quickly his girlfriend fell pregnant—it hurt," I continue. "It still does."

"I can imagine. Well I can't imagine, but I … I'm sorry I kept asking if you were still in love with him. I just knew there was something going on." He touches my cheek with his thumb and I realise he's smoothing away a tear. "Something you were holding back."

"I'm not bothered about Tom. I'm over it. I have

been for a while. The baby stuff." I pause. "I think I was worried in case me not being able to give you more children made you …" I swallow and stare out at the moored boats bobbing gently and the bright lights of the harbour.

He turns my face towards him, his eyes a shade darker than before. "I don't need more children, Jo. I just want you!"

"You said you did the other day, before you knew. Are you sure I'll be enough?"

"You are so much more than enough, oh-um-Jo!" He's holding both of my hands in his. "It's like an angel sent you to me or something." In that moment, I can't help but think of Jen, somewhere in heaven. I hope she can see how beautiful, smart and funny her daughter is. How amazing Ben is with her, but most of all I hope she can see that I'll take care of them both, with everything I have.

Chapter Sixteen

I rouse in Ben's arms, where I'd fallen asleep. We were awake most of the night making love, so there was no early morning run today. Something transitioned between us last night, after I opened up to him about not being able to have children. It's as though our bond strengthened. Everything I'd been holding back was laid bare and we're no longer two lines of parallel rope, coiled round the other to form individual knots. Our free ends have been pulled, sliding us together to make a double knot. This strong, yet simple connection now impossible to untie.

Today, Ben and Poppy are due to fly back to the UK, and I wish they didn't have to leave, or I was going with them, despite wanting to spend more time with April, of course. It's only a few weeks until Christmas I try and tell myself, but feel a tear swell under my eyelid that I swallow down, and sigh.

"That was a big sigh!" he says with a croaky voice, reflecting last night's lack of sleep.

"You're awake?"

"I was only dozing, enjoying the feel of this beautiful woman by my side."

"Is that right?" I lean down to kiss him.

"Do I really have to fly home today?"

I stroke his stubbly cheek and say nothing, continuing to look into his eyes, which are searching every inch of my face. My mind retraces every step of making love to him, storing it for the weeks until we're together again.

"This whole trip has been just perfect …" he says so lightly it's as though he breathed the words into existence.

"It has, hasn't it—?"

"Move in with us, permanently, when you get back? I mean, you've been practically living there anyway."

"Are you serious?" I lean both my arms on his chest, my face inches from his.

"Deadly!" His gaze is fixed on me.

"You don't think we're rushing things?"

"Well, I'm not planning on going anywhere, are you?"

I shake my head, smiling widely. "… I'd love to."

He rolls me over, so he's on top of me, before kissing me slow and firm. Hearing the door fling open, I quickly jump to the side as Poppy enters the room, carrying Pinky under her arm. She reaches the bed and climbs on top of the duvet, the bird now perched in her lap, a sleepy expression resting on her perfect features.

"Good morning," I say, drawing the duvet up under my arms to shield my naked body.

"Morning, Pops."

"What about Pinky?" she asks, her hair all ruffled, her eyes half open. One of my favourite sights.

"Morning, Pinky," we both say in unison, making a smile spread across her face.

"Hey, Pops, I've got some great news …" He looks at me and I nod. "When Jo gets back from Australia, do you think you'd like it if she lives with us?"

I hear her inhale first. Then her eyes roll upwards, as if she's looking at the ceiling. "I kinda thought she already did?"

We both erupt with laughter and Poppy looks even more confused.

"Well, that's settled then. Jo stays."

Poppy jumps to her feet. "Yippee!" she shouts, bouncing high, rocking us from side to side. Then she practically jumps into my arms, squeezing me. I pull her closer into my embrace and my heart swells with such joy, I fear it might explode. When I glance up at Ben his eyes close briefly and I think I catch a glimpse of a tear.

April's set out breakfast in the kitchen and my nostrils don't know which smell to savour first. The sweetness of pancakes and waffles, or the saltiness of bacon. Then I see a bowl of fruit and smell the freshness of melon and sweet strawberries. There's filter coffee dripping into a glass jug, which smells invigorating and I need it this morning.

"April, this is amazing!" I squeeze her arm as I pass.

"It's just a little send-off for Ben and Poppy's last morning here in Oz," she says and I can sense she, too, is sad to see them go.

"We really appreciate it. Thank you for letting us stay here and gatecrash your girl time."

"I'm a girl, Daddy," Poppy says, her tiny fingers pawing at a pancake. Ben lifts it up, putting it on a plate, directing her towards the table.

"You certainly are. It's me who's the imposter."

"Well, I've loved having you both here. Please come over again. There's still so much you haven't seen yet."

"Oooh, can we, Daddy?"

"We'll have to save up for the flights again, Pops, but we'd love to come back. If Jo doesn't mind us tagging along again one day!"

"Jo does not mind in the slightest," I say, handing him a steaming cup of coffee, followed by April's, and then I cup my hands around my own and sip, knocking back my head at that first taste.

Seated around the table, we dig into our feast. I've joined Poppy in smearing chocolate spread over my pancakes, and we arrange our fruit into faces on our plates, comparing and smiling at one another. *I'll miss this!* I stare at her long after she tucks into her food. When I look away, Ben catches my eye and I can tell he's reading my mind because he offers a reassuring smile. Shaking off my pang of sadness, I plan on trying the bacon and eggs next, along with a waffle. I did happen to work up a large appetite after all.

"So, is it straight back to work when you get home, Ben?" April asks.

"I'm afraid so. I've got plenty to keep me busy, even though it's low season. Ronnie's holding the fort for me while I'm away, so I'm hoping he's made a start on the paperwork, but it's not his strong suit."

"Who's Ronnie?"

"My employee and best mate. He text me a couple of days ago to say everything was good and to remind me I'd volunteered to help at the fundraiser coming up."

"Fundraiser?" I tilt my head to the side.

"It's at the Esther Centre and Ronnie's shaving his hair off for charity."

"Wow!" I jerk my head back and notice April eyeing me curiously. "Ronnie's a long-blond-haired, blue-eyed, ripped surfer dude," I explain.

"Oh come on, that's hardly fair. I mean he looks like that, yes, but he's more than just a surfer dude. *I'm* not just a surfer dude."

"Sorry, I love Ronnie." I rub his arm, "I was just trying to explain to April why it's such a big deal that Ronnie's shaving his head."

"He's done it before for charity. It tends to raise quite a bit and some of our mates enjoy daring him to do these things."

"Well, if a bit of male ego raises money for charity then I'm all for it. I'd probably shave my head for the right cause." April looks skyward as though she's thinking what would entice her to be that bold. I can't imagine her without long hair. Unlike me, she's never cut her hair short before.

"You'd still look stunning. A Natalie Portman vibe," I say.

"Thanks." She swigs from her mug.

"What else is at this fundraiser that I'm missing?"

"Missing! While you get to sun yourself here and I get wet sponges or gunge thrown at me."

I curl my lips. "I was picturing more a bake sale, raffle prizes, that sort of thing."

"I wish. Though a couple of years ago, when Jen …" His voice trails off and he smiles at Poppy. "You're mum made Daddy into a raffle prize. I was sold to this little old lady called Betty for the afternoon."

April and I both giggle at the image. "What did she have you do?" I roll my top and bottom lips together, as April and I try and pretend we're not being childishly rude.

Ben's tongue lifts to rest on the corner of his mouth and shakes his head. "She had me mowing her lawn, hanging picture frames, fixing broken cupboards. Hardest day's work I've ever done."

"Well, you do hang out at the beach all day, surfing," I say.

"That is not all I do."

"It pretty much is, Daddy!" Poppy talks through a mouthful of waffle.

I high five Poppy and April follows suit.

"Right, thank you for breakfast, but I'm going to

shower and pack, because you ladies are tag-teaming me."

Ben smiles the widest smile and we practically heckle him from the room.

I'm quiet on the drive back from the airport with April. The air is cool this evening and I'm wrapped in a cardigan, watching headlights of oncoming cars pass us on the other side of the road.

"So you're stuck with me and I feel as though we left your heart back there at the airport," April utters into the silence.

"I'm sorry. I want to be here. I—"

"I get it. I've seen you guys. This little family unit you've become. It almost makes me want to settle down myself."

"Wow!" I tilt my head back, not that she can see me.

"I said *almost*, don't get too excited. I'm still a self-confessed bachelorette."

I roll my eyes. If April ever told me she was in a relationship which might stay the course, I'd probably think it was a joke. An April fool, as it's so aptly named. I can't actually imagine her settling down. She's such a free spirit. Happy in her own skin, and I love that about her.

"Maybe one day, Cuz!" I say.

"I'm happy for you, Jo." Her voice has taken on a sentimental tone. "I hated what that business with Tom did to you. I'm sorry again, though, that I outed the situation to Ben. I just didn't expect him not to know."

"Don't worry. I should have told him sooner. I knew he'd understand, deep down, I just … I dunno."

"It hurt you. Tom hurt you with his decision to leave. I could have killed him back then."

"I don't blame him for wanting children of his own. I often wonder what I would have done if things had been the other way around, you know."

"You would have stayed. I know you would." The sound of the indicator fills the silence.

"Perhaps, but my desire to be a mum was so over-whelming at the time." My shoulders lift, then fall as though being held down by tiny weights. We drove to the airport at dusk and now the car is in darkness, aside the glow from the roads and traffic. It feels cosy, the same way a blanket, pulled high up beneath your chin, tucked under your toes, does on a cold winter's day. It reminds me of being in the car on the way back from Wincastle. Ben had called and I'd driven straight to him. I knew then how I felt. How very *not casual* this was.

"How do you feel about being a mum to Poppy?" April's question cuts through my thoughts and I feel as though the hairs on my neck are standing on end.

"Oh my goodness, April. We're living together, not

getting married. I'm not her mum. I don't know what I am. Her friend. Her dad's partner?"

"Yes, but one day you might be her stepmum. Is that exciting or terrifying? I mean, I'd be a little terrified." The car swings into her parking space at the apartment block.

"It's both, I guess. I don't know if I'm ready to let myself have that kind of attachment to her. She can be taken away from me so easily if things with Ben don't work out. I mean, he might even change his mind before my time here's done … I'm scared of loving her any more than I already do, to be honest. Does that make sense?"

"It makes perfect sense …" She's looking at me now, in the dimly lit underground garage. "I never told you about Aaron, did I?"

"Wasn't he the guy you started dating when you first got to Australia?"

"Yeah."

"The record-breaking six month relationship!" I tease.

"Shush." She warns, flipping the car key over in her fingers.

"What about him?"

"He had a daughter, Olivia. Livi."

"What?" I double take, spinning around so my knee is bent, my ankle beneath my leg.

"She was four at the time, from his previous relationship. She lived with her mum, but they shared weekends, so I got to know her really well. I …" She sighs. "I knew that Aaron and I weren't right for each other, not really, but I stayed longer because I got attached to that little girl. I still think about her now, from time to time. Wondering what she looks like, how much she's changed."

"April!" My breath hitches. "Why did you never tell me this?"

"I dunno. I tried to pretend I wasn't bothered. I'm … me; independent, no strings attached April. It's probably the only time I've ever considered what motherhood might be like."

"And now?"

"I'm happy." She sighs, in a way which tells me she's not entirely. "If I get broody I'll buy a turkey baster and sperm. I mean, you're a nurse, aren't you? I'll get you to help me if I can't manage it!"

"What a terrifying prospect!" I clutch my hand to my chest, laughing. Knowing she's making light of her feelings. It never occurred to me that April may, indeed, want children someday. Not that she wouldn't be an amazing mother; she's just, April.

"What I'm trying to say is, be careful." She playfully taps my nose, something I'd seen her do with Poppy, and I can see it, how April must have been with Livi. "If I can get attached that easily," she continues, "then you, my sexy-ass cousin, are screwed, and I mean that in the nicest possible way."

"And I love you for it," I say. April climbs out of the car and her words circle through my mind … what if I get too attached to Poppy and things with Ben don't work out? I'm not sure I can take another failed attempt at motherhood.

Chapter Seventeen

April's birthday is upon us, and we're relaxing by the pool on the roof of this ridiculously expensive hotel in the heart of the city, where we're staying the night for free. Apparently, April is friends with the owner. To be honest, with her lifestyle, she's always getting freebies of one kind or another. 'Rich people like to give you stuff,' she always says. This five-star hotel is exquisite. I've never been somewhere so lavish. The infinity pool we're relaxing by overlooks Darling Harbour and the city skyline. The sunbed on which I'm lying is mink-coloured, with a blue and white striped towel, and I could practically dip my big toe into the turquoise refreshing water from here. There's a bar behind us and some shaded tables and chairs, which are unoccupied. Only April and I are staying the night; a handful of her closest friends have been given access to the hotel in order to spend the day with us. All of us slicked up with factor fifty suncream and moving only to roll over, cool off in the pool, or sip cocktails brought to us by waiters.

"I could get used to this," I say, before sipping my drink. The fresh mint dances with the zesty lime on my tongue as the ice cools my fingertips and lips.

"Cheers."

"Yes, cheers to you, my cousin." I chink my glass against hers and she beams at me, her gorgeously tanned skin glowing in her army-green cropped-top bikini.

"I'm so happy you're here for this. I know you're missing a tall-dark-handsome-man inexplicably. Not to mention a cute-as-a-button, red-headed-little-girl."

"I am missing them terribly, but absence makes the heart grow fonder and all that." She clinks my glass with hers once more.

"That's my girl!" she says, but I'm downplaying my feelings. The truth is, this past few weeks since Ben and Poppy left, my heart feels hollow. So often I want to tell him about my day, or when I've seen something I know she'd love, I feel a pang of regret at being so far away. Especially when I realise it's too late, or early, to call, miscalculating the time difference. I even miss making her sandwiches for school and singing together in Bumblebee as we drive there. My body resides in this big, vibrant, beautiful city, but my heart climbed into a suitcase and boarded that plane several weeks ago. We seemed to manage keeping in touch at first, but now our schedules clash, what with me starting shifts again, the aforementioned time difference, his work and Poppy's routine. I haven't seen his face for almost two weeks. I spoke to him briefly on the phone a couple of days ago, alongside Poppy, who monopo-lised the conversation, and then it was time for her to go to school. We've mostly resorted to texting rather than calling, or FaceTime. The other times I'd tried him, I'd not manage to connect. A text normally comes through later, explaining he'd been getting her ready for school or bed, which I thought would be the case. I know their busy timetable. The truth of the matter is that alongside the rising excitement inside me that it's only six more days until I see him, there's an uncharacteristic insecurity, growing each day we spend apart.

Our suite is breathtaking, with panoramic views over the harbour. There's even a bath in front of floor-to-ceiling windows. Although we're going out this evening, there's a huge part of me which wants to stay in and video call Ben from the suite to show him.

"Penny for them?" April cuts through my thoughts as she enters the room.

"I'm just relaxing." I lift my right shoulder.

"Everything okay with Ben? I've made reference to him several times today, but you've not made one gushing remark in return."

I sit forward as she joins me on the sofa, cross-legged, listening to me. "I thought, you know, after how we left it—"

"You two shacked up for life, you mean?"

"Well yeah, how he'd asked me to live there permanently, and how connected we were before he flew home. I thought there'd be more contact, or just …" I pause, looking up at the cloudless sky through the windows.

"More declarations of undying love and protracted 'missing you' calls?" she says.

"Frankly, yeah. I thought maybe that's how it'd be."

"Ben doesn't really strike me as the type, and you've never needed that before now."

"No, I haven't. I'm here with you, enjoying my time and I'm settled in the knowledge that I love him and he loves me, but … I'm not, for some reason, this past week. I'm not feeling settled." I rub the skin behind my neck.

"Maybe you're just not used to missing someone … some *people*, this much. He's probably giving you space to enjoy yourself and not seem as though he's a needy boyfriend. I like his vibe, to be honest."

I run my fingers through my hair, twirling a strand around my fingertips. "You're right. He's giving me space to enjoy myself and he's always busy, I know that."

"You know what I think's wrong?"

I turn my head to look at her.

"I think being honest with him before he went home, about not being able to have children, has left you feeling vulnerable again. Which is completely understandable. He made you feel for the first time in a long time you're worth being with and I think it scares you," she leans closer, placing both hands on my forearm, "how much you love him … How much you love her."

'Love her.' The words reverberate through me. I'm

terrified. Not just of feeling this way for Ben, but every time I admit to myself how I feel for Poppy, it's worse. I once loved the idea of being a mummy so deeply it almost destroyed me when it didn't happen. As I reach for April's hand, she squeezes it. "Ben loves you. Poppy loves you. It's plain to see and you need to allow yourself to love and be loved."

"Thank you. How do you know me better than I know myself?" I gently touch the skin beneath my eyes, shaking my head to stop any tears coming.

"Because I'm Am-az-ing!"

"Modest, too." I laugh.

"Seriously, though. If I found someone who was made for me the way you two are made for each other, I might just relinquish my independence."

I pull my upper body away, widening my eyes for effect.

"I'm probably one to many Disaronnos in to have you hold me to that," she adds and we laugh. I'm intrigued by her repeated claims of 'being part of something', instead of perpetually alone, though I'd never push her to talk about it. April is a bit like an onion, many layers, which need carefully peeling back and it's usually better to let it be her decision to start. I'm grateful for her and all her complexities. I always have been.

"Now, how do I look?" she says, standing with a spin.

"Stunning!"

"Let's go celebrate." She drags me to my feet.

We spent the first part of the evening having drinks

on the very apt thirty-fourth floor, watching the skyline lit up as far as the eye could see. I was more than happy, sitting there, a gin in my hand, getting to know April's friends. I'm in the unique position of being able to compare being a nurse back home and here as we swap stories of the career we love to hate. My mind casts back to the 'what if' I'd moved here when April did all those years ago. What would my life look like now? I wouldn't have met Ben, and I can't bear the idea of that. I wouldn't have met Tom either, which is altogether more appealing. I'd still be infertile, though, and whoever I was in a relationship with would have had to accept a life with no biological children. Tom couldn't; even the idea of adoption was closed off for him. I was more open to it, but I always worried about forming a bond with a child who wasn't *yours*. Of course, at the time I had no reference point. No Poppy in my life to teach me how quickly your affection could grow for a child. I thought I'd need to see myself in their reflection, to feel close to them. Pick out traits from my own family—myself, to find joy in their actions. When Poppy mirrors me, even if it's how I'm sitting, cross-legged, or holding her cup the same way I do. Or when her little fingers, all slicked up with cream, rub the lengths of my shins, as she had on my birthday when giving me a massage. My heart aches with joy, warmth, pride—love. Of course, she's at a cute age and isn't full of premenstrual hormones, which does concern me slightly. My mum takes great pleasure in reminding me how I threw a bottle of nail polish at my dad and missed during a premenstrual strop. I also worry what effect losing her mum so young will have on her, even though she's never known any different. Will that absence cause her to falter later in life? Am I good enough to fill that void? I've so many questions and uncertainties and when my mind runs away with me, as it is right now, I'm pleased for the distance, to try and work out how I feel before involving myself in their lives more permanently.

After an incredible three-course meal in a local restaurant, also run by one of April's friends—sadly, not another freebie, aside from the bottomless drinks— we had a cocktail-making class. I was grateful when the food joined the alcohol in my stomach, helping to absorb some of it. Especially given the activity didn't allow for slowing down. Flames and plumes had emerged from behind the bar as the mixologist, which I'd no longer been able to pronounce correctly, showed us how to create the most delicious concoctions I'd ever tasted, or seen. April had been in a similar state to me and all the girls had laughed so hard we'd struggled to catch our breath. It had been exactly the release I'd needed after stewing so much about Ben, and I knew April had had the best time. Sharing the evening with her made me so happy.

Now, back at the hotel, full to the brim with food and alcohol, I'm sitting by the window, on a sofa, looking out towards a black sea. April crashed out on the bed in just her bra and pants, full face of make-up, with a dozen numbers from guys she'll never call.

Happy. I press to dial Ben. It's two a.m. here, so it's lunchtime there. To my delight, he answers on the first ring.

"Hey," I say, more slurred than I'd have liked.

"Hey, it must be the middle of the night there. Everything okay?" There's a touch of concern in his tone.

"Everything's great. It's April's birthday, remember?"

"Course, sorry. She had a good time?"

"The best time. It's been perfect. Only more perfect would be you here, enjoying the view." I'm not sure my sentence held up as grammatically correct, but I don't care.

"You've had one or two of the gins, I hear?" There's now a lightness in his tone, which I've missed.

"Honestly," which I pronounce 'honsley', "I've never drunk this much."

"Drank this much," he corrects.

I laugh—more of a giggle really—and I hear him huff out a laugh too.

"I miss you," I say, sighing heavily.

"I miss you." His tone drops at this, his words almost fading as they're spoken, just as the lights in the far distance seem dimmer and hazy. "Did April find herself a nice man this evening?" he asks.

"Several, but she didn't entertain any of them."

There's another subtle huff of appreciation. "What about you? Any admirers?"

"I had my fair share." The line is quiet, as though he isn't there anymore. "Ben?"

"I'm still here."

"I didn't entertain any of them either. I'm kinda taken." I close my eyes, wishing he was here to make drunken love to me on this very sofa, where we could fall asleep under the night sky around us. "Are you okay?" I ask when he doesn't say anything.

"Yeah, just missing you."

"I'll be home soon. In six more days to be precise. I love you."

"Are you sure you want to come home for Christmas?"

I pause, wondering if, perhaps, in my drunken state, I've misheard his question. "Why wouldn't I be sure?"

"It's just a long way and you shouldn't feel you have to."

"But you just said you missed me?"

"I do."

"So why wouldn't you want me to come home?" I sit bolt upright, strikingly sober all of a sudden.

"No reason. I'm only thinking of you not interrupting your trip. Now, drink two pints of water and get some sleep, okay?"

"Ben?"

"I've got to go. Customers." With that, I hear silence. Checking my phone screen, not quite believing he hung up so quickly, I see my wallpaper—the selfie of the three of us at the Eden project. The one with the bunny ears. The nagging sensation I've had about something not being right is now a full-blown sucker punch and I curl into a ball and sob.

Chapter Eighteen

I woke in my own bed, at my parents' place, fully clothed, and had to drag my jet-lagged self out from underneath the covers and into the shower. The morning after April's birthday, Ben apologised via text, followed up by a phone call a couple of days before my flight, where he didn't elaborate more; we just slipped into regular conversation about mundane things and then Christmas plans. We're going to spend Christmas Day with my parents and then, on New Year's Eve, we're taking Poppy to the fireworks display at the harbour. I'd told him my dad could pick me up and not to meet me at the airport, because I didn't want Poppy having to traipse out late at night. To my surprise, he didn't fight me on it. Despite our 'business as usual' conversation, there was nothing usual about how he sounded, either that, or my insecurities are still playing tricks on me.

As I walk down the concrete ramp onto the beach, I pull my faux-fur-lined green parka coat around me, shielding my body from the cold that seems to reach beneath my clothes and search out my bones. In the past couple of months, my skin's forgotten what having heavy denim fabric against it feels like. The only familiarity is the way my boots sink into the sand, making my pulse rate quicken. He'd mentioned being at the shop today, sorting stock and that he'd see me later, but I wanted to surprise him early. My emotions have been vacuum-packed so tightly inside me, the outside pressure pushing them down stronger than the inside pressure trying to push them to the surface. Now I'm within feet of him, I stop fighting to keep them inside. Bubbles form in the pit of my stomach, similar to when I'd stood here on the second time we met.

Pushing open the door, I see Ronnie, with his back to me, his head shaved, wearing dark wash jeans and a blue hoodie. He's bending over the desk, scribbling on some paper, and I smile, wishing I'd been there for his head shave. Hoping someone filmed it at least.

"Hey, Ron," I say, pausing as he turns to look at me.

"Jo!"

"Ben! What happened to your head?"

He rubs his scalp. "Charity head shave. Ronnie didn't think I'd do it, but I proved him wrong."

"I … um. How come you didn't tell me you shaved your hair off?"

"Sorry!" He walks over, scooping me into his arms. "I didn't think you'd mind."

"I don't mind. Of course I don't. I mean, I loved your hair, but I just …" My eyes narrow and I shake my head ever so slightly. "It's taken me by surprise, is all." I touch his scalp and feel little bristles of hair, which actually feel quite satisfying underneath my fingertips. It's not the fact he's bald, but my insides feel like the weights of a hot air balloon have been removed long enough to leave the ground, only to be instantly tied down again and I'm struggling to figure out why.

"So, do you still fancy me with no hair?" he asks, tipping his head to catch my eye. He still looks as handsome, if not surprisingly more so, because you can see his sharp jawline and cheekbones on his square-shaped face. Each angle from his forehead to his chin is equal, and his eyes have taken on being even more stand out without his mop of black hair. "It'll grow back, so your Aidan Turner fantasy can be satisfied," he says and I realise I'm still staring.

"I still fancy you. You'd look handsome whatever," I say and mean it as he draws me into his chest and I whisper, "I've missed you."

"I've missed you, too," he says, kissing me.

After school, we pick up Poppy together, and as soon as she sees me, she's in my arms and I sniff her hair for a familiar scent. It only takes a brief inhale to return calm to my senses.

"Did you miss me?" I say.

"Lots and lots. So has Pinky. He was wondering if you can read us a bedtime story tonight? He likes it when you do the voices and so do I. I tried to get Daddy to do them, but he only has one voice and that sounds like when he's being the wolf in *Little Red Riding Hood*." I laugh and look at Ben, who's staring out in front, but catches sight of us and laughs, too.

"I'd love to read to you. It might help keep me awake."

"Are you going to shave your hair off for charity?" she asks, in the way kids change conversations without even a pause to signify the end to the previous one.

"I wasn't planning on it, no. Why?"

"April said she might. When we were in Australia."

"Ah, yes." I give one nod of my head as I remember the conversation. "She said she might for the right cause."

"What's a cause?"

"It's something worth doing, or giving to, because it helps people," Ben says.

"So you and Uncle Ronnie shaving your heads helped people?"

"Yes."

"I think it suits him better, but I like how yours feels, Daddy."

"Thanks, sweetheart, I think," he says, rubbing his chin. His eyebrows narrowed, then raised.

Everything is as it always has been between Poppy and me, as though the time since our airport goodbye until now has evaporated like water on the shoreline. However, something between Ben and me feels misplaced still, despite the 'normal' moments today.

He's quiet and not as playful. There were so many highs when we were last together in Australia, perhaps this is just 'normal life' resuming. That level of intimacy and closeness can't be experienced every day, of course, I know that. Plus, this is our longest time apart since we met. He must sense some of how I'm feeling because he wraps his arm around my shoulders and, in that moment, its warmth offers some relief.

Poppy's laughter fills the room as I finish off on my best witch's voice and the story ends. Ben is leaning on the doorframe, leaving us girls to our fun, but watching with a bemused smile on his face.

"Can you read me another?" she asks, sitting forward, pushing her hair from out of her face with the palm of her hand.

"Tomorrow. It's late now," I whisper.

"Please," she says with an elongated 'ease' sound and a toothy grin.

"Not tonight. Jo's tired from her flight," Ben says, his voice deep and full of authority. I've forgotten how much I like no-nonsense Ben. It's sexy.

She sticks out her bottom lip, and I smooth her hair behind her ear as she gives in, lying down. Ben strides over, leaning in to hug and kiss her, and I do the same.

"Goodnight," I say.

"Say goodnight to Pinky," I hear.

"Goodnight, Pinky." I pull the door to and descend the stairs, finding Ben curled into the sofa. He raises his arm, inviting me to join him.

"I can't get over seeing you with a shaved head yet. I'm sorry if I keep staring."

"It's okay. It'll grow back. I'm known to do these things from time to time—especially if Ronnie goads me like he did at the fundraiser."

"I remember you telling me once how precious you were about your hair. I think big, fat ugly tears were mentioned."

"Oh, there were very nearly tears as he shaved it off. Tears of laughter from the crowd! I'm sorry, though, I should have mentioned it on the phone. I just didn't want you upgrading me for a long-haired Aussie surfer." His tone is light and playful, but there it is again, the unexplainable churning in my stomach.

"Are you okay?" I ask, finding the courage to address the enormous pink elephant in the room. "You've seemed distant lately. I thought it was just the time difference, but I—"

"I've just had some stuff. There's a ton of paperwork to do at the shop—always is this time of year, and I've left it to build up as always. Plus, I had a run-in with my parents while you were away and you know how they put my hackles up."

"What happened?"

"The usual lectures really. I need a better job, she needs a better school. It was irresponsible of me to take her out of school to go gallivanting to the other side of the world on holiday."

I blow out my cheeks and then release. *Who are these*

people, or more specifically, who do they think they are. "… and what school do they prefer?"

"Boarding school."

I pause then. "Did you go to boarding school?" I ask. Thinking it strange I didn't know this, but then he doesn't talk about his childhood, or his parents.

"Yeah, and it was a blessing to be away from them. I think it's the only reason I managed to turn out okay. I had great mates and some really good teachers—not that I necessarily knew it at the time."

"I can't believe we've never talked about this before."

"I didn't think it was important, I guess. Sorry." He scrubs a hand over his head.

"No, it's okay. I just realise we don't talk much about your childhood. Where were you at school?"

"Surrey."

"Ah, that's why you have a southern and not very Cornish accent. I imagine there were lots of Kate Beckinsale accents in Surrey?"

"Did I ever mention how much I loved boarding school—well, the surrounding town. It was an all-boys school!" His eyes sparkle then and it feels nice.

"Do they know about me?" I ask, but instantly regret it as I notice him look away, shaking his head.

"It's okay."

"I'm sorry."

"You don't have to apologise," I say, but although I completely get his privacy, I feel a little pang of sadness from being kept a secret. His frame has stiffened. He's tense again and I feel as though I've ruined the moment. This is the change I've been feeling. His easy-going, relaxed nature. It's missing.

"I don't really want them knowing my business, Jo."

"I get it. I do." I sigh. "Did Poppy see them, too?"

"Yeah, that was the worst part. Mum made some scathing remark about Poppy having her mum's genetics and not 'our side' of the family's."

I gasp, my hand flying up to my mouth. "What did she mean by that?"

"Her ideal for Poppy is to be the daughter she never had. Horse riding, piano playing and a pretty frilly-dress-wearing doll. Not digging around in the garden and hanging around the beach with me, like a bum. She thought her mum was a hippy who was trying to save 'every lowlife going', as she likes to refer to people in need."

"Ben … I."

"You don't have to say anything. There are no words to cover it."

"You should have talked to me on the phone. Told me what happened!"

"I didn't want you to worry. Besides, I'm used to it. I just feel a bit stressed right now. I'll be fine once I've caught up."

"You sure that's all? I thought you might be changing your mind about us?"

"I'd never change my mind about us!" He spins to face me.

"You still want to live with me when I'm back?" I can't bring myself to look at him as I ask.

"Course I do." He dips to meet my eye and I see it as his face softens. My Ben. We kiss. The kiss I've been waiting for since I landed. The kiss I've been pining for since he left.

I've been back from Australia a couple of days and Christmas is just over a week away. Poppy is so excited, and it's the first Christmas where I get to experience a child's exhilaration in the run-up to the festivities. Ben's been busy with accounts and a backlog of paperwork, so I've been giving him some space, figuring he's right and he'll be less stressed once he's on top of things. Hopefully over Christmas and New Year things will settle and we'll actually get to spend some time together.

I've been trying to help out with Poppy. We've been reading our way through every Christmas book on her bookshelf, which involves numerous tales of elves, reindeer, the odd duck, sheep and cat. It's more magical than I could have imagined, and just as exciting as when I'd been a child. I find myself wishing I were there for every bedtime, and to see her in a morning, when her hair's all straggly, her voice quiet and she's even more snuggly than during the rest of the day. I think back to April's confession in Australia about Olivia and how much she felt for her in just six months. Then I take a deep breath and hope, once more, I wasn't wrong to become so attached. It's a deep-seated fear lately. One I can't shake, because it's not a normal relationship where you stand to lose just one person. Here, I lose one, I lose them both.

Tonight, I'm alone at home in my room, trying to sleep, but all I can do is think about Ben and Poppy, so I decide to try April. There have to be some perks for being awake in the night, when your cousin is on a different time zone. Lounging back, I pull out my phone and dial her number.

"Hey, Cuz."

"Hey, why aren't you sleeping? Jet lag?"

"Something like that. I can't switch my brain off." My back sinks further into my cushions.

"More Ben angst?"

I sigh.

"Have you sat him down yet, told him how you feel and asked him what's wrong?"

"I ask him what's wrong all the time. Borderline needy girlfriend levels of pestering." I rub the palm of my hand down my face.

"You haven't told him how *you* feel. He's a bloke, so he won't know unless you spell it out."

"So, you're the man expert now?" My eyes widen, my head cocked to the right as I lean into my phone.

"Hey, just because I choose to be single doesn't mean I don't know how men operate."

"It's just not like him. He's always been so open and friendly. He barely flirts with me anymore and I don't get it. Has the honeymoon phase worn off already? Was Australia our 'honeymoon'?" April just listens, as she has numerous times in the past month, while I was over there and since I've been home. "I'm not this person! I don't obsess over relationships and men. I have my worries and doubts, as is only human, but I resolve things. Face things head on. I can't work out why I'm so afraid of confronting him …" I rub my thumbnail between my two front teeth, listening to the scraping sound it makes.

"I think you know exactly why."

"You're right." I drop my hand and sigh. "There's two things I fear happening. First is that he's changed his mind in the cold light of day and he does want a future with children in it. Second," I touch my lips with the back of my hand, "is losing Poppy from my life."

"You're bound to have those doubts. You said it yourself, you're only human and this isn't you obsessing over relationships. This is a vulnerability you have. We *all* have them."

"April, what if he's cheated on me while I was in Australia? He's met someone else? I dunno. I'm losing my freaking mind here." I lift a front section of hair, tug at it and tilt my head backwards.

"Okay, so now you're sounding a little crazy. Ben's not a cheater," she says, her voice steady.

"Again with the 'know all about men' vibe." I rub my temple. I'm not trying to be mean. I'm relieved she has such faith in my boyfriend. I'm annoyed with myself for having so little.

"Talk to him! Maybe, just maybe, he's picked up on your insecurity since you flew home, and he's worried you've changed your mind about him and Poppy! You're a catch in this relationship, Jo. I'm not saying Ben's not, but a gorgeous, sexy nurse, who loves his kid and wants to be a mum."

"Yeah, I guess he could be feeling insecure." I gloss over her compliments.

"But if he has cheated on you, I'll cut off his penis and make him eat it."

"Graphic!" A beat. "April, do you think he's going to end it?"

"That's not what my guts telling me." Her voice is soft.

"Love you."

"Love you, too, now sleep."

I've probably been asleep for little under an hour when I startle awake. I'm hot, having fallen asleep in my dressing gown, with my duvet up to my chin. I strip back the bedclothes and yank off my robe. I look for my phone, but I can't locate it at first. Eventually, I see the edge poking out from underneath my bedside table, no doubt where it slid off the bed following my call with April.

Nine missed calls and one text message: *In ED with Poppy, please come.*

After dressing in haste, grabbing a pair of leggings and an oversized jumper, I shove on my boots and grab my coat. My mind floods with images of Poppy, sick or hurt. It's three a.m., so she might have woken unwell in the night or something. It must be bad if he's taken her to the hospital. I think of all the childhood illnesses it might be and pray she's not got anything serious. If she were being sick, he would have sat with her until it passed. If she had a fever, he'd have given her medicine. On the journey to the hospital, I've tortured myself enough. A colleague shows me to where they are, but we're not in paediatrics as I'd expected. I push back the cubicle curtain and see Ben lying on a metal trolley, his skin translucent, curled into a ball, and I freeze.

"Jo!" His voice is weak and apologetic.

"Ben, I don't understand!" I swallow and look around the small space for Poppy, but she's nowhere to be seen. "Where's Poppy?" I ask.

"Hi, Ben. I'm Bex, one of the ED doctors," she says, nodding at me. I'm friends with Bex, we've been on nights out together. Why is she addressing my boyfriend like he's a patient? And why the sympathetic look she cast my way before she started speaking to him. My mouth feels dry and I'm hot all of a sudden. I pull at my jumper, trying to loosen it at my neckline.

"So you started with a fever a couple of hours ago?" she continues, taking his history.

"Yes."

"Any other symptoms? Nausea? Vomiting?"

"I've vomited a few times."

"How many in the past twenty-four hours?"

"About four or five."

Why is he sick? Maybe he's eaten something. Where's Poppy? I search the room again, expecting to find her, but she's still missing.

"When was your last treatment?"

"A week ago."

"And that was your first dose?" Bex asks.

"Excuse me," my throat is so dry I can barely utter the words, "what treatment?"

Bex looks at me, her eyes narrowing. "His chemotherapy." Her body stiffens as she speaks.

"I'm sorry, did you say chemotherapy?" My mouth drops open and I feel a cool sensation travelling up my arms and through my stomach, lodging itself there.

"Jo," he whispers, my gaze meeting his. I see his hand rubbing at his wrist. "I've got cancer ..."

I shake my head, gripping the foot end of the trolley. Bex moves beside me, as if she might need to hold me steady, and I step back, away from her. He doesn't move, he's no longer looking at me. I can't hear anything else, though I'm not sure anyone's talking. A silence fell among us after Ben's words, as though we were actors and someone had forgotten their line. *Cancer.* "I need a minute," I say, rushing hastily from the cubicle. Leaning on the nearest wall, I try to calm my breathing, which is shallow and fast. My feet make an attempt to move back towards where Ben is lying, but I'm rooted to the spot. Every thought in my mind is scrambled and nothing makes sense. "Sarah," I say, stopping the colleague who showed me to him. "Did his daughter come in with him?" My words are ringing in my ears. I need to know where Poppy is and if she's all right.

"She's with Suzy in the relatives' room." I thank her and move past before she can speak further, stumbling around the corner. I need to find her and make sure she's okay. Her daddy's sick and she's probably terrified. *Cancer.* My mind whirls as though it were one of Poppy's spinning tops. I replay the past few weeks and try to find anything I've missed. Signs, symptoms, but there's nothing aside from his distraction and low mood since I got home. I've spent so much time obsessing whether he's gone off me, I didn't even notice he's unwell.

Outside the door to the relatives' room, I wipe the tears from my cheeks, willing myself some composure. As I push back the door, she opens her eyes and rushes straight towards me.

"Where's Daddy?" she asks, crying as she sees me. "He was being sick in the toilet and shaking. I got him a blanket, my pink unicorn one, but it didn't help." She sniffs. "He asked me to get his phone and then he called you, but he said you were probably sleeping, so he called an ambulance. I heard the siren and I opened the door for them. Daddy couldn't move from the bathroom." I push the palm of my hand into my face and move it over my lips as her head presses into my stomach. Crouching low, I look into her eyes and see so many emotions for such a young age.

"Daddy's poorly, but the doctors and nurses are going to help him get better. You did amazing tonight. I'm proud of you!"

A half-smile forms on her face. "Are you his nurse?" she asks in a smaller voice than I've ever heard.

"I'm going to stay here and look after you," I say, and she hugs me tight, the relief of having each other flowing between us both.

I'm not sure how long we've been lying on the sofa, Poppy tucked into my side, sound asleep, with me listening to her small breaths. Hearing the door open, I lift my finger to my lips to Kate who's standing there.

"They're moving him to a bed on the ward soon. The day staff are here. Do you want me to sit with her while you see him? He's been asking for you," she whispers.

Nodding, I edge off the sofa, making sure the pale green blanket covering Poppy is still in place.

As I stand outside the cubicle, I can't make myself lift my hand to slide the curtain to one side. I don't know what's happening. It was just an ordinary night just a few short hours ago. I'd poured out my soul to April, coming to the conclusion my boyfriend was cheating on me, or he'd decided I wasn't the woman for him. He's got *cancer*, and he hid it from me. Now I'm standing here, with a blue paper curtain between us, wondering what I'm going to say to him.

"I can see your boots," I hear him say, his voice sounding stronger.

"Hi." I finally push the curtain aside.

"Hey." I see the line hanging down from his fluid bag, and the needle in his right hand. He's shirtless and I notice his weight loss. I don't know why I didn't notice this before. There are tabs on his skin from where they've done a tracing of his heart. I'm not sure they'd find a rhythm for mine if they looked for it right now.

"I'm sorry." His voice trembles as he speaks. "Is Pops okay? I really scared her."

"She's not the only one, but she's fine. Sleeping." I perch on the edge of the trolley, taking his cold hand in mine. "Why didn't you tell me you're sick?" I pause, my throat feeling as though it's tightening. Suffocating. "I'm a nurse. I'm your girlfriend." My mouth opens to say more, but nothing comes.

"At first I didn't want you feeling as though you needed to come home." He swallows. "I was stupid. I thought I could get through this without anyone finding out. I didn't want to worry you, or Poppy. I don't know why I thought I could hide it. I didn't think I'd get this sick. Not so soon anyway … I just needed more time to process it."

"When did you find out?" I ask, hearing his words, but scarcely believing we're having this conversation.

"I had a lump before we went to Australia. It was painful after Ronnie and I'd been drinking one night, so I went to the doctors and he sent me for a scan. I got called in after we got back from Australia for more tests and a biopsy."

"Where's the lump?" I ask, clutching my fist against my chest.

"In my neck and another in my armpit." He points to the left side of his neck. "It all happened so fast, I barely had time to think."

"The hair," I say, it dawning on me why he shaved his head. "It wasn't for charity?"

"No." He gives a slight shake of his head. "I knew from talking to the specialist nurse the chemo would make me lose my hair, so I got Ronnie to shave my head at the fundraiser, too. Make it easier to cover up."

"So he knows?"

"Yeah. I'm sorry." His chin sinks onto his chest.

I roll my lips together, pressing them tight and nod. He starts to cry, his shoulders juddering up and down, and I wrap my arms around him, kissing his fresh, salty tears from his ashen face, my heart splintering beneath my ribs.

"I was so scared. I couldn't move off the floor and Poppy was so brave. She shouldn't be looking after me. I'm supposed to take care of her, of both of you. Jen would be so mad with me for doing that to her."

"Stop! No, she wouldn't." My voice is shaky. "You didn't know. You aren't sick on purpose. I'm here … You don't have to do this alone. I'm not going anywhere." As I speak the words, I'm praying, so hard, neither is he.

Chapter Nineteen

I'm cuddled into the sofa, with a silver teddy-fleece throw over my legs, waiting for April to call at midnight, UK time. We've always spoken when it turns Christmas Day here, though it's already morning for her. I think it started when I was on night shifts nearly every Christmas Eve. Now, though, even when I'm not, I wait for her phone call. It's become somewhat a ritual. She knows about Ben, after a brief WhatsApp conversation, but we haven't spoken on the phone yet. There hasn't been the time. After spending a few days in hospital, Ben's home and his antibiotics have almost finished. The consultant was pleased with his recovery, and had told Poppy she helped make Daddy better quicker by helping him the night he got sick, which she was pleased about.

I hear the manic high pitch tones of a FaceTime call and answer, seeing her wide smile, already her hair wavy and a full face of expertly applied make-up.

"Merry Christmas," she says, and I notice her festive Santa earrings dangling from her ear lobes, swaying happily.

"Merry Christmas, Cuz." I aim for some cheer, but

244

I'm exhausted; emotionally and physically. Looking after Poppy alone for the past few days has opened my eyes to what it's like being a single parent. It's a wonder Ben coped all these years, alone.

"How are you?" April asks.

"Aside from my boyfriend having cancer, you mean?" The words don't make the situation feel any more real. It's as though I'm dreaming. A really bad dream.

"I still can't believe it. He seemed so healthy when he was here."

"I know." I give a sad, slow nod.

"You should be getting an early night. I wouldn't have minded you cancelling our call. You look done in."

"Gee, thanks!" I roll my eyes and look down.

"You know what I mean. I'm worried about you."

"Honestly, I'm not sleeping well anyway. As soon as I lie in bed, things just keep going round and round in my head. I normally end up on the sofa, watching reruns of old gameshows until I'm so tired my brain has to surrender. Is it odd I'm finding Dale Winton's voice comforting?"

"Yes! Very. Please stop!"

I laugh, then immediately cry at the almost forced release of emotion.

"Oh, Jo!" Her eyebrows pull down and her tone is soothing. So much so, I wish I could crawl through my phone screen and reach out to hug her. "Did you get to speak to his consultant?"

"She said he has a very treatable, early stage Hodgkin's Lymphoma." I wipe my tears with the back of the blanket. "I'm holding on to her optimism with both hands," I say. Because whenever I think of the alternative, I can't breathe. My throat feels as though it's closed up. Every muscle in my body squeezes so tight, I feel as though my head might lift off under the pressure.

"Treatable and early stage is good news. He'll beat this, Jo." She pushes her shoulders back. "I know he will. Ben's the toughest guy I've ever met."

I let her words pierce through my shell, trying to absorb them. I need all the positivity I can find. All the 'he's young and strong', 'he's a fighter', 'everything will be okay' pep talks people will dole out, because when I'm alone with my thoughts at night, when the rest of the house is sleeping, all I imagine is losing them both.

"Jo, these are yours." Poppy hands me two small square boxes wrapped in black and golden striped paper with a thin black bow. "I helped Daddy pick them," she says, bouncing on her knees beside me and leaning forward to watch me open it. Inside the first box is a daisy flower charm and I know my mum helped wrap them. The neat folds and too much Sellotape scream Linda Mitchell's handiwork.

"Because they're your favourite flower," she adds.

"I love it," I say, tracing my fingers delicately over the silver.

"Open the other." Poppy's excitement cannot be contained. I open the second perfectly wrapped gift and it's another white pop-up box, with a starfish and sea shell dangle charm inside. "It's because you know all the names of shells and you taught me them." She points to the silver shell resting behind the mint stone-encrusted starfish. "It's a scallop, see. They didn't do a dog whelk one." Her shoulders sag, the sort of sag which would normally be accompanied by a huff, but there was none.

"It's perfect," I say, my eyes biting back hot, happy tears as I hug her. "I love them." When she releases me, I lean up to where Ben is resting reluctantly on the sofa and whisper, "Thank you." Sealing it with a kiss. I turn back to Poppy and give her a small box. This time it's wrapped in bright pink paper, with a white bow—I learnt to wrap gifts from my mum. As she opens it, I see her face light up.

"A charm bracelet! Thank you, thank you, thank you!" Her small fingers trace the tiny charms already hanging from it.

"Daddy and I thought the poppy flower and the bee would be a nice reminder of your mummy," I say softly, lifting my gaze up to meet Ben's, seeing a flash of pain sear through him. We'd bought this before we went to Australia, after making the bee garden, because she kept admiring my own charm bracelet.

Back then, it had felt right. The perfect gift. Ben agreed. Now, though, it feels as if it's adding to his distress. I can only imagine what's going through his mind.

"Please can you put it on?" She holds her wrist out, passing me the bracelet, and I loop it around and clasp it together. She's beaming. "I'll never take it off," she says, planting a soft kiss on my cheek, before doing the same to Ben. He doesn't say much, just wraps his arms around her, lingering in an embrace, until she wiggles away.

"There's a set of dolls over there, I for one, can't wait to play with. Shall we get them out before we get dressed to go to my parents'?" I ask her as she flops on the floor beside me.

"What time are they expecting us?" Ben looks pale and tired.

"I said we'd be there about eleven-thirty. They may have some presents for a certain someone." I poke her belly and she giggles.

"More presents!" She yelps. "Can we get dressed and go now?" Poppy jumps to her feet.

"Soon. Now, which doll shall I be?"

The smell of stuffing, lemon and turkey wafts in my direction the moment we enter the house. As we near the kitchen, the spice from the mulled wine reaches me and I feel the much-needed comfort of a family Christmas. Mum has prepped all the trimmings in pans and steamers. A meat carving knife sits happily by the side of a silver platter where the turkey and beef will go. There's a salad spinner on the draining board, and as I open the fridge, placing a bottle of Mum's favourite rosé Cava in the door, I find prawn cocktails, all made in the crystal dishes we've had since we were kids. There's mackerel and crab sticks in a white ceramic dish beneath them—part of my favourite course, the fish course. I love the smoked, sweet taste of peppery mackerel, with the freshness of firm, juicy prawns, smothered in seafood sauce with a sprinkle of paprika on top. My mouth's watering already and it's a while yet until we eat.

"Merry Christmas," she calls out, appearing in the doorway to the kitchen.

We embrace one another in hugs and kisses and Mum lingers on me, for which I'm grateful, but I have to work twice as hard not to break down and cry in her arms.

"Go into the lounge. Santa's been."

I hear Poppy's excitable chatter to my mum as she follows her keenly. I'm grateful for them. Grateful for them making it Christmas at a time when neither Ben nor I can seem to muster up the strength to sustain it.

I'm standing with Mum as the vegetables finish boiling. The meat is carved and we're almost ready to serve the main course. The starter was, as always, delicious and, to my surprise, I ate well. It's the first time I've felt hungry all week, since the stress stole my appetite. Ben had hardly been eating, too. If it weren't for cooking meals for Poppy, I doubt I would have bothered to eat properly at all. I'm certain Mum's cooking will change that, at least I hope Ben finds his appetite today. He skipped the starter, it wasn't what he fancied, and there are foods he needs to avoid while on chemo, in case he gets food poisoning, shellfish being high on the list. The specialist nurse had referenced the list of foods to avoid being like a pregnant lady's diet, which stung a little. She didn't mean to upset me; no one knows the little triggers you have, when you're unable to have children. They lurk in unspoken corners, creeping up on you when you least expect it. Most of them are such everyday occurrences, phrases, comments, expectations, that the wounds they cause go unnoticed, like little nicks on the skin. Only those who know your inner turmoil guard against things more carefully, though that in itself brings pain—mostly because you wish people didn't have to, or wish they wouldn't treat you differently. People in general don't know how to deal with things such as infertility, so invariably get it wrong, but then again, perhaps there is no right or wrong in something like this.

"Did the chat with the consultant reassure you?" Mum's voice breaks through my thoughts.

"I guess so." I slip my hands into the front pocket of my apron.

"He still looks pale."

"Yeah, he's feeling better, but not fully. I don't think he expected to be hit so hard. The trouble is, chemo takes away the body's ability to fight infection and he was unlucky enough to get one after his first treatment."

"I still can't believe he never said a thing in Australia." Mum isn't trying to sound accusing. I know she's just as shocked as the rest of us. It's a lot to process.

"He said he felt tired a couple of times, but put that down to jet lag. He had no reason to think it might be cancer, Mum. Ben's too optimistic for that. I wish he'd told me, instead of going through that first treatment alone."

"Poor Poppy, seeing him like that. She must have been so scared, little love."

"She's a strong kid."

"Ben's strong, too," she says. *Those* words again. I absorb them, as though they're rays of sunshine, seeping into my skin.

"I know." My eyes fill once more, and it's only through looking up and blinking I stem the flow of tears.

"When's his next chemo?"

"Day before New Year's Eve. He has to have four treatments, two weeks apart, and then another scan. If he responds, he has another two treatments and some radiotherapy. It was caught early by him seeing the GP about the pain in his neck after drinking alcohol."

"Thank goodness for that, at least." She touches my arm.

Shortly after, we're seated at a long table, my parents either end, and Ben and I opposite Poppy who is admiring my mum's silver glitter reindeer table decorations. Ben has a genuine dislike of glitter. Won't have it in the house. Says it's not strictly the glitter he doesn't like, but more that you find it, days/weeks later, stuck to your face. He positively recoils when opening cards, especially Christmas cards. Hands me or Pops the envelopes at even a whiff of the stuff. We secretly enjoy winding him up, saying how we're going to glitter-bomb him one of these days.

The centre of the table is taken over with succulent meats, surrounded by silver place settings, with round plates brimming with vegetables, roast potatoes, stuffing, pigs in blankets, and roasted Brussels sprouts with chestnuts and lardons. I have Buck's Fizz in a champagne flute, as is tradition with my parents for the dinner itself. Ben is sticking with squash, like Poppy, and his plate is more modest.

"I've not overfaced you, Ben, but there's plenty more if you wants seconds."

"Thank you, Linda. It looks and smells delicious."

To my delight, Ben tucks into his food and manages to clear his plate. We're all wearing our Christmas hats. Poppy traded her blue one for her dad's pink one, and was very happy with this.

"What do you call a boomerang that doesn't come

back?" They all stare at me in anticipation. "A stick." I give a shrug of my left shoulder and flatten my lips into a smile.

"That's terrible," Ben says, his tone more energised. "What's yours say, Pops?"

"What do Santa's little helpers learn at school?" she reads, before pausing.

"I don't know," says my mum.

"The elf-abet!"

Laughter drifts around the table and Poppy looks chuffed that she made us laugh, though she could have said any number of terrible jokes and still made us smile. The perks of being little and oh so terribly cute.

"Read yours, Daddy!" She places her hands on the table, leaning in.

"Okay." He turns over the small strip of white paper. "Why are pirates great?"

There's one or two furrowed brows, and I have to admit I can't see where this is going, for once. He scans our bemused faces.

"They just aaaaaarrr!" he says in the best pirate tone I've ever heard and the table erupts with laughter. The smile on his and Poppy's faces are my favourite moment of Christmas, because it's normal; how I'd expect them both to sound and look and I hold on to that normality for the remainder of the day.

One week later, and we're getting dressed. Ben had his treatment yesterday, but aside from retching over his breakfast and sleeping in longer this morning, he seems okay. The meds seem to be taking the edge off things better than last time, he said. The plan for the evening had always been to go into the town for the fancy dress party. It's a big thing, the New-Years-Eve fancy dress fireworks display at the harbour. It's more or less a massive excuse for underage teenagers to get drunk in the street, spill beer and wine over one another, wearing stupid clothing. The atmosphere is great and it's relatively kid friendly, if you stay away from certain groups.

"Are you sure you're up for this?" I check with Ben for what feels like the gazillionth time.

"I don't want to disappoint Poppy, she loves New Year's Eve."

"I get that, but I don't want you back in hospital in a week like last time."

He rubs from the tops of my shoulders to my elbows, our eyes fixed on each other's.

"Last time I was stupid and ignored feeling ill. Plus, I hadn't told my super-hot nurse girlfriend, like some idiot." His eyes briefly flick up to the sky. "This time she knows and can look after me."

"Good use of flattery, but the slightest hint you're not well and we're leaving early, okay?"

"Deal." He kisses the end of my nose and pulls me into his arms, where I breathe in his aftershave. The single squirt he sprayed on his Adam's apple. It smells like energy, fun and happiness. It smells like Ben.

Poppy is dressed as a flamingo. White long-sleeved T-shirt and leggings, with a giant pink ride-on flamingo, which is attached to shoulder straps. It's soft and tutu like, with dangling legs and finger loops for the wings. Upon her head is a fluffy pink crown. I'm Little Red Riding Hood and Ben is Maverick from *Top Gun*, dog tags and all—he looks hot, despite his recent weight loss and the drawn look on his face. His aviators hide this well, as does his smile. His bald head makes him look even more military, but not at all like Tom Cruise. Outside, it's fairly mild and mostly dry, so we're in for a good evening. As we reach the centre of town, the crowd swells. I'm nervous because the specialist nurse had advised against crowded places, but I try and push that aside and focus on the costumes people are wearing. I love seeing how inventive some are. We have giant Minions, many Harry Potters, super-heroes, pirates, Pink Ladies and sea creatures—I particularly love the clear umbrellas that people have transformed into light-up jelly-fish. My favourite, however, and for good reason, are the bananas. The reason I love them so much is because there is a group of over-excited gorillas waiting to pounce on them. Every time we spot an unsuspecting banana, we wait with amusement for the panic as the gorillas start chanting 'Narna, narna, narna' and then bear hug the person wearing the costume. It's a poorly thought-out costume choice, if ever there was one, but I can't stop laughing and it feels good. Good to see Ben and Poppy laugh, too. She's been quiet since her dad was in the hospital and we explained about his cancer. Ben nudges me and I look up.

"Narna, narna, narna, narna!" the gorillas shout and the person in the banana skin makes a run for it as three hairy beasts set off on the chase.

"Poor thing!" I say to Ben, who's watching me intently and not the charade in front of us.

I look into his eyes and he draws me in, just like the very first time, all those months ago on his sofa.

"I'm sorry for this. It isn't what you signed up for."

"It's not what either of us *signed up for*, but then we fell in love and that's what I'm going to do. Love you, no matter what." I shake my head, my eyes rolling upwards. "I love you, Ben Campbell, and I love that little girl over there …" Poppy is playing on the sand, in her pink, sparkly wellies, drawing lines and love hearts with a stick.

"Will you do something for me?" There's a shaky, uncertain look on his face and his voice wobbles. "It's important."

"Anything," I say.

"Will you adopt her for me?"

"What?" I say too loudly, because Poppy looks up, so I wave at her and smile. The sounds around me seem muffled all of a sudden, as though I've been standing too close to a bomb blast, which has thrown me backwards and left me with some hearing loss.

"I know this probably isn't the time to ask such a

thing, but I don't feel as though I can leave important conversations anymore." His words are clearer again as I focus on what he's asking of me.

"Ben!" I inhale.

"No, wait! Let me get this out … if anything happens to me." He's staring at me, his neck muscles contracting. I lift my hands to the sides of my face. "If anything happens to me." He takes my hands in his. "I don't want her to be alone. There's no one else. My parents will try and take her—send her to boarding school and I don't want that childhood for her. She'll be swallowed up and the spirit sucked out of her."

"What about Ronnie? He's her godfather."

"She needs a mum, Jo. She needs you."

"She needs her dad!" I shout, but there's so much commotion, no one notices us. No one notices the man I love making plans for the worst-case scenario.

He nods, his nostrils flaring and he swallows. "Please, I need to know she's gonna be okay, with, or without me."

My gaze drifts to Poppy, who's saying hi to a puppy who's rolled over to have his belly tickled. I think how much I love her and how close we are. For years, I've wanted to be someone's mum—I would have given anything to be, just not this.

Chapter Twenty

Since Ben asked me to adopt Poppy at New Years, it's been intense. As was the phone call to the duty officer at the local authority, but she was very helpful and shed some light on the process. My brain is awash with information, alongside all of my concerns for Ben and keeping up with Poppy's schedule. Right now, I'm struggling to concentrate on April's voice, asking me questions I'm not entirely sure I know the answers to.

"So it's a possibility?"

"Sorry, what?" I ask.

"Adopting her?"

"We have to pay a fee, they allocate a member of the team to assess me, and they provide a report to the court."

"And how long will that take?"

"Anything up to two years, she said on the phone, but it depends on how busy the courts are."

"I'm sure it will be quicker," she says. "What does Ben think?"

"We haven't talked it through fully yet, he's still sleeping off the chemo he had a few days ago. It's usually now it hits him. Honestly, April, it didn't sound as though we've been together long enough. She talked about stability and cohabiting for a year or two at least before applying." As we talk, I'm busy googling step-parent adoption, trying to see if there's any more information to make me feel as though we're not wasting our time, or our emotions.

"Don't they assess each case individually? Surely his diagnosis plays a part in them understanding why he wants this to happen, now?"

"I don't know. Even though we technically tick the 'living together as a family for six months' box, I'm not sure it's enough to have the application approved. She talked about it being simpler because there isn't another living parent to contest things."

"What normally happens if there is another living parent?"

"They have to give up their rights to the child."

"Wow! Okay. I can see why it's simpler." She's probably pulling and twisting her hair as she takes in everything I'm saying.

"Yeah. She also spoke about alternatives to adoption, such as a parental responsibility order, which would give me the same rights as a parent, but it wouldn't make me her mum." I stroke my left eyebrow, then rest my head on my hand. My skin is pinched beneath my fingertips.

"But … I know there is one," she says.

"… I don't know if I can do this right now. It's so important to Ben, and I don't want him to have to worry about this on top of everything else." I stare at the muted telly, some property programme I wasn't really watching.

"How do you really feel about it? Not the supportive girlfriend answer. The answer you'd give me if we were drinking gin in my apartment, eating olives and chips?"

My eyes search the black keys of the laptop open in front of me. "I can't think about it. Thinking about the implication of what I'm doing means I have to consider a possibility of him dying. I know his cancer is curable. I know that." I'm breathing quickly, my words tumbling from my lips in haste. "There's a part of him that's scared enough to plan for the future, a future that doesn't involve him … I can be her mum, April, with him by my side, but how would I even know where to begin doing that by myself? I've been in her life all of five minutes and I'm pretty sure that's what the social worker person thought on the phone."

"Anyone would see you as a stable, reliable person who has so much love to give a child." Her words rush out all at once. "And as for where Ben's at," she slows now, her tone more measured, "he lost his wife when he wasn't expecting it. She wasn't supposed to die and she did, suddenly. He's preparing for the worst because the worst happened to him once. I get it."

"I get it, too, but he's leaving me his daughter. By asking me to do this, he's trusting me to be her mum and potentially her sole parent without him. He's arranging to have the house put in joint names, and he's told me all about the trust fund he set up for

Poppy after Jen died. We've talked about life insurance policies and stuff I don't want to think about." I tilt my head back and take a breath. "I guess I imagined one day we'd get married, and I'd be her step-parent. Trust funds, Wills, and adoption on the other hand …" I massage the bridge of my nose.

"Adoption was always a possibility when you found out you couldn't have kids."

"I'd talked myself out of adoption because I thought it would be too complicated and more painful if it didn't work out."

"Will Ben consider that parental responsibility thing instead? If it's simpler and gives you the same rights as a parent?"

"When I mentioned it to him, he disregarded it. He wants her to have a mum. I don't know where his head's at. It's all over the place." I rub my index finger along my jagged, bitten-down thumbnail.

"Marrying you will make you her mum."

"April!" I close the laptop and it snaps shut. "I'm not suggesting that."

"Has he not considered it?"

"It hasn't come up." My tone is curt. "Sorry," I say. "Marriage, adoption, cancer … it's just not the stuff I thought we'd be facing so soon."

"Would you say yes if he asked?"

A beat. "Not if he asked me right now, no." I hear a knock. "April, I'm sorry. There's someone at the door. Can I call you in a few days?"

"Of course. Hey, Cuz, it'll all work out. I promise. Love you."

"Love you, too," I say, but this is the first time in our entire relationship her words don't reassure me.

"Just a second," I call out, trying to be heard, hoping Ben sleeps through the disturbance. I check the clock, as though it will magically tell me who's at the door.

"Can I help you?" I ask the couple standing in front of me.

"We should probably ask you the same question, young lady." The sternness in her tone surprises me and I don't respond. "Where's Benjamin?"

With that, the penny drops and I'm suddenly aware these are his parents. "You must be Mr and Mrs Campbell?" I smile.

"Yes, and you are?"

"Jo, Ben's girlfriend."

"The nurse who didn't notice my son had cancer!" It was the harshest statement I'd ever heard from a complete stranger. I draw back my head and swallow.

"I'm sorry, is Ben expecting you?" I ask, trying to regain some composure.

"I imagine not, and if he did, he would most likely ignore us, as he has done for the past decade."

"Well, he's sleeping at the moment, so you might want to come back another time. I'll let him know you popped by." With that, I close the door in their faces and can't help but feel even ruder than they were, if not a little bit satisfied.

I hear the sound of clapping behind me and I turn, seeing Ben emerge from the staircase. "I'm impressed.

There are few people equipped to handle my mother the way you just did. I'm deputising you from now on."

"I feel awful, but seriously, what *was* that?" I lift my hand.

"That was Margaret Campbell at her finest."

"She blames me for not noticing you have cancer! I didn't even know she knew about it, or me?"

"I called her a couple of days ago. I wanted them to hear I'm sick from me and to ask them not to try and get involved, because I'm getting the best treatment. Seems they listened, as always." He rolls his eyes, which have dark circles beneath them. "I mentioned I was in a relationship, that you're a nurse, and …" He shakes his head. "If there's one thing my mother does well, it's blaming everybody else."

"Maybe she's right. I was so focused on Australia, I didn't notice the lump, or your tiredness. I remember you saying you had an ache in your neck when we shared that bottle of wine, but I just didn't—"

"Jo, you couldn't have foreseen this, or changed anything. We caught it early and I'm getting treatment to deal with it. Please don't let my mother get inside your head like she does everyone else. I told her because it was the right thing to do. I don't need their help because I have *the* best nurse looking after me." He pulls me into his warm body and my shoulders slump. Everything feels cosmic levels of big and scary, though when he holds me, it melts away and I feel invincible. Here in his arms, I feel as though I could do anything.

We sit at the kitchen table, where I fold my right leg under me. "Do they know about the adoption?" I take a long breath in.

He shakes his head, firmly. "No!"

"Because they wouldn't approve?" My eyes narrow and there's this constant dull ache in my temple.

"They would say the only place Poppy belongs if anything happens to me is with them."

I stand and make my way to the sink, where I lean against it, staring out into the garden. It's a bleak day. Grey skies, with droplets of rain running down the window in the interval between downpours. The vibrant flower beds we planted in the summer have lost their life, at least until spring, which feels an eternity away right now. His arms slide around my waist, as he always does, and he kisses the nape of my neck, making my skin tingle slowly down my spine.

"The social worker might ask them what they think about me becoming Poppy's mum. They interview people. They'll interview me, you, Poppy." I puff out a breath, just as the wind howls and the rain beats down on the glass once more.

"So we tell them we don't have contact with them. We explain what they're like and why it's nothing to do with my parents. We won't be the first to have estranged family members." His tone is light, trying to inspire me to be the same, but I can't.

"What if it's not enough?" I pause, listening to the kitchen clock ticking in the silence. "What if *I'm* not enough?" I spin to face him, my heart pounding in my chest.

He slides his hand gently down my face, lifting my chin. "You are more than enough, oh-um-Jo. You're everything." I look away, so he dips his head until our eyes meet. "And I'll keep telling you how enough you are, for the rest of my life."

With that, sobs rage from me, as though the barricade holding them back had been blown to pieces, the debris now flying everywhere, uninhibited. "I'm sorry," I say. "I'm supposed to be strong for you. You're sick and I'm the one falling to pieces."

"Please don't apologise. You've been strong for me since you found out. You're only human, Jo, and I know I've put too much pressure on you, asking you to consider adopting Poppy."

"No, no!" I grip his arms. "I want to… I'm… I'm just so scared of losing you. Of making a mess of being her parent. I feel like you're planning to die and, it's not like you're leaving me your cat, or car. You're leaving me your daughter!"

Ben takes both my hands in his, pausing. "I'm not planning on dying. Jen died after giving birth. She was young, fit and healthy—she didn't have cancer." His eyes are dull, just like the weather. Cancer has robbed him of his sparkle.

I close my eyes.

"So I prepare for the worst now. I'm a glass-half-full kinda guy, but what happened to her made me prepare for the worst. I need to know what sort of life Poppy would have if another one of her parents were taken from her. *You*," his posture straightens, his chest pushing out. "*You*, will give her the life I want for her. I can't control what happens to me, but I can make sure my daughter has the best mum and the best life." There's a flicker then of light in his eyes. Subtle, but there.

Unremitting tears wash my cheeks. "I will love her as if she were mine, Ben … I already do!" I swallow, feeling as though my throat is closing in. Bile burns my insides as I gulp it down.

"I know. I know," he says and I fall into his arms.

Every inch of the house has been dusted, including all the skirting boards, coving, lampshades and door-frames. I've used three bottles of bleach, two packs of antibacterial wipes, and hoovered the carpet until it's almost threadbare. The kitchen smells of homemade bread and chocolate brownies—possible overkill—but I haven't been able to sit still all day. It's just after one p.m., and any minute a lady called Paula will knock on the door and want to ask me questions about my intentions to adopt Poppy. Ben is upstairs resting; he had chemo yesterday and was up in the night feeling sick, but it's settled now. I don't want to wake him, but she'll want to speak to us both. Poppy is at school and my parents have offered to collect her if the meeting runs long.

I perch on the edge of the sofa, drumming my fingers on the arm rest, pressing the home button on my phone to illuminate it and check the time. It beeps and I look again, noticing Emma's name on the notification: *Good luck. I'll be thinking of you. Let me know how it goes. E x*

I don't reply. She'll expect the meeting has started and it should have, though I imagine the social worker is very busy, and my wanting to adopt Poppy is the least of their worries. My fingers go back to creating an erratic beat when I hear a car pull up and the engine stop. I stand, drawing in a lungful of air, and check my appearance in the mirror above the mantel. My knee-length dress is respectful, patterned with cinnamon florals, featuring long sleeves edged with lace cuffs and an embroidered neckline. It doesn't require any jewellery and I thought it gave me an elegant, mother-like look. Motherlike as in off a very 'this is not real life' TV show or movie, but I wanted to make an effort. I'd spent so long on the phone trying to get this meeting, being rejected numerous times before speaking to, Paula, the team leader. The policy is clear that the couple has to be in a relationship for a couple of years, but when I explained some of our situation, she agreed to meet.

Finally, the doorbell chimes and I move towards it, trying to steel myself.

"Hello, I'm Paula. We spoke on the phone." A lady with half up, half down dreadlock hair stands before me, carrying a file in her arms and with a pleasant smile on her face.

"Hi, I'm Jo." I reach out to shake her hand, which she accepts before I gesture past me into the house. She follows and I lead her into the lounge. "Please, take a seat." I pause, watching her ease down into the sofa. She's wearing a grey skirt and blouse, with a cardigan over the top, and she smells like my mum's favourite perfume, Angel by Thierry Mugler. I joke with Mum that she wears Angel perfume because she is one. Now I'm praying Paula is one, too. She's older, mid-fifties I'd say. Possibly with a bad back, given how she sat so carefully, and some other underlying health issues, given her legs are slightly swollen. I don't try to assess people, it just sort of happens, involuntarily. "Can I offer you a drink? Some brownie?"

"No brownie for me, thank you, but I'd appreciate a glass of water." Her voice carries a subtle Jamaican accent.

"They're homemade, and delicious, according to Poppy." The words are out before I can claw them back.

"I'm diabetic, but thank you. I'm sure they're love-ly and certainly smell good," she says good-naturedly, but I slink off to the kitchen feeling as though I've just been caught sucking up to the teacher, making my insides jeer. Filling a half-pint glass, I step back into the lounge, placing it on the coffee table beside her. Claiming a seat on the chair, I put both hands in my lap and wait, as though it were an exam.

"So, Jo. We're meeting today to discuss the step-parent adoption order you and your partner," she looks at her notepad, "Ben, wish to make in relation to his daughter, Poppy?"

"That's correct."

"Is Ben here?"

"He's upstairs resting. He had chemotherapy yesterday and spent a good part of the night feeling unwell, but I can get him. He told me to wake him when you arrived."

"I'm sorry he's not well. Why don't we have a chat first and then we'll go from there?"

I nod and force a smile.

"Ben has stage 2A Hodgkin's lymphoma, is that correct?"

"Yes."

"I'm just making notes as we go along, okay?"

I nod again.

"He's receiving chemotherapy, followed by radiotherapy and his treatment is to cure his cancer?"

"Yes." My voice sounds shaky. I lean back into the chair as she scribbles, but immediately sit forward.

"You spoke on the phone about meeting Ben during a surf lesson and you grew close quickly, meeting Poppy after a few weeks."

"Ben and I had an instant connection, but we were cautious in the beginning. I knew how I felt for him early on. I also knew I wanted to meet his daughter and get to know her."

"And how did that go?"

"We met at the beach and walked along collecting shells. Poppy is so bright and easy-going." I smile. "We got along straight away, which was a relief. I wouldn't have rushed it, though. I was prepared for it to take however long she needed to build a relationship."

Paula looks at me, placing both palms on her notebook. "Jo, just breathe, okay?"

"Okay. Sorry." I puff out a long breath and there's barely a moment before she resumes her questions.

"You can't have your own children, can you?"

"No, no, I can't," I answer, but telling me to breathe and then jumping in with that question was a little poorly thought-out.

"Did you ever consider adoption before now?"

"I did. With my ex-partner, after finding out I wouldn't be able to have any of my own."

"Can you share with me what happened there?" Her tone is level.

"Our relationship ended because he wanted his own children and didn't want to look at other options to have a family."

"I'm sorry. These interviews delve into your personal life and can be quite obtrusive." She holds the notepad to her chest, her big chocolate-brown eyes meeting mine. There's compassion in them at least, alongside the business-like edge.

"It's fine, I was expecting as much. I'll answer anything you need me to."

"Do you want to adopt Poppy, Jo?" Paula pauses, examining me. I feel heat rising up my neckline.

"Yes, I do. Very much."

"You're not feeling obligated because your partner has cancer and are trying to respect his wishes?" Her head is cocked to one side.

"You're asking if I feel a sense of duty to do this?" The heat and colour have now reached my cheeks. I want to touch my face, but fear it will say something negative about me or the situation.

She nods.

"Don't get me wrong, my initial reaction, when he suggested it was shock. Mostly because I didn't like the idea he was planning for the worst-case scenario."

"His death?" she asks.

"Yes." I swallow. Her words are so blunt, I try not to let the emotions stirring inside me take hold. It's like I'm in some sort of soldier boot camp interrogation and the aim is to break me. "No one wants to think about the worst-case scenario, do they? Ben lost his wife and so he feels as though he needs to make plans for Poppy."

"His late wife." She looks again at her lap and the paper notes.

"Jen," I say.

"Jen." Paula's eyes meet mine. "She died after childbirth?"

"She did."

"Does Poppy talk about her mum?"

"All the time. Ben's always made sure Poppy knows about her. We made a bee sanctuary in the garden last summer as a place to remember her. Apparently, Jen was a big coffee drinker and when we went on a family day out to the Eden Project, we learnt about how bees are essential in making sure some of our foods don't run out. Such as coffee. Her mum used to keep a pretty garden, but Ben hadn't been able to keep it up for the past few years. With the help of some friends and my parents, we restored it."

There's a curve to her previously straight lips now as she observes me. "How lovely." Her eyes narrow. "So, your parents have a relationship with her?"

"They've been helping out with Ben being ill. Poppy loves it when they collect her from school, if I have a shift, or she takes their dog, Cassie, on walks when we visit their guest house."

"What sort of dog is she?"

"A Lassie dog." I smile and the curve of her lips widens too.

"You say about having shifts. Are you back to work after your sabbatical now?"

"I've been taking casual shifts around what Ben and Poppy need. My old job has been seconded while I've been away."

"Are you planning on going back to Australia to finish your sabbatical?"

"No, I'm home for good now."

"It's a bit of a change, though. Travelling around to settling for family life." She scribbles.

"I was homesick after only a few weeks away from them both, so it was unlikely I'd have gone back after Christmas anyway, regardless of Ben's illness. My time away showed me what was important. Where I want to be." My breathing quickens, but I notice her give me an approving nod and hope my answer was enough.

"What do your parents think of the adoption?"

"They're in complete support and have grown fond of Poppy themselves, treating her as if she were their own grandchild." My mind replays the first time, in the guest house when I slipped up and called my mum Grandma to Cassie.

"I'll ask Ben more fully about this, but his own parents are not in her life?" She flicks over another sheet of A4 paper in her notebook.

"They have been on and off, but I've only met them once and Ben doesn't have anything to do with them. I believe he used to allow them to see Poppy when she was younger, but when she started to complain, he didn't make her."

"Poppy herself has objected to spending time with them?"

"Yes. She chooses not to. Ben said they looked after her for the day in one of the school holidays before he met me, but Poppy cried when she got home, saying she didn't enjoy spending time with them."

"Did he say why?"

"I think they're very well off, but he always says his childhood was stifling and that he doesn't want her sprit sucked out of her by them."

Paula doesn't say anything to this as she writes more down.

My armpits are wet and I'm pleased the patch of sweat is hidden in the floral pattern, as Paula's line of questioning feels as though it's drawing to a close. I can't count the times she's flipped the page in her notepad and I'm hoping it's not a bad sign. The round of questioning about our sex life was not something I'd expected, nor was me telling her about the shower sex we'd had in Australia. I shake my head replaying the conversation.

"Jo, I'll be frank," she says, as though this is new and not the entire approach so far. "We spoke on the phone about expecting a couple to be together two years before the adoption process. This is to ensure the relationship itself has been tested and proven to be enduring. However, I appreciate the circumstance you're in with Ben's ill health, and the fact that Poppy has no close family relationships, and no mother to relinquish her rights as a parent. It also sounds as though you have a good bond with her already. All of these things are favourable to your application. There'll be extensive background checks, police checks, a medical and we'll need references, but I'll write a report for the court."

My chest caves in and I breathe out far louder than intended. My legs are shaking and I think my blood sugar just decided to plummet.

"Now, let's meet Ben, if I may? And I think I might try one of those brownies," she adds and I could cry.

I'm in bed, staring at the shadows resting on the ceiling above me from the moon seeping through the curtains. Ben's asleep, as is Poppy. He managed to speak with Paula, then climbed straight back in bed. From what he told me there was solidarity in our replies at least. I hear a subtle vibration on my bedside table and retrieve my phone.

I have two notifications. One from April. The other Emma.

I scroll to April's first, who wants an update about the meeting. I reply with a short 'I'll call you tomorrow, too tired tonight' message, and sign off with a kiss. For whatever reason, it's Emma I want to debrief with. I carefully climb out of bed, sliding on my dressing gown, and head downstairs into the kitchen.

"Hey," she answers on the first ring. "Sorry, I should have messaged you earlier. Long day!"

"Don't apologise. How did it go?"

"Honestly, I'm not sure." I let out an elongated sigh. "It was like taking your driving test, where the instructor gives nothing away, but I didn't get to know if I'd passed or failed at the end." I push my hand through my hair.

"Harsh."

"It was brutal!" I rest the phone between my ear and shoulder as I open the fridge, retrieving some milk.

"What happens next?"

"Police checks, a medical—which takes an age to get the report from the GP apparently—and references," I say, pouring myself a tall glass of milk.

"I'll happily be a reference. Chris, too."

"Thank you … Also, they want to speak to Tom!" I move to the table and sit. This was another reason I wanted to chat to Emma. April seethes whenever I say Tom's name and I needed a more grounded response to this.

"Really? Why? How do you feel about that?"

I smile a little that Emma never manages to ask just one question. "It's part of background checks. It's like being recruited for the secret service. School history, job history, previous relationships, how I spent Christmas and Easter as a child."

"Does it help if you believed in the Easter Bunny, or not?"

I laugh, knowing it's her way of lightening this for me. "Ha-ha, no idea. I guess they're trying to uncover anything in your past that triggers you to open up about important things. Maybe it tells them if I had a safe, happy childhood and I'm capable of providing Poppy with the same. I dunno." I shake my head.

"Well, that box is well and truly ticked."

"Yeah. At least that's one interview I don't have to worry about. My parents are definitely a bonus." My heart warms then, as though a patch of sun has found its way through the gloominess. The sort of moment where you turn your face up to meet it.

"Will you call him?" She pauses. "Tom, I mean, warn him about the interview?"

"I think I should give him the heads-up. What do I say, though, Em? Hey, Tom, a social worker's going to call you, to see if you have any dirt on me that might make me unsuitable to adopt the daughter of my boyfriend, who, by the way, has cancer and doesn't want his daughter left an orphan if he dies, like her birth mum did."

"I mean, when you put it like that … I just want to hug you right now!"

"Thank you. I would love that so much … I didn't tell Ben about needing to speak to Tom. I think he'd worry too much about putting me through it."

"I get that. What did April say?"

"Haven't told her either. You know how much she hates Tom."

"Something about fire and suns, if I remember correctly?"

"Yep. A line from one of her favourite movies, *10 Things I Hate About You.*"

"I loved Heath Ledger in that film," Emma says. "In general really."

"April was a huge fan … There was that video," I say.

"I know the one."

"Heath Ledger was at some awards or something and a fan screamed when she saw him, so he planted a kiss on her lips and she fell to the floor in a fake faint."

"I love that video. It makes me so happy and sad.

The loss of him … tragic."

I pause. A chill goes through me as though ice water is running through my veins.

"I'm here for you, Jo. In any way I can be."

"I know."

I feel better for our chat, and although I'm completely drained, it's been nice to share things with her. To laugh, even in spite of all the heaviness. I don't want to end it, despite the weight of my eyelids threatening me, because I know as soon as we hang up, my mind's going to focus on Tom, and how I might feel speaking to him. What I'm going to say, and if what we had, once upon a time, is enough for him to help me?

Chapter Twenty-One

The forecast for the end of January was supposed to be cold, with a chance of snow, but today it's bitter—like Arctic Circle cold, or so it feels to me. I'm wearing bootcut jeans, a brown long-sleeve top, with leather boots and a cosy cream poncho, which is keeping me snug. Ben's in the passenger seat beside me, wrapped up in a hat, gloves, scarf, jeans and a thick winter coat. I've not known him feel the cold this much. Normally, he wears shorts all year round, but lately he's freezing all of the time.

"You're quiet?" he says as I indicate, turning into the hospital grounds.

"Am I?" I reply, but know he's right. After I drop him to his chemo appointment, I've arranged to meet with Tom for coffee, to explain the situation.

"Are you okay?" I can feel him staring at me from his side of the car. Luckily, I'm driving and can't meet his eyes. My face would give me away for sure.

"Yeah, just thinking about what I need from town. Poppy needs new polo shirts for school, and I said I'd make pizzas with her for tea." I notice his shoulders roll forward and he swallows. "Sorry, I know food makes you feel sick at the minute."

"It's okay. I'll probably have soup again, if that's all right?"

"Sure. I'll make you some, and buy that soft bread you like from the bakery." I knock him a sideways smile.

"Could you get some more Bonjela, please, ready for more mouth ulcers?"

"Of course." I touch his knee as we pull up in the drop-off space outside the chemotherapy unit.

"Well, here goes number four." He doesn't make any attempt to get out of the car, other than release his belt.

"You're doing great." I lean over to kiss him on the cheek. He doesn't offer me his lips. It's nothing personal. He has a metallic taste in his mouth and it's been sore a lot lately. Ulcers. Thrush. More side effects of the chemo. "Later on, I'll look after you and do whatever you need me to."

"There was a time I'd have the rudest thing to say to that, but honestly, I'd settle for a cuddle in front of the TV."

"Done. We can save the rude stuff for another time." I wink at him, though it only raises a half-smile and his eyes remain expressionless.

"I better get inside."

"I love you," I say.

"Love you, too." I watch him walk in the direction of the building and I sigh. Wishing he was through this already. Wishing I could do something, anything, to make him better.

Both April and Emma messaged me early this morning, wishing me luck. April said a few more choice things, but I shrugged those off. Today is about Poppy and the adoption. My relationship with Tom is ancient history. Ben and Poppy are my future; this is just a small hurdle to get over on the way. The drive back from the hospital gave me too much time to go over and over what I'll say. So much so, my stomach is a knotted mess and I wish gin were on the menu and not coffee as I walk the five-minute walk from the car park to the coffee shop.

I'm instantly relieved when I push open the door to the mostly empty café and feel the warmth of their heating, alongside no sign of him. Tom was never on time, so it's no surprise. I wanted to arrive first, to give myself time to order and settle myself. What I don't want is an awkward ordering for each other, offering to pay for drinks and over-complicating this whole thing. I feel uncomfortable enough, even before his presence. It's like waiting to be reunited with an old friend, one that knows the in-depth intimacies of you, but who no longer should—no longer deserves to. Nothing can erase who and what you were, once upon a time. Only time itself can help you feel removed from the person, as things fade into a hazy background. It's like watching your favourite childhood Christmas film— mine was *Santa Claus: The Movie*, the one with Dudley Moore. We would watch it every Christmas Eve, without fail, though when I watched it as an adult it didn't arouse the same emotions. I remembered them, vividly, but it lacked impact. The result of which is a strange mix of both nostalgia and unavoidable disappointment.

I find a seat towards the back where there's two comfy high-backed floral chairs either side of a low mahogany coffee table. Ironically, where I last saw Tom sitting with Sarah all those months ago. It's a bit like returning to a crime scene, but without Frank today—I didn't want to explain this to him. The space feels secure, or rather, it makes me feel more secure. It's also away from earshot of the staff. This conversation was going to sound odd enough for just two pairs of ears, let alone more. Each time the door dings open, I look up, but it's another person popping in for takeaway hot drinks. There are a few more seated customers, but it's still sparse. The next time my eyes lift from the table in front of me, I see him. He looks shorter than I remember, still taller than me, but would pale beneath Ben's stature. His hair is cropped shorter than usual, but is wispy around the ears, as though he'd rushed to be here. His style hasn't changed, still wearing grey chinos, with a black parka coat zipped up. At first, he doesn't see me, and I take a deep, savouring breath.

"Sorry I'm late," he says, resting his coat over the back of his chair as though it were yesterday we were last in each other's company.

"No worries," I say, hearing April in my head with

her Aussie accent and wish I were on the beach with her right now.

"Can I get you another?" He points to my cup, which is still brimming full of hot liquid and I think the question is as redundant as we are.

"I'm good. Thank you," I say. The pleasantries making my insides squirm uncomfortably. As he excuses himself to grab a drink, I'm pleased for the moment to gather myself. I didn't know how seeing him properly again would feel. There was so much emotion in our parting and the year prior to our split. When somethings been so highly charged, you wonder how you'll ever act normal, or at least that's what I feared coming here today.

It's not long until he's sliding into the seat opposite, taking a tentative sip of his hot chocolate, which gives him a moustache that he wipes away with the back of his hand. This sends a reflex through me, from when he'd first wiped whipped cream from my top lip on our first date. It wasn't here, but it was at another coffee shop in town. We'd both had a deluxe hot chocolate and I should have been mortified I'd made such a mess, but his simple movement back then made me realise how much I'd liked him. I remember the spark and the way it had felt, but the same way Christmas movies no longer excite me, neither does Tom.

"Thanks for agreeing to meet with me." I place both hands on the table, which is clean, but has a tackiness to it.

"Sure," he say, with a 'deer trapped in the headlights' look, like when we get student nurses in ED and they don't quite know where to stand and what to do. I haven't gone into details about why I wanted to meet, only to say it was important and he'd agreed.

"It's hard to find the words, really." I stare up at the clock above the door and think of Ben, in the hospital.

"Are you all right?" he asks, leaning forward. "You're not sick are you?"

"I'm not sick." I shake my head.

"Phew!" I notice his shoulders relax as he eases back into his chair. "I thought you were going to tell me you'd got cancer or something," he says, lifting his drink.

"I don't, but my partner does."

"Crap!" He returns his cup to the table, without taking a sip. "… Is he gonna be okay?"

"It's curable, but he has a daughter, Poppy. She's almost eight."

"Wow! Okay." His gaze flits from table to window and back again. I've seen this look before. It's his completely floored look. One he had at our final hospital appointment.

"I'm trying to adopt her as her step-parent and the social worker needs to speak to people. Family, friends … exes." I talk quickly, so I don't have to think, or remember.

"Ah, so me?" He grazes his fingers over his stubbly cheek and top lip.

I nod. "I'm sorry, I wish they didn't have to, but

they do significant background checks."

"You sure it's not because you're being recruited to the secret service?"

The very joke I'd made with Emma a couple of weeks ago, which speaks of how in sync we once were, and my heart lifts, but a tear catches in my eye. "I think that'd be easier." I huff out a laugh.

"I don't mind talking to them. Doesn't the kid's mum want her?" His gaze is focused on me now.

"Her mum died when she was a baby," I say softly, the words never failing to make my insides quiver.

"Crap!" he says again, his eyes bulging, and I watch him trying to come up with something to say. Ben would know how to deal with this situation. He wouldn't have to think about what to say next. It's then that I miss him. Wishing he were here, sitting beside me. I don't know this man before me anymore. Tom is nothing more to me now than a time in my life. A series of lessons and opportunities to grow as a person. How I feel now, for Ben and Poppy, is far greater than anything I shared with him.

"I'm sorry if I'm not quite with it. The twins were up most of the night and …" He shrinks back, his crumpled brow tells me he regrets mentioning his children.

"It's okay," I tell him and smile.

He nods, his eyes flickering with a lost sense of emotion as they meet mine. "It wasn't about you," he says quietly.

"We don't have to do this." I run my hand through

my hair, resting it behind my neck.

"I want to." His eyes look watery as they meet mine. "My decision to leave … It wasn't about you," he repeats.

I concentrate on taking slow, steady breaths. "I know." My voice isn't as level as I'd like.

"It was a hard time for both of us. The trying. The tests." He shakes his head.

"It was hard," I agree. The pain and disappointment we both felt back then floats in front of us, as though being played out on a negative photo reel.

"Are you enjoying being a dad?" I ask with a genuine smile.

"Yeah!" He nods, unable to hide the love and pride he feels from his face. "They're cute. Tiring, noisy, but very cute. Wanna see? I'll understand if you don't," he quickly adds.

"I'd love to," I say and I'm not trying to be polite. I do want to see how his kids look. What his life looks like now.

He scrolls to the camera roll and through several adorable pictures of a tiny boy and girl in various stages of undress, with a slight covering of a shade lighter hair than him. Some are of them sleeping. Some with their toes taking centre stage. All show them bibbed and happy.

"I'm pleased for you, Tom. I truly mean that." I place both hands on my chest.

"Thank you." His watery eyes have now been replaced by a warm glow.

"Do you have a picture of your step-daughter?"

Hearing him call her my step-daughter, although inaccurate, gives me a sort of fizzing sensation in my stomach. "I do," I say, taking out my own phone, mirroring the exchange we just had over pictures of his kids.

"Wow!" He tips his head to one side "She's beautiful."

"She really is." I keep scrolling, knowing the camera roll to be full of pictures of Poppy and none of Ben or me lately. Not since Australia.

"I reckon your fella's gonna have a job on his hands when she's older, keeping the boys away."

"Tell me about it." Hearing him refer to any kind of future with Ben still in it makes me feel as though he's just taken one of my cartoon sandbag weights from my shoulders. The load feels ever so slightly lighter.

"They say having children changes how you think and see things, but I never got it until the twins were born."

I nod. I may not have my own children, and Poppy might not be my biological daughter, but I know what he's talking about. How differently it makes you feel and how the world seems to shift on its axis.

I sip the rest of my coffee as the space around us fills with the smell of toasted cheese, salty bacon and deep, rich coffee. There's the sound of banging metal as the barista empties and fills the coffee machines. The loud hiss of steam from the milk frothing spout makes us raise our voices to engage in chitchat, as we catch up on the lost period of each other's lives.

"Anyway, thank you again for meeting me and for understanding. I appreciate it." I go to stand, bringing our time together to its end.

"Jo." His hand's on my wrist, his touch familiar and yet strange. "You'll be a great mum. I'll tell them that when they call me." He nods, pushing out his lips slightly as I see a tear again behind his cobalt blue eyes. "I hope Ben's okay," he adds. "Sounds like a great guy."

I close my eyes, fighting back pools of tears, and I feel his arms pull me towards him, holding me in silence. I'm not sure what I expected from our meeting, but kindness and compassion wasn't it. Not that that wasn't who he was, he was a good guy. We just weren't meant to be as a couple. I know if things had been different, if it were him sitting here with a sick partner, asking me for a favour and breaking down in front of me, I'd hug him, too. Whatever's passed between us, we were once great friends. As we part, I realise this meeting was long overdue for us both. Everything which once unified, then destroyed us, has slipped away and I know we've parted friends.

Chapter Twenty-Two

Poppy's upstairs getting dressed for school. I've finished a run of long day shifts at work, though I'm still not officially employed, as the person doing my job is on a year's secondment. I've had a few bank shifts in ED and my parents have been helping out when I've been at work, as Ben has his good and bad days, as to be expected. In many ways, we've got into a rhythm and routine with this altered way of living.

"What time's your scan?" I ask him, trying to hide the wobble in my voice. I'm not sure who's more worried about it, him or me.

"Nine-forty-five. Then I'm going to pop into work and see how Ron's getting on with some bits I emailed him."

"Are you feeling up to it? Chemo hit you pretty hard this time and it's not even been two weeks." It had been his worst session so far, since the hospitalisation after the first.

"I'm good, honestly," he says, scanning the kitchen worktops, and I slide his phone and keys towards him. "Thanks."

My hand rests on his phone as he goes to take it.

"Your immune system's at its lowest right now," he looks at me, "so please be careful and make sure Ron doesn't have anything wrong with him before you go see him." My words are pleading. A little nagging, like a parent to a child. I think somewhere along the way we've slipped into new roles.

"Sure."

I release my grip and clasp my hands together. "Ben, I'm serious!"

"I promise I'll behave." He gives me a two-finger salute and I puff out a long breath, saying nothing else. These days, he's either quiet and withdrawn, or joking around and making light of everything. I, on the other hand, see infections and danger everywhere. "Poppy, sweetie, we need to leave now or you'll be late." She appears, frowning on the bottom step. "What's wrong?" I ask.

"I want Daddy to drop me at school!" She sounds mulish and out of character, with one hand on the banister.

"Sweetheart, Daddy has to go to the hospital this morning."

"Humph." She crosses her arms in front of her chest, frowning at me. Borderline a scowl.

"Poppy, don't be like that with Jo." He pauses by the front door.

"I don't want to go to school." She races back upstairs, crying.

Ben goes to rush after her, but I place my hand on his chest. "You need to make your appointment. I've got her." He looks at me, his eyebrows almost touching. "Go." I give him a reassuring nod.

Ascending the staircase two steps at a time, I pause outside her room, hearing the rhythmic sobs filtering through the door. "Hey, it's just me," I say softly, my hand pushing open her door, which lets out a small squeak.

"I want Daddy!" she says, muffled by the pillow attached to her face.

Perching on the bed beside her, I rub her back, between the shoulder blades. "Poppy, do you want to tell me what's wrong? Why are you so upset?" I feel a burning in my chest.

"I miss Daddy," she wails.

"He misses you, too, sweetheart, but he's trying to get well, so he can go back to spending time with you. Poppy …" I ease her off the pillow and her face is splotchy and red. Her eyes even more green than usual behind a film of tears. "Talk to me."

"I heard him arguing with Grandma about who gets me if he dies. He's going to die, just like Mummy, and then I'll be alone, living with Grandma and Grandad." Her face hits the pillow once more and the sobbing intensifies. I bow my head, pulling her into my arms.

"The doctor said they're going to make your daddy better and …" I hesitate, unsure if I'm supposed to reveal this to her just yet. "I'm going to adopt you." She looks up at me, wiping her nose with the back of her hand. The silence is deafening. "I'm going to adopt you and be your mummy, just like Daddy's your daddy, and I'll always look after you, with him."

"Are you allowed to do that?" She almost pricks up her ears, as an animal would to focus their attention on a novel sound.

"Yes, but it might take a while. There's lots of rules." I inhale and release slowly. "Daddy was going to talk to you about it, plus there's a nice lady called Paula, who will want to ask you some questions."

"What kind of questions?" Her head tilts to one side.

"Nothing bad. She just wants to know how you feel about me being your mummy."

Poppy doesn't say anything, she just sits, staring at me, the rise and fall of her chest lessening with every passing second until she's composed.

"They'll let you be my mummy?"

"Yes, but only if you want me to be." My head lowers, our eyes meeting.

I see the corners of her eyes turn upwards first, followed by the curve of her lips, which grows. Her eyes glisten and she reaches her little hands behind my neck, pulling me into a hug. "I've been praying for you to be my mummy."

I laugh. It's a form of release.

"… So that means I can stay with you, if Daddy dies?"

"Yes, darling," I say, wanting to remove some of her fears and comfort myself at the same time. The fact this sweet little girl has to even think about a parent dying, let alone two, makes me feel as though I've been stabbed, deep, with something so blunt I feel it push through every layer of skin. How can I promise her he won't die, even if it's unlikely? Yet, I just promised her she could be with me if he does, and there are no certainties there either. Not yet at least.

It's one p.m. when I arrive at the beach. It's early February and cold, but not freezing today. I'm not being blasted by sand, as I have been on previous walks on the beach to find Ben. He hasn't been down here much lately, working from home on his good days. Ronnie's been holding the fort. The surf school isn't just busy during the summer months as you would likely think. They open seven days a week from March to November, and from May-September they run coasteering, sea kayaking and paddleboarding on a sister beach. The shop is also online, so there's always orders to fulfil. Ben's built up this business and it's thriving, but I know he's been worried and felt useless for weeks now.

"Hey, Ronnie, have you seen Ben? I haven't heard from him since his scan this morning." I lean on the desk.

"Hey, yeah, he was in here twenty minutes ago."

"Did he say where he was going?" Ronnie doesn't

meet my gaze, instead his fingertips stroke his eyebrow. "Where is he?" I ask, more sternly than intended.

"He's gone for a surf!" His shoulders droop.

"He's what!" I almost gasp. "And you let him?" I go outside, craning my neck to see him in the water, but I can't.

"I told him it wasn't the best idea. Said I'd go with him, but—"

"I need a wetsuit!" I practically shout.

"Jo, you know what he's like when he wants to do something." His words are rushed. "There was no way he was gonna listen—"

"I know. I'm sorry for snapping."

"I'll go and get him."

"No." I place my hand on his arm. "I need to."

The sand is cold and so, too, is the water settled on top of it. I can see Ben's form, sitting on his board, bobbing around on top of the water. Even though I can feel the cold on my feet and face, my body feels as though it's on fire as I march quicker towards the tide. I wade in without stopping, and as soon as I'm deep enough, I start to swim. The cold water catches my breath, but I don't stop. He's not that far out and I reach him with ease. The sea's calm, not a day you'd expect him to be trying to catch waves.

"What are you doing?" I'm panting, my lips tingling as my mouth puffs out cold air.

"What are *you* doing?" He reaches for me and I rest up on his board.

"I came out here to see why you think it's a good idea to be surfing, twelve days post chemo."

"I'm not surfing. You have to have waves to surf." His words are pointed. Like the 'I'll behave, promise' from this morning, and his two-finger salute, which I'd shrugged off.

"It's funny, is it? The concept that you might get seriously ill again!" I snap.

"No, it's not funny. None of this is funny. Being prodded, poked and sick. Losing weight and having no hair. None of it is funny." His jawline tightens.

"Ben!" I inhale, my lungs burning.

"I came out here to think, alone. I needed to breathe some damn air!" He lets out a forceful sigh.

"I'm sorry." I swallow, but instantly regret it, tasting the salt water leave a trail down my throat, adding to my queasiness.

"What if it's not gone? The cancer … what if the scan's bad news?" His quiet words drift away on the bobbing waves, as though it wasn't really a question, more a thought, spoken aloud.

I rest my hand on his, but it's numb. I feel nothing and, I imagine, neither does he. "You still have two more treatments and radiotherapy," I say, answering it all the same.

"I'm tired, Jo. I miss my life." His eyes close and my heart squeezes.

"I know you do. I know … come on, we need to go in. It's freezing out here! We can talk in the warm."

We're in his truck, dry, clothed and being warmed by hot coffee and the blowers on full speed. Neither of us speaks at first. Ronnie had asked me how he was when we reached the shop and changed. I'd shrugged and rubbed his arm, giving a half-smile. I know he's as worried as I am, and feels just as helpless at the moment. Ben hasn't opened up to him lately, which is unusual in their friendship.

"Is Poppy okay?" he asks, staring down at the coffee in his hands.

"She scared and misses you."

I see his head shake from side to side, his eyes fixed on the calmest ocean I've ever seen. It's as though it, too, has no fight left today.

"I'm afraid I did a terrible job parenting her this morning and might have told her too much."

He looks at me, his head cocked back.

"I told her about the adoption plans." My voice is low, monotone, as I cast him a sideways glance. "She heard you arguing with your mum on the phone and thinks you're going to die, and she'll have to go and live with them. I'm sorry. I shouldn't have, I know it was the wrong thing to tell her." I circle my finger around the top of the plastic cup in my hands.

"Don't apologise. I should have stayed to see if she was all right. I'm the one doing a terrible job as a parent right now. Poor kid." He huffs. "I had no idea she heard that conversation," he says, shaking his head slowly from side to side. "I've lived with them, and it's not an experience I'd wish on anyone, so I understand why she's upset."

"I know, but I basically promised her I'll be her mum."

"You will be." His half-thawed fingertips trace over my skin.

"We don't know if I'll pass the adoption assessment," I say through blurry eyes. "Paula was clear about proving it's in Poppy's best interests and that we're in an enduring relationship." I watch the bus climb the hill, the same way I've watched thousands of buses climb it and I know how much effort's involved. How easy it would be to take your foot of the pedal and roll backwards to the bottom.

"She needed to know, especially with her interview coming up. I should have talked to her myself about it before now, but I just haven't had the energy … I think you did the right thing. You did what any parent would do. You made her feel better and gave her hope."

I shake my head. "I feel like I lied to her." A sob leaves me then.

"Jo," he strokes my face, "I would have done the same. We lie to protect our kids sometimes. Until the worst happens and then we deal with it, hoping we won't ever have to. You shouldn't feel guilty about making a seven-year-old girl feel better today. You were being a mum."

There's more silence between us. Navigating all of this would be a challenge for any couple, but especially since our relationship hasn't yet seen the passing of each season. We're in the winter solstice of our relationship; the least daylight, and longest of nights. It's the harshest winter I've ever had to endure.

"It's Poppy's birthday next week and I want to do something nice for her, before I get my scan results," he says, cutting into the quiet and lifting the mood with his warm tone.

"She really wanted a teepee tent sleepover party with Jessica, or that's what she told me last week," I say. "I have a friend who runs a party business. They set it up in your house, in any number of themes. Balloons, sweets, bunting. The works. I've even seen pink teepees on her Facebook page."

"Would you help me organise it?"

"I'd love to." I smile, a small tingle of excitement flushing through my stomach.

"Okay. Least it's just one friend, right?"

It's the weekend and two days before Poppy's birthday. Ben was a soft touch and one friend turned into three: Jessica, Sophie and Flossy. My friend helped me pull it all together last minute, and the set-up looks amazing. So much so, I wish I could fit into the tiny pink teepee beds. Each one is covered with pink blankets, and round rose gold pillows, with a unicorn teddy. There's pale pink bunting across all four teepees, and hot pink, blush pink, white and gold balloons filling the space above. All four beds have tables, each with a pot of sweets and a LED candle inside a lantern. Poppy's has a light box with *Happy 8ᵗʰ Birthday, Poppy* on hers. In front of the TV, the lounge floor is covered with scatter cushions, ready for the girls' two chosen movies. First though, it's pizza time and afterwards I've promised to give them all pretty hairdos and painted nails. I think I've got my work cut out for me.

I've not long since finished the cupcakes, with Barbie pink frosting and decorated with either a party ring, Jammie Dodger or white chocolate disc covered in sprinkles and a variation of pink or white chocolate mice, flumps and mini marshmallows. Ben's got the fire pit ready in the garden, so the girls can make smores later. I apologise in my head, in advance, to their parents for the sugar intake, but then immediately think we're the ones who have to get them to go to sleep tonight. *Rookie mistake.*

"These look amazing." Ben kisses my cheek, his arms wrapped around my waist. He presses into me more than he has done in weeks and I feel flutters in the pit of my stomach.

"Hey, no funny business with four kids in the house," I joke.

"I know. I just haven't felt well enough lately for *all that*. I—"

"I miss it, too." I nod, slowly. Our eyes meet and I feel more intimacy in this moment than I have in a long time. "You'll be better soon and then we can make up for lost time."

"Is that a promise?" One of his eyebrows lifts.

I wipe some pink icing on his lips and use my tongue to lick it off. He gives a throaty cough before inhaling. "I'm gonna take that as a yes."

I bite my lip and he smooths his thumb over them in such a familiar gesture that the present fades away and I'm left with only memories of better times. The moment's short-lived, however, when four sassy girls waltz into the kitchen, spotting the cupcakes.

"Wow!" more than one of them says. "Can we eat them?" Flossy asks.

"Not just yet. It's pizzas first, which are ready in about five minutes. Why don't you all go and wash your hands and then come sit at the table, ready." My mind wanders back to my parents' kitchen, when Poppy had asked to eat some of Mum's baking, and I'd hesitated with my response. Now I'm fending off four children wanting to spoil their appetite with ease.

There's a table in the kitchen, decorated with a pink and white spotted table cloth, party hats, poppers and balloons. The plates, napkins and cups are all flamingo-themed. I couldn't leave Pinky out from the party, after all. When Poppy sees Pinky at the table with a hat on, she looks at me and smiles so brightly it makes my year. My mind captures the moment and her expression as though my eyes are the lens of a camera. Something for me to hold onto in the darker days. Not, I'm hoping, that there will be many more of those.

A couple of hours later, after a marathon nail-painting and hair-plaiting session, I left the girls all cuddled up on pillows and blankets in the centre of the room, watching movie number two. I breathe a sigh of relief when I slump next to him on the couch in the other room. He'd wanted to help more, but I didn't want him to be too close to the girls while his immune system is low. Though I'd practically interviewed all their mums, two of whom I know well. The third, Sophie's mum, looked at me like I was a little odd, before I explained about Ben's illness. Then her posture went from leaning back to leaning in, and I could feel her sympathy. I think I preferred the panic over the pity.

"I haven't seen her look that happy in weeks. Thank you. You made an almost eight-year-old girl's day … year even."

"I'm exhausted, but I've loved every second." I flip my legs over his and he starts rubbing the soles of my feet. "It's the sort of party I'd love now, as a grown up, let alone when I was a child."

"I'll remember that for your next birthday then." He winks at me. *I've missed this lightness.*

"I'll hold you to that."

"Oh, the works." He wafts his hand in the air.

I laugh. "Today's been a good day," I say.

"It has, hasn't it, and not just because of Barbie pink iced cakes—which were delicious by the way—but because it's the first time life felt as if it were about more than my stupid illness."

"Life will be more like this again really soon. You'll see." I take his hand in mine with a squeeze. We hear squeaks of laughter through the walls and I look at Ben and huff out a laugh. "Sounds as though they're enjoying the film."

"Yeah." He pauses. "Jo." I watch him, seeing the words forming behind his lips. "I hope I don't upset you by saying this, but if things were different, I'd want this."

"This?" I ask, but I know what he's about to say.

"Four giggling girls in the next room. Poppy and three 'mini yous'."

"A boy, perhaps, just so you have some solidarity," I add, my heart thumping in my chest.

"Okay, three girls and one boy then." The corners of his eyes crinkle with his wide smile.

I close my eyes, pushing down any sadness trying to surface in order for the joy of this moment to win for once, but to my surprise, there is none. This isn't something to be unhappy about. The man whom I love loves me enough to want more of me in his life, but he also loves me enough without it, too.

Chapter Twenty-Three

We're sitting side by side, next to a brown wooden desk with a single computer on standby and a faded royal blue swivel chair in front of it, which is pushed out. There's an examination couch on the back wall, covered in a roll of white paper. The sink sits to my left, beside the door, and there's a small rectangular mirror on the wall in front of me, in which I can see my reflection. My eyes have dark circles under them. My skin is a shade lighter than usual, tinged yellow in the harsh strip lights above us. It's a grey day outside. The sun hasn't graced us with even a hint of brightness, which matches the subdued mood between Ben and me. It's been a couple of days since Poppy's actual birthday—another great day—where we went to the cinema and out for a meal. What was even more special is that she wanted my parents to join us for dinner and they were delighted. Mum and Poppy have grown close since Ben's illness. My parents love their new grandparent role and I think Poppy enjoys it. She likes to go to the guest house and play with Cassie, even choosing to have a sleepover one night, where Cassie slept on the floor beside her bed all night. Ben joked that we'd be having to get a dog ourselves next, which I actually love the idea of. A family dog.

I'm sure we've only been sitting here for five minutes, but it feels as though time may be going backwards. We're at the top end of a long corridor, in the farthest away room, and there's no noise outside. A little hustle and bustle would be a welcome sound against the muteness in this tiny space. It's the kind of silence you seek out to prepare yourself for something, or to reflect in. A bit like an athlete before a huge race, gathering focus for what's expected of them. Ben's sitting with his elbows on his knees, his hands in a praying position in front of his face, rubbing his pressed-together index fingers over his bottom lip.

We were up most of the night, talking. Sometimes random nonsense, other times going over the things he needed me to know. He'd written a Will, a copy of which was placed in his bottom bedside drawer. I said it perhaps needed to be somewhere safer, but he kept talking, as though he needed to impart everything to me with urgency. He'd told me where all the paper-work was for Poppy's trust fund, and the mortgage documents, including the transfer into our joint names. I knew it was blind panic, almost irrational, because he knew he wasn't going anywhere the next day, even if the scan were bad news, but I'd let him speak. I'd let him say all he needed to, in order for him to feel as though everything were in order, just in case. The one thing we didn't talk about was the adoption, or the fact I still have no legal rights with Poppy. She'd had her chat with Paula and didn't say much about it, other than that the lady was nice. We didn't pump her for information either, wanting her not to worry, or sense we were. As far as Poppy's concerned, I'm going to be her mum, and she can't see why anyone would not agree to it. For Ben, however, I think he's filed the adoption away for now, alongside other things out of his control; his cancer, for instance. He's focused on the practicalities and I think this is because when Jen died, Poppy was just a newborn and there were so many things to sort out, while grieving and raising a baby. I have the feeling he's trying to protect Poppy and me from having to deal with these things. He's making it simple for us, just in case.

"Good morning, Ben," Dr Jai LaLa, pronounced Zi, his consultant haematologist, greets us with her usual warm, full smile and pleasant Indian accent. She's small, with short dark black hair and glasses, and normally wears a shirt with black formal trousers, today being no exception. I've liked her since our first meeting. There's something about the way in which she speaks; she connects with you straight away and makes you feel as though you have her full attention, and there's genuine care behind her eyes.

"Morning." Ben grabs my hand and the blood circulation to my fingertips is compromised in an instant.

"How are you feeling?" She tilts her head to one side.

"With respect, Dr LaLa, I'd really just like to hear

the results of my scan."

"Of course. It's excellent news, Ben. The cancer has gone. You're in full metabolic remission." She widens her arms, bringing her palms together into a clap in front of her.

My own hand's blood supply returns so quickly I'm left with a tingling sensation. Turning towards him, my face aches with a smile so wide it must look fake. I gulp down the relief sitting in the back of my throat, trying not to cry, but fail miserably. The words are dawning on Ben, too. His eyebrows are no longer pushed together, his eyes brighten, his jaw relaxes and a smile springs from his cheeks as he grabs me.

"You're sure? I mean. What does that mean?"

"You'll have one more cycle to consolidate the treatment, and then some radiotherapy, but that's it. Then you're finished. We'll keep a close eye on you, of course, in follow-up, but you'll get your life back." Those words, 'life back'. They almost reverberate around the room, as though we're sitting at the entrance to a cave.

Ben kisses me so hard he makes my lips burn afterwards.

"It's almost over!" he says, as though he's talking to himself more than us. "I can't believe it. Thank you, Dr LaLa, thank you." He shakes her hand and I can see he's resisting the urge to bear hug her. She's nodding, her eyes glistening, and I can tell she feels this with us. I'm also resisting the urge to hug her.

As we leave the room, Ben appears as though he's

gliding down the corridor. The heavy weight weighing him down, now gone—he left it back in that consultation room right beside my own. When Dr LaLa spoke the word remission, I felt my shoulders relax for the first time since I saw him lying on that trolley in ED. I've been 'on duty' ever since, even when I'm off duty. Making sure he takes his medications and gets enough food and fluids. Monitoring his temperature, wiping down surfaces and washing my hands until they're sore, cracked and bleeding. Since that first infection, I've tried to protect him from catching anything else, and I can't believe it's almost over. I feel hot tears prickling behind my eyes again, but this time I don't succumb. There's been enough sadness.

"We need to tell Pops," he says, pausing by the passenger car door. "Let's get her from school, make up an appointment she has," he says in haste.

"Okay, I'll call the school and say she's got the dentist."

"It's really almost over?" He pulls me towards him.

I nod, slowly, not daring to speak, for fear of it all being ripped out from beneath us, this solid ground we've found.

"I love you," he says, before kissing me, long and slow.

"Here's to the future and your health, Ben," Mum says, raising a champagne flute above her head. We all join her. I partake in the fizz Dad opened. Ben has a sip of mine, but sticks to orange juice with Poppy. Cassie is by her feet, waiting expectantly for her to play.

"Thank you," he says. His smile builds and lightens up his face. "I just wanted to thank you as well for helping out with Poppy these past few weeks. It's been so good of you all." He looks at them and then turns to me, moving close by my side. "I'd like to make a toast." He lifts his glass. "To Jo—I couldn't have survived this without you, and I know I've got more treatment tomorrow, but right now, I feel so very lucky. Thank you." He kisses me, his free arm around my back.

"Who's for a slice of my homemade chocolate cake?" Mum asks, her eyes shining, locked on Poppy.

"Me!" Poppy's hand is straight in the air as though she were in class and we all laugh.

"Come on, honey," Mum says, wrapping her arm around her shoulder and I watch as they move to the counter top and portion the cake together, as though they'd been doing this Poppy's whole life.

"Thank you." He turns to me. Our noses are inches from each other's.

"You said that already." I cast him a wide smile. My face aches, the way it had when we first met, from smiling so much. Oh, the hope and relief in his eyes. On his entire face. It's priceless. It's everything.

"I know, but I mean it. You stuck by us and made sure everything was okay. I know how stressful it's been for you."

"It's worth every new grey hair, for you to be better." I yank at a strand, beaming at him.

"You don't have any grey hairs." His hand slides down the side of my face, his fingertips grazing my lips, and I kiss them softly.

"I feel as though I should have." I huff out a laugh and raise one shoulder to my ear as a tingle escapes down my back.

"Well, I'll still love you when you're grey and wrinkly."

"Is that right?" I lift my chin high.

"I promise," he says, our eyes locked. In them I see everything which has been missing since that last morning in Australia, when our future had felt full of excitement and promise.

The afternoon is spent making calls to people, letting them know the good news. I have to wait to call April as she'll be asleep, but I phone Emma and Chris, who are so relieved. Poppy snuggles up to her dad for an afternoon movie and I watch them both more than the film. In truth, I can't take my eyes off them. My little family. My heart's so full it can't take it. It's surreal, how quickly the fears left, being replaced with pure contentment. I don't think Ben's dreading his last two treatments, for his final cycle, so much now he knows it's almost over. Knowing the side effects will soon be gone, too, and it's been worth it for a cure. I know it wasn't the news he was expecting. The glass-half-full-man is in there somewhere, but he wasn't present in that consultation room this morning, and he's been missing for weeks now.

When Ben takes Poppy up to bed, I head upstairs and into our room, perching on the edge of the bed, trying to absorb everything. Ben's in remission—I can't quite get my head around it. I'm so thankful and relieved it's almost hard to quantify just how much. As much as I prayed for this, I hadn't allowed myself to hope, feeling as though to do so would have jinxed it. I know this is how Ben had been feeling, too. Not allowing himself to think about being cured. It had been about managing all our expectations, and thankfully, mine have been exceeded. Our prayers answered. There's another feeling which I can't quite place, sitting shoulder to shoulder with my relief. All I know is that my mind is questioning whether Ben will still want me to adopt Poppy, now that his fears of leaving her alone are unnecessary.

My phone vibrates next to me and I see April calling.

"Hey, you're up early." I sink into my pillows.

"I've got a job with an early start, but I saw your text saying call me and I was worried. Is Ben okay?" I can hear panic in her voice.

"Ben's great. We got his scan results this morning and the cancer's gone."

She inhales loudly. "Oh that's amazing news, Jo.

I'm so happy. So, no more chemo?"

"He has two final treatments to complete his course, then some radiotherapy, but it's worked. I don't think I've ever held my breath for as long as I did in that consultation room, waiting for the doctor to come in and tell us the news. I've never seen Ben look so scared before, either."

"He's so chill about everything, it's hard to imagine."

"This cancer has really affected him. I think it's even surprised him, how vulnerable he felt with it all. I just hope he can find his way back to his old self now."

"Are you okay?" she asks. Miles of distance doesn't stop her sensing something's not right.

"It's nothing, I feel stupid for thinking anything other than how relieved I am—"

"But?"

"The adoption … Don't get me wrong, I'd trade adopting Poppy in a heartbeat to keep Ben alive, but I'd settled my heart on becoming her mum."

"Aw, sweets, you're already her mum. A piece of paper isn't going to change how that little girl already sees you. It would just make it legal, is all. I can't see how Ben would want to go back on those plans. Poppy certainly won't. She's one little lady who knows her mind."

"Ha-ha, I love that about her. Ben says it's Jen, though I think it's a bit of both of them. She's so much more like her dad than he can see. I think seeing Jen in Poppy brings him comfort, so I don't say much."

"She is like her dad, for sure," April agrees. It's nice she knows them. That we spent time together. I think April fell for Poppy as quickly as I did and I can hear how relieved she is for Ben.

"You know what Ben said to me the other week, when it was Poppy's party?"

"What did he say?"

"He said if things were different he'd want us to have four kids. Three girls and a boy."

"How did that make you feel?"

"A little sad, but mostly it made me happy. He loves me enough to stay. He could see a future with more kids in it. And yes, it's different for him too now he's had the chemo, but he chose me, so I can look at *what could have been* with him and smile at the idea for how lovely it sounds."

I hear her sniff. "Okay, so you've made me cry and now I look like a panda and need to redo my make-up."

"I'm sorry, Cuz," I say, wishing I could give her a tight squeeze. "At least pandas are cute!"

"Very!" she agrees. "And don't be sorry. You inspire me. Hold on to this family of yours with both hands." There's emphasis on every one of her words.

"I will. I promise. Now go redo your face!"

She laughs. "Love you."

"Love you."

Chapter Twenty-Four

It's been a week since Ben's last chemotherapy treatment and I've just arrived home on a Saturday evening after covering someone's shift who's off sick. There's flu going round and despite many of the staff being vaccinated this year, it seems people haven't been protected by the vaccine with the strain of flu in circulation, and there's quite a few nurses down with it. Poppy had been given strict instructions from me to make sure Daddy rested, and of course, I'd left them with movies and pizza. Surprise, surprise. Though Ben hasn't regained his appetite or taste and hasn't been eating well this past week. He's beyond tired now, too, and I think the fact this was the last time he has to endure feeling this way is the only thing pulling him through. I felt bad saying yes to a shift, but they sounded desperate. I'm pleased to have only been on the afternoon shift and it flew by, especially with thoughts of my little family—and a hot bath with my name on it—waiting at home. I imagine both Ben and Poppy will be in bed now, unless he's let her wait up for me. It makes me feel special that she wants to, and I love kissing her goodnight.

I creep upstairs in a still and quiet house, not wanting to disturb them. Poppy's light is still on, so I push the door back and see her lying there, staring at the ceiling.

"You're still awake? Where's Daddy?" I creep beside her.

"Daddy wasn't feeling very good, so I sent him to bed, and I've been waiting for you to get home to give you the handover." She sits forward, cross-legged.

I smile, knowing she's referencing being Daddy's nurse for the evening and that at work nurses have handovers between shifts, to tell the next team of staff how the patients are.

"Go for it."

"He ate two slices of pizza and drank a whole glass of water. Then we sat on the sofa and he fell asleep to the film, but I didn't wake him, only at the end to tell him to go to bed."

"Great job. Did you remember to brush your teeth?" I touch her chin.

She nods, smiling and showing me her toothy grin.

"Even better!"

"Can you read to me?" Two bright eyes beg me, but I'm too tired.

"Not tonight, darling. I've got to get a bath, because I'm all smelly from being at work." I scrunch my face up and waft my hand in front of my nose, which makes her giggle.

"Okay. Night, night," she says, pulling Pinky in closer to her as she lies down.

I kiss her forehead, tuck her in tight and turn out the light on my way out of the room.

Stepping into our bedroom, I see Ben lying on the bed, asleep. He's snoring quietly for now, which is a contrast to the other nights this week, when in the middle of the night the noise coming from him was louder than a freight train passing by. I decide to shower instead of taking a bath, as it will be quicker and I don't want to wake him.

When I'm dressed in my pajamas, my hair twizzled up in a hand towel, resting precariously on my head, I re-enter the bedroom. I'm greeted by Ben's snore, which is different—his breathing heavier than usual. I go over to his side of the bed and observe the exaggerated rise and fall of his chest. I reach out and feel his forehead. It's warm. I gently rub his shoulders and he stirs, but doesn't fully waken.

"Ben. Wake up, please. You're really warm. Ben!"

"I'm not warm, I'm cold," he whispers, shivering. Only half opening his eyes.

I go in his bedside drawer and pull out the black case holding his thermometer, pressing the tip into his ear … *thirty-nine degrees*. I scroll through my phone to the emergency contact number given to us in the chemotherapy unit and dial.

"Hello, yes. I'm phoning for my boyfriend, Ben Campbell."

We waited only twenty minutes for the ambulance to

reach us, but it felt as though it were far longer. My mum came over straight away to be with Poppy, who's sound asleep still, having slept through the sirens blaring out as they drove down the street. Not even the heavy footsteps on the stairs, or the hiss and bleep of their radios disturbed her, thankfully. The crew who pitched up were two guys from work, who I know and trust. They thoroughly assessed Ben en route to the hospital as I sat in the back with him, wishing I'd not gone to work. Knowing I could have caught this earlier if *I'd* been there. The gold standard for treating sepsis in a post-chemo patient is to administer intravenous antibiotics within one hour. I don't know how long he's been like this, or if he bothered to check his temperature when he started to feel unwell. For the last part of the journey, he was so out of it. I'd held his hand, praying harder than I've ever prayed that he'd be okay.

An hour later and I'm by his trolley in ED. It feels as though we've come full circle and are now back where this all began. My colleagues have been amazing, to both of us. I'm sipping tea from a disposable paper cup when Ben turns his head to look at me.

"Sorry I scared you … again." He coughs. It's a new cough, and I don't like how it sounds.

"It's okay, as long as you're all right."

"Is Pops okay?" He takes a deep, pained breath and closes his eyes.

"Mum said she slept through all the commotion, hasn't stirred even a little. She's going to sleep on the sofa and listen out for her."

"Well, that's something. At least I didn't scare her again like before."

"No, I'm pleased of that, too, but she said you went to bed not feeling well. Why didn't you call me when you started to feel poorly?" I take his hand.

"I just thought I was tired. It came on really suddenly." He coughs again.

"I don't like the sound of that. When did you even start with a cough?"

"My throat felt a bit tickly all yesterday, but I didn't start coughing until now."

I puff out a breath and rub my temple. "I've probably brought germs back with me from work. It's too risky with your immune system. Everyone's off with flu."

"It's not your fault. You always get changed at work, and shower the second you're home. You have the immune system of a horse."

"But you don't, and that's the point." I stand and pace the room.

"It could have easily been Pops bringing germs home from school. We always say kids are germ factories. Stop torturing yourself! This is just one of those things." He holds out his hand as the door to the side room opens and in walk two doctors, the ED consultant, Dr Brown, and a junior doctor called Luke.

"Hello Ben, Jo," he greets us.

"How are you feeling?"

"Like a bus ran me over," he clears his throat, "but

better for the meds."

"You're lucky you live with a nurse and she got you in quickly." Dr Brown looks at me, smiling.

"I am lucky," he says, squeezing my hand, but I still feel responsible.

"Ben, I think you've got flu, but the swabs should confirm this."

"I had my vaccine." He scratches his face, resting his knuckles over his lips.

"I know. It's been quite the season this year and it's just unfortunate. I'd like to keep you in for a couple of days, so we've asked for a bed. There are none yet, but they might be able to make one in the morning."

Ben flops his head back onto his pillows. "Okay, thank you."

"Thank you," I say as they leave the room and know that, despite his disappointment, it's the right thing for them to do.

"You should go home," Ben says when we're alone.

"I'm not leaving you." I jerk my head around to look at him.

"You've been working all afternoon, and it's late. You need sleep." He looks at me, in the way he does with Poppy, when he's right and she won't be told.

"He's right," Kate agrees, walking in with a bag of intravenous fluids. "I'm here till morning. I can keep an eye on him until we find a bed. Make sure he behaves." She winks at him and he makes the effort to smile, weakly.

"I don't have my car. I rode in the ambulance."

"Mel's on a twilight. She finishes soon and is over your way, so I'm sure she won't mind dropping you." There's unplanned solidarity between the pair of them and I sense I'm not going to win this one.

"Okay." I breathe out. "Your phone's in the bag, as is your charger. Are you sure—"

"I'll call you if there's any change," Kate assures me.

"What about—"

"I'll hand over to the ward to call you, too." She doesn't need me to finish my sentence to know what I'm going to say. I nod. My gaze drifting between them both.

"Love you." I kiss his forehead, my bottom lip quivering as I pull away. On my way past Kate I squeeze her arm.

Mel drops me at the door to our house and we say goodnight. It's late and we're both tired, but she did her best to keep the conversation going. Aside from asking how I am, and a brief talk about Ben, we kept the topics light. When we'd run out of anything to say, we fell quiet and enjoyed the remainder of the journey in peace. I'm grateful I didn't have to drive, or walk to the car park alone. The hospital is eerie at night; all corners of buildings, lurking shadows and dimly lit paths.

Luckily, my house keys were in my bag, which I'd grabbed on my way out to the ambulance earlier—I didn't want to wake my mum, but as I step inside, she's in the hallway. Her super bat hearing hasn't faded with age, it seems.

"How is he?" she asks, rubbing her eyes and blinking, suggesting she'd been asleep after all.

"Stable. Talking, which is more than he was when we left here. I think we got him in in time. I'm so pleased he doesn't have any more treatment after this, because I'm not sure how much more worry I can handle, Mum." I look down at my feet. "Did Pops stay asleep?"

"Sleeping like a baby. Though I don't know why people use that saying, given babies normally keep you awake all night, like you did."

I muster a small laugh and squeeze her arm.

"Bed. Go on." She points to the staircase.

"I think I'm going to get a cuppa first. My brain won't switch off."

"Are you still not sleeping?"

"Honestly, I can't remember the last time I did." My voice sounds breathy, as though I'm amused by my own statement, when actually it's not in the least bit funny. "If I'm not worrying about Ben and the future I'm waking up trying to remember if I've washed Poppy's PE kit, or bought her a top with a number on it for 'Numbers Day' at school, or RSVP'd to a friend's birthday party. I check and recheck the calendar for appointments for them both, and then I can't remember when I'm supposed to be at the dentist, which I missed the other day." My shoulders slump and my arms droop by my sides.

"I'll put the kettle on," she says, turning towards the kitchen before I have chance to object.

"I could have made it, Mum. I pull out the bar stool to sit on as I watch her move around my kitchen as though it were her own.

"It's no bother. I could do with one myself. Your father and I often wake in the night and he puts the kettle on. Sleep doesn't come as easy when you're our age, or at least it comes, but then goes quickly too."

I laugh softly and so does she.

"What did they say at the hospital?" She sets two identical cups on the counter. Real china ones which she bought me, because tea tastes better from a china cup. I didn't get this when I was younger, but I do now.

"They think he's got flu."

"Poor love." She frowns. "He's not had things easy these past few months."

I shake my head. "No, he hasn't. I don't know how Poppy's going to take the news in the morning. She worries so much about him." I lean on the breakfast bar, resting on my fist.

"She's such a sweet little girl." Mum opens a drawer and sets a spoon beside the cups.

"The things she's been through, though. I know she doesn't know any different, not having a mum, but she feels the void. And with her dad being sick. It doesn't seem fair."

"Life rarely is, but she's got you."

"I love you, Mum." I slip off my stool and wrap my

arms around her as the kettle bubbles to a stop.

"What's that for?" She hugs me back, her soft smell of bar soap and talcum powder making me feel like a child. Her arms are still the only arms which truly comfort like no other.

"I never fully appreciated how hard a job parenting is and how effortless you made it seem."

"Well, I love you too, honey." She softens a strand of lose hair from my face. "And you're making parenting look fairly effortless yourself." A beat. "It's hard, even without Ben's illness to contend with. Parenting is relentless, but as clichéd as it sounds, so rewarding. Especially when your kid turns out like you."

"Oh Mum!" I say, swallowing the lump in my throat as she releases me.

"You miss it when it's over, the hustle and bustle." She waves a metal spoon around as though it were a wand or a conductor's baton. "It's intense in the midst of it all, but it passes ever so quickly." She stirs milk into the two cups set before her.

"You really think I'm doing okay?" I whisper.

She nods, all glowing eyes and gentle smile as she passes my tea, its warmth comforting my cold finger-tips and her words comfort my soul.

Chapter Twenty-Five

The side room on the ward is chilly today, or perhaps it's just the fact I'm tired. Four night shifts back to back, with a neighbour doing DIY during the day tired. I wrap my woolly cardigan around me tighter and rest my head back on the light green recliner chair I'm sitting in. I have a day off today, so at least I didn't have to cancel any shifts, though I might in the coming days. My mind reflects on how I'd underestimated how hard it is having a sick loved one. As a nurse, I've spent time with hundreds of families and always been sympathetic, but unless you've experienced it, it's hard to fully understand the toll it takes. The perpetual worry, gnawing anxiety, and the worst of all, feeling utterly helpless. It's my job to help people, but when it comes to Ben, all I can do is hold his hand and support him. What I want is to be the one treating him. I watch the nurses taking his blood, or placing cannulas in his veins. My fists tighten when they struggle, because I want to take the needle off them and do it myself. When his pump signals his intravenous fluids are finished, I want to silence it, reset it, get the next prescribed bag and attach it. When he's in pain, I want to fetch his painkillers, or simply give his antibiotics on time, not an hour late because the poor staff nurse is rushed off her feet with too many equally sick patients to look after. I want to feel useful. With my own patients I can order tests and check results, all with the click of a few buttons. As far as Ben goes, I have to speak to his nurse for information, ask questions, probing and possibly irritating them because I'm the millionth relative they've dealt with today, and not the most important job on their ever-expanding list. At work, I have control. Here I have none.

The iPad rings on Ben's table, so I pick it up. He's gone for a chest X-ray, but shouldn't be much longer. I'd asked Mum to help Poppy FaceTime her dad this afternoon and I hadn't realised just how late in the day it is.

"Hey, Pops," I answer, smiling at her on the screen. Her shoulder slump, her eyebrows pulling in.

"Where's Daddy?" Her lips meet in a straight line.

"They've just wheeled him for an X-ray."

"What's that?"

"It's like a special picture that shows the doctor Daddy's lungs."

"Urgh, gross!" Her face wrinkles.

"It's not anything gross. Don't worry. Here he is now," I say as the porter pushes the bed feet first into the room, pushing the plug back into the socket, and applying the brake. I turn the camera to Ben and he rouses a smile.

"Hey, my little Popsicle."

"Hey, Daddy. Did you get to see your lungs?"

His eyes narrow as he looks at me.

"I told her an X-ray is a special picture of your lungs. She thinks it's gross."

"No, I didn't see anything—" Ben coughs and can't finish the sentence. His chest is far worse than when he was admitted.

"Bad cough, Daddy."

"Bad cough!" he replies, croakily. It's something he's always said to her when she's had a cough. Their repertoire. I pass Ben his cup and he sips the water.

"When are you coming home?"

"We're not sure, but hopefully soon. Daddy just needs more medicine," I answer for him, trying to maintain my smile.

"Can't Jo give you the medicine at home? She's a nurse." Her voice drops.

"Aw, I wish I could, darling. Daddy needs to rest in hospital for a few days and then we can look after him when he's a bit better."

"Do you want me to send Pinky in, to keep you company?" she says and I see a tear bubble in the corner of his eye.

"You look after Pinky and hug him whenever you miss me, okay?"

"Okay. Love you!" She blows him a kiss.

"Love you more!" He curls the corners of his mouth into the widest smile he can muster, but after she ends the call Ben erupts into a coughing fit and can barely catch his breath. I fetch his nurse from the corridor and she checks his observations. His oxygen levels are low, as is his blood pressure. I hold his hand as she hooks him up to some oxygen and he settles, breathing into the mask.

"Your blood transfusion's ready, Ben, so I'll start that shortly. Try and relax with the oxygen and I'll recheck your observations when I bring the blood in."

"How are you feeling?" Ben tries to take the mask off and I stop him. "You need to leave it on." I'm stroking his cheek.

"I don't feel good, Jo." He squeezes his eyes shut.

"Just relax. Breathe and relax." My insides churn and my lips tingle as I take his hand, knowing we haven't yet beat this thing.

He's on his second bag of blood and the nurse changed his oxygen to a nasal one instead of a mask, so he can talk when he wants to.

"Jo," he says. I realise he's awake and that I must have been dozing in the chair beside his bed.

"Yes?" I lean forward, my eyes blinking awake as I take his hand.

"I need you to chase Paula and the adoption." His words are rushed and half-formed, but I know what he's asked.

"Ben, you scare me when you talk like this. I'm not going anywhere. With or without a bit of paper."

"But you don't have any legal rights." Each word takes a little more of his breath away.

"Ben—"

"Maybe we should get married."

"What?" My head goes back, my shoulders forward.

"If we get married, you'll have more rights."

"It wouldn't give me more rights as far as Poppy goes. Not really. I'd still need at least a parental responsibility order. I'll chase Paula and a court date, if it'll put your mind at ease, but I—"

"I know—" He coughs more, leaning forward until it passes. I rub his back gently, up and down. "I know," he goes on, "it doesn't sound very romantic … Proposing as I cough my lungs up in a hospital bed." His breathing is rapid and nasal as he tries to take in the oxygen. "I'm sorry. I just … I'm scared, Jo." He swallows and I offer him some water, but he shakes his head. "I thought this was over." His face is pale, with dark purple circles under his eyes. Tears bundle together in the corners, like a dam backed up and ready to burst open. "They have weddings in hospitals all the time on telly."

"Ben, you need to stop talking, you can—"

"If it helped give you more rights," he pauses, "as my wife … we could do that and I'd marry you properly later?"

"They do a lot of unbelievable things on telly. Now stop talking and catch your breath. The only thing you need to be thinking about now is getting well."

"So, we can't get married here?" he continues, each word separated by a breath.

"Not unless you're dying and you're not." I gulp,

feeling as though my heart's just dislodged itself. It's risen up my throat, landed on the bed beside him, where it's beating slower, and slower, until is arrests, right there on the white linen.

"Just rest, okay." I hold his hand tight. "Leave everything else to me. I'll look after her, no matter what," I say and he closes his eyes.

When his nurse came to do some checks, Ben decided I should go home to relieve my mum, and spend some time with Poppy. The staff agreed to call me with any changes and the transfusion seemed to have started to perk him up. I didn't argue. I need time to process the conversation we just had. He asked me to marry him like he was asking me what flavour ice cream I wanted at the beach. I don't blame him for it; I get it. He's scared and feels every bit as helpless, if not more so, than I do. He's worried for Poppy like I'm worried for him, but I know he's not thinking straight. He's never been this low in his health, both physical and mental. The treatment has overwhelmed him and he can't see anything else at the moment. I want to be his wife and on any other occasion I'd say yes, if the circumstances were different, but right now I need to focus on helping him recover and looking after Poppy.

After seeing my mum off, I wander back into the lounge and find Poppy holding a picture of her parents in her small hands, stroking her dad's face.

"Pops …do you want to talk about it?" I ask quietly.

"I just miss him," she says, her eyes puffy and tinged red.

"I know you do and he misses you just as much." I rub her back.

"He said the cancer had gone away, so I don't get why he's still sick?" Her voice, normally so bright and cheerful, sounds strained and small.

"Well." I sit beside her. "His body's a bit weak and so he's not able to fight off germs the way we can. It won't be this way forever, he just needs time to recover."

"Won't those special X-ray's make him sick too?"

"The radiotherapy?" I stroke her soft long hair, smoothing it from her face.

She nods, her lips puffed out.

"Not in quite the same way. He'll be tired and there may be a few other things, but hopefully he won't get any more infections."

"I hate cancer!" she says, huffing out a fierce breath.

"Me too. Me too." My words are accompanied by an ache in my chest. "Do you know what I think we should do?"

"What?" She sits up, facing me.

"I think we should put on your dad's Bon Jovi music and have a dance party."

"But I feel too sad and Daddy's not here to join in."

"It'll help let the feelings out, and would definitely make Daddy laugh when we tell him."

"We could send him a video of us dancing, to cheer him up!" Her spirits rally and I laugh, wishing I hadn't suggested it now, but know she's right and, as usual, I'm unable to resist the warmth radiating from behind those big beautiful eyes.

With the camera set to selfie mode, I aim it towards where we're standing. The music is ready and she presses play, choosing *Livin' on a Prayer*. As the intro builds, I close my eyes, seeing him so vividly; flicking his long hair, a mischievous look in his eyes—one that I miss and took for granted. My heart's back there with him, feeling this undeniable pull towards him as I crossed the room where he'd taken me in his arms. I knew that night how special he was and how I was completely falling for him. When the chorus kicks in, Poppy and I jump around, our hands linked, wafting our hair and singing loudly to the words. I'm not the only one who knows it off by heart. As I watch her, the top of her unicorn pajamas lifting to show off her belly button, her smile reaching the corners of her eyes in the moment, she reminds me so much of him. With his performance replaying in my mind, and hers in front of my eyes, everything slows as I see their duet. They're side by side, trying to outperform each other and breaking into fits of laughter as they do. I wished we'd done this. I wish I'd filmed them together, or we'd turned the camera on ourselves like Poppy and I are doing now. We'd sing and dance until we were breathless and deliriously happy, then he'd kiss me and she'd push between us, saying we're the bread, and she the ham to our sandwich. I want that memory so badly.

By the end of the song, we're lying on the floor in a heap, laughing so hard my stomach hurts, and I have tears streaming down my cheeks. I pull her little frame into my side and our laughter tears turn to real ones as our sadness finds its release. In each other's arms, we cry a while and it's exactly what we both need.

Sleep claimed me surprisingly easily afterwards, Poppy too. The next thing I remember is hearing the dull vibration of my phone on the bedside table and the louder than necessary ring tone accompanying it, which I snatch and answer. "Hello," I say, sitting bolt upright.

"This is Annabelle, the staff nurse calling from the hospital. Can I speak with Mrs Campbell?"

"I'm Jo, Ben's partner. Is he okay?" I remove the phone from my ear to check the time. Seven a.m.

"Oh, I'm sorry." There's a pause, which lasts longer than is comfortable. "Ben's condition has deteriorated overnight and he's been asking for his wife." Her words sting in an unpleasant *I've got a papercut* kind of way, taking me by surprise.

"His wife died eight years ago. How unwell is he?" I ask, feeling her answer before she gives it.

"… I think you need to come."

I'm not entirely sure what I said after that, or how I managed to find some clothes and dial my mum's phone number, but I did. Now I'm walking down the longest corridor on my way to the ward. My feet feel as though they're floating along a moving walkway, rather than stepping on the hard floor beneath me. I don't hear anything, aside from a loud ringing in my ears, despite two porters pushing a blue-covered trolley passed me. From experience, I know there's a deceased patient inside. When they've passed me, I lean up against a wall and dry retch, breathing in through my nose and out of my mouth a few times, until I'm composed enough to start walking again. As I arrive at the ward, the nurse, Annabelle, finds me.

"We're just about to transfer him to intensive care." She cups my elbow and my hand flies to my chest.

"Why, what happened?"

"He's septic and struggling to maintain his oxygen levels. The X-ray shows he's developed pneumonia. Has he ever smoked?"

I shake my head, struggling to register her question. My brain is still on the words 'intensive care'. "… I think so, yes. A while ago now. Why? Are they going to have to ventilate him up there?"

"Possibly," she says lightly and I feel a sudden ache in the back of my throat. I try to swallow, but it's as if something's in the way and after several attempts I'm panting. I place both hands over my mouth as if it were a brown paper bag and breathe through my fingers, gaining little control. His bed travels towards me and I rush beside his lifeless body, covered in tubes and wires, with pumps and oxygen, being transported beside him on sheets stained with his spilled blood.

"Ben." I grab for his hand. "I'm here," I say. His eyes widen, flickering momentarily up at me, but then they close and my legs buckle as he's pushed past me and slides through my fingertips.

"You need to sit," Annabelle says, guiding me to a nearby chair. The ringing in my ears is back and even louder than before. I see her mouth something as she pushes down on my shoulders when I try to stand.

"I need to follow him," I say, trying once more to stand, but my legs don't cooperate.

"You need a minute." The sound of her voice is less muffled as the ringing subsides. "Let them settle him. I'll take you up once they're sorted, okay?" Annabelle offers a sad smile.

I'm back to sipping tea again from a disposable paper cup, asking myself when this nightmare will ever end? How did we go from the happiest news of his remission to him being rushed off to ICU with pneumonia? I just don't understand. I'd lowered my guard too soon. The fear had begun to wane, with hope starting to replace it. So often in the weeks leading up to his scan, as I sat beside him, comforting him as the effects of the chemo took their toll, my mind would force me to imagine a life without him. The thoughts were not conscious ones. They would creep up on me and take hold when I least expected them. The gut-wrenching agony felt so real in those moments as I tried to reject them for what they were, just thoughts. No longer was this flawed reasoning born out of fear. Facing a life without him is never more real than in this moment and I'm waiting for the agony to strike; the same twisted knot to form in the pit of my stomach, hardening with no release, but what comes instead is worse. Nothing. An abyss so wide I feel as though I'll fall into it and disappear forever. Not one part of my body feels as though it belongs to me. Not one part of my brain is capable of responding. My eyes scan my surrounding as though I'm lost, with no clue as to where, or who I am. Void. Blank. Alone.

"Jo?" My head lifts to the nurse crouched in front of me, saying my name. She's wearing blue scrubs, her dark hair pinned back into a tight bun. We're in the relatives' room on the Intensive Care Unit. It's small, pleasant, purposeful, but not cosy. She's still talking to me, the nurse. It's the 'what to expect seeing your loved one attached to so many tubes and machines' talk. I know this, but don't tell her. I let her talk. Let her think she's preparing me. I don't need the talk, because I know there's nothing she, or anyone else, could say that will prepare me for seeing him—unconscious, a machine breathing for him.

"Are you ready?" she asks, coming to the end of

her script—this isn't a criticism, all nurses have them. We default to well-used phrases to help us cope emotionally when faced with supporting others in their own distress. I nod and follow her out of the room. She swipes her badge through a set of double doors and I notice how quiet it is. There's background noise from the machines working and the blood pressure cuffs droning as they inflate to time. There's no conversation in this part of the unit, just the beeping of monitor alarms. It's still, controlled even. Nurses measure and record, moving around their patients as if it were a choreographed dance.

As we draw near to his bed I close my eyes, a lump swelling in my throat. My mind fills so quickly it's like instant reversal of amnesia. What am I going to tell Poppy? I didn't even get to show him the video of us dancing from last night. Wishing I'd said yes to his proposal, as hasty and unthought-out as it was. What are my rights with Poppy if he dies? Ben had been planning for this, planning not to be here. I know he and April both said it was because he lost Jen, but I feel as though he didn't expect to survive.

The ventilator is a rhythmic sound, mixed with the other beeps, some long, some short. The nurse doesn't leave me, instead she guides me closer to him and into the chair set beside his bed.

"He'd hate this." I wring my hands. "He's always so strong, far stronger than me. He'd hate being this dependent and weak."

"Now you're the one who needs to be strong, Jo,"

she says, brushing her hand over my forearm.

"Thank you," I say, making eye contact with her for the first time, as though her words have pulled me back from the darkness of the deep hole. I reach out and touch his fingertips. Another nurse is at the far side of the bed, charting and measuring as per the routine. He's got a central line hanging from his neck, an arterial line in his wrist and the tube of a catheter from his bladder, feeding into a bag hanging over the side of the bed. The numbers on the monitors don't all make sense. I'm not a nurse here—that side of my brain hasn't restarted. Here, I'm out of my depth as I focus on the mechanical rise and fall of his chest. Here, I wait and pray.

"Excuse me!" I open my eyes and rotate my neck because I realise I'd fallen asleep awkwardly in his chair and now it aches. A nurse is standing beside me, waiting patiently for me to respond.

"Sorry, I must have closed my eyes," I say.

"Ben's parents are here, but I need you to step outside for them to come in if that's okay?"

I shake my head, swallowing. "He doesn't really get along with his parents. I don't know what he'd want me to do."

"It's up to you. You're down as his next of kin."

"… Okay. Let them see him, but don't let them stay long, please."

She nods, once, rubbing my shoulder.

I head out into the corridor and see them. Mrs

Campbell, surprisingly, opens up her arms to me, and even more surprising than that, I step into her embrace.

"My dear, how is he?"

"Stable, for now, but he's very sick." My voice breaks on the last word.

"You look exhausted, dear. Why don't you go home and rest for a while? We can sit with him." Her expression is thoughtful.

"I'd rather stay, but you can go in and see him."

"How's Poppy?"

"Upset, but doing okay. My mum's with her at home." My muscles feel weak.

"Well, if you need anything."

I nod. To be honest, I'd expected more venom from her. The sympathy and kindness was unsettling, but despite her lack of bite, I'm cautious. Pythons may not be poisonous, but they're large and powerful creatures who kill their prey by suffocation—this I know.

The nurse shows them inside and I go for a walk around, on autopilot. At first, I'm not sure where I'm going, ending up by the chapel. Pushing the door open, I step inside the bright, airy room, which faces large glass windows overlooking a courtyard. Seated in a purple fabric chair, I lower my head. My thoughts are silent and so, too, are my prayers.

After leaving the chapel, having been woken by the chaplain, curled up on a row of seats as though I were on an airport layover, I'm unsure how long I'd stayed. I buy a large, extra shot white Americano from the coffee shop in the glass-fronted main hospital atrium, which is also bright, making my eyes feel the strain of just waking up. My body and mind want to shut down, alongside my muscles. I want to be in bed, asleep before the phone call which led me here. Before seeing him in that hospital bed being kept alive by drugs and machines. I feel a small vibration from my back pocket and retrieve my phone.

"Hi, Mum."

"Jo, I'm so sorry." She sounds out of breath. "They turned up and took her."

"What, who took who?" I hold my breath.

"Ben's parents. They came from seeing him at the hospital and insisted Poppy go with them."

"What, no!" My stomach feels rock hard. "They were here just a second ago. I saw them. I left them to visit Ben. No, you're kidding."

"They told Poppy you'd asked them to collect her, so you could look after her dad, but I knew that couldn't be true. She didn't want to go, but her grandma was so convincing. I couldn't stop them, not without upsetting Poppy."

"Mum, it's not your fault." I stumble backwards and a passing gentleman catches my elbow. My scalding hot coffee splashes onto my hand.

"Are you okay?" he says, not releasing his grip straight away.

"Yes. I'm fine. Sorry. Thank you," I hastily add.

"Jo, what can I do?" I can hear the stress in her voice.

"Nothing, Mum. You can't do anything and neither can I. I need to go." We hang up the phone and I dial April, even though I have no idea what time it is there, nor can I even think straight to figure it out. It rings forever and I almost give up, then I hear her sleepy voice.

"Jo," she says. "What's wrong?"

"I'm sorry to wake you." I'm shaking now.

"No. What's happened, tell me!"

"It's Ben, he's in intensive care on a ventilator and Poppy's grandparents have taken her. I don't know what to do. April, what do I do?" I blurt out as people pass me at a distance.

"Jo, I need you to take some deep breaths for me, okay?" April breathes in and out and I copy her, but feel lightheaded. "What actually happened?"

"My mum was looking after Poppy while I was at the hospital with Ben and his parents turned up, first at the hospital to see him. She was being so nice to me, it should have made me realise she was up to no good." I close my eyes. "Then she went to the house, told Poppy I'd sent them to collect her for a few days."

"Okay, Jo! You need to listen to me … You need to call Emma and Chris. They might know someone. They can help you. I'm all the way across the world and I can't get to you right now. They can. *Please* call them."

"I will." My voice cracks. The bridge of my nose is

burning with tears, wishing she were here with me.

"I love you," she says, the words equally soothing as they are heart-wrenching.

"Love you."

Chapter Twenty-Six

Chris is on the phone in the next room. Emma's beside me on the sofa, holding my hand as we listen to the hum of his voice, but I can't hear his words, or I'm trying not to. When I left the hospital, the nurse said we'd know more with how Ben responds in the next twenty-four hours. I should be there, not here, trying to work out how to get his daughter back from her thieving grandparents. *Our daughter,* I hear my brain say. Except she's not mine yet. He'd be so mad right now. I give a shuddering breath and Emma squeezes my hand.

"Jo," I hear her say.

"Sorry, what?" I look up at her.

"Can I get you anything?"

"No, thank you." I can't remember the last time I ate. I've had several cups of tea, because people think tea solves everything. I was guilty of the same, especially at work with my patients and their families. No amount of tea will fix this, though.

"Talk to me!" she says.

"Ben would be so mad, Em. I was supposed to look after her. He didn't want this. He didn't want his parents to be anywhere near her." I press the palm of my hand to my lips. My throat feels thick.

"This isn't your fault, Jo. They made sure you were at the hospital and found out where she was, so they could go and get her. It's manipulative and taking advantage of their own son being seriously ill." She recoils.

"I told them where she was. I practically gave her away." I grit my teeth together … "I've lost them both, haven't I?" I sit, silently staring at my dry, chapped hands. I'd washed them over, and over, to try and keep Ben safe from germs these past weeks. My knuckles are cracked, with lines of dry blood sitting on top of the skin.

"You haven't lost them." She clasps my hands in hers, her eyes meeting mine. "Ben's a fighter and so are you! You're gonna fight for Poppy. You have rights." I try to pull away, but she holds tight. "The social worker passed you. The courts just need to award you the adoption order. Ben's wishes couldn't be clearer."

"I've tried phoning the Campbells, but they don't answer. I just want to know she's all right. I don't know where they live, or I'd drive over there myself … not that they'd let me in."

Chris emerges, trying to look optimistic, but his gaze ping-pongs, avoiding eye contact. "So, the police said it's a civil matter, as they're her grandparents and there's no child protection issues. My solicitor said we can fight them taking her because of the adoption order, but you need that to have her removed from their care."

"What if they try and get an order to keep her?" I'm still holding Emma's hand.

"They have no pre-existing relationship with their grandchild, so the courts will favour you, who's been Poppy's caregiver—particularly since her dad became sick."

"She's probably so scared right now. Her dad in the hospital and me unable to be with her." I sob and Emma wraps her arms around me. "She's going to think I lied to her and I've sent her away, to the one place she didn't want to go."

"My solicitor's firm is seeing how we arrange a court hearing to get the adoption order as soon as possible. It's special circumstances, Jo. Have faith, okay?" He dips his head to meet my empty gaze.

"Thank you," I say to him, still coiled in Emma's arms, but faith I'm running a little low on.

"Try calling them again," Emma suggests as I ease away from her. "They can't ignore you forever. Poppy will be asking to speak to you, to find out how her dad is."

I scroll to my last dialled number and wait, expecting to hear voicemail, but a small voice answers.

"Poppy?" I stand.

"Jo, where are you? How's Daddy?"

"I'm going back to the hospital to see him soon. The nurses and doctors are taking good care of him. How about Grandma and Grandad, are they taking good care of you?"

"They are, but why am I not with you? Grandma says I have to stay here because Daddy's not well. You promised you'd be my mummy." She's crying now. I close my eyes tight. The sound of her small sobs pierce through me, one by one.

"I will be, darling, soon, I promise. Just let Grandma and Grandad look after you for a few days while I look after Daddy, okay?" I try to hide the anguish from my voice. I want her to feel this is normal and not have to deal with any more heartache.

"Okay." Her voice drops and she goes quiet.

"Please can I speak to Grandma?" I ask in a level tone.

"Okay," she says again.

"I love you," I say.

"Love you," I hear back, but then the phone goes dead.

My hand touches my throat. I'm frozen, listening to the deafening silence on the other end of the phone as another piece of my heart shears off.

"Jo, what did she say? Is she all right?" Emma is sitting on the edge of the sofa.

"She hung up on me." I shake my head.

"Poppy?"

"No, Grandma. Poppy's upset and full of questions, but that's to be expected. I can't believe she didn't take the phone and speak to me. Coward," I hiss, pacing in front of the hearth.

"She knows she's in the wrong, that's why!"

"Does she! I'm not sure, given all the things Ben's told me about his childhood."

"Were they abusive?"

"No, nothing like that." I wave a hand, then smooth hair from my face. "I just think they were judgemental and nothing was good enough. They saw things one way and anything outside of that wasn't right. Ben felt suffocated by them. He always said he didn't want Poppy's spirit sucked out of her, the way they tried to with him."

"Well, it's a good job she's got you then." She meets me in the middle of the room.

"They're loaded, Em." I go to sit, but immediately stand again. "They can afford all the legal help and fancy solicitors in the world. They'll fight me."

"Yeah well, so are Chris and I. We'll fight back."

"I don't have that kind of money to repay you."

"You don't need to. I always said if there was a way I could return your generosity to me, for the time I lived with you in Cornwall, then I would. Let us return this favour, Jo. Poppy will be home with you soon. I'm sure of it."

"I'm so grateful to you and Chris for dropping everything to be here and dragging you away from Stephen."

"We wouldn't be anywhere else. Stephen's quite happy with his grandma, he'll hardly notice we're gone. I just wish there was more I could do."

"You being here is enough and Chris taking control of the legal stuff. I can't think straight. I need to be with Ben, but I can't stop worrying about Poppy."

"We're not going anywhere. We'll sort it." Emma takes Chris's hand and they both look at me with such solidarity it's comforting.

Later that night, Chris and Emma are asleep in the spare room. I'm sitting on the edge of our bed, near Ben's bedside cabinets. I didn't want to leave the hospital, but there is literally nothing I can do. I held his hand and talked to him, but I couldn't find the words, because I didn't want him to hear Poppy was gone. I didn't want to hear the machines and his rhythmic artificial breathing, or see the nurses changing bags of fluids, taking samples from his lines and charting his condition. There has been no improvement, according to his team. No deterioration either, so he's stable. I'm supposed to find comfort in those words. A word I use with no thought, thinking it's a soothing, hopeful word. It's not. I open his drawer to take out one of his jumpers, feeling as though the smell of him will heal me. As I lift it up, a pile of envelopes drops onto the floor. There's a few addressed to Poppy, all held together with an elastic band and one with my name on it.

Darling Popsicle.

Sorry, by the time you read this letter, you'll be a woman and will most likely cringe at my pet name for you. You used to when you were a kid, too, but I think you secretly liked it. At least I hope you did.

Happy 18th Birthday, gorgeous girl.

I wish I was there to spoil you. I'd take you shopping and out to dinner, or stay in and make pizzas together, for old times' sake. I wish I was there to see what sort of woman you've grown into. I love you so much they didn't even invent the words for it yet. I've loved our little life together, too; you and me against the world for all those years. What adventures we've had, right? You taught me more being your daddy than anything else in life ever would, or could. It was my greatest ever achievement, and I'm so very proud of how funny, smart and caring you are. You reminded me so much of your mum when you were a little girl and she would be as proud of you, too.

We both left you far too soon, and I'm sorry you had to go through that, but I know Jo will have made a wonderful mother. Looking after you and loving you, as your mum and I would have. Remember all our good times, Pops, and don't be sad today. Celebrate life and love and be happy.

Mummy and I will be smiling down on you, raising a glass of something.

Love you forever,
Daddy
xxx

My trouser leg is wet from fallen tears, which I wipe with the back of my hand. My eyes are so blurry, I only just make out the line of kisses along the bottom of the paper. I push it to one side, along with the others in the pack, unable to bring myself to read the envelope entitled, 'on your wedding day'. Ben wrote us letters. Death letters. Letters from 'beyond the grave'. Or whatever you want to call them. There was always that part of him which thought he wouldn't survive and he couldn't shake it. No matter how positive I tried to be, or he acted. I pull his jumper to my face and breathe in deeply—his scent engrained in the fibres. I picture him, wearing this jumper, lying beside me on the sofa, tickling my ribs just so he can hear me laugh. I would roll over on top of him, and we'd kiss as though we were teenagers, until we had to come up for air. I keep my eyes squeezed shut so that the memory stays with me, and when it fades, I wipe my face with some tissue and hold the letter addressed to me. Every part of me wants to shove them back inside the drawer and pretend they don't exist. Pretend I never stumbled upon them. Pretend he never wrote them, but I can't. It's like an itch that has to be scratched, and so I begin reading.

Dear Jo,

If you're reading this letter, I guess this thing's beat me and I'm sorry! I'm a blubbering wreck right now, so I'm pleased you're at work and Pops is at school, because I just finished writing to her and my heart ripped into tiny pieces. *I hope she never has to read them and you never have to find these letters. I don't want to leave you both, but I wanted to have the chance to say some things, if these are to be the last thoughts you ever hear from me. When the time's right, please give them to her for me.*

That day you walked into my shop, looking for surf lessons ... I'll never forget it. My heart stirred for the first time since Jen, and I couldn't stop thinking about you. I never thought there would be another woman for me, but you changed that. When you returned the next day, oh-um-Jo, I knew I had to take you surfing myself. I needed an excuse to find out about the woman behind that smile of yours. What a woman you are! You've turned my world upside down, or right side up. I dunno. I should have married you already. A shotgun wedding in Vegas, or something—you've never seen my Elvis impression, it's far better than my Bon Jovi. (I know you're smiling right now and that's okay. Don't ever hide that smile of yours. The world deserves to see it.)

The truth is, I didn't want to rush things, even though I knew I wanted to spend the rest of my life with you. I also didn't want it to be shrouded by my illness. All I can say is, Poppy and I are beyond lucky to have you in our lives and I only wish I could have been there to see the rest of the journey. You don't know how much I'm praying I will be.

I know you wanted a child of your own and how painful that part of your life has been, but trust me when I say, YOU ARE ENOUGH! If there were no Poppy, and only you and I for eternity, you would be the life I want. The fact that I got to share that life with you both, even for such a short time, was a bonus.

Take care of her like I know you will. Make sure she knows how much I love her! She's yours now. I couldn't imagine leaving her with anyone less special than you.

My heart is with you forever. Even if I'm not.

I love you.

Ben.

xxx

Chapter Twenty-Seven

Today would have been a joyous day, if things had turned out differently. I woke early, or more to the point, I rose early. After spending much of the night awake, staring at the shadows on the pillow beside me. Ben's pillow. The moon seemed so much brighter, as though it knew the darkness inside me and it was trying to compensate. No amount of brightness would, of course. I chose a black calf-length chiffon dress, with a round neck and wide puffy sleeves. Underneath is a cotton V-neck jersey dress. I'm wearing tights because it's cold outside, paired with plain black heels. I'm not sure why you have to dress smartly for these things, but it seems ingrained to do so. We're all dressed in smart clothes, even Ronnie, who I've never seen in a shirt and tie before.

We're gathered on a large landing. It's not really a room, because you walk up one flight of stairs into an open plan area, with adjoined green fabric chairs outlining the space.

"Jo, why don't you sit down?" Emma says, touching my forearm.

I sit beside her and immediately stand again, the

floor beneath me showing tracks where I've been pacing, my heels leaving their mark in the carpet.

Chris touches my shoulder and I halt, looking to where his eyes lead mine. April's striding towards me, her arms around me faster than I can compute what she's doing here.

"April!"

"I got here as soon as I could. I'm sorry it took me so long." I hold her for the longest time. In fact, I'm squeezing her so tightly I hear her breathing become laboured, but my arms don't show any signs of release.

"I'm so pleased you're here."

"Have I missed it?" She looks as flustered as she sounds.

"No, we're still waiting," Chris says, and she takes my hands, sitting beside me.

"Hey, April." Emma looks round me to her. They've never met in person, only virtually, when I used to FaceTime while Emma lived with me.

"Great to meet at last," April says, smiling up at both Emma and Chris.

We're given the signal and I know it's time. I stand, but my legs feel weak and I can't put my foot forward. Ronnie takes my arm, gripping it tightly and almost lifts me from the spot, carrying me forward with his momentum, April on the other side.

There's hardly anyone in the room, just us really, and a couple of officials. Until the door opens to the left of the platform and the judge walks in, taking a seat behind a raised desk. It was supposed to be a grand celebration. We were supposed to come here together, with our friends and family to receive the adoption order. Poppy would have been allowed to sit behind where the judge is now, on the platform and wear her wig. The entire event would have been captured in photographs. April is seated beside me, no camera in her lap. Not waiting for the go-ahead to start snapping the shots. My parents are behind me, with Chris and Emma. They gain a grandchild today, their first and only grandchild. I'd imagined my mum wiping away tears of joy and my dad swallowing down pride at his perfect growing family. I can see Ben looking at me, with so much love behind his gaze. I listen carefully and hear whooping, claps and cheers as they pronounce me her mum. Poppy throwing her arms around me with such force she tilts me sideways. We pose for April, who captures the three of us, smiling widely, as a family.

The reality is somewhat different. The courtroom walls are panelled with light oak to match the desk behind which the judge resides. There's a crest on the wall behind her. It's sombre and devoid of excited chatter and celebration. I don't look at anyone. I want to hold the other reality in my mind. Seeing things happening that way, not this. My ears are ringing as though they're on a different frequency and I don't hear any of the words being spoken by the judge. I'm praying she doesn't ask me anything, because my voice feels as though it's been buried somewhere deep in the pit of my stomach, and I'm afraid no words would project. To my relief, I'm handed the order and as quickly as she entered, the judge exits. Emma and April cocoon me from both sides, my mum from behind. As they release me, I look up to where they're all watching me.

"You're her mum, Jo. We can get her back," Chris says, beaming.

As we walk towards the door my legs feel tingly, as though they're on a conveyer belt and I have no control of the speed or direction I'm travelling. With everyone beside me, I stop inches before the door.

"She's coming home!" I say, before everything becomes hazy and I collapse.

They tried to stop me coming to the hospital after I fainted. My parents wanted to bring me here to have me looked at, but I wanted to see Ben. The solicitor was arranging for Poppy being brought home, to try and avoid involving the police. I didn't want to upset Poppy. I'm sitting at his bed, the bed he's been in for a matter of days, but it feels longer. His nurse said they were going to start weaning him off his sedation and they have. He's breathing a little on his own—the infection finally responding to the medication. He still hasn't opened his eyes. How I miss those beautiful eyes, so full of confidence and mischief.

I'm used to the noise now, sitting here in the ICU. The place of no rest, or distinction between day and night. Eventually you drown out the decibels reached by the machines, until it's just background noise. Like the chime of the old grandfather clock in the house next door to where I used to live. At first, I heard the passing of every half-hour and hour. Over time, I didn't even notice it anymore, and when I did, it was oddly comforting. The machines attached to Ben are oddly comforting as well, because they signify life. He's still alive. Thanks to his team, who've worked continuously to make him better. I'm grateful for the care he's received here, the attention and monitoring and I've a new found respect for my nursing colleagues who do this work—I know I could not. The nurse looking after him steps away from her chair by the computer and I'm alone with him.

"Sorry I've been quiet," I say, bringing my hand into a fist, my knuckles resting against my lips as I try and find the words. "You're not going to like what I have to say, or at least the first part … A couple of days ago." I mutter, hanging my arms by my sides. "A couple of days ago, your parents took Poppy from me and refused to let her come home. Somehow, I don't really know how, to be honest, mostly down to Chris, I went to court this morning and they granted me the adoption order, so she's on her way home any time now … I'm her mum, Ben. I can't get over those words. It's the first time I've said them aloud." I pause, wetting my lips with my tongue. My mouth is so dry. "I'll never replace Jen. I wouldn't want to, but I'll love her as though she's mine. I'll show her a mother's love, you know I will, and make sure she remembers her." My words sound rushed, so I slow them. "Being parted from her these past couple of days, worrying if I'd lost her, taught me just how much she means to me." I reach out, placing my hand on his, stroking his cold fingertips. "I wish you'd wake up to share this with me. We should have gone to court together today, as a family. Celebrating our future," my voice breaks, "not like this," I whisper and swallow. There are no tears left inside me, just the feeling of them floating somewhere below the surface. With my free hand, I draw a line across my forehead and down my temples with my thumb and finger, circling back under my eyes, pinching the bridge of my nose. As I massage the skin there, I feel something move underneath my other hand. My gaze darts to his hand. "Ben, can you hear me?" I ask, the pitch of my voice rising. I wait, watching intently and I see it. His finger moves. "Ben, can you squeeze my hand?" I ask, pushing my hand under his. It's subtle, but it's there. His grip tightens and releases.

"He's waking up," I call out to the nurse.

It's dark, but not late as I race through the front door to our house. The sound of small feet thundering towards me grows, until she's in front of me, charging me with the force of a small rhino, almost leaping into my arms like a lemur.

"Jo!" she calls out and I pull her as close as I can manage. She's showered and smells like strawberry shampoo and I can almost hear my heart pop under the pressure of being reunited with her. My blood's fizzing through my veins.

"I'm never being away from you again," I say.

"Promise?"

"Pinky promise." We link our little fingers. "Now where's Pinky?" I smile at her, taking in every inch of her face, holding it between the palms of my hands as if to inspect it more thoroughly.

"He's in the kitchen, with everyone."

"Well, let's go. I have something to tell you."

We skip into the kitchen and I'm greeted with the sight of my favourite humans. Emma and Chris are perched at the breakfast bar. Mum's by the kettle, which is already steaming from the spout. Dad is leaning on the worktop beside her and April is almost upon me, drawing me into a hug. She slides her hand down to meet mine and I clasp my other around it, as Poppy retrieves Pinky from Ronnie's arms. I give him a warm smile.

"Would Pinky like to go to see Daddy tomorrow at the hospital?" I ask, noticing a room full of probing gazes on me.

"Can I?" Her voice is shaky and soft.

"Well, I dunno. Let's ask him shall we?"

I place my phone on the workbench and press ring. He answers with a hoarse voice, barely audible, but it's enough to make everybody in the room gasp and then tear up.

"Daddy!" she yells, jumping up once on the spot.

"Popsicle!" he mutters.

"Everyone's here, Ben. We're all here, waiting for

you to come home to us." I place a hand on my chest.

"Great to hear ya, boss." Ronnie shouts and I can hear a small chortle sound.

"Daddy needs to rest still, so we'll say night and see him tomorrow."

"Night, night, Daddy. I love you so much!"

"Night, kiddo. I love you so much, too." I can hear the strained emotion in his weak voice, but I can tell he's happy.

"Say night to Pinky."

"Night, Pinky," he croaks.

"We love you!" I call out and hang up the phone.

"Daddy's awake?" Her eyes are big and bright as she leans towards me.

I nod, tears unwittingly roll down my cheeks as she thunders into me once more, her head hitting my stomach, leaving me breathless. I wrap my arms around her head and rub her neck. I see Chris pull Emma into his embrace and Poppy holds out her arm for April and Ronnie to come and join us. My parents, too. My mum kisses my cheek, her lips are soft and tender. This moment is so unexpected after the way the day began, as I look at Poppy, laughing hysterically as Ronnie tickles her sides, and April comes to her rescue. I woke this morning thinking no amount of brightness could compensate for the darkness of today. I was wrong. I was forgetting just how bright my *daughter* is.

Chapter Twenty-Eight

Winter is well and truly behind us now. We're heading towards the end of spring and the evenings are light. The daffodils have almost gone, having sprung up everywhere, including in our garden, which I look out over while waiting for the kettle to boil to make Ben a cup of tea. Our yellow and orange daffodils bow their heads, bobbing in the gentle breeze. The mixed colour pansies and cyclamen also returned, but are starting to fade. I'm looking forward to summer this year. To seeing the bee garden flourish and spending time together outside as a family. I hear the kettle click off and pour the hot water into two cups sitting side by side, stirring in the milk before walking through into the lounge.

"You need to sit back down on the sofa." I place both cups on coasters and direct Ben back to the cushions and blankets he's just pushed aside to stand up.

"I've been lying down for weeks. Or at least that's how it feels." He huffs.

"Ben, you almost died. You've not long since fin-ished your radiotherapy. Now do as you're told.

Please," I say, sounding like a mum.

He relents and plops back down. Dr LaLa said everything was looking good. He's been given a follow-up appointment and instructions to let his body recover fully. I haven't relaxed just yet, though. Still wary for any more complications, I suppose. I know he's much better. The radiotherapy made him tired, gave him a sunburn like rash on his skin, but nothing quite like the chemo. The mother hen in me, activated by both Poppy's presence in my life and Ben's illness, is unlikely to power-off anytime soon. They never tell you when you become a parent you'll worry constantly. It will be a relief when I no longer have to about Ben.

"Thank you," he says as I hand him his cup.

"It's only tea."

"I don't mean thank you for the tea."

"What for then, bossing you around? I need no thanks, I secretly enjoy it." My voice takes on a villainous tone.

"Secretly enjoy it?" he scoffs. "There's nothing secret about your pleasure, miss." His eyes glow and his tone is sexy, reminiscent of old Ben.

I lift both shoulders to my ears and smile in a *what-can-I-say* movement.

"Seriously though, thank you for looking after me through all of this and I'm sorry for the stress both I and my parents put you through." I see the muscles in his neck tighten. "They had no right to take Poppy like they did and when I'm better—"

"We've talked about this. Don't get worked up

about that right now. If you want to confront them when you're stronger, then by all means, but now's not the time."

"I can't help it. Every time I think about how they thought they could just take her." His eyes grow cold.

"They didn't win." I touch his arm.

He's shaking his head. "This is not what you signed up for. I mean, you just wanted surf lessons. Not a sick boyfriend and parents who kidnap their grandchildren."

"When you put it that way," I lift my eyebrows, "it does sound a little bit soapesque. And there was me, only interested in paddling out with a sexy instructor."

"Is that right?" he asks, his lips parting as I lean down and kiss him.

"You, me, Poppy. All healthy and happy. This is what I want. I nearly lost you both and I don't want to live without either of you, ever again."

"So, does that mean if I were to ask you a certain question, you'd say yes? I promise it won't involve hospital gowns this time." His steady gaze is fixed on mine.

I cock my head to one side and fold my arms. "I mean I'd have to think about it and it'd have to be quite romantic. A girl like me needs some convincing, Mr Campbell."

"Okay, oh-um-Jo. I can do convincing." He kisses me again and I forget the last few months and how sick he's been. We pull apart to the sound of the front door opening and Poppy and April appear in the lounge, all laughter and conversation.

"Good day at school, kiddo?" Ben asks.

"Yep." She drops her bag by the sofa.

"Thanks for picking her up, April."

"No worries. I'm making the most of it before I have to fly home." She scruffs the top of Poppy's head, who ducks away from her, giggling.

"I don't know what I'm gonna do when you leave. I've got so used to having you around." I link my arm in hers, resting my hand on her forearm.

"I know. I know, but I've got work lined up."

"You've not done so bad making money here these past few weeks. Photos can be taken anywhere." I give her my best pleading face, but know she has a life to get on with.

"Well, you'll just have to give me a reason to come back again soon." She winks at Ben and he smiles at me, knowingly.

"Can we go to the beach for ice cream?" Poppy interrupts.

"Oh, sweetheart. Daddy still has to rest."

"Dr LaLa said get back to some sort of normality. What could be more normal than a walk along the beach ... I could do with some fresh air," Ben says, his pleading face more effective than the one I'd tried on April. I purse my lips to one side and see the three of them, awaiting my reply, like a brood of children asking for sweets from their outnumbered mother.

"If you promise to not overdo it and not bother Ronnie about work if he's there."

"Promise." He gives me a scout's salute, but I don't believe him.

We're standing on the beach and Ben takes off his shoes, pushing his toes into the sand as though he were plugging himself in. I see him tilt his head back and sense every bit of his energy. This place is his life source, his home and place of healing. It was right to bring him here and even I feel my own anxiety levels diminish. I've made him cover up, wear a hat, too. He doesn't need sun exposure following his treatments, especially as the sun has actually graced us with its presence today.

April is chasing Poppy in the sand and we watch, holding hands.

"Boss!" Ronnie appears, giving Ben a man-shake-hug-thing they do. "It's good to see you out and about."

"He's taking it easy, though, Ron," I warn.

"No arguments from me." Ronnie salutes. I think he's still terrified of me from the day I yelled 'wetsuit' at him. "As soon as you're better, though, beers and a BBQ at my place."

"Sounds just my sort of thing." April appears beside us and I think I see Ronnie blush for the first time since we met. "Do I get an invite to this barbie then?" They've seen each other a few times now. At the court, at the house when Ben had woken up and a couple of times before that. I don't think they've shared much in the way of conversation, but they certainly look good together.

"Sure thing," Ronnie says.

"I thought you were heading back to Australia soon, Cuz?" I give Ben a discreet nudge and my lips press into a straight line, which is creeping up at the corners.

"I didn't say right away." April dismisses me and I can't help but think she'll eat him alive. Poor guy.

"Right, I promised this gorgeous little girl of mine ice cream." He touches her nose.

"Dad, I'm not little anymore, remember."

"Oh, of course. I forgot." He shakes his head, in a *silly me* way and we smile at the normality of the situation.

We take a slow walk with our ice creams across the sand. Once Poppy's demolished hers, she starts doing cartwheels and I'm praying we don't see her ice cream again. April joins her and I'm amazed her stomach can handle it too.

"She's so good with her," Ben says, before pushing the last bite of his cone into his mouth. I love seeing him eat. I love that he wants to and how healthy he's starting to look.

"I know. They've become little besties since our trip to Australia. I'll miss her when she goes back, unless Ronnie has anything to do with it!" We laugh. "Seriously, though, It was hard enough saying bye to Chris and Em when they left, and I can visit them whenever." We walk along, to keep up with Poppy and April.

"Well, we'll have to try and make our trips more frequent."

"It's a long way to go for just a couple of weeks and neither of us can take longer off work. Plus, we can't keep taking Pops out of school."

"So we go for two weeks and suffer the jet lag. It'd be worth it. Or we ask April to come over here more. It's not like she can't freelance, like she has been. Your parents have a B&B or she can stay with her folks again, or even us if she wants."

"It would be nice to see her more and Poppy would love it. I think it's surprised April just how homesick she's been. I know my aunt and uncle have loved having her home."

"Do you think she'd ever move back permanently?" he asks.

"I doubt it, you've seen the life she leads out there. It wouldn't be an easy thing to leave behind."

"Neither are you, though." He stops, his eyes on mine.

"Speaking from experience are we …?"

"I'm never leaving you again," he says, kissing me.

It's peaceful today, walking together by the sea front, back in the place this all started just over a year ago. Here on the sand where my heart first found him, the pain of the last few weeks melts away all of a sudden; like the passing of winter to spring—it seems far off to start with, then it's here before you realise anything's changed.

"Jo, come help us look for shells," Poppy calls out over the hum of other families flying kites and siblings playing together, making the most of a pleasant afternoon now that school's over for another week. I can't believe it will soon be another Cornish summer. It's odd, given I missed the May ball in Wincastle this year, though I wouldn't have wanted to go without Ben. Poppy's been asking when she'll be old enough, and even though it'll be way off in the future, I can't wait to take her shopping and get her hair styled for these things. For now, I'm happy collecting shells, reading bedtime stories and tucking Pinky into sleep beside her. I'm no longer daunted by being her mum. As we move into different seasons in her life, I'll learn what to do, just as I have with this one.

We search around in the sand for shells, looking for our favourite. I bend over to collect all varieties, but not the elusive white dog whelk.

"I found one," Poppy announces, her arm up high, though the shell is too tiny to make out from where I'm standing. I see her give it to Ben for safe keeping, while she goes on searching. I smile at him and catch up with Poppy and April, who have an almost half-filled bucket and I add mine to their collection.

Ten minutes or so must have passed when I look up to find Ben, but he's nowhere to be seen. My eyes scan in all directions, my heart rate accelerating irrationally. I look back to the shop to see if he's sneaked away to bother Ronnie about work, but I can see Ronnie from here and Ben isn't standing beside him.

"Pops and I are going to go up on the cliff and take some pictures of the waves crashing."

"Okay. Have you seen Ben?"

April points her finger over to just beneath where the cliff is and there's Ben, standing between some boulders which were brought in on a spring tide.

I breathe out, willing my heart rate to slow. *Isn't it supposed to be Poppy who wanders off, not him?*

April and Poppy ascend the rocks and pause at the top. It looks as though April is teaching her how to use the camera properly. Ever since Australia, Poppy's insisted she wants a camera for her ninth birthday, so she can practice her photography and become a photographer when she's older, just like April. It would have been nice if she'd wanted to be a nurse like me, I'd told Ben, laughing, but I love that I'll get to see what she becomes and have the opportunity to help shape and guide her, whatever it may be.

The beach down where Ben's standing, is almost empty, aside from a few dogs bounding over the waves.

"Are you all right?" I walk the last few steps in haste, breathless.

"I'm perfectly fine." He touches my arm.

"You walked off and I couldn't see you. I was worried."

"I'm sorry. I just wanted to go for a walk on my own." He takes my hand and we walk beside each other to where the boulders lie. As we near the rocks I see, *Will you marry me?* written in the sand.

"Aw, look, someone's prop—" I turn, seeing Ben on one knee, ring between his finger and thumb.

"Oh-um-Jo. I know you think I tease you too much with that name, but that day, when you walked into my shop looking for surf lessons, stumbling over your own name, I knew there was hope for me. I never thought I'd love again, or find the happiness you bring into my and Poppy's lives. I wouldn't have survived the past year without you, and I know it's not the year we planned, but it's made my heart completely sure that I want to spend the rest of my life making you as happy as you make me. I'm so in love with you. Please will you marry me?"

My mind flashes back to the letter I read and the symmetry in some of his words. It's been the hardest year, but in many ways, the most blessed year of my life.

"Yes!" I shout, which carries on the air. He scoops me into his arms, kissing me. As we part, he slides the precious diamond ring onto my finger, then puts a thumbs-up in the direction of the cliff and I realise why Poppy and April went up there. They went to take pictures of Ben's proposal.

"Did they both—"

"Help me plan this … absolutely!" His smile is full of mischief.

"Who else knew?"

"Ronnie. Your parents."

"My parents?" My head jerks back.

"Well, I had to ask your dad's permission."

"How very traditional of you." I bow my head, beaming at him.

We kiss again and I place my ear against his chest, hearing the strong thuds of his heart and relish the sound and the life it signifies.

Chapter Twenty-Nine

The bay is surrounded by high cliffs, with fields on top of them. With most of our guests arriving this afternoon, the day before our big day, we had a welcome BBQ in the garden, before descending to the beach for drinks. Then, after dusk, there'll be a fireworks display. We didn't plan for a huge number of guests, but we did plan it to be a spectacular party. In the morning, everyone will receive a breakfast hamper from the bride and groom, to see them through until the wedding breakfast.

The beach is well sheltered and the golden sand soft between my toes. There's a blanket of dark green seaweed at the water's edge, which is calm, and the sound of gentle lapping waves on the shore can be heard amongst the chatter of friends and family. The headland curves to the right, and in the distance I can see a cluster of white-fronted properties, so happily situated near the water. Poppy has already taken many landscape shots on April's camera; she seems to have an eye for things.

"How are you feeling, soon-to-be Mrs Campbell?" Ben asks and my heartbeat quickens.

"It's not a done deal yet. I may still change my mind." My chin lowers to my right shoulder and I flutter my eyelashes at him.

"Is there anything I can do to, you know, tip things in my favour?" he says, sliding his hands behind my waist, the thin fabric of my cotton maxi dress ill protection from the sensation traveling along my skin. In a swift, gentle pull, our hips meet, his mouth inches from mine as I inhale. In that moment, I may have forgotten to breathe, but as his lips meet mine, my chest relaxes and my lungs deflate, as though air was being released steadily from a balloon.

We move with our drinks to a flattened rock by the water's edge, watching as the stone darkens where the water flows over it. He's sitting behind me, his arms around my frame, as we watch the sun slowly fade, its circular form blurred behind wispy clouds painted in various shades of orange. The darkest hue where it rests on the horizon casts a line over the shallows, resembling a laser beam cutting a straight path.

"Do you want to give Poppy her gift this evening?"

"No, I think you should in the morning," he says.

"Are you sure you don't want to see her face when she opens it?" There's a fluttery feeling in my stomach, thinking how she'll react.

"I don't need to, I can already picture it. It's your moment with her. I just can't wait to watch you both walk towards me." He inhales and I feel his chest cave in.

"Me too." I kiss his forearm and he kisses my

shoulder, sending an electrical surge down my arm. "We should head back soon, round everyone up for the fireworks."

"Just a bit longer," he whispers in my ear, making me shudder.

"You're not turning all wistful are you, Mr Campbell!" I bump him.

"Well, only because my soon-to-be wife is." The fire inside me is stoked by the word wife, so strange, yet so welcome.

"Get a room, boss!" Ronnie's familiar bellow rings out and we see him appear, with Poppy, April and Cassie dog in tow. She makes a bound for the water and Poppy chases her, both of them sandy, damp and gloriously happy, as are we all.

"The fireworks are going to start in half an hour. We're heading back up to the BBQ to toast marshmallows." April says, catching Poppy as she runs by.

"Come on, miss," I say, Ben helping me to my feet. "Let's get you dry and a warm pair of clothes before it starts." I hold out my hand to her.

As I look out from the balcony of my hotel room, I see glorious blue sky, with a gentle breeze bringing in the salty sea air. From here, I can see the top of the white teepee where our wedding reception will be. To one side, rows of white chairs either side of the grass aisle leading to a floral archway of yellows and whites, draped with tulle and fairy lights, to blend in with the starlit sky, come evening. There's rattan tables and large square parasols dotted about the lawn, in and around the teepee, and a trail of gardens, surrounded by tall, lush trees and greenery that slope all the way down the beach. Last night, the fireworks had lit up the bay and Poppy's face. After which, she'd grown sleepy and Ronnie had helped carry her back to my parents' room, where she had a sleepover. Ben bunked in with Ronnie and I shared the bridal suite with April and Emma. I'd always pictured getting married by the sea, so this was the closest thing to a beach wedding we were allowed in this country, giving us everything we wanted from our special day.

Although it's September, it's warm during the day, dropping cooler in the evenings. We thought we'd have to wait at least a year to book this place, preferring it to all the other venues we viewed, but when we were offered a cancellation, we took it. It just meant we didn't have long to arrange everything. Not that a longer timeframe would suit me, or a very overexcited Poppy. I liked the idea of wedding planning. The reality was somewhat more stressful and I'm pleased the day has finally arrived. Especially now I've got my hair and make-up done, my nails manicured and a glass of gin in my hand. The bridesmaids—April and Emma—are on prosecco, but I wanted something stronger. Poppy, has orange juice in a champagne flute to make her feel as though she's part of it. Stephen is my adorable page boy in shorts, a white shirt and yellow bow tie. Mostly being kept in check by the toddler whisperer that is my dad—who knew! Emma has already asked him to be their live-in nanny, making us all laugh.

My bridesmaids are wearing daffodil yellow full-length chiffon dresses with spaghetti straps and a silk empire waistline. Poppy's is a flowy chiffon dress to match the others, with a scoop neckline, ruffled sleeves, and a daisy headdress—her hair long and wavy. She has a white basket full of rose petals to carry. Both my adult bridesmaids have a plait across their fringe and loose waves. I'm still wearing my silk dressing gown, embroidered with the word Bride.

"Could I get a shot of the bride and bridesmaids?"

We line up for Sian, April's best friend from school, who is our official photographer, given that April is busy with bridesmaid's duties. She's keen on jumping in later to take some shots, but for now, we have Sian—who's a staggering six feet tall, with blonde hair the length of her back and eyelashes straight from a supermodel magazine. If I were an insecure person, I'd never have her within ten feet of the groom on my wedding day, but I know where Ben's heart lies. I did, however, catch April giving Ronnie a scowl when she'd introduced him to Sian and I'm not sure what's going on there, but I'm looking forward to the debrief later.

"Beautiful, and one of just the bride and Poppy, please," Sian directs.

"Come on, Mummy." She takes my hand, and as she steps in front of me, I rest my hands over her shoulders, smiling at how perfect this feels. Even weeks on from when we told her the adoption had been finalised, I still get a flutter in my stomach when she calls me Mummy. At first, I'd look around, or forget to respond, unused to the title. Eventually, though, the word flowed in our everyday lives and so, too, the deepened relationship it brought with it, cementing our affection for one another and uniting us as one family. We hadn't managed to have a celebration, the one that had been planned the day the court awarded me the adoption order. We made the announcement over chocolate-covered waffles one breakfast and I ended up smeared in it, just like that photo, all those months ago, after she pounced on me. Today, we plan to celebrate everything the past year robbed from us.

April hands me a small white gift bag and Sian lingers with her camera. I bend down and Poppy turns towards me.

"Your dad and I got you a gift for being our bridesmaid today." I look at her, trying not to tear up.

Her beautiful green eyes are glinting in the bright sunshine. "What is it?"

"You'll have to open it and see." Her tiny fingers slide open the pale pink ribbon and she reaches inside and pulls out a black square box. Opening the lid reveals a heart-shaped locket, which looks so dainty I can't imagine it fitting more than a doll. "Look inside," I say, peering into the box with her.

As she opens the heart, there's a tear in her eye. The locket holds a photo of her mum.

"I love it," she says with the composure of a much older girl and I take a deep breath as I blink and swallow.

"You can keep her close, because she'll always be your mummy, too." My voice is wobbly, each word I have to push forward.

"I'm lucky," she says, her fingers holding the heart between them and I smile, waiting for to go on. "I have two mummies looking out for me. One in heaven." She looks skyward. "And you." She bundles into me, knocking me sideways, not least with her words, and I put one hand onto the floor to steady myself, before wrapping both hands around her tightly.

My wedding dress is bohemian style, with a low V backline and delicate beadwork on the plunge bodice. The skirt is chiffon, panelled with French lace. It's floaty and beach worthy, which is what I imagined for my big day. I'm wearing a whimsical forest herb flower crown, which is simple and suits my face and short hair. The bridesmaids have daisies braided into their plaits.

"You look stunning!" April appears beside me and Emma hands her a tissue before taking one for herself. My mum third in line. All three women are dabbing their eyes, with their best attempts at preserving professionally applied make-up.

"Don't you all start, or you'll set me off." I place

my hand over my stomach, trying to keep the emotions inside.

"It's time!" my dad says calmly, passing me a posy of daises tied with pale yellow ribbon. "You look beautiful, Jo." He kisses my cheek. I turn to take Poppy's hand and she clasps mine, her basket in the other. We make our way down a winding staircase and through bi-folding doors onto the path leading to where the ceremony will take place. We pass other guests and staff who smile and gush, especially over Poppy, who looks so tall and grown-up, even in the eighteen months since I met her.

"Remember to breathe, Mummy," she says, squeezing my hand, before joining the other brides-maids who take their formation. Poppy's first in line, with a chalkboard sign over her wrist that reads: 'My daddy's so lucky!' and I can't wait to see Ben's face when he reads it. Our entrance is to a simple piece of instrumental music, nothing popular. Just a calm, gentle song which fills me full of hope, joy and new beginnings whenever I listen to it. My heart feels light, beating steadily as I see Ben's face break into the widest smile at the sight of Poppy stepping closer and closer to where he's standing, Ronnie by his side. Wearing sand-coloured linen rounded lapel suits, shorts, not trousers, white shirts, with no tie, and yellow handkerchiefs. The smile breaks into a laugh as he reads her sign, turning to Ronnie, who joins him. Ben blows Poppy a kiss as she steps to the side with Emma and April, then his gaze finds me. My feet are on autopilot, stepping on the soft grass. A surge of warmth floods me from my belly upwards and my heart rate quickens. I grip my dad's arm tighter, my gaze fixed on Ben's—that invisible wire pulling me ever closer, the same way it had in the beginning. His hand finds his chest and I bite my lip, which makes him give the slightest shake of his head, so subtle only I would notice. Now, inches from my place beside him, I wrinkle my nose affectionately and smile.

"Wow! You look *beautiful!*" He gulps and takes my hand. My dad kisses me and shakes Ben's other hand and the guests are seated. He turns to me again, eying me once more. "Wow!" he repeats, the dimples of his cheeks unable to stay hidden.

I turn to Poppy, who steps forward to take my bouquet, winking at her, and then the ceremony begins.

The afternoon slips by in a haze of photographs, drinks, warm embraces and some highly amusing and emotional speeches. There's no one speech which stands out as my favourite, obviously Ben's because it was full of adoration when he addressed me, and his usual wit and natural charm shone through. My dad's was heartfelt and simple, wishing us as many happy years as he and my mum have shared, making my eyes glisten. Ronnie regaled us with a tale about Poppy's seventh birthday party, where they'd all gone roller skating, Poppy and her friends all dressed like princess- es, and when Ben, the man who makes surfing look easier than walking, glided on one foot, pushing off with the other, keeping both hands by his side with more grace than a ballerina. Ronnie struggled to speak at the memory of ballerina Ben, which was his nickname for a good few weeks apparently, and we all cried with laughter. There's video footage somewhere and my first mission as Ben's wife is to find it. The poignant part of Ronnie's speech was his tribute to Jen, saying how much she would have liked me and how proud of Poppy she would be, which made her climb on to Ben's lap. I swear Ronnie stole the show right then.

As the evening draws in, the sun is fading and we wanted to get some family shots on the beach. Hoping for another magical sunset, we take April with us, who snaps away at every piece of natural interaction as we pose together and apart, even drawing a huge love heart with our names written inside for one of the photos. Ben pulls me close, kissing my forehead, before Poppy climbs between. We shout, "Ham sandwich!" at the camera and April laughs.

Ben crouches down in front of Poppy, giving her another box. This one is tied with a white bow.

"I already have my necklace," she says, surprised.

"This is something for your charm bracelet."

"A charm?" she squeals excitedly and pulls open the box.

Inside lie three hearts, two silver and one rose gold. The smallest, a rose gold heart, says Poppy on it, the larger silver heart, Daddy, and the middle-size silver heart says Mummy. I crouch beside them both and see a tear in her eyes, which I know is happy and not sad. Poppy wraps her small arms around our necks and we lift her up, holding her close, not bothered we're now all covered in grains of sand.

"This is the bestest day of my life," she says and I agree. For I'm the mummy of this special little girl and the wife of her father, the man I love. Ben attaches each charm to her bracelet, which dangles as her hands find ours. She's in the middle of us as we walk towards the water's edge, the orange sun resting on the horizon once more. A perfect Cornish sunset. This was the final shot I wanted April to capture. The three of us, holding hands, walking together into our future, as a family. With the realisation in my heart that *this* is enough for me. This is the life I'm meant to live.

The End

Acknowledgements

This is the easy part of writing a book, as I get to thank all the amazing people who've helped me along the way (and pray I haven't forgotten to mention anyone). However big or small your input has been, thank you. I could leave it there, but I'm not known for being short of words (essential for a writer, as you can imagine). This book is testimony to this, as it's at least thirty thousand words longer than my debut, *Meet Me in the Treehouse*. You, my readers, are the reason there is a second book. I hadn't thought about writing more than one, when I set out on this author journey. The dream was to be a published author (tick). With all your support and amazing reviews, it's made it possible for me to write and publish, *A Perfect Cornish Sunset*. So, to my wonderful readers, bloggers and bookstagram-mars, the biggest, heartfelt thank you. I smile every single time you tell me how much you enjoy reading my books. This will be something I never tire of hearing. I hope book two lives up to your expectations, because I wrote it with you all in mind. In the hopes you'd fall in love with this story and the characters as much as I did.

Writing is a solitary business, but there are so many people who play a part in a book going from an idea in my mind to what you read on the page. As always, I want to thank the Romantic Novelists' Association

(RNA), New Writers' Scheme (NWS). I doubt I'd be a published author without you. The organisers and members who all support and encourage one another have taught me a great many things since joining. I specifically want to thank, Janet Gover, our NWS co-ordinator, who is moving on from her role. Janet we will miss you! I've certainly appreciated all your help and would like to say what a fabulous job you've done. Thank you. To my NWS manuscript readers, of which there were two for *A Perfect Cornish Sunset*. Your advice helped me to not only shape the book, but to bring out more of my writing abilities. It truly is a wonderful scheme and I thank you for the time and care you showed to me in your feedback.

Thank you to Hilary Johnson, my copy-editor. I've come to value your opinion greatly and looked forward to working with you again on this book. To Paul Salvette at BB eBooks for his fantastic formatting service. Thank you to Rachel Gilbey of Rach Ran-domResources Blog Tours, for arranging my blog tour again for this book!

Big thanks to Sue from work, who spreads the word about my books more than anyone I know. I don't think she lets a single person who shows even a hint of an interest in books leave without a plug. You're a star. Special thanks to Suzanne Snow and Leonie Mack, both fabulous authors. I've had the privilege of knowing Suzanne since she reached out to include me in her Live event after reading *Meet Me in the Treehouse*. You've always taken the time to advise and support me, even though you're super busy. Thank you. I love being part of the writing community because of people like Leonie and Suzanne. Thanks for reaching out to me and letting me run cover and blurb ideas past you both.

To my best friend and number one Beta reader, Ruth, as always to have your support is invaluable. You never tire of being my sounding board and I'm so grateful for your friendship. Thank you. To Joan, my mother-in-law, and number two Beta reader, you are a constant encouragement to me. Thank you, as always, for reading the first drafts of the book and believing in my writing ability. My father-in-law, Les, is lucky enough to have his own audiobook performance of my novel when you read it to him. I love this! To my sister-in-law, Lauren, thanks for listening to me waffle on about writing, covers and blurbs and generally shaking me when my confidence plummets and I want to give up. You rock!

With many stories, you often need specialist knowledge of the themes within the book. I had some amazing people advise me on aspects of the plot which I wanted to be as authentic as possible, especially as they're such sensitive issues. Thank you to all who helped me; Bev, Jennie, Katie, Jo and Dr Lala, who not only helped me, but agreed to a character in the book being named after her!

Thank you to my mum and dad for everything you've done for me in life. Your love, support and the memories I have through life shape the characters I create and the way I write. You will find scenes in my books which reflect the love and happiness I've experienced growing up and in life, and that is a reflection on you, as my parents.

Thank you to all my wonderful friends (you know who you are), who I don't see as often as I'd like. You are also the people I often think of when creating my beloved characters and draw upon times we've shared to bring magic to my words.

Thank you to my amazing sons. Being your mum is my entire world and I will never be prouder of any achievement in life, but strive to make you proud to call me your mum. I wish for you both to be happy and healthy in all you choose to do in life. I love you both.

My wonderful husband, James. No one believes in me more than you. Thank you for allowing me to reach my full potential. Never holding me back and for inspiring such deep-seated confidence in myself, my resolve holds fast, even when the world and life tests us. You're my secret weapon. I love you.

About the Author

Kelly Tink is a cancer nurse, writer and hopeless romantic, living in Cambridgeshire. She enjoys exploring fun outdoor places with her husband and two sons, especially if it involves eating ice cream by the sea.

She's an avid reader, loves a good film or TV series and drinks lots of tea. *A Perfect Cornish Sunset* is Kelly's second novel. Her debut, *Meet Me in the Treehouse* was published in 2020 and is available on Amazon. She can be found tweeting at @kelly_tink or on Instagram: kelly.tink.

It would mean the world to Kelly if you would consider taking a few moments to write a review. These reviews let new readers know what you thought of her books. Thank you.

Copyright

Printed in Great Britain
by Amazon